IS AN ALL-VOLUNTEER ARMY
The Second Fixxer Adventure

It's the late 1990s—and Hollywood wants to take over the world!

Those in the know in Hollywood know that if they need a dark deed done or a sticky personal or professional problem "fixed," they can call upon The Fixxer. Mysterious and dangerous, with wit and aplomb, The Fixxer works the fruitful fields of Hollywood, fixing the sins and correcting the stupidities of the highly paid and well-paying denizens therein.

Whether you are a successful comedy film director whose "art" has never truly been appreciated because the country's most important film critic has held a grudge against you since college, or you are a neophyte and naive screenwriter who resents the professional blackmail she has just suffered, you call upon the Fixxer.

But not all problems are as simple as they first seem. Just exactly what does it mean in Hollywood to join the Communion of the Golden Arse? And why does the secret elite group, The Enclave, want with the movers and shakers in Hollywood?

PRAISE FOR THE FIXXER ADVENTURES

"Steven Leiva not only promises but delivers. Beautifully written. Bravo!" — **Ray Bradbury**.

"*Blood is Pretty* is a wonderful read, a highly entertaining and impressive debut novel." — **Richard D. Zanuck, Academy Award-winning Producer of *Jaws* &Driving Miss Daisy.**

"Steven Paul Leiva takes a dash of James Bond, the ghost of noir, a splash of Hollywood and stirs it into *Blood is Pretty*, an adventurous, fast-paced first novel." — **Melodie Johnson Howe, Edgar-nominated Author of *The Mother Shadow*.**

"The Fixxer has the mystery of the Shadow, the sophistication of James Bond, and the street smarts of Sam Spade." — **Stuart Nulman, *Book Banter/CJAD, Montreal*.**

"The Fixxer is a fascinating character. Intrigue, murder, and mayhem in a fast-paced, action-filled adventure." — **E. V. Le Roux, *Silver Moon Magazine*.**

"*Blood is Pretty* "...funny, kind of dark, and has many biting things to say about Hollywood. I urge people to check it out." — **Jeff Cannata, *DLC Podcast*.**

"Leiva's immense gifts for mystery and suspense are matched only by his wry, biting wit in skewering the Hollywood he clearly knows so well." —**Paul Provenza, Author of ¡Satiristas.**

"At last, Leiva has given us a second Fixxer adventure...Leiva mines his firsthand knowledge of the community he toiled in...with the same wry humor, intellectual insight, and terrific storytelling that are the consistent signatures of his work." — **Ken Kragen, Legendary Hollywood Producer/Manager.**

"A fast-paced thriller with more twists than a box of Rotini pasta. Leiva ratchets up the action to a nuclear level following *Blood is Pretty*. — **L. Dean Murphy, *The Big Thrill Magazine*.**

IS AN ALL-VOLUNTEER ARMY
The Second Fixxer Adventure

IS AN ALL-VOLUNTEER ARMY

The Second Fixxer Adventure

Revised Edition

STEVEN PAUL LEIVA

Magpie Press

Dedication to the 2010 Edition

For
Peter Anthony Holder
&
Stuart Nulman

Early Readers. Early Fans.
Friends Forever.

Dedication to 2023 Edition

For
Phil Proctor

A funny man. A talented man.
A good man. A kind man.

CONTENTS

IS AN ALL-VOLUNTEER ARMY
The Second Fixxer Adventure

1
FAIRLY FREAKY

We are often disconcerted by what we see when we look in the mirror in the morning. Gravity is an unkind force on our faces after eight hours of horizontal unconsciousness. But imagine how even more disconcerting it is when you look in the mirror and see not yourself but somebody else. Now imagine what it would be like if that someone else was famous. What if, on your shoulders, you found a head that was a Monday through Friday morning habit for three million Americans here toward the end of the twentieth century? Worse than that, a head which, in its original form, holds little inside to be in awe of.

"Fairly freaky," Roee said as he wheeled in a room service cart.

"Fairly freaky, indeed," I said.

"A damn masterpiece, if you ask me, Fixxer," offered Michael Slayton, the Hollywood makeup man I had flown to New York to effect this transformation.

"We are not questioning your talents, Michael. Indeed you can take our reactions as a compliment. Still, I wish it had been Bryant Gumbel."

"Robert Jordan isn't a semi-regular on the Today Show, you're taller than Bryant Gumbel, Gumbel hasn't been the host for years, and he's black," Roee reminded me.

"Yes, but he's a better interviewer — and what does being black have to do with it?"

"Swanee, how I love you, how I love you, my dear old Swanee..." Roee began to sing quietly.

"Really, Roee, you ethnic and/or cultural minorities should become less sensitive. Here I have altered my appearance to that of a gee-shucks, midwestern, all-American, white Anglo-Saxon Protestant, and no one seems offended by that."

"Being a gee-shucks, midwestern, all-American, white Anglo-Saxon Protestant is offensive enough."

"Jeez. Centuries of power, and where does it get you? No respect."

Roee just sighed a sigh he had worked to perfect and announced, "Your breakfast."

"What's on the menu?"

"A three-egg omelet with fresh cut basil, Kalamata olives sliced into perfectly even quarters, and feta cheese left, as you prefer, in large chunks," Roee revealed the meal with a flourish as he lifted the silver dome from the plate.

I allowed myself a moment to gaze, smell, and salivate. "You made it yourself, didn't you, Roee?" I queried with the proper measure of delight I've learned he expects.

"Kitchen privileges are not hard to come by when you can speak intelligently about sauces. And for you, Michael," Roee lifted another silver dome, "since you made no particular request, I took the liberty to whip you up some sourdough pancakes from a starter I once acquired in Alaska. As for embellishments, you can choose Canadian Maple syrup, a fresh raspberry compote I've made, or— and please don't scoff, just try one bite—sour cream and honey."

Michael was amazed. "How did you know sourdough pancakes are my favorite?"

Roee smiled. "How do we know that you've been collecting the underwear of a particular stripper at Bodies 2000 out in North Hollywood for the last six months?"

The slam of this information reformed Michael's face. "Oh. Yeah. I forgot."

"By the way, Michael," I said as I took my first bite of the omelet and the full force of its hot flavor blessed me, "she's got a drug habit—very nasty one, and despite the delicacy of her visage and the smoothness of her skin, both, I admit, very appealing, she is very, very dumb and dangerous. Best forgotten at this point, don't you think?" I looked up at Michael and answered my question with, I hope, a subtle force.

Michael stared back at me. Then he looked down. Not in shame, I assumed, but in the dumbfounded wonder of it all. "You're doing me a favor, aren't you?" he asked sadly.

"Yes, Michael. The pit of your stomach is telling you something different right now, but yes, I am."

xx

I was in New York on a job. It had come to me, as all my jobs do, when my business manager, Norton Macbeth, called me up on the secure line of The Phone.

"Larry Lapham," Norton said without preamble.

"Desperate to be Mr. Film Comedy, but somehow always comes in just shy of that," I launched into what I knew. "His films gross well, which certainly impresses, yet he remains somewhat unknown by the general public and not accorded the respect he probably feels he deserves by the industry."

"He wouldn't argue with any of that."

"So what does he need fixing?"

"Just that, he, he, he." Norton often punctuated his sentences with a bit of staccato laughter."

"What am I supposed to do? Blackmail Hollywood into respecting him?"

"He thinks he knows the source of his troubles."

"Really?"

"You want to talk to him?"

"Will he make me laugh?"

"Not unless you pay him, he, he, he."

"I was thinking of the unfortunate humor involved in the reverse."

"He can afford a lot. You can take it seriously."

"Then I can talk to him."

xx

Norton had arranged for me to see Larry Lapham at three that day. I was to meet him at his building on Washington Boulevard in Culver City, across the street from the Sony Lot.

Now there's an example of the glamour of Hollywood gone shiny instead of lustrous. Instead of the old dream factory that was Metro-Goldwyn-Mayer, the original occupant who built the studio lot, you expected a "Sony Lot" to be pumping out the gleam of many gadgets housing transistors, light emitting diodes, microchips, and other mysterious ways to manipulate electrical energy. Not true, of course; the lot still made movies. It was, I guess, just a name thing that bothered me. And possibly the fact that the lot had been refurbished and now had the look of what you might dream a movie lot should look like—if you were a star-struck, semi-literate farm girl in 1935. There is just something a bit discomforting about all the new façades they put on the office buildings to make them look like the golden-hued simple life of Anytown, USA, that politicians keep getting elected to lead us back to. But my comfort was not much considered when the pricey American management team the Japanese had hired to run the place convinced them that if they genuinely wanted to buy into Hollywood, they had to buy into fake—and love it. Of course, that management team eventually petered out. Now, as we sit here in 1999, ready to close out this twentieth century, the "Century of the Movie," there's a new team running the show. They probably think the façades are real.

I much prefer Lapham's building. Although he makes comedies with goofy yet charming characters who are cleverly made to slip on metaphorical banana peels and who are often participants in humor derived from the various ways the mammalian body expels waste, the building that houses his company, Painted Dessert Pictures— Lapham's from Arizona—is all clean, gray concrete, shiny, clear glass, and cold, highly reflective steel. It's a serious business making the hoi polloi laugh.

4

You enter the building from the parking garage, where a charming guard greets you respectfully. Then you take an elevator up to the first floor, and it opens onto a spacious area illuminated mainly by the natural sunlight streaming through the two-story floor-to-ceiling glass window in front of you. You almost don't see the receptionist sitting at a semicircle desk against the glass as the view of the giant movie posters for upcoming Sony releases on the fortress wall of the studio across the street diverts your eyes. Right now, the posters were proudly hailing, The Day My Dog Died, a Sundance Festival anointed little independent film made by a guy in Montana that Sony's classic division had picked up, and Blood Brothers, the new hit romantic comedy about twin vampires.

"May I help you?" asked the young woman behind the desk. She was cute and almost marketable—but that's not unusual here.

"I have an appointment with Larry Lapham at three."

"Your name, please?" Cute asked.

"My name is Mr. Lapham's three o'clock appointment, "I said sternly.

"Oh, well..."

"Has he got more than one three o'clock appointment?"

"Oh, well, no, but—"

"There you are."

"But how do I announce you?" There was confusion and worry and the hint of being yelled at often in the past for "fucking it up."

"As Mr. Lapham's three o'clock appointment, emphasizing that I am the three o'clock appointment. Not the three-o-five or any time thereafter."

She did so and was obviously told to send me right up.

I ascended a broad, sweeping staircase leading to a second floor of balcony offices that overlooked the reception area. A smiling, well-tailored woman greeted me at the top of the stairs and showed me into Lapham's office. It was a large, bright, L- shaped room with a desk at one end, an extensive conversation pit of couches and chairs in front of a media center at the other, and a concrete and glass conference table in between at the bend of the L. Lapham was standing behind his desk, backed by a large canvas seemingly painted by Picasso. It took my eye as it probably took the eye of everyone who entered for the first time.

"It's not real." This was most likely Lapham's opening greeting to every first-timer to his office.

"Yes, I know. The rather inattentive brushwork points that out clearly. Nor is the Mark Rothko behind your assistant's desk real. Both props, I believe, from your art world comedy, Abstractions, wherein Chevy Chase manages to destroy the treasures of twentieth-century art in one four-minute slapstick bit."

You know my films?"

"I have a VCR," I said in a noncommittal way.

"Well...." He lost his words here. He had to grope. "Listen, I don't really know why you are here."

"I assume you asked for me."

"Well, no, not really. Look, I just took on Norton Macbeth as my business manager. The last one I had was getting me into these weird investments and—"

"Norton is very conservative."

"Well, yeah, that's what I thought, but then—well—you—uh... Look, I was blowing off steam to Norton, and maybe I said too much, but he started to tell me about you, and he pressed me to have this meeting and... Look, I don't want any rough stuff."

"Rough stuff?" I said with as incredulous an air as I could manage.

"Well—you know...."

"Tell me your problem, Larry," I said like an old friend. A transparent technique but often effective.

"Let's, uh, let's go sit down."

He led me to the conversation pit and sat in what I assumed was always his chair, the significant one perpendicular to the two couches facing each other. I sat on the couch to his right, on the end farthest from him, to observe from a distance. Already I had perceived that Larry Lapham was a geek grown successful. The Spielbergian beard he sported could not hide a bucktooth horsy face that could have comfortably housed the vocal tones of Disney's Goofy going, "Gorsh!" When he walked to the couch, his mid-section led the way, almost as if some invisible hand was pulling him by his belt, but when he sat, he sat with the style of a man grown used to power and control. Nonetheless, you couldn't mistake the unsatisfied air about him. Some "little" thing was pissing him off.

"You know who Robert Jordan is?"

"This country's top film critic. The only one whose opinion can sell tickets, thus make a film's success."

"Or stop the sale of tickets."

"Thus breaking a film. Yes, unusual. The power the New York Times used to have over Broadway, he seems to have over Hollywood. Why do you think that is?"

"He's damn good, really knows film, but he also knows how to play to a crowd. Without being too slick about it. He's never given up his credentials for glamour, and he's got that damn TV show, his regular appearances on This Day, and his books. Gives him a hell of a lot of power. And that fucking 'royal rating system' of his: We are very not pleased; We are not pleased; We are indifferent—that's probably the most damning one—We are pleased; We are very pleased. What the hell is that?"

"I take it none of your films has gotten beyond his indifference?"

"No. None of my films have gotten beyond, 'We are very not pleased.'"

"Nonetheless, you're still successful."

"'Successful' is a relative term."

I looked around his office, making a point. "I suppose we are talking about the difference between a rich relative and a very rich relative."

"That's part of it. I had the shock of my life when a Wall Street analyst told me that if my films had gotten raves from Jordan, the 'winning' atmosphere that would have built around my films would have effected a positive energy not just on the potential audience, but on the studio, the marketing guys, the exhibitors in the field making the decisions on how long to book my pictures. That energy, this analyst said, could well have equated to 21.4 to 33.7 million dollars more in gross per picture."

"Those are very precise figures."

"He's a very precise man."

"Whom you were talking to because you were thinking of taking Painted Dessert Pictures public."

He bore down a little now with his eyes. He was wondering how I knew that. I didn't. It was a logical guess, but it impressed, nonetheless."

"Yes, that's right. And I didn't because I and my work were valued less than what I felt was appropriate. A value derived from the numbers, a misvalue derived from the perception."

"And now you need..."

"I have a new picture coming out in a few weeks. I need Robert Jordan to give me a sterling review."

Lapham said it as if he was reporting needing a can of beans off a supermarket shelf. I was pretty sure that Jordan was no can of beans.

"Well, outside of bribing him..."

"No. He can't be bribed."

"If we could find a dark secret, blackmail is usually effective."

"I wouldn't condone that."

"And you said no rough stuff."

"No rough stuff."

"Then I guess you just have to hope he likes your picture."

"Why? That doesn't seem to have affected his reviews of my work in the past."

"I assume there's a story behind that statement."

Lapham nodded—and looked inward. This is where he was deciding whether to commit to a relationship of information with The Fixxer. Norton always does his job well. He had told Lapham that I would keep his confidence—keep it to use as I saw fit in the future. That this was part of the deal. What he could get in return, however...

Lapham finally spoke. "A couple of weeks ago, a guy I went to college with was visiting L.A. We were roommates in the dorm during my freshman and sophomore years at Penn State. I left after two years to get closer to home and study film at USC. I hadn't heard from him since. He called up the office, assuming I wouldn't talk to him—people's warped sense of what Hollywood success does to you. I was delighted to hear from him. I immediately invited him and his wife up to the house. We had a great time reminiscing. Then he mentioned how he had run into the other famous person from our dorms connected to film on a business trip to New York. I was completely stumped. I had no idea who he was talking about. 'Robert Jordan,' he said."

The way of human nature is clear enough. "So what did you do to Robert Jordan when you were an 18 or 19-year-old college kid to make him hate you all these years?"

"I snubbed him, I guess. That's all. Look, my friend had to put him into context for me even to remember him, but then I got it. He was Bobby, this little, fat nerd on the floor above ours. He had tried to force his way into our circle, but, you know, I wasn't much more than a nerd myself—and from Arizona. I wasn't looking to make friends with people with umbilical cords but people with tow-ropes. Do you understand?"

"You wanted to befriend rather than be friends."

"Yeah. My sights were high. There also seems to be something that, I swear, I never perceived, but my friend says is true. I guess Bobby had homoerotic feelings towards me."

"Unrequited love can be sad on several fronts."

Lapham ignored that statement and continued. "It all makes sense now, though. For you see, the ironic thing is, I think that Robert Jordan is the finest film critic we have, the finest one in years. Yes, he's a bit of a showman, but his views are solid, well thought out, and grounded in a love of film. I have rarely disagreed with one of his reviews, except for those of my films. I was never able to understand why he didn't appreciate them. I thought I knew his tastes. Hell, I've made creative decisions based on what I thought Jordan would like. Most filmmakers won't admit to it. But we are all playing to more than just the audiences."

"So you believe Jordan probably really likes your films but continues to review them poorly out of unresolved adolescent spite."

"Yeah—and it pisses me off. Outside of what he's doing to me, it's dishonest."

"Dishonest?"

"I may not be the greatest filmmaker in the world, but I do love film. I have a regard for it." Having made that clear, Lapham paused. He looked down at his expensive loafers. Then he made his decision. "I would like to have this situation fixed. I would like for Robert Jordan to be found out—in as personally and professionally an embarrassing a manner as possible. I would like him to lose something. I would like him to lose the respect he's gained. I would like him to lose his credentials and position, but not before he admits that he's always liked my films. Now that, Mr. Fixxer, is a tall order."

"And one not so simple as bribery, blackmail, or rough stuff. But one far more vicious."

"Norton didn't tell me you were a judgmental person. Nor that you had any right to be."

"You're a fairly humorless man for a comedy filmmaker, Mr. Lapham."

"I put it on the screen, Mr. Fixxer."

If he wanted to be serious, I decided I would be serious. "A million dollars."

His eyes widened just slightly. "You're kidding?"

"Plus expenses."

"I don't believe you can help me." He started to get up.

"Sit down!" The sharpness of my tone was enough to stop him. He sat. "Don't ever walk away from a meeting with me. What you want, I can give you. It will not be easy; the details will be elaborate, the planning will be precise, and I must have your full cooperation. I can do it for one million dollars plus expenses, a mere fraction, I would guess, from what you will personally realize if you can take Painted Dessert Pictures public at the value you put on it."

"I might make fifty million."

"Two percent, then."

"A bargain, you're telling me.

"What guarantee do I have?"

"You pay nothing until the job is done."

"Then what guarantee do you have that I'll pay once the job is done."

"Mr. Larry Lapham, you may have some moral objections to rough stuff. Know that I do not."

2
BLUES+JAZZ

Lapham agreed. It was too good of a deal to pass up. I explained to him that I already had the bare bones of an idea, but it would take some 'feasibility study.' That seemed like a term he would appreciate. From his end, I needed the release date of his new film and when and where Jordan would be screening it for his review. He said he would call the studio publicity people, get the information, and pass it on through Norton. I also told him to be prepared to appear on the This Day show to promote the film and not bother the studio about it. I would take care of everything.

"Forget it. We've never been able to get a booking on that show. Each time they make up some flimsy excuse to hand the publicist. Now, of course, it's understandable. Jordan got me blackballed there."

"Really? Maybe I can make the blackball a little less black."

xx

When I got down to the Porsche 911 in the garage, I got in and thought for a while. There's not much in a parking garage to divert your thoughts. There was a large contingent of people I would need for this commission. Not to mention the cooperation of the weather, assuming...

I started the car and left the garage, turning right onto Washington Boulevard, then a quick right onto Motor. I decided to drive through Cheviot Hills, a prettier drive than taking Overland. I picked up the phone and called Roee.

"Talk." It was Roee's standard greeting when he answered The Phone.

"What's the weather like in New York right now?"

"Well, it's the dead of winter."

"Yes...?"

"Lots of snowstorms—pretty miserable."

"Likely to keep up for a couple of weeks?"

"What are you doing? Running a numbers game based on the weather?"

"Roee...?"

"Should I get a Farmer's Almanac?"

"How accurate is that?"

"I don't know. I'm not a farmer."

"I need something I can rely on."

"Fixxer, surely you've heard that the weather is something people can talk about but not do much about."

"Yeah, I've heard, but I'll bet Petey hasn't."

"Oh, yes. I'll patch him in on the scrambler."

Petey still worked for the old place near the nation's capital, and although The Phone is very secure, I could never guarantee that their phones were. Suddenly he was on, speaking in his customary near shout.

"Fixxer, you old lady killer!"

"I thought you said you'd never bring that up again. Besides, I paid the death benefits."

"Sure, sure! How are you?"

"I'm okay for a man in my condition."

"And what condition is that?"

"The human condition, Petey, the human condition."

"Ha-ha! I fall for that every time!"

"So, how's the Veritas Bear Rug Program holding up?" Veritas was a software that could have changed the world if greed for power and money had not interfered to corrupt it—and I had not interfered to stop the greed. It was an amusing, if hazardous, bit of fixing I had done a while ago. The Veritas computer program was essentially a dream machine. Petey's favorite dreams were wet ones.

"Oh, Fixxer, it's great! Guess who I made love to last night?"

"That's a guess I don't wish to hazard."

"Eleanor Roosevelt!"

"Eleanor Roosevelt?"

"Yeah, I mean, I was trying for Sharon Stone, but I've been reading this book on the Roosevelts, and I couldn't get her out of my head. You know, Fixxer, she wasn't bad!"

"Fine. Petey, do you remember—"

"You know what they say about still waters running deep, as in thro—"

"Yeah, Petey, that's just great, but—"

"I mean, there was a certain appeal to her—"

"Petey—"

"Of course, it started to get kind of weird when I heard the ever-so-subtle squeak of a wheelchair—"

"Petey!"

"So you need something, right, Fixxer?"

"How's the weather back there?"

"Brutal."

"That's nice."

"You can talk! You're in California! Say, do you need me out there?"

"Sorry."

"Damn! So you called about the weather, so I told you, so goodbye!"

"Petey, I'm worried that the weather will let up back there in the next couple of weeks."

"Boy, you're just plain mean!"

"For a particular reason, and on a particular day, I require the worst winter conditions possible—especially in Manhattan. I'd be willing to have it confined to the West '70s."

"That's big of ya!"

"I'm remembering that time in the thaw between East-West relations when our masters didn't want it to thaw so quickly."

"When we had to keep their foreign minister snowbound in Moscow for a day or two."

"That's the time."

"Oh, yeah."

"You concocted a cloud seeder much better than the normal dry ice or silver iodide."

"Yeah! I called it Super-Seed!" Petey said with justifiable pride.

"Got some in your stores?"

"You know, Fixxer, it's a pollutant."

"I only need a little."

"And it is only Manhattan, after all."

"So if, on this particular day if there is an unwanted break in the weather, would you be able to repair that break?"

"Assuming there are enough super-cooled clouds in the sky?"

"Okay, assuming that."

"Well, I could take the day off. Hire a plane. Sure, why not?"

"And if the weather is already bad, maybe just this side of brutal?"

"Then I could make it more than brutal. A real blizzard for the books."

"Really?"

"Yeah. I love to set records. Ten grand for the seed, you pay for the plane, call it five grand for my time."

"Okay."

"What, you're not going to negotiate me down?"

"I was going to offer 20 and 10. You need to value yourself higher, Petey."

"Fixxer, you're a bastard! A beautiful one, but a bastard nonetheless."

"Well—pays the bills. I'll contact you soon."

xx

I returned home at about 5:30, turning the Porsche over to Frank, the Iranian Beverly Hills High School senior on duty in the underground garage.

"Good evening, Sir," he said very right and proper to me. "Sir" is the only way the building's staff can address me. For my name is unknown to them—as it is unknown to everyone except Roee.

"Good evening, Frank. Have the car washed; I've been south of Pico," I said as I made my way to the elevator bank.

"Uh..."

There was a bi-level fear of reprisal in his voice. I stopped.

"Yes, Frank?"

"Uh..."

"Frank," I took a few steps back towards him, "'...How can we regulate events, of which we yet know not whether they will happen? And why should we think, with painful anxiety, about that on which our thoughts can have no influence?'" I enjoy quoting the good doctor from Litchfield.

"Wha—what?"

"Speak up, Frank. If I get angry, I get angry, and there's not a damn thing you can do about it. Whereas, obviously, since you've had some courage even to utter your shaking 'Uh...' you must feel quite compelled to say something to me."

"Mr. Roee told me to keep the car here, as you will probably want to go right out."

"Oh, Mr. Roee said that, did he?"

"Yes, sir. He just called down."

"You know Mr. Roee is Jewish?"

"Uh—yes, sir."

"How do you know that?"

"He won't let the building deliver anything to your floor after sunset on Fridays."

"Yes, damn inconvenient. The point, though, is you wouldn't be making this up to get a Jew into trouble, would you?"

His eyes went a beautiful fearful. "Uh, no, Sir. Wh—why would I do that?"

"You're Iranian."

"But I've been in America since I was three."

"And Islamic."

"No, Sir. We're Presbyterian. Well, at least my parents are. I—

I don't go to church."

"So you're not out gunning for Salman Rushdie?"

"Who?"

I smiled. I'm not sure it relieved him. "All right, Frank. Keep the car available." Then I turned and headed for the elevators.

I already knew all these salient points about Frank. I had got him the job in the garage, as I had gotten his older brother, Joe, the same position two years before, although neither knew that. I made a mental note to call his father and scold him for spending too much time away from home lecturing on the good old days under the Shah. Frank needed a little infusion of his cultural identity (sans any prejudices), or he was doomed to become too typically American.

When I got home—the whole 15th floor in a Westwood high-rise on Wilshire Boulevard—Roee greeted me as the elevator doors opened.

"I think you should go out and see Mike."

Roee is never much one for the little ceremonies. He just stood there, effectively blocking the entrance into my home, his sharp face and the arrow of his dusty red hair seeming to be pointing the way out.

"Mike? Mike who?"

"Newsstand Mike," he said in his matter-of-fact way.

"Newsstand Mike? Why should I vacate hearth and home so close to dinner to see Newsstand Mike? If he has any information, get it and pay him."

Newsstand Mike worked the Sherman Oaks Newsstand on the corner of Van Nuys and Ventura in The Valley. He was one of my "Fonts of Wisdom," a core group of people whose information, from salacious gossip to cold hard facts (often the same things), helps feed the database in my computer on the people and personalities of Hollywood. "Information" is a bit of a hobby for me. Newsstand Mike might seem an odd font of such information. But he is a showbiz fanatic, nosy, tenacious, and a bit like a bartender to his customers, including many Hollywood foot soldiers who are usually pissed off about one thing or another. Or, more importantly, one person or another is usually a person more powerful than themselves. Hollywood has the highest per capita percentage of well-paid pissers & moaners in America. Washington, D.C., of course, holds the overall record for pissers & moaners, but they are not that well paid.

"It's not information he has, but a problem," Roee elaborated.

"If Mike has a problem that needs my help, he doesn't have the income to pay for it—so what's for supper? I believe, this morning, you said something about lamb?"

"It seems to be a problem a friend of his has."

"Does Mike have any friends that could pay my fee?"

"I doubt it."

"It was a new recipe; I think you said."

"Fixxer—he's a valuable resource."

"And I pay for that value."

"Norton agrees that you should go out."

"Oh, Norton does, does he?"

"Yeah. He had a good long talk with Mike."

"A talk?"

"Yes."

"A good one?"

"Yes."

"And a long one?"

"Yes."

"I can't tell you how impressed I am. Something about a sauce made from crushed pomegranate."

"I didn't make any supper tonight."

"You didn't—"

"Thinking of Newsstand Mike, I was reminded how much you like the food at Blues+Jazz."

"Which is right next door to the newsstand."

"You have told me they make an excellent ham dish."

"Which you, of course, won't make for me."

"My God is not a forgiving god."

"It was good you thought to tell Frank to hold the Porsche."

"Forethought is one of my strengths."

"And I bless you for it, sir. If anybody should happen to call, I'll be at Blues+Jazz."

Then I turned around and reentered the elevator. I stopped the doors just before they closed. "Roee?"

"Yes?"

"Don't go to bed before I get back. We've got much to talk about on the new commission from Lapham. I want to brief you tonight so you can start things early tomorrow."

"You're going to make me suffer, aren't you?"

"Yes," I smiled a big and, I hoped, wicked smile. "but it will be good for you. Bye."

xx

Frank had the Porsche running and ready for me to leap right in, which I did. I quickly got onto Beverly Glen and went over the hill to get to Sherman Oaks. It was a pleasant, clear, L.A. winter evening. A three-day storm had just ended the day before, and it had remained cool and breezy enough to keep the vision-impairing particles of pollution from creeping back into our air and souls. So once I got onto the dark canyon curves of the Glen, the sky was there and nicely black, and what stars could be seen had about as fine a clarity of twinkle as they ever get over L.A. I took Beverly Glen down to Ventura Boulevard, made a left there, then a left onto Van Nuys Boulevard, placing the Porsche right in front of the newsstand on the west side of the street. I parked in the No Parking zone but knew Mike would protect the car.

Mike saw me when I pulled up. I saw him hand over the responsibility of the cash register to one of his coworkers as I got out of the car. Mike walked over to me quite nervous, evidenced by the slight tremble of his jaw, which wagged his long, gray-streaked chin beard. When he got to me, he looked up at me and took his dirty Sherman Oaks Newsstand baseball cap off his head. A sign of respect he had never shown me before.

"Hi, Fixx. Gee, I really want to thank you for coming on out."

"And I want to thank you for making me miss what I assume was going to be a lovely lamb dinner."

"Fixx—this is important. Other—otherwise, I never would have called Mr. Macbeth."

This was a Mike I had never seen before. Where was the confident little man always so sure of himself and his facts—the character comfortable with his role in the scheme of things? Mike was the kind of person you never assumed had a personal life, either at home or even inside his head. He was one of those people who flowed in and out of your life to give an accent to it, the kind of person you never thought about existing except during those times. He stood here now, though, Newsstand Mike, his eyes pleading, nervous, concerned over something. Something "Important." It seemed I couldn't help myself. I had to take him seriously.

"Okay. Let's talk."

He walked me over to the little pizza-by-the-slice joint south of the stand and offered to buy me a cup of coffee. I passed. That left him nowhere to go but to start.

"There's this girl, uh—" He corrected himself, "Young woman. Bea—Bea Cherbourg. She's been a customer here at the stand since she got into L.A. a couple of years ago."

"From?"

"Back East. Connecticut. She graduated from Yale. She came out here to work in film."

"She's an actress?"

"No, anything but. She wants to write—and direct."

"Oh. A *filmmaker*."

"Yeah. I could tell because she bought all the film magazines. I mean from *Film Comment* to *Variety*. The whole range."

"I see the problem."

"No, no, actually, she was doing pretty well. At Yale, she had been in the Gamma Phi Epsilon sorority. It's really a film club."

"Yes, I've heard of it. Created to create an 'Old Girls Network,' I believe."

"Yes, that's right. And it works. It got Bea a job at Olympic Pictures."

"Because Sara Hutton's running the place."

"Yeah. And she went to Yale."

"And was president of Gamma Phi Epsilon her senior year."

"That's right. So she's always interested in talent from there."

"And Bea is a talent?"

"She's brilliant."

"That's not what I asked."

Mike looked down. Then back up at me. "I don't know. I mean, how would I know? But she thinks she is. Anyway, she didn't get hired for talent at first. Not that kind of talent. Hutton hired her as a reader and made it clear that she would personally groom Bea into a top-flight motion picture executive."

"Mike, where is this leading?"

"Well, I—I'm not any good at explaining it. She should explain it. I—I want you to help her Fixx. I want you to talk her out of something."

"Out of what?"

"Out of using your services."

"Mike, that's somewhat antithetical to doing good business and a habit I don't want to get into.'

"Well..."

"How does she even know about me to want the services I have to talk her out of?"

"Oh, well, you know, she knows the rumors. You know, I mean, you know, you're one of those rumors."

"Yes, thanks to good marketing I pay dearly for. But, usually, people at her entry level..."

"Ah, well, I got to bragging that I knew you, and—you know.?"

"Mike...?"

"I know, I know, it's against our bargain, but—Fixx—I love her."

Mike is about thirty-seven or thirty-eight. Short, no more than five-three, wiry, with a tattoo on his left shoulder proclaiming the superiority of the Rebel Alliance and one on his right that says: Rosebud. As I mentioned, he sports a long, black-and-white chin beard and loves his old Sherman Oaks Newsstand baseball cap too much. The women he appreciated the most were those prominently featured on the cover of the magazines closest to the cash register. The ones with names like *Juggs, Girls On Girls, Cum Agin',* and *Hot & Horny.* If I had ever taken the time to imagine what Mike thought would be the dream romance for him, I would have guessed a plot wherein Mike rescues from the low life and a drug habit the ex-child star of a late '70s sit-com, now just a hint of her once irrepressibly cute self. But enough of a hint for Mike. I would not have imagined he would ever fall in love with a Yale graduate climbing the Hollywood corporate ladder.

"Does she love you?"

"Of course not," he said as a painful matter of fact. "And she doesn't know that I love her, but—but I do." He paused for a moment. Then he took a deep breath and said, "Something happened, and she's very angry, and she came to me, and she wanted to know if I could get her in touch with you because she wants to hurt people, she wants to hurt them really bad. Especially Sara Hutton." He was quiet for another second while he got another breath. "She's pure, Fixxer. She's a pure person, and suddenly there's this hate eating her up, and she's going to try to attack and hurt people who could—could squash her. I don't want to see her hurt. So I want you to talk her out of it. I want you to talk some sense into her."

There was a glistening in his eyes, a potential for tears.

"Where is she now?" I quietly asked.

"She's in Blues+Jazz. Waiting for you."

"Do you want to come in and introduce us?"

"No. I'll take you there. I'll point her out, but—but no."

"Okay, Mike. I'll take care of it."

"Fixx, thanks; I mean, I owe you, man, I really owe you. The next really juicy information, free of charge. Free of charge."

"Well, we'll talk about that at the time."

Then we walked up to the corner of Ventura and Van Nuys, passing the newsstand, to stand in front of the large, rusted-looking metal door of Blues+Jazz. It was the design choice of this small restaurant that featured live blues and jazz combos within its used brick walls and under its fake corrugated metal roof. I opened the door and allowed Mike to walk into an open area dominated by the kitchen, which stood—cooks busy with their tasks—for all to see. Next to this area was the main dining room with black top tables, each with four simple chairs. And a small bandstand up against the west brick wall. There were just a few scattered customers, most looking at menus. A tall black man with used-up eyes tuned his bass; another black man sat at the drums looking bored, and a white guy I pegged to be a jazz instructor at a local community college looked nervously over sheet music at the piano.

"That's her there." Mike pointed to a young woman sitting off to the side, a coffee in front of her which she seemed to be staring into. I gave her a good look. The assessment came quickly. If Vulnerability were ever to have a poster child, she would have been it.

I walked over to her table and said, "Bea Cherbourg?"

3
TO KISS THE GOLDEN ARSE

I had walked up quietly, and the sudden mention of her name startled her. But only slightly. She looked up at me. She had a good, strong face. The vulnerability was mainly exposed in her brown eyes, magnified just shy of distortion by glasses. The frames of her glasses were not stylish, but I assumed they were—somewhat consciously on her part—reaching for a personal style. They were oval, almost eye shape, making them mask-like, which was probably the intent. She had a long face with a strong jaw, but not one that made her look mannish. She had a long nose complimentary to her face, a good complexion, and thick, ginger hair that fell with a slight wave onto her shoulders. Her mouth was set straight with lips that were together and which were not quite thin but certainly not sensuous. You could imagine, though, that when she smiled—if she smiled—it would be a pleasant one.

"Oh, hi. You're Mike's friend?"

"It's probably more accurate to say Mike is my friend."

"Oh."

"In any case, I am here at Mike's request. May I sit?"

"Yes, of course."

I sat and waved the waiter over.

"Let's order dinner. I'm starved."

"Do you want to stay here? I mean, is this place okay? We'll have to shout when the band starts to hear each other."

"Yes, that's true, but it also means that only we will hear each other."

The waiter came over, and I ordered the baked ham dinner. She ordered a salad. The kind one picks at rather than eats. I also ordered a vodka tonic with a lemon twist. She asked a Sam Adams lager.

"What do I call you?" she asked after the drinks had arrived and the music had started. It was some cool jazz. Mellow.

"What have you been told to call me?"

"Mike calls you The Fixxer."

"He has been granted that privilege."

"And me?"

"Tell me your story. Answer my questions. You will probably not need to call me anything."

"I don't really know where to begin."

I started to speak, but she cut me off.

"Yes, I know, at the beginning. It doesn't seem to me to be as simple as that. And yet, I consider myself a storyteller. I mean, all I've ever wanted to do was to tell stories. From the time I was about eight. Stories that moved people. 'To tears and to action,' as one of my teachers used to pound into us."

She said the last words with a slight laugh, slightly proud, slightly embarrassed. Then she paused as if looking for something in her head—or for permission.

"Continue," I said, giving it.

"Film—film is the storytelling medium of our day, of this century. Do you understand? Film, for better or for worse, is it."

"You sound defensive."

"Do I?"

"Yes."

"My mother wanted me to be a novelist."

It made sense. Bea Cherbourg looked like a novelist. "Why aren't you one?"

"I think in images. I can't help it. Even when I read a novel, even a great novel, I see images; I don't see words, I don't even hear them in my head."

"Sounds like Evelyn Wood Speed Reading to me."

"No, it's more than that, it's—look, when you grow up now, you grow up surrounded by the moving image. Movies, TV, newscasts, and music videos. It's how we communicate."

By "we," she meant, of course, her generation. Whatever that was, she was implying by her tone that I was not part of it.

"I never imagined I could tell stories in any way but as a filmmaker."

The waiter came with the food, set it down, and asked if we had everything we needed. Bea smiled when she looked up at the waiter and responded yes. I had been right—about the smile.

"You know, Bea, I'm getting to know who you are, but not what your story is."

"All story starts from character." She smiled again. The eyes now peeked from behind the mask.

"The same teacher?"

She nodded. "He was brilliant."

"And you had an affair with him," I stated.

She blushed, but she admitted it, "Yes." The color from the blush was complimentary. It brought to her face a certain loveliness—a particular old-fashioned attractiveness. I had a thought: I would love to see her smiling in clear, bright, windswept sunlight.

"But it ended?"

"Yes. I wanted to stay. Get my master's. Teach. Be with him."

"But he said you had to come out here. To Hollywood. Make a difference."

"Yes. When I came out here, I thought I would waitress or do temp work. I was looking forward to it, you know, the struggle before the success. I thought I would meet up with other struggling filmmakers; maybe get involved in a low-budget but interesting film. Wind up at Sundance. But I got a job right away as a reader at Olympic Pictures. I didn't even go after it. They called me."

"Gamma Phi Epsilon."

"Yes, how...? Oh—Mike. He's sweet."

"He's concerned about you."

She repeated, "He's sweet," then picked an olive from her salad and ate it. "Anyway, I was suddenly making good money. More than I thought I would be making at this point. I don't come from a rich family."

"You got to Yale on a scholarship?"

"Yes, so earning this kind of money was great. I leased a condo right up here on Dickens. Got a car, a BMW. You know, used but nice."

"How was the job?"

"Interesting," she furrowed her brow when she said it as if the word was not quite adequate. "At first, anyway. Then it became kind of—frustrating. Boring. You can't imagine how many terrible scripts are submitted to the studio. To have to write reports making sense of them is a real chore. Out of a kind of self-defense, I took to being kind of—I don't know— funny about them, I guess, sort of Dorothy Parker-like. After about two months, I was called into Sara Hutton's office. I was terrified. I mean, she's the president of the company. I had seen her around the lot, but—but it turned out okay. I guess she liked my reports; she liked the barbs I threw in on the really bad scripts. She told me that she had personally hired me as a sister of Gamma Phi, which was very important to her. She also told me that I had been assigned only scripts that were coming in from the smaller agencies representing the weakest writers. It had been sort of a test, and I had passed with flying colors. She said this as she gave me a big hug."

"A big hug?"

"It was creepy."

"Was it sexual?"

"Absolutely. She's a lesbian, you know."

"That's not true."

"Well, later, she even tried to—"

"She's bisexual."

"How do you know?"

"I have it on good authority."

"Well, what's the difference?"

"Are you homophobic?"

"No! I just don't want to be violated—taken advantage of—by

anybody."

"Is this what you are angry over?"

"No. I can handle passes. I'm angry because she blackmailed me."

She quickly ran through the rest of the story, how Hutton had scripts from more established writers assigned to her, how she had begun to groom Bea for a development position, and how Hutton had given her a raise. It was all exciting yet frightening. She wasn't sure it was what she wanted, becoming a motion picture executive. Then she decided to write her own script as a test to help her decide which road to take. It took her eight months of late-night writing, but she was happy with it when it was done. She had consciously taken the high-concept elements she knew the studio was looking for but tried to place them in a well-written, character-driven script, one with a strong female protagonist. She showed it to a young agent she had been dating, and he loved it. He made up a pseudonym for her and submitted it to Olympic. Bea made sure it was assigned to another reader. It did well, moving up the studio system, and the studio got excited and wanted to buy it. It was then that the agent revealed the actual name of the author.

"I don't think Sara was happy about it. She acted happy, but—"

"It wasn't her game plan for you."

"Yes, exactly. I mean, she said, in a joking sort of way, but in a creepy way—"

"Like her hugs?"

"Yes—she said, 'You know, I was just weeks away from inviting you to kiss the golden arse, but now I'm not so sure.'"

"To kiss the golden arse?"

"I had no idea what she met. When I mentioned it to others, people either didn't know or reacted strangely, in, you know, in a funny sort of way—but no one would explain it."

"Where does the blackmail come in?"

"She said I couldn't stay at the studio, they would consider it a conflict of interest, but she said she would go out on a limb and pay more for the script than they normally would and make me co-producer on the film. It all sounded great to me. So I left the studio that day, thinking I would have a check for the script in a few days and would start on the rewrite. The studio always orders a rewrite. The negotiations, though, dragged on forever over small points. For five months. I couldn't believe it. During that time, I didn't earn a dime. I had savings, so I was okay for a while. The deal finally closed, but most of the money was tied up as bonuses; I got very little upfront. Then, after I signed the contract, they announced they wanted somebody with more experience to do the rewrite. I was shocked."

"You shouldn't have been."

"I know, but that didn't stop it from happening. Anyway, as a co-producer, they asked me to the meetings with potential writers. It was obvious from the way they interviewed the writers that all they really wanted from my script was the concept. Then, after a writer was hired, in the first story meeting, Sara told him—it was a *him*, of course—to throw out my main character and create a character who was just, well, just a girl. I protested. Loudly. I told them I wrote the script to portray a strong female who could triumph alone. Who had an inner strength of character mixed with human frailty. I was most proud of having created a well-rounded character. All story comes from character, I told them."

"How did they take being lectured to?"

Sara shot a look at me, taking what I said as censure. But a slight pulling back of her stare made it clear that what I said was not unjustified.

"Sara turned to me, smiled, and said, 'I know what you were trying to accomplish with this character, but I think we ought to go for the cliché.' I was stunned. Not that she would want to do this, but that she would so gleefully announce it. As we walked out of the meeting, this little shit VP, Don Gulden, leaned into me and said, 'You'll never be asked to kiss the golden arse acting that way.'"

"The golden arse again."

"Yeah. When I got home, there was a message from my agent on the machine. I called him. He said the studio called with an ultimatum. If I wanted my producer's development fee check—which wasn't much, but it was the only extra income I had coming in—I couldn't go to any more meetings. 'But it was my story,' I said. 'Not anymore,' he said. 'But what about the contract?' I asked him. He said it didn't matter. What was I going to do, sue Olympic? I had no choice; I had no money left, so I agreed."

"That was the blackmail?"

"Yes, I was appalled. Then he said they wanted me to know Sara Hutton was very disappointed in me. As if that was information that would make me feel bad."

"It's information that might frighten some."

"Sure, but this was as if it was supposed to hurt me. You know, on an emotional level. Like I had let her down."

She had hardly touched her salad, but she ordered another lager. "What can I do to get back at her?" She finally asked, her eyes dropping down as the question came up.

"Someone once said that success is the best revenge."

"I don't want to wait that long." She looked back up at me. "I want to hurt her now. Mike said that that's the kind of stuff that you do."

"Mike doesn't know what I do. He only knows what he thinks I do."

"So, you don't...?"

"I fix things, Bea. Problems people run into in their careers and lives in Hollywood. Sometimes the problems are due to their own stupidity, greed, or hubris. Occasionally, they are due to harm being done to them by other people's stupidity, greed, or hubris. Now and then, they are just perceived problems standing in the way of wish fulfillment. Those I handle on a case-by-case basis after due consideration of the potential outcome and the potential profit. Those are the cases I charge the most for."

"And you charge...?"

"A lot. It is always, from anyone's perspective, a lot."

"So I can't afford you?"

"It's unlikely that you could, but more germane to our discussion is that there is nothing here to fix."

The shock on her face went from insult to injury in something less than a flash.

Each human ego has two great desires: To be recognized for its uniqueness and to be taken seriously. The second is essential for the first to be a recognition of honor, something for the mantelpiece. These two desires are easily self-fulfilled—too easily, in fact—but the desires are never truly satiated until others fulfill them. The struggle to make others come around is every human story, from the child desperate for a parent's regard to a mass murderer crying out from the middle of the mass to a star personality from entertainment, sports, or politics knowing how to work the public. It's not just an old story; it's the oldest story. Yet each of us somehow thinks it is just their story. Bea Cherbourg had gotten herself so worked up over her personal injuries that it was a blow for her to see that I did not share her outrage.

She removed her glasses and wiped the half tears—the only ones she was willing to allow—away from the corners of her eyes. "Okay," she said in acceptance but with defiance at the edge.

There was a bit of Miss Jones creeping into my head. A bit of *Why Miss Jones without your glasses you're...* The mask was away.

"Look, Bea, you must understand that Hollywood is an all-volunteer army. No one is drafted into the business, and enough has been written about Hollywood that no one should come here without knowing that war is possible. You've had an unusually charmed basic training. You landed a good studio job without trying. You have one of the most powerful people in the industry willing to mentor you in what has become the second most important business in America. Okay, so there are some 'creepy' elements about her. You can't hold that against a person in this town. You were in a good position. Many people were waiting in line for that position if you didn't want it—and you didn't. Okay. I admire people who know what they want. From a great position, you took a chance and shifted and won. You sold your first screenplay. There's another long line at the recruitment office dreaming of your life. Then you get buffeted by the process, bumped, and bruised, but you had the integrity of character—or the temerity—to say, 'Hey! Quit rocking the boat!' The point is, though, it's their fucking boat. They can rock it all they want, and if you don't like it, fine, get out—for now. You're still going to be paid. You'll most likely get a first-position writing credit. You'll have a career."

"But my story—"

"Is not your story anymore. It's been bought and paid for. Bea, take my suggestion; let them have this one. After all, it's just movies."

She stared at me—deeply—as if she intended me to look away. I did not. Then she put her glasses back on.

"If I had the money to pay you—"

"It's not about my fee. I have worked on commission before. I will, from time to time, invest in a person's potential."

"You think I have no potential then."

"I think you are too young, too much at the beginning to be consumed by hate. Anyone who can afford my fee has probably been through periods when they had no recourse to slights, big and small. So they learned to take it. Those who could see the comedy in it all took it slightly better. They developed hard, thick calluses, not festering sores. Then when the time came when they could ask me to do something about a problem, they did it as a matter of business. With dispassion, not with hate."

"That's the most frightening thing I've ever heard."

"Give it time. It'll eventually wind up low on your list."

XX

I paid the bill, and we left the restaurant, walking up to Mike at the cash register of the newsstand.

"Is everything okay?" he asked.

"Yes," Bea said. "Your 'friend' doused me with reality quite effectively. I will go home and practice grinning and bearing."

Mike caught the pain of the comment. "Do you want me to walk you home?"

"No, thank you, Mike. I would really prefer to be alone."

Bea Cherbourg turned to me, saying nothing at first. Possibly she was trying to memorize the aspects of my face—or allowing me time to memorize hers. "Goodbye," she suddenly said in a neutral tone, then turned and walked down the street, heading towards Dickens, leaving the full light of the newsstand for the intermittent illumination of streetlamps and headlights. I looked after her and noticed for the first time what a fine and shapely body she had, revealed by a well-cut and attractive suit. Shame on you! I would have said to myself had I not enjoyed this atavistic attention to my genes.

"Do you think she'll be all right?" Mike asked.

"Mike, I see where the love lies."

He was embarrassed. "Hey, you didn't say—"

"Of course not. If you are satisfied with the unrequited, I am satisfied for you. I'm just acknowledging the universality of your feelings."

"Yeah, fine, but will she be all right?"

"I don't know, Mike. She's a romantic and an idealist. That doesn't bode well. She's young, and that's a debit. On the other hand, she's young, and that's a credit. See how complex it is? The whole thing revolves around whether she's a survivor or not. And there's no way to tell that until she's survived a few setbacks—or doesn't. At least for now, I've dissuaded her from getting Old Testament about the situation. As was the request."

"Yeah. Thanks—thanks a lot, Fixx. I really, really appreciate it."

xx

I drove home wanting to think about the Lapham commission, but I couldn't get Bea Cherbourg out of my head. I kept wondering if I had, perhaps, presented reality as a little more razor-sharp than it truly is. But I couldn't find fault with myself. Reality is something I'm possibly too familiar with—in much more than just its Hollywood incarnation. Indeed, one of the appeals of doing business in this town was the opportunity to avoid realities far more razor-sharp and cutting than this one, with all its well-worn tinsel, glitter, and gold.

By the time I came to the corner of Beverly Glen and Wilshire and stopped at the red light prepared to make the left turn towards my building, a Los Angeles high-rise of rare architectural interest, I had convinced myself that it had been a good deed well done.

TO KISS AND MAKE UP

When I got home, Roee, as instructed, had not gone to bed and was waiting for me. You have to appreciate what a sacrifice this was on his part. For Roee, going to bed is not just going to bed. It's when he writes, so his wont is to "go to bed" fairly early whenever our evenings are not taken up with a commission. Roee is a failed playwright, but that doesn't stop him from continuing to write. What is failure anyway? The measure of a bank account—or the mismeasure of a man? Roee's work is abstract, absurd, obtuse, full of veiled references to the Talmud, and completely asexual. Not destined for the lights of Broadway, but then, such lights Roee would find too harsh as they might reach back and illuminate his past—something he could not afford to happen.

He greeted me in the dining room, sitting at his usual spot, which was set with a place mat and a silver spoon, as, indeed, was mine. Between the two settings was a silver pitcher.

"How was dinner?" he asked.

"Delicious, an excellent high culinary insult to your god."

"I'll be sure to pass that along. How was the rest of the evening?"

"Have Newsstand Mike report to Norton," I said as I sat down, "who can then pass it along to you. I would rather we talk about the Lapham commission, which, I think, will be a great deal of fun. Not to mention highly profitable. Now, what am I looking forward to here?" I asked, indicating the setup.

"Well, since I knew we would be up, I made you some peach cobbler. Served with heavy cream, of course."

I was delighted; peach cobbler is one of my favorites. "Well, thank you, Roee. That was sweet of you. It's that sensitive homosexual side of you, isn't it?" Of course, I was saying this to a man who, in the line of duty, had dispassionately dispatched to their various gods more than a few disrupters of civilized society.

Roee stood up abruptly, pushing his chair back several feet. "Fixxer, you ever call me sweet again," he said as his eyes contacted mine, "and I'll have your guts for garters!" Then he rolled his eyes up and did a dead-on impression of Truman Capote. "Nice red ones with a frou-frou of white lace."

I laughed generously. After all, I am the only audience Roee might ever have.

xx

Roee brought out the peach cobbler; I poured on the heavy cream, I threw my palate into an ecstasy of sweet sensations, then laid out the particulars of the Lapham commission and my basic plan, including Petey's potential part. Then I went over my needs.

"By tomorrow, we should know when and where Robert Jordan will screen Lapham's film. My guess is one of the screening rooms in the Tribeca area. He screens films alone, probably, most of the big critics do. Be prepared to fly to New York at a moment's notice. You'll need access to the screening room. If you can't get it through financial means, then use stealth. Be sure to take the Bag O' Tricks, and check out the night equipment before you go, especially the AN/PVS-4 scope. While in New York, negotiate for and secure the real estate, personnel, and equipment needed. Of course, we'll use Michael Slayton, but we'll fly him in just before the job. Call tomorrow and make sure he's not on a film right now. If he is—get him a couple of days off. Who's our person on the *This Day* show?"

"A young PA named Andrea."

"Has she been reliable?"

"She's only been there three months, but she's fed us some good stuff."

I found it advantageous to have placed on every network morning show, on the Leno and Letterman shows, and on several of the crews on *Entertainment Tonight* and the *E!* channel, representatives of, shall we say, my interests. These are people with a healthy interest in cash, who keep their eyes and ears open in the green rooms, the makeup rooms, and on-location shoots for the little slips of action and information that can come when guests are too nervous or too relaxed waiting to go on. Often little rumors are stated, opinions are expressed, and accusations are made when scenes are played out with wives, husbands, or lovers. Who has a drug habit? Who subscribes to an offbeat religious or political notion? Who orders the fat sucked out of their trophy wife's butt? Most of it is frivolous information, but Roee and I dutifully enter it into a data bank on our computer. You never know when circumstances will make silly rumors timely information.

"Have her start taking a full set of photographs. I want every inch of the studio covered. Where is she from?"

"Ohio. A town called Worthington."

"Ah. The kind of place where one can build character."

"Exactly."

"Tell her to tell her bosses it's for Mom and Dad back in Worthington. Also, find out from her Jordan's schedule of appearances on the show and when he will be doing his on-air review of Lapham's film. We gear everything around that date. I think that covers it. Got any questions?"

"No."

"Good. If all goes well—and it will—we'll take the next day off and relax. Providing Petey gives us a break in the weather. You'll be able to visit Tom."

"That would be nice."

"And I can continue my search for Gilgamesh Paul. I may have a lead."

Roee did not hesitate to display his disapproval. "When will you give up your obsession to find that guy?"

"I wouldn't call it an obsession. I started something. Now I'm going to finish it."

"How much time have you wasted here on it?"

"He obviously can't be found in L.A."

"So you think you'll have better luck in New York?"

"Makes sense, doesn't it?"

"No. Why? Gilgamesh Paul is a forgotten man. There is no one left to care for him."

"I care."

"How can you? You really know nothing about him."

"I know what I've heard. I'm intrigued. I think he's a man I want to spend some time with."

"He's a man from the past."

"True, as, in many ways, so am I. Look, I've never asked you to get involved in this."

"Wrong. I had to check out the Santa Barbara lead."

"I was down with the flu at the time."

"It couldn't have waited?"

"The lead was fresh."

"And false."

"What, you didn't enjoy the day in Santa Barbara?"

"Well...."

"You got back really late."

Roee rolled his eyes up. He then smiled. I got up quietly, having decided to leave him with his memories. "Oh, by the way," he said, stopping me.

"Yes?"

"Anne Eisley called."

"Anne? From Australia?"

"Yes."

"Interesting."

"I told her you were out, that we had some business to take care of this evening when you got back, but that you would be available to take a call—" Roee stopped and consulted his watch. The Phone rang. "Just about now. I'll get it, shall I?"

"Oh, yes, please do."

"Fine. If you'll but retire to the library, I'll send the call through."

I had not heard from Anne for quite a while. Indeed, until that moment, I did not expect to hear from her again—outside of my monthly commission checks. I had done a job for her a while back, a little Hollywood pest control. Then I asked her aid in another job I was doing, the same one that had introduced us all to the wonders of Veritas. For that job, I had a particular use for her extreme beauty. The kind of beauty most men fall in love with upon first sight. Yes, love, not just lust. Lust is a knee-jerk reaction—emphasis on the Jerk. After the job, we—"Stayed in touch" is the appropriately delicate way to put it. It was a fantastic time. I couldn't chronicle it if I wanted to, but it has its neural net in my brain, which I like to throw out now and then to capture my imagination.

The phone rang in the library, and I picked it up. "I thought you said you never wanted to talk to me again?"

"No," came her voice, thrill-inducing waves of perfect pitch. "I said I never wanted to see you again. I'm not seeing you. I'm just hearing you."

"So, when you return to L.A., we can only have phone sex?"

"I don't know. What's your credit card limit?"

"I'll hock Roee."

There was a sudden quiet on the other end. Except for the breathing that seemed an airy manifestation of thoughts trying to be gathered. "Fixxer, I, uh—I just thought you might like to hear that I've missed you."

"Can't say I blame you."

"Oh, god, you're infuriating!"

"Oh, god, you're enchanting."

"You're insufferable!"

"And you are indescribably beautiful."

"Yes, well, I know, but that's my trade, right?"

"Don't undersell your acting ability."

"Fixxer, I am not the female lead in *Return of the Road Warrior* because of my acting ability."

"I heard you only got the job because you had paid-up

insurance."

She laughed. A little. Then it stopped. "You were not very kind to me when we last saw each other."

"I was honest."

"Honest? How can you call yourself honest when you have no name or past? Or, at least, won't reveal them to me."

"Never explain the mystery."

"Even to me?"

"Even to you."

"But I, but we—"

"That's a condition I can't help. Nor, I assume from the fact that you called me, can you. We are just going to have to deal with it."

"Or not."

"Or not."

"Goodbye," Anne said softly.

"Goodbye."

"Sweet dreams" were her last words before she hung up. I believe it was a sincere sentiment.

It's the life I've chosen for myself, or maybe the life chosen for me. I try not to dwell on the fine points.

XX

A week later, I met Larry Lapham in his office at 4:45 in the morning.

"Why are we here so fucking early?" he asked, expressing the pique he had probably been rehearsing since his shower an hour earlier.

I looked at him briefly, focusing on his goofy overbite, then orally punctuated the look. "I do not allow my clients to ask questions."

"I am paying you a million dollars plus expenses and can't ask questions?"

"Ignoring for a moment that that is another question, I'll simply state that because you are paying me a million dollars plus expenses, you should rest in a wonderful and blissful state of quiet confidence and know that you do not need to ask questions." I handed him a small slip of paper. "Dial that number and put the call on the speaker. Say nothing. I will do the talking."

Lapham unhappily took the paper. Like most people in his position in Hollywood, he is usually surrounded by a financially tied, thus loyal, staff that does everything for him, including a great deal of mundane thinking. Sitting in the familiar surroundings of his glass and gray cocoon at an odd time and with a stranger whom he considered dangerous instead of the comfortable, warm, helpful bodies he usually relied on brought out the defenseless child in him. He fumbled the phone slightly, forgetting, at first, to dial 9 to get an outside line, but he finally got it, and Roee's voice came through hushed but clear.

"Talk."

"Are you secure?" I asked.

"Yes."

"Has the target arrived?" Lapham darted me a look on that one.

"Yes."

"The equipment is functioning properly?"

"Everything checks out. All test positive. The lights were lowered just a moment ago. The night vision is clear."

"The target is in sight then?"

Lapham jumped in, "You mean Jordan?"

I nodded yes while sternly motioning him to be quiet.

"Report once you have a positive on the shooting," I instructed.

"I will be happy to do that."

The line then went quiet. Lapham, worry widening his eyes, began to speak. I hushed him, stared him down, then casually and quietly sat, unmoving. After about fifteen minutes, during which I practiced specific deep breathing relaxation techniques and Lapham sweated, Roee returned on the line.

"The target is down—"

Lapham jumped up, screaming. "What the hell have you done, you bastard? You shot him, didn't you? God damn it, I said no—"

I had pulled a gun out of my jacket and pointed it at Lapham's heart. It was a Russian Tokarev TT-33, short-barreled, light, but with a lovely muzzle velocity far surpassing a Colt 45. I like to think of it as a silencer—of hysterical nincompoops.

"May I finish now?" Came Roee's voice laced with exasperation.

"Please do," I quietly said, keeping my aim steady.

"Thank you. The target is down, rolling on the floor with laughter."

"Literally?" I asked.

"Well, metaphorically—but close."

"Excellent. Keep shooting. I want the whole thing documented for posterity."

"Your wish: my command."

The line went dead from Roee's end. Lapham still stood, staring at the Tokarev. "You can hang up now," I said.

Lapham slowly turned to the phone and pushed the speaker button off. Then he sat and said, ,What the fuck...?"

I put the gun back into my jacket. "I am constantly being misunderstood. I carry this for clarity."

Lapham seemed to have nothing more to say. So I spoke. "All films for review are screened for Robert Jordan at the Rizzoli Screening room in midtown Manhattan, always at eight in the morning. The booking for screening your film was set for today. One of my agents, who, of course, I shall not name, flew to New York three days ago and was able to arrange with certain staff members of the screening room to allow him full access to the room and other connecting areas of the building. At this moment, he is sitting in an empty office two floors above the screening room, watching a video monitor connected through a thin fiber optic line to a digital video camera outfitted with the excellent AN/PVS-4 military night scope. The camera has been surreptitiously placed in the screening room. It is directed at and focused on Mr. Jordan, documenting every he-he, every ha-ha, every ho-ho, and, most importantly, every guffaw he is expelling in an immediate, instinctual, and unguarded response to your film. If he continues to respond to the rest of the film as he has responded to the beginning, we will have documented proof that he finds this particular 'Film by Larry Lapham,' at the very least, quite funny, and at the very most, knee-slapping hilarious. If he so reports in his review, then there is nothing left to do, and, indeed, I will charge you only ten percent of the agreed-upon fee, plus expenses, of course. However, if our reading of Mr. Jordan is correct, he will not review your film positively. He will go on the air and slam it. I have arranged that he review your film on the *This Day* show before he reviews it on his syndicated show. Imagine now, if you will, that shortly after slamming your film on the *This Day* show, Charlie Wise, the host, will suddenly introduce you to come out and face your accuser. This will take Mr. Jordan by surprise and, I assume, make him nervous. But it is live television; what is he going to do? He will have to roll with it. You will face your accuser by running the video images of Mr. Jordan 'losing it' to the mastery of your comedic touch, which are currently being electronically laid onto digital video tape, thus exposing his complete lack of professional integrity and ethics over live, national television to a viewership of 15 million people."

During my speech, Lapham's jaw had slowly separated from his overbite, and his mouth now stood fully open in awe and wonder. He held that momentarily, then broke out into a large and loud laughing fit. It offered a certain balance to the continent: Robert Jordan in New York laughing at Lapham's film; Larry Lapham in Hollywood laughing at Jordan's coming extreme embarrassment.

Lapham finally got control of himself and asked, "How—how are you going to get Charlie Wise to cooperate?"

"As I have tried to convey to you, I never give answers, so questions are superfluous."

xx

A little over a week later, Roee and I, in the guise of Charlie Wise, arrived on the set of *This Day* at 5:30 in the morning to do a last-minute check, ensuring the staff had everything clear and that all equipment was functioning correctly. On the way over in the Limo, Petey's blizzard started kicking up. We put a quick call into him up on the plane.

"Super-Seed seems to be doing the trick," I said, looking out the car window and watching the visibility slowly fade.

"What? Maybe you expected I wouldn't come through for you?" Petey shouted.

"Petey, I've never lost faith in you."

"I should say not!"

"It occurs to me, though, that if Manhattan was slated for a blizzard anyway, I'm paying you for nothing."

"Hey, didn't you read my weather report? Without me, New York would just be having a normal miserable snowfall. Now it's got a blinding blizzard of history-making proportions! Do you know how much money this area will lose just in the shutdown of commerce alone!" Petey seemed to be taking delight in his minor deity-like position. "Neat, huh?"

"I like a man who takes pleasure in a job well done."

"Damn right! That's what made America great!"

xx

Andrea greeted us when we arrived at the studio. She was nervous and wide-eyed staring at me, or not me, but him, or not him, but...

"Jesus," she said.

I brought her back to clear thinking by addressing her in my own voice. "Get over it if you want to remain on the payroll. I need you to be operating in the mundane of the ordinary. Only the blizzard has made this day different."

"Yes—yes, sir."

Then I addressed her in the gentle, Midwest wind of Charlie Wise's voice. "Would you be so kind as to get me a cup of coffee, Andrea?" I gave her Charlie Wise's patented kind smile. "I'd really appreciate it."

"Of—of course—Charlie," she said, her brain screaming orders at her legs to get a move on while simultaneously sending out urgent messages to all the senses asking for some rational explanation.

After our check of things and a little talk with the staff, I looked at my watch, saw that it was 6:33, and said, "Roee, it's time to make the call."

Roee stepped over to a phone and dialed Robert Jordan's number. "Hello, Mr. Jordan? It's Joe over at *This Day*. We have a hell of a problem here, and we really need your help. Well, you see, the blizzard has screwed everything up. We've just found out that our guests for the first half hour can't land at the airport, so we need you to come in now and do tomorrow's segment today—Yes, I know, Charlie mentioned that you always review films on your show first, but he would like you to bend that rule today, it would, get us out of a jam—Look, what Charlie wants to do is have you review the film right after the weather, then sit down with him for the rest of the half-hour and discuss whatever you would like about current films. You know, any pet peeves you got going right now, that sort of stuff. Charlie says, in the circumstances, it could be quite entertaining. He wants to give you a lead in, then turn the rest of, say, eight minutes, over to you—Yes, well, yes, I know, well, we called you because you're only a couple of blocks away. Well, yeah—yeah—no, no, we know you can't walk to the studio, we got a car heading over there now—Sure, sure, we've got the best drivers in town, they can drive in this muck—Yeah, yeah, we already got your review on the TelePrompTer, we were all set up for tomorrow—Oh, that's great! That's really good of you. Look, the car should be there any minute if you can get ready right away. You go on the air at 7:15." Roee hung up and turned to me. "He expressed pique until I piqued his interest."

"Eight minutes of airing your cultural pet peeves on network television to 3 million people. For a man like Jordan, that's high-grade heroin."

xx

"Andrea!" I shouted into the air after Roee left for makeup.

She materialized in a zip of point A to point B action. "Yes, uh, Mr.—uh—Charlie?

"Larry Lapham?"

"He's been picked up at the hotel, the Limo has him, and he's on his way."

"And when he gets here...?"

"I'll—I'll greet him and take him immediately to the green room.

"Thank you, Andrea."

xx

At precisely seven o'clock, I went on air as Charlie Wise, opening with his signature two words, *This day*—then continuing with the month, the date, the year, then—*is a brutal day here in New York City*. I explained quickly how a blizzard of unprecedented proportions had ground New York City to a halt, affecting businesses large and small, including the *This Day* program, which was working with a skeleton staff and valiant substitutes, such as Harry Stoner from our local affiliate, who would do the newscast, sitting in for our regular Mary Magnolia, who's stuck somewhere between Connecticut and our studios here in Manhattan.

Roee committed himself rather well, doing the news. Even if he did spend an inordinate amount of time reporting on a Festival of Samuel Beckett plays. He also did double duty and covered the weather, the lead story being "The Great Blizzard." Just as he was coming to the end of the report, detailing the record highs in Los Angeles, I saw the short, bald bulk of Robert Jordan being rushed into the studio, stripped of his outerwear by Andrea, then placed into his little reviewing cubby hole of a set that featured a simple, yet oddly royal, red velvet mock Victorian chair. He sat down and just had time for a deep breath of calming air, a quick sip of water, and a glance at the TelePrompTer when he was given the cue to begin.

"As the grand old actor said on his death bed," Jordan started in his well-known high-pitched voice, "'Dying is easy; comedy is hard.' Well, boys and girls, I'm not sure in all cases that that is true, but it certainly is for Larry Lapham, who's latest opus—I use the word opus because it's the name of a flightless bird—whose latest opus, *War of the Wimps*, is scheduled to hit the theaters on Friday. If the theaters have any good sense at all—they'll duck! You know, I've tolerated Lapham's regurgitations of American film comedy highlights for several years now, and I've tried to do it with, well, with good humor. Still, even my normally beatific forgiving nature can't stretch this far. What in the confines of Mother Nature's grand good Earth gave Lapham the idea that he could take Jean-Claude Van Damme and turn him into Buster Keaton? Except in the locker room scene where Jean-Claude is in drag, a cinematic moment to be missed—as often as possible—reaches more for Diane Keaton than Buster Keaton. And the dialog! Larry, I've got to be straight with you. English is not Jean-Claude's native tongue. It wasn't fair of you to ask him to deliver lines that would ruin Robin William's career. I would blame the writers, but I happen to know, for a fact, that the writers on a Lapham film are basically stenographers! Which makes the director a dictator! Hey, Larry, dictatorships are passé, haven't you heard? Next time, let some good, funny writers write some good, funny stuff. Stuff funny enough that even you can't mess it up. This is Robert Jordan saying, regarding *War of the Wimps*, I am very much not pleased. *This Day* will return after these messages."

People scurried, repositioning cameras, retouching make-up, getting Jordan's small mic unplugged, leading him to the host's area where I sat, and plugging him back in.

"Thanks for coming in, Robert," I said, smiling at him.

"Well, I'd like to say it's my pleasure, Charlie, but I've got to tell you, I live only a couple of blocks away, but I felt like Scott racing Amundsen to the South Pole." His voice was still dripping with the inconvenience of it all.

"Ten seconds, gentlemen," came the word from the floor manager. We both gathered ourselves up and:

"Welcome back," I said to the camera. "I'm here with Robert Jordan, our resident film critic and culture creature." I turned to Jordan. "So, Robert, *War of the Wimps*? I guess it's not going to make your top ten list."

"Or anybody else's, I would guess."

"Really? Lapham's films don't do that bad in the box office, do they?"

"The miracle of modern marketing, Charlie. In the old days, hucksters were checker-suited, fast-talking men relegated to the back roads of America pushing useless patent medicines to the local yokels as quick cures for 'what ails ya.' Now they're Armani-suited, face-lifted communicators of cinematic glitz. You know, there used to be a plethora of patent medicines sold in America."

"Whoa! I'm glad you don't review television."

"*I'm* glad I don't review television." I did Charlie Wise's well-known chuckle in response. "Although, these days, some of the writing for television puts Hollywood features to shame."

"Really?"

"Yes, I think so."

"Well, let's put that to the test. We have a guest television reviewer today." Jordan was jolted into perplexity. You could see it in his face, magnified, I'm sure, on the television screen. "For a look at the current state of television film criticism, here's film producer and director Larry Lapham."

With panic now peppering the perplex, Jordan noticed the electronic Lapham on the monitors and, worse, the flesh-and-blood one over on his set sitting in his red velvet chair.

Lapham was calm and natural on camera—and just a tad vicious. "Being a big believer in turnabout is fair play; I would like to review the review you have just heard of my film, *War of the Wimps*. I found Robert Jordan's review to be extremely well-written, witty, and pungent in that pure Jordanian manner of his. I found his delivery and comedic timing impeccable, as always, but I found it disturbing that the content of the review was dishonest and deceitful."

Jordan turned to me and growled out a whisper, "Charlie, what the—'

"Keep smiling, Robert; you never know when the director will cut back to us."

Lapham was continuing. "Of course, I could be accused of not being objective in this, as Jordan's review was of a film that I spent a year of my life on and am, quite frankly, proud of, but I didn't say his opinion was wrong. That is not for me to say. I said it was dishonest. For I happen to know, for a fact, that Robert Jordan loved *War of the Wimps*, or, at least, liked it enough to spend most of the time while he was screening it in the throes of laughter. As this videotape clearly shows."

The tape ran on all the monitors, and Jordan looked wide-eyed at his electronic self in the green light of the night video, laughing heartily every few seconds; an excellent round laugh, an old-fashioned laugh, the kind of laugh that is almost a pleasure in itself, as well as a vocalization of pleasure. Yet it was eerie. For he was alone in the theater, and one man laughing alone can't help but seem—mad.

I leaned over to Jordan and whispered, "Out of courtesy, we edited out the times you picked your nose."

Jordan stood up, intending to leave, but Roee was right there to put a powerful pinch onto his right trapezius muscle, which tends to make one want to sit again.

"I'll do that to your testicles next time you stand up without permission," Roee said quietly to Jordan. He wasn't fooling. Something Jordan—I could tell from the open mouth stare he gave Roee as Roee walked off—did not doubt.

The tape ended just as Lapham came over. He sat and joined me in looking to Jordan for an explanation. Jordan wiped the flop sweat off his brow. Then he took a deep breath and tried to remember, I'm sure, just who the hell he was.

Jordan chuckled nervously, "As good a time as any to go to a commercial?"

"Don't need to," I said. "This portion of our program is being brought to you as a public service by Mr. Larry Lapham, director of *War of the Wimps*, coming soon to a theater near you."

"Well, what can I say?" Jordan was trying his best not to look cornered. "Except this is the most outrageous behavior I have ever seen in fifteen years of broadcasting, and you will be hearing from my lawyer." He was starting to give in to his anger. "That tape— that tape could well have been made when I was reviewing, uh, uh, I don't know, uh, Mel Brooks' last film."

"Well, that's hardly likely," I had Charlie Wise say with uncommon sarcasm. "Before we march off to court, why don't we hear what the dean of broadcast journalism has to say, shall we?"

The monitors came alive with the avuncular face of his gray eminence. "This is Walter Cronkite."

Everything opened wide on Robert Jordan: eyes; mouth; bowels, most likely.

"Unbeknown to Robert Jordan, I was in attendance and observed the screening that you have just seen a video record of, and I can attest to, indeed could swear to in a court of law, that that video is a true and accurate record of Robert Jordan's reaction to the film, *War of the Wimps*. Robert, no one has been more dismayed over the recent diminishing of standards in broadcast journalism as I have, but, my god, man, when that lack of standards filters down to film criticism, you can only ask one question, Where goeth the world? And that's the way it is."

"Thank you, Walter," I said as the monitors went blank. "It's always good to hear from the most trusted man in America." I turned to Jordan. "Robert?"

Jordan was in a state of shock. He seemed unable to talk. Lapham happily filled the vacuum.

"How many of my other films that you gave rotten reviews to did you really like, Bobby?"

Jordan came back to us—realization having slapped him in the face.

"Yes," Lapham said. "College. Same dorm. You wanted to be my best friend, and you've been carrying this grudge ever since because I didn't let you."

Live television pressed on Jordan from all sides, sapping one kind of strength, giving him another. "*Litigators.*" Jordan finally said.

"What?"

"Your film, *Litigators*, I truly didn't like that one."

"Yes, well, I didn't like it much either, to be honest with you," Lapham admitted.

"But all the others—all the others I have adored. Each one fulfilled the promise I knew you had back then in college. Me. Not any of those others whose friendship you desired so passionately."

"Well, then, for Christ's sake—!" There was a little emotional stumble here by Lapham. You could see it in his eyes, in the false start of angry words and the successful quiet stating of a pleading one, "Why?"

48

"It's my right as a human being to hate. It's my right to be petty. Sometimes it's the only way to feel we have control over some little corner of the world. You know that now yourself, don't you? Your hate has ruined me. You have destroyed my career."

"I have done no such thing. This is the wages of your sins, not mine."

"And on that melodramatic turn of phrase," I said, turning to the camera that stood in for 3 million people, ,I think it's finally time to go to a commercial."

The red light on the camera going off was, to Jordan, like a gong being struck. He leaped out of his chair and sprung onto the still-sitting Lapham, knocking him and his chair over. He started beating at Lapham with his fists, screaming incoherently— although it is logical to presume that profanity was involved. Lapham, a good six or seven inches taller than Jordan, kept a defensive posture throughout, deflecting blows while trying to talk Jordan into stopping.

I got up, and Roee came over, and we stood over the two flailing bodies. I was amused by an analogy Roee struck between the two beneath us and the mating practices of a particular species of squid that fornicated in a frenzy of violent movement.

After the drawing of some of Lapham's blood, we decided to break it up. "Now, why don't you both just sit and catch your breath," I suggested.

Jordan, the broadcast professional, looked around at the smiling, interested, yet idle crew. "Don't—don't you have to go back on the air."

"I don't see why. We never were on the air." Some of the crew couldn't help but laugh.

"What?" Lapham blinked with confusion.

Ignoring him, I continued. "Therefore, Robert, your career has not been ruined. Not that I couldn't arrange that if I wanted to." I pulled off the "Charlie Wise" makeup, hair, face, the whole illusion, shocking not just Jordan but Lapham, who had had no idea.

"Fixxer? What the fuck...?"

"I don't answer questions!" I shouted, using my natural voice. "Now, both of you sit!" They did so. "You are not in the broadcast center of the *This Day* show. You are in a perfect replication in a warehouse three blocks from that center. The people you see around you are my employees, loyal to me. They can be trusted. Not a word of what has gone on this morning will ever get out— if you both cooperate."

"But I want it to get out!" Lapham's anger was tactile and hot. "That's what the fuck I'm paying you for!"

"I don't always deliver what I'm paid for."

"Then I'm not going to pay you."

"I deliver something better."

Jordan watched this exchange, confused, which was understandable. His world had gone from warm, familiar, cozy, supportive, and solid to the slippery deck of a ship lost at sea, tossed by waves, and threatened by the monsters that *Be Here*. He must have had a million questions, but he was drawn to and asked only two, which he addressed to Lapham: "You paid to ruin my career? How much?"

Lapham looked at him, irritated, as if Jordan had suddenly become an annoying child. "A million dollars!"

"Plus expenses," Roee felt compelled to remind.

"Plus expenses," Lapham confirmed. "Which," he glanced around, "will come to a lot, I assume."

"Oh, maybe another million," I informed.

"Another million!"

"You're paying two million dollars to ruin my career?" There was an element of being impressed in Jordan's voice. "I'm—I'm touched."

"Touched?"

"To think you—you thought that much of me."

"I thought you were a damn fucking schmuck!"

"Yeah, but one worth two million dollars to ruin."

"It's true, Mr. Jordan does think a lot of you," I said, taking over the conversation. "He told me he thinks you're the finest film critic in America." Lapham cringed a schoolboy cringe. I guess I wasn't supposed to say anything. "It's bothered him for years that you, a man whose critical acumen he admires, did not like his films. So you now have what you've always wanted: Larry Lapham to desire you as much as you once desired Larry Lapham."

"And it's only going to cost me two million dollars!"

"Lapham shut up, or I will have my associate here crush your windpipe." Roee smiled and walked forward. Lapham shut his mouth.

"Here's what you're getting for your two million dollars." I turned to Jordan. "Although we were not on the air, we did videotape. The tape will be placed in my archives. If you don't follow my instructions to the letter, I will release the tape to various news agencies with the wonderful story of how Robert Jordan got 'stung.' It will ruin your career. To avoid this, you will go home now and rewrite the text of your show that airs tonight into a reconsideration of the films of Larry Lapham. You will tell your audience how, in viewing the brilliance of *War of the Wimps*, you were forced to reassess all of Lapham's previous films. You will publicly apologize for the pans you gave those films in the past, stating that now, with far more mature eyes, you realize that Larry Lapham is the premier master of the comic film in our era. You may, of course, exclude *Litigators* from your reassessment. We wouldn't want you to be anything but honest. You will follow up tonight's broadcast with your actual scheduled appearance on tomorrow's *This Day*, during which you will give *War of the Wimps* the rave you genuinely think it deserves. Thus, you will set things right with Mr. Lapham, making him both a current success and rediscovered genius. As a residual benefit to yourself, you will enhance your reputation as a critic who is not only willing to reassess but has the depth of thinking to look beyond considerations of good and bad box office to see the actual value of a body of film work. For once, an American critic will have been there before the French.

"As a residual benefit for you," I said, turning to Lapham, "I'm going to give you a private viewing of this tape so you can see yourself as a victimizer, as a man so consumed with self-righteous outrage you would stoop to this repulsive method of embarrassing and ruining a fellow human being. Vengeance—" Lapham's eyes began to wander. "Listen to me!" I said it loud, snapping him back to me. "Hear me," I said softly, "for I speak truth born from experience. Vengeance is only attractive in the conception—never in the execution."

Lapham and Jordan stood there thinking, slowly moving their eyes to each other, looking for the tie that now bound their fates together.

"So," I said. "Don't you think it's about time for the two of you to kiss and make up?"

5
THE GREAT WHITE PAUSE

Robert Jordan left to go home and write what was to become an Emmy-winning episode of his syndicated film review program, *Meet Me at the Movies*. Roee attended to the under-the-table payment of the staff in the cold hard cash of lore, soon, I'm afraid, to be entirely replaced by digital denominations—more death of romance. I thanked Andrea, a lovely girl becoming a woman. Without sacrificing the ominous, I tried to give her the proper positive reinforcement for a well-done job. She may prove valuable in the future. Lapham hung around—like the nerd he once was, he seemed reluctant to leave the party. I had no choice but to approach him and say, "These fine people will have to rush while striking the set, and you will be in the way."

"I wanted...."

"Yes...?"

"I wanted to ask you some questions, but...?"

"The job is over. I believe I can agree to a few questions."

"Was that really Walter Cronkite? Because, you know...." He pointed to the remains of "Charlie Wise's" face that I still held in my hand.

"Does it matter?"

"I'm curious."

"Yes—if that satisfies."

"What? My curiosity, or—"

"Something deeper and darker?" He had no answer, nor did I. "Anything else?"

Lapham looked around him at our very reasonable facsimile as it dissipated. "I can see all this has been expensive, but a million dollars?"

"Do you ask this question when the studio pays the bill?"

"Yes, I do," he asserted.

"Do you know what it costs to arrange a blizzard?"

"You arranged the blizzard?"

"How else was I going to camouflage the city to get Jordan here instead of the actual studio without him noticing?"

"Yes, well, but arranging a blizzard?"

I just smiled as Roee walked over.

Lapham shook his head. "You do like adding to your legend, don't you?"

I smiled again. The most innocent one I could manage.

"How Hollywood of you," Lapham stated.

Was it a curse or a compliment? I decided not to ask.

"I suppose you'll send me an itemized bill?"

Roee answered, "I suppose you'll just forward two million dollars to Norton Macbeth within three days. He'll find the proper way to account for it in your tax return."

"And if I decide that a million in expenses is not justified and I refuse to pay the full amount, you'll—"

"Arrange for you to have the legal right to use handicap parking spaces." I had stated it as a mundane point. "Right?" I asked Roee.

"Oh, absolutely. Debilitating physical damage. At least that's what we've always done in the past."

"It always seems to have worked."

"Yes, no reason to innovate now that I can see."

Lapham looked at us. I could tell he wanted to laugh, but whether at us, with us, or existentially, I hadn't a clue.

xx

Getting back to the hotel was a major task, but then, that was my own damn fault. Nevertheless, we made it, got into our suite, sat by the fire, I with a vodka tonic, Roee with what he considered an adequate Merlot, and allowed ourselves to toast (in two ways) and feel satisfied.

"I enjoyed that," I said.

"Did you?"

"Yes."

"What particular aspect about it did you enjoy the most?"

"Sometimes we are but a circus of clowns."

"Indeed?"

"To be the ringmaster in a circus of clowns."

"You find that enjoyable?"

"I find it amusing. I enjoy being amused."

"You don't miss the blood of lions?"

I looked at Roee. He is often so damn perceptive. "Well—I don't miss the lions. They are not amusing."

"And the blood?"

"Say, that reminds me, I'm hungry."

We ordered lunch—Roee was only slightly critical of it—and watched the blizzard slowly disappear. Petey had promised a clear day for tomorrow. I hoped he would deliver.

xx

The following day was bright and clear, and I decided to move Petey from minor to major divinity. The view of Central Park from my bedroom window was stunning in its Winter Wonderland aspect. The sky was blue beyond human comprehension. The deep-in-the-center feeling of joy at being alive was overpowering. It made me hungry for many things.

xx

Roee was off to meet with Tom, a stunningly handsome young man I had met only once but had immediately liked—a Midwestern boy charmed by that which was exotic in Roee. Hearts,

I'm afraid, were going to be broken here.

As for me, I was determined to find Gilgamesh Paul.

xx

As I left the hotel, I stopped momentarily to appreciate the grand gift I had given Manhattan. Quiet. It was so hushed— wonderfully so; eerily so; wonderfully, eerily so. There was very little if any, traffic, and what there was moved to a muted soundtrack. I stepped out from under the hotel's awning, and the crunch of snow my footfall caused seemed like a celebratory cheer. Then I noticed other crunches at other volumes around me caused by other hearty souls out to see their city in its great white pause. A short pause. It would only last for a matter of hours before dirt would demand its due; dogs would, in olfactory panic, begin to remark their territories, and slush would laughingly settle in, waiting to freeze up overnight to cause someone bodily harm the following day, as is its purpose in existence.

I had planned to take the subway, but this was no time to be subterranean. It would be a long walk, but it would be one in a benign and fresh alternate universe. The subway would do for the trip back.

I went to the corner of Central Parks West and South and turned down Broadway. Before me was an inviting corridor. I took the first step and never looked back.

Sometime later, I entered a small shop on Broadway close to Twelfth Street, which I was relieved to find open. At about three-quarters of the way, I had the sudden fear that no one would be there, prevented by the conditions from getting onto the island. That would have been ironic. The door opened with the old fashion tinkling of a bell, though, and an ancient face looked up and greeted me.

"Good morning," the man behind the counter said.

"Good morning. Glad to see you're open."

"Why shouldn't I be?"

"A blizzard is a good excuse to take some time off."

"Dying is taking some time off. Until then, I'll work."

"I'm interested in finding the whereabouts of a Gilgamesh Paul. I was given to understand that you might—'

"Gilgamesh Paul," he said with some awe. "That is a name I have not heard in many years."

"So...?"

"Haven't a clue. Not here. Not for years. No one's interested."

"I'm interested."

"Make's you odd, then, doesn't it? Have you ever—"

"Never."

"Not surprising."

"But he sounds like—"

"Yes, so others have told me. I only remember one thing he said. He was at a summerhouse in the Hamptons and was asked if he wanted to go for a swim, and he answered—let's see if I can remember this—he answered, 'The act of swimming should only be committed if one happens, by accident, never by design, to be in water of sufficient depth to reach from the bottom of your big toe whilst *en Pointe*, to the bridge of your nose at its highest possible elevation.'" The old man laughed. "I always liked that." He laughed some more. "You see—I don't swim."

"You don't swim?"

"Don't swim."

"You live on an island."

"A meaningless point if you never leave it—and I never have."

xx

Disappointed, I left the shop, looking for the nearest subway entrance. I suddenly noticed that the New York offices of Olympic Pictures were directly across the street, housed in a violently Art Deco building. It had been their New York offices since the founding of the company in the early Twenties. Of course, the Olympic Pictures of then is not the Olympic Pictures of today. The Olympic Pictures of then was founded by George Pangalos, a Greek fishmonger who had developed a passion for the nickelodeon and photographing shorthaired flappers in short skirts.

In contrast, Sveriges Riksbank, the central bank of Sweden, owns the Olympic Pictures of today. Of course, the Sveriges Riksbank did not particularly want to own Olympic Pictures; it did so by default. Specifically, the default on a billion-dollar loan they had given to one of their least moral and least sane countrymen, Per Hjalmar, who had developed some of the same interests that had inspired George Pangalos, thereby creating, with the bank's money, a continuity of a sort after Olympic had been gutted in the Eighties by a fat financier from Atlantic City who sold off most of Olympic's film library and all of its Hollywood studio facilities, leaving behind nothing but the husk of its logo, a brightly burning torch grasped in a strong hand. That is what Per Hjalmar convinced the Sveriges Riksbank to bank on, as he knew that Hollywood was becoming very brand-name-conscious. It was pure sleight of hand. A particular officer of the bank—no longer with the bank, of course—was charmed by Hjalmar into keeping his eye on the hand with the logo in it rather than Hjalmar's other hand, the empty one, the one that was supposed to be holding collateral.

The rumors had it that, after several years of new management headed up by Sara Hutton, the Sveriges Riksbank was ready to sell, hoping to recoup at least the billion dollars of the original loan, if not the near billion they had had to pay to keep Olympic up, running and producing pictures to make it marketable enough to—

Speak of the devil.

As I was standing there musing on the recent history of Olympic Pictures, Sara Hutton emerged from the building. She was bundled up against the cold, but there was no mistaking her. Sara Hutton was more unattractive than any other person I could think of. Although unattractive may not be the right word, she did attract—enough to have lovers of both sexes, enough to climb the Hollywood corporate ladder, which is surface sensitive, and enough to make more money than most. Nonetheless, she had a face that, by comparison, made the ugly look plain, the plain look beautiful, and the beautiful look divine. This was demonstrated the second Bea Cherbourg followed Hutton out of the building. She was radiant, beaming. She and Sara smiled at each other; laughed; linked their arms the way women do, and began walking up the street.

It seems another couple had kissed and made up at my suggestion.

xx

The flight home offered no amusements. The movie was one of those vanity films forced into production by a still gleaming star of action and sex determined to reveal the deep soul within. The screenwriters and director, though, had had a hard time finding the deep soul within, although I'm sure they looked just about everywhere, for the film was just simply small, dark, and quiet, but not at all soulful. Roee spent the time scribbling on a new play, so conversation was out. I had been hoping for Gilgamesh Paul, of course, but... As we were traveling in the guise of the Chairman & CEO and the president of Prosthetics of Providence (Roee had put on our business cards the legend: *Let Us Give You a Hand*), we were not even graced with the solicitous attention of a VIP flight attendant. So I slept.

And dreamed of Bea Cherbourg.

It was a strange dream. It was flesh. Bea's flesh. I could see it, feel it, smell it, taste it. It was the center and all that surrounded it. It was soft and warm and gave when I pressed into it. It was well-shaped and fit. It was not naked. Naked had no relevance. It just was. Then it was her eyes. Then her smile. Which smile? The one that she had given the waiter? The one she had given Sara Hutton? Hey! Where's mine? The flesh is given. The smile is not. The eyes condemn—

The rude sound of landing gear locking into place woke me up. I took a deep breath, scrub-cleaned the old brain with recycled oxygen, and stretched. Then there was a momentary sense memory of Bea Cherbourg's flesh in my arms—then it passed. Reflex wanted me to lunge out to pull it back, but I conquered Reflex, a dark and impulsive god.

xx

59

Several weeks passed. I did not dream or think of Bea Cherbourg during that time. Nor did I give any thought to the fact that I wasn't dreaming or thinking of her. I forgot the matter.

A few small commissions came our way. The most interesting one was from Bill Baker, a film producer who had been hoping to direct his first feature. He had line produced the last three pictures of Joe Waugh, a current hot one in Hollywood, the last two films being the first two of a planned fantasy trilogy. Waugh had directed the first; he had turned over the reins to another director for the second and had promised Baker the third. Although Waugh was the acknowledged genius of these high box-office grossing films, much of their story and elemental details came from creative jam sessions Waugh and Baker had had when they were near nobodies working on their first film together: a low-budget road picture that became a sleeper hit. Baker felt that being able to direct the third film was his justified reward, but, unfortunately, the second film had gone way over budget, mainly due to the director's demands, but Waugh blamed Baker. As Waugh was himself financing the second film out of the profits of the first, that blame carried weight. Waugh decided to direct the third film. Baker was devastated, but he swallowed his pride—or squirreled it away in his cheek—and begged to, at least, stay on as the producer. Waugh agreed, and preproduction began for a shoot that would spend 16 weeks in the Brazilian rain forest, which was to double for the fantasy realm of Thunnorak. That's when Baker decided to find The Fixxer. He had heard of me but wasn't sure I existed. He chose to believe. It was important to him to believe. It took him eight weeks of searching before someone connected him with Norton Macbeth.

Baker explained everything to me in a meeting Norton arranged at the Children's Museum in Downtown Los Angeles. This was three days before the production was to move to Brazil. I knew a lot about Waugh. Anybody who had become as famous as him, I get to know a lot about. I immediately told Baker that I could, for a price, fix his problem. And by the time he left for Brazil in three days, he would be the film's director.

The solution was simple. I didn't even have to go into the computer database. It had been reported that Waugh never made a move without consulting Mary Anne Richardson, the all-American homemaker psychic/astrologer who worked out of her house in the Encino hills and had quite a list of "A" talent clients, who had all spread the word about her remarkable, natural gifts. This is not unusual in Hollywood; it is, in fact, far too usual, but such Hollywood normality was useful if you knew how to take advantage of it—and I did. I happened to know that Mary Anne Richardson of Encino started life as Clara Brown of Southampton, England. She left her native land ten years before when her New Jesus evangelical message wasn't bringing in enough sucker donations there to make it pay. So she came to America for the fruitful fields of the local suckers she had always heard about. Unfortunately, she found a preponderance of evangelicals running around sucking on the suckers. Too crowded. She tried to make ends meet by running a pyramid scam. Unfortunately, the ends met in prison for eighteen months, where she picked up various American accents. Looking for a new gig once she was out of prison, she had a revelation standing in a supermarket checkout line. She saw the stars—the ones in the zodiac and the ones on the big and small screens. She saw them merging under the protection of a spreading tabloid banner headline. Just converge the celestial stars with the Hollywood stars, she thought, and let the brilliance illuminate the path to gold. It worked. Another immigrant made it big in America.

I paid her a visit. I paid her a substantial fee. The next day she warned Waugh that if he were to travel any time in the next three months, doom would be his name. The film was ready to go. Considerable investment had already been made. A crew was waiting in the middle of a Brazilian rainforest. He couldn't publicly delay the film giving his psychic's warning as the reason. Baker got to direct.

Roee was congratulating me on a good job swiftly and lucratively done when the call came informing us that Bea Cherbourg's body had been found in a snowdrift on the frozen Bering Sea just off the Seward Peninsula in Alaska.

6
THERE'S NO PLACE LIKE NOME

The call came from Norton Macbeth.

"Do you remember a while back, Fixxer, when you did a favor for Newsstand Mike?"

"Talking sense to his unrequited love."

"That's right."

"Obviously, I do. Bea Cherbourg. Oddly enough, I saw her—"

"She's dead."

Dead is a word analogous, for many reasons, with an inalterable period or, as the British like to say, a full stop—which I did for half a beat. Then I asked if it was murder, although I knew the answer.

"Looks that way, he-he-he." Norton's laughter was not gleeful; it was nervous tittering. "How did you know?"

"Why else would you be calling me? If she died of natural causes or a simple accident, as unfortunate as that would be, it is not something you would take up my time with."

"Her body was found in Alaska. Nome, Alaska, of all places. In a snow drift."

"That's a little bit more than strange."

"That's what I thought."

"I assume Mike is devastated."

"Very. That's what prompted him to call me, he-he-he. He was reluctant, but he wants your help."

"I assume it's in police hands?"

"Yes, but they won't communicate with him. He's not a family member, after all. Also, he's convinced they won't investigate—and he has information he won't give them."

"Why?"

"You'll have to ask him that. He says he'll only give it to you. Now, I know this isn't really any of your business, and there is certainly no fee involved, but—"

"Is Mike available now?"

"Uh, yes. He's at the newsstand."

"Tell him I'll meet him there in half an hour."

"Okay, but are you—"

I hung up. "Roee, I'm going out."

Roee had gotten the gist of things from my end of the conversation. "Do you want company?"

"No, but you can call the Captain and alert him that we may require information on the case."

"Okay, I'll do that."

xx

I made the quick trip to Sherman Oaks, wondering about Bea Cherbourg. What had gotten her killed? In Nome, Alaska, "of all places." Nome, a small berg at the end of America whose city motto was, unsurprisingly, "There's no place like Nome," was not the sort of place one would expect a Bea Cherbourg to vacation. Even to run away to—and I had just seen her with Sara Hutton, happy, it seemed, problem solved, what was there to run away from? Was it research for her film, then, or location scouting? I didn't know what her script was about, so there was no way to tell. But it was a reasonable assumption that a woman who would describe herself as being somewhat Dorothy Parker-like was not going to tell a story that takes place in Alaska, rural Alaska at that.

Mike was waiting for me at the curb, reserving, by his presence, the parking spot. "I got us a table set aside at Blues+Jazz," was his greeting.

"Fine," I said and followed him to the restaurant. We entered just as a jazz trio finished a set with a not-half-bad rendition of Carmichael's "Stardust" (ah, Hoagy, not wholly forgotten, The Best Years of Our Lives, indeed, Mr. Bond.) We sat as applause showed appreciation, and the players expressed their thanks. We ordered drinks. Mike was particular about the kind of whisky he wanted.

Mike started by asking, "Mr. Macbeth told you?"

"Bea Cherbourg is dead. Murdered. In Alaska."

"Yeah." He choked on the word.

"Mike, your grief will be as unrequited as your love if you don't get control of your emotions and deal with this."

Mike sucked in a long, moist breath through his nostrils and said, ,You know, Fixxer, there's no goddamn justice in the world."

"Yes, I've noticed."

He was angry. "Oh, you have, have you? You've noticed injustice? When did you ever notice injustice?"

I nodded toward the three musicians packing up to go home. "The day I realized that Rock was more popular than Jazz."

Mike looked at me with a high level of hate. "You probably think I'm a silly little man, right? Silly little man in love with a beautiful young woman who would never—"

"I think nothing of the sort, and what I do think, you'll never be able to divine, so don't try. Look, I'm not here as a grief counselor. I won't hold your hand and witness you beating your breast. I am here at your request to receive information regarding the murder of Bea Cherbourg, which you, for some reason, are holding back from the proper authorities. I am also here to advise you that that is a criminal offense. So tell me the story. Sequentially, please."

Mike was not apologetic nor acknowledged the dressing down I had just given him. He just reported the facts, as requested.

"Bea—Bea was really depressed for a couple of days after you met with her. Then, suddenly, she was feeling better. She said she had decided that you were right, and she would call Sara Hutton and apologize for being so uncooperative and beg her, if she had to, to let her back on the project. You know, she said it in such a way that...."

"That what?"

"I don't know. It was—chilling."

"She got back in the good graces of Sara Hutton."

"Yes, and she said Sara was cool about it. She took her back on the project and even took her to New York for a trip. She started spending a lot of time with Sara, I mean, you know, outside of the office, so to speak."

"Do you think it was sexual?"

Mike looked deep into his drink. This was not comfortable for him. "I know it was."

"Okay. Keep going."

"A little over a week ago, she asked me if I would take care of her cat again."

"Again?"

"I did it when she went to New York. I mean, I'm here close by."

"I see."

"Her cat's name is Mr. Woollcott. Stupid name for a cat."

"Not so stupid if he is the friend of Dorothy Parker."

"Who?"

"Never mind."

"This time, she said she was going away for a few days on a retreat with Sara, some other Olympic executives, and others in the industry. She—she seemed quite excited about it."

"Where was the retreat held?"

"She wouldn't tell me. She said she would only be gone two nights, and could I please feed Mr. Woollcott, take in her mail, and water her plants? As she gave me the key to her apartment, she said—with this scary smile, Fixx, this really weird scary smile—she said, 'I'm off to kiss the golden arse.' I didn't understand that."

"You probably don't want to."

"Well, anyway, when she didn't return when she said she was going to, I got worried, so I called Sara Hutton's office and asked if the retreat had been extended. They said no. So I asked if Sara Hutton was there, and they said yes, but she couldn't speak to me. Of course, I was a nobody calling, so I couldn't have gotten through in any case. So I asked if Bea was around. They told me Bea no longer worked there. I said I knew that, but was she just, you know, physically there? Did she come back there after the retreat? They said they hadn't seen her, and anyway, as far as they knew, she had not been invited to the retreat. It's very exclusive."

"So she wasn't an official guest."

"I guess not. Anyway, that's when I called the police."

"What for?"

"To file a missing person's report."

"Did you really think she was missing? Maybe she had just decided to stay on for an extra day of R&R."

"No, I knew it, I knew something was wrong, but there was nothing I could do except this. At least this was doing something."

"I see."

"I even thought they wouldn't take a report from me 'cause I'm not a relative. I thought I would have to fight with them, but—but they did."

"Too many missing persons these days for them not to."

"Yeah. So I gave them all the information, you know, who she was, height, hair, eye color, what she was wearing when I last saw her, all that. They said fine; they'd put it in the system. Every day she didn't return, I called the police, but they said nothing had turned up. Finally, after about the fourth day, they called me and asked if I knew who her next of kin was. I asked why, and they wouldn't tell me. They said they had to talk to a family member. I told them I knew she had parents back east somewhere, and I would try to get their phone number. So I went into her apartment and looked all around, found the number, and called them back, and gave it to them. I also asked them to please give my name to her parents and ask them to call me at the apartment, saying that I was Bea's friend and I was taking care of things. Then I hung up—and cried."

"You knew."

"What else?"

"The parents called?"

"Her dad—about an hour and a half later—nice sounding guy. All he would tell me is that they had found Bea in Nome, Alaska, dead and that, in the opinion of the people up there, it looked like she had been murdered. I tried to get more out of him, but he said no, he didn't really know me and didn't want to talk about it anymore. He said he was getting on a plane to come here to meet—the body—and close the apartment, take the cat. I met him at the newsstand the next day. He was pretty upset, of course. He thanked me for taking care of things and tried to give me some money, but I wouldn't take it. I gave him the key. It was like Bea. It was like giving him back Bea."

Mike stopped talking. He was staring at some insubstantial thing in front of him: the ghostly image of the key, most likely, a key in the shape of the shapely body of Bea Cherbourg.

"What did you find in the apartment when you were looking for the parent's phone number that you don't want to show the police?"

Mike was not surprised that I had figured this fact out. He pulled a small bound notebook out of his coat pocket and handed it to me. "It's—it's something like a diary, I guess. Read the last couple of entries."

I quickly scanned the last pages. Then I turned to Mike. "Why didn't you want to give this to the police?"

"If Sara Hutton had anything to do with it—even if, you know, she's arrested and put on trial—do you think she'll be convicted? What justice did Vic Morrow ever get, or Nicole Brown? The rich, the powerful—and in this town, the movies are the power— they can influence, buy themselves out of anything. I don't even want to give the police the opportunity. But you can take care of this, Fixx."

"Well, these pages are hardly evidence that Sara Hutton had anything to do with the murder of Bea, but even if they are a good hint and I could track down the facts, what makes you think I wouldn't just turn them over to the police? I'm not an avenging angel, Mike."

"Because it's your responsibility."

"My responsibility?"

"You should have taken her on as a—as a charity case, and you should have fucked over Sara Hutton, and then this all would have been over, and she wouldn't be dead!"

"Interesting point of view. Considering it comes from the man who asked me to dissuade Bea from seeking to hurt Sara Hutton."

"Well, you didn't do a very good job, did you? So, it's still your responsibility. You're as guilty as anybody for murdering her!"

I don't believe in guilt. It's a lousy emotion that rarely leads to satisfactory action. If anything, it prays on the mind and leads to inaction while it gropes for a convenient excuse, as an addict gropes for a needle. I do, however, believe in responsibility and owning up to it. Did I share some responsibility for this outcome to a life of potential, now forever unfulfilled? I didn't know, but this "silly little man" thought so, even if that thought was born of tortured grieving hormones. Still, I felt it would do no harm to show respect for the man and his pain.

I pocketed the notebook. "Mike, if I find anything I think will satisfy you, I'll let you know. If I decide that there is an action that I can take that I think might satisfy you, I'll let you know."

Mike looked again into his glass, empty now but for a drop or two. "Okay, Fixx. Th—thanks."

I finished my drink and left.

This is what was written in Bea Cherbourg's notebook:

I have fucked Sara Hutton. Although I don't like that word, I never have. I have had carnal knowledge with Sara Hutton. Sounds too demure. Like I'm averting my eyes from the fact. It also sounds like an old movie. Was an old movie. Mike Nichols. With Nicholson and that guy who used to sing with Paul Simon. I have made love to/with Sara Hutton. There was no love. I have had sex with Sara Hutton. Dry and factual. I have had a lesbo relationship with Sara Hutton. That would have turned Sam on. Poor Sam. The master. What little you know now compared to your student. It was not revolting/repulsive. Stimulation of the clitoris is stimulation of the clitoris is stimulation of the clitoris. A rose is a rose is a rose? Gertrude! Shame on you! It was— what it was. I was shocked by how quickly she took my call when I called her. She knew. People with/in power know. She knew I was coming with my tail between my legs. She liked my tail. I did good. I almost convinced myself. It was really comfortable being "liked" by her again. The corporate jet. The suite. God, it's easy to believe that if you have access to these things—a right to them—then you must be right.

SHE IS PUTRID!!!!!!!

*I will get her. I will find out something. There is something. There is
something— dark at her core. If I find it, there must be something there I can
use. She wants me to meet Max. She's been starting to talk about this Max.
I don't like what's in her eyes when she speaks of him. Maybe he's her guru or
something. It's creepy. I will find it out. Then I will fuck her! Now I like the
word.*

"Looks to me like she died of an excessively melodramatic
nature," Roee said after I had updated him and he had read the
pages.

"Well, she was young, passionate, idealistic, and absolutely
convinced she had the moral high ground—such afflictions lead to
melodrama. Especially since she didn't have the good sense to
vaccinate herself with cynicism."

"Surely, you jest?"

"Might have saved her life if she had truly become a Dorothy
Parker."

"Yeah, but then she would have drunk herself to death."

"It's slower than homicide."

"Do you think Mike is right? Do you think Sara Hutton had
something to do with it?"

"I don't know, but it's an intriguing enough possibility that we
should look into it."

"So what's Mike going to pay with? Day old copies of the
trades?"

"You don't think we'll gather information about one, maybe
more individuals that will prove useful in the future? I think dark
deeds have been done here."

"True—and I'm not opposed to showing Mike some
consideration, but, Fixxer, on occasion, you get obsessed—"

"I am not obsessed. I'm intrigued."

"That may be worse."

"Nevertheless...."

"Nevertheless, I called the Captain. He said he would have
information for us in the morning."

"Good. Well, I think I'll go into the library, crack open the data bank and catch up on the biography of Sara Hutton.

xx

Sara Hutton was the only child of a clown. Hamilton "Ham" Hutton, known professionally as Hammy the Clown, started his career just after the early days of television at a little station in Williamstown, Massachusetts. It was just an afternoon children's show, but Ham put his all into it, innovating out of joy as much as necessity due to the low budget. He was happy putting on the costume and make-up and wig and prancing and talking in a strange voice caused by constricted vocal cords. He was happy creating weird characters in puppets, drawings, and full-body costumes. He was happy creating a world and writing dialog for these characters, giving them outrageous, funny, energetic life. He became a local sensation and might have remained local if it hadn't been for the Williamstown Theater Festival, that summer event that brings the royalty of New York theater out every year to perform for six weeks or so. Often, they had children in tow. The children found the show. They talked of nothing but Hammy and wanted to meet him. The parents, being good parents, had it arranged, met Hammy, saw the show, and were charmed. Hammy became the talk. Network people, taking a summer break to see some plays heard of him. Soon he had a network show. He was placed in the early evening because a savvy programmer saw how all the sophisticated theater folk responded to him. Hammy was a hit. He was successful. He was "In," and before he could become "Out," he was saved forever by the good fortune of having the "In" stretched into "Institution." He became part of the fabric of contemporary America. Thus he was rewarded with riches.

Sara Hutton grew up in a fifteenth-floor apartment on Central Park West overlooking the park and a massive house in the Hollywood Hills overlooking the city. She had puppets and other strange creatures for siblings, and she probably wasn't her dad's favorite. After all, as far as he was concerned, she was only a co-creation. She went to private girls' schools because her mother did not want her to face the unfair competition of boys. She excelled academically. She was her class president. She had her pick of Ivy League colleges, and she picked Yale. She graduated with honors, decided not to pursue a higher degree, returned to Los Angeles, and got a job in the mailroom of William Morris, her father's agency. Everything was ascendant from there. She moved from the mailroom to working a desk for that moment's hot agent, to becoming an agent for a few years, to moving over to Paramount as a junior development executive. At Paramount, she quickly moved up the ladder of larger offices until she was a Senior Vice President with nowhere to go, as the President and Chairman of Paramount were firmly planted, well regarded, and, worse, good at their jobs. Then the once fabulous Olympic Pictures, now not much more than a shell owned by a bank, came calling. They needed a new president. They wouldn't get an "A" player but a young, aggressive, hungry woman with a very showbiz name. It was a good, politically correct fit. She took the job after protracted negotiations that ended by shocking the town over how much she got the Swedes to pay her. It seemed to have been worth it, though, for she started to bring Olympic back with reasonably budgeted popcorn movies starring hit TV actors doing exactly what they did best on TV. Big-screen action films for small-screen action actors. Big-screen dumb comedies for small-screen sitcom actors. It became known as the Hutton Formula.

And the dark side? People didn't like her, or rather, artists didn't like her because she had a supercilious attitude towards them, contemptuous and chilly—she thought all of them were nothing but clowns. That's why she was most successful working with those who, if they wanted what they wanted—as opposed to those who had much too much of what they had always wanted—had no option but to grin, bear, and bitch about her in private while they smiled, sought out, and pursued her in public. Then, of course, there was the sex. The rumors were of many, varied, and young—dangerously young on occasion. The talk was of leverage, power, and force, brutally applied occasionally. The blind eye was well-turned, though—out of strange industry courtesy.

Was she capable of murder? Roee thought that all motion

picture executives had the potential for violence, but that was just the playwright in him. Murder is probably the least effective—and indeed the messiest—way a motion picture executive can put a crimp in the career of a creative person. How could it possibly be satisfying? Death tends to desensitize a person. What joy was there for a motion picture executive in contemplating the cessation of suffering?

7
A SNIPPY PIECE

The following day I got onto the line with the Captain, my "employee" at the LAPD. We never mention or use his name for obvious reasons. He is well placed in Internal Affairs, which makes him valuable to me, as the latitude that gives him becomes a far-reaching tool. He could give me the details on the secure line of The Phone.

"The body was found just outside of Nome, Alaska, in a snow drift on the Bering Sea. The drift was being moved by a snowplow clearing an area for golf."

"Golf?"

"Yes, they play golf on the frozen sea up there. Use orange golf balls. You know, because white balls—"

"Yes, the obstacles to normal play are not hard to imagine."

"Anyway, they try to ricochet the balls into sunken, flagged coffee cans before losing them among built-up chunks of ice. Big golf classic every March brings in players from all over the world. This was just for locals, of course."

"Who found her?"

"Guy by the name of Don Henderson of Arctic Circle Snow Removal."

"I assume that's a business that suffers no depression up there."

"Yeah. Anyway, he was plowing away when he caught sight of some color and stopped for a look-see. Was rather shocked to find the body. Knew immediately that it wasn't a local."

"Sure. Small town. He must know practically everybody."

"Well, it wasn't that so much, as she was wearing a Donna Karan evening gown and high heels. Not your typical dress for Nome, where even business people prefer the layered look and good, sensible walking shoes."

"She wasn't killed in Alaska, then."

"Yeah, even the local police figured that out. They called in the Alaska State Troopers, who flew the body down to Anchorage for the autopsy. No coroner or medical examiner in Nome."

"What was the autopsy report?"

"Cause of death: electrocution."

"Electrocution?"

"It gets odder."

"Okay. Continue."

"The mechanism of death was instantaneous ventricular fibrillation of the heart caused by the electrical current passing from the point of contact, through the heart, then on down to the ground, and the manner of death—"

"Homicide?"

"Obviously. The accidentally dead and suicides don't usually take a vacation trip to Alaska postmortem, so to speak."

"Where was the point of entry of the current?"

"Her lips."

"Her lips?"

"They were burnt clean off."

"And the grounding point?"

I had a guess. It was, unfortunately, correct.

"Her knees."

"Her *knees*? Plural?"

"Correct—both. Identical burn marks."

"To kiss the golden arse," I half whispered.

"What?"

"Nothing. If it's something fruitful, I'll share it later."

xx

The Captain also reported that the Anchorage coroner could not even estimate the time of death as the body had been frozen in the snowbank, delaying decomposition. However, given the condition of the body, especially that the fixed lividity—that is, where the blood had been taken by gravity to settle and, eventually, clot—was somewhat unevenly distributed throughout the body, and that there was no discoloration of the skin, the coroner had concluded that she had been dead less than 24 hours at the time she was frozen and that the body had been moved in "sort of a bundled state."

The coroner also noted that the victim had motor oil stains in various spots on her clothes and skin, that grains of sand were found under her fingernails, and that she had had sexual relations within twenty-four hours of her death.

"There was no identification on the body, but when the troopers read through the missing person notices from other states, it wasn't hard to match up the body with the report on Bea Cherbourg. They called the LAPD, and you know the rest."

"Yes."

"But my question, Fixxer, is, how do you know it?"

"Bea Cherbourg was a friend of a friend."

"This Mike guy from the newsstand?"

"Yeah. So how's the investigation going?"

"Not much. We talked to her friends; her last known employer—"

"Olympic Pictures?"

"Yeah."

"What did they tell you?"

"That she no longer worked there, although they were developing a script of hers, there had been no meetings on it lately, and no one had seen her recently."

"Did anyone talk to Sara Hutton?"

"Yeah—the lead was provided by this Mike. Her answer was the same. She had been busy traveling, running an industry retreat, and she hadn't seen Bea since the last meeting on her script, which she admitted did not go well, and Olympic and Bea Cherbourg were having 'creative differences' on it. We told her we had a report that Bea Cherbourg attended the retreat. She categorically denied it. It was for executives only, and, as she was no longer an executive...."

"You should get a list of who was at this retreat and question them. Although, it will probably be to no avail."

"We did. It was."

"You might want to check out the pilot of the Olympic corporate jet about a recent trip to New York, but I'll bet he'll report what he's been told to report."

"You know something we don't know, Fixx? Because, at the moment, with the information in hand, the word is Olympic is a dead end, and we are to leave it that way."

"I don't have anything I can give you with confidence."

"Then we'll have to leave it that way. You, however...."

"I'm not in the business of solving murder cases, Captain."

"Fixx, even over the phone, I can see your nose twitching. By all accounts, she was a lovely girl. Hate to see her become a statistic under the heading: Unsolved."

"Are you offering unpaid aid and comfort?"

"You know my number."

The Captain hung up.

xx

It was evident that Sara Hutton was somehow involved in the murder of Bea Cherbourg. It was also apparent that she had less than competently covered her tracks through effort and influence. The finding of Bea's body on a frozen sea Alaskan golf "green" had to have been a mistake. Not enough of one to give the police the means, maybe the desire, to overcome her influence, however. As far as they were concerned, Bea was a malcontent screenwriter (a far too natural assumption) who had done something silly— probably some stupid, weird Hollywood sex thing—to get herself killed by someone with the ability to move her body north to Alaska, hoping to get rid of it. They would continue to investigate, but it would be frustrating, and cases that seemed easier and quicker to solve, offering lovely Skinnerian positive reinforcement, would dictate their behavior.

Poor Bea Cherbourg. Her screenplay would never get made now. Poor Bea Cherbourg.

Poor Bea.

I was suddenly hit with the fact that a small part of me, most likely a tiny part of me, but a part nonetheless, was in love with what was left of Bea Cherbourg.

Which, of course, was nothing but people's memories of her. I had no idea who the Bea of her parent's memories was. Mike's memories were idealized, and as charming as they were, they were of a woman Bea herself would probably not much have liked. Sara Hutton's memories were distorted, I was pretty sure, through a lens with a massive flaw in it. My memories were not extensive. Yet they were sharp with the clarity of a smile that supported two sad eyes. I sat back from myself and wondered about this small part of me suddenly in love with a smile supporting two sad eyes. It was curious. I had never been aware of this part of me before. Possibly, when this love dies—it was so fragile, I assumed this was its fate—possibly I would lose all future awareness of it. For now, though, it begged to be considered.

There was a memory missing. Not one I could share, but one I could be informed of. I needed that information.

"Roee?" I called him over the intercom system. He answered from the kitchen. "I want to take a little trip to New Haven, Connecticut. To Yale University. I want to speak with a teacher or professor named Sam or Samuel. I don't have a last name. He's probably with their film program. Make the arrangements, would you."

"Of course. Now would you like breakfast?"

"Yes, something hot and nourishing. Something that would make me feel happy on a cold, miserable winter's morning."

xx

"His name is Samuel Farber, called Sam by all, and he teaches,

79

among others, a course on film analysis in the Film Studies Program," Roee walking into the library later that day and, dispensing with any former greeting, reported to me. "Now, I don't know the syllabus for this course, but I assume it has something to do with investigating and delineating the multifaceted layers of film's various emotional problems and suggesting a cure or cures for them, or, at least, controlling them through some form of drug therapy."

I looked up from the computer screen, where I was going over some detailed, and usually secret, financial information regarding Olympic Pictures. "Roee, are you sure your mother was not once near mortally frightened by a mad and homicidal film projectionist in a movie theater in downtown Tel Aviv?"

"My mother was not that kind of woman," Roee stated with some umbrage.

"To attract the mad and homicidal?"

"To go to a movie."

"I see. All right, let's contact Mr. Farber and schedule an appointment."

"With whom? Federal Agent Harrington?"

Federal Agent Harrington is one of 52 identities that I can assume. Each one is fully backed up with all the necessary documents. Some require makeup. Some don't. Some are scary. Some aren't. One my mother would have recognized—but I'm not sure I would.

"No, I'm sure Mr. Farber is cut from that part of the college cloth that finds anything Federal suspect. That would not be conducive to getting him to open up. How about J. W. Crick?"

"The freelance reporter?"

"Yes, on assignment from Vanity Fair to investigate the death of Bea Cherbourg."

"Bea Cherbourg was hardly famous. Why would Vanity Fair be interested?"

"True. Not Dunne at all. All right, a general snippy piece on Death in Hollywood—the death of dreams, death of ambition, death of people, and, more importantly, for Mr. Farber's sake, death of Art. You know, the rot in the underbelly. That should attract him. Tell him the death of Bea is just serving as a metaphor for my larger purpose."

"For tomorrow?"

"Yes, late afternoon. I'll take the redeye tonight."

"Why the redeye? I can get you an earlier flight."

"No, the redeye will be fine. It will help make me naturally disheveled. After all, I assume some romance is left in journalism."

xx

The next day, after a flight as disheveling as one can imagine—Roee, in the spirit of the enterprise, booked me into coach—I met Samuel Farber at the Film Studies Center of Yale, located in a building on Crown Street, which is, essentially, the southwest border of the campus proper. So 305 Crown Street faces out to reality—if one wanted to think of it that way—instead of into ivory towers, which Yale claims not to have any of.

Farber greeted me in his small office, desk facing the wall, bookcases filled haphazardly, books and papers taking up space on the guest chairs and small guest couch, the graying computer on the desk clothed comfortably in a thick cloth of dust.

Farber was a tall man of maybe forty-five who probably jogged every morning to keep him fitting into traditional cut jeans instead of the loose fit ones that were his right by age. They did look good, however, especially with close-fitting T-shirts, like the one he was now wearing, which featured the key art poster for the Polish release of Bonnie and Clyde. He had a head of hair so generous and thick you just knew that somewhere in the world, at least ten men suffered congenital baldness to compensate for the fact. He was undoubtedly handsome; all could agree on that, male and female, the old and the young, those with 20/20 vision, and even the blind.

"So," Farber said with a smile that seemed like a hug from a buddy wearing a cashmere sweater, "you're from Vanity Fair?"

"I'm a freelancer on assignment for them. I don't normally cover Hollywood, but Graydon thought I could bring a fresh perspective to an old story."

"The Death of Art in Hollywood?"

"Yeah."

"And the death of Bea."

"Were you shocked to learn of it?"

"Of course. I've never lost a student before."

"*You* lost her?"

"I meant that Bea is the first student of all I've taught who's died."

"You've been teaching...?"

"Twenty years."

"And you know the whereabouts of all your past students and their current states of health?"

"Well, I suppose I meant students who had been special."

"Students who saw you as what? The master? A guru?"

He smiled and slowly shook his head as if in pity for this outsider who didn't understand. "As a friend with a mind compatible to their own."

"Just minds?"

"I have a suspicion as to what that question relates to, but maybe you should elaborate."

"Did you have an affair with Bea Cherbourg?"

"Well, if I had, I truly apologize if it caused the Death of Art in Hollywood."

"Would you be sorry if it had caused Bea's death?"

He took a second to think—but only a second. "I doubt that very much."

"How come you never went to Hollywood?"

"I have too much respect for film."

"And you teach that respect to those students compatible with your mind?"

"I think that's probably an adequate description of my job."

"Is film an art?"

"It can be."

"A powerful medium?"

"Obviously. Whether it's an art or not."

"What's your assessment of Hollywood filmmaking today?"

"I assess that the Hollywood film today has sunk into the

multinational-mega-corporation-think cesspool. The art in the American film has not so much died as it has been put aside as irrelevant to the goals of the multi-national mega-corporations. Product with a shelf life is their concern, not human interactive communication regarding the shared human condition."

H obviously had given the question some thought.

"'Interactive communication regarding the shared human condition,'" I quoted back to him as I wrote it down in a notepad. "Is that your definition of Art?"

"You have a better one?"

"Yet, despite your opinion, you teach film studies."

"Well, doctors study disease."

"To find a cure?"

"Yes, I suppose so."

"Was Bea Cherbourg the first special student you sent to Hollywood?"

"What makes you think I sent her to—"

"Sort of as a mole, to borrow a term from my usual journalistic beat. Except she wasn't so much a mole, which is a gatherer of information, you were probably hoping she would be more of an agent provocateur, a spreader of information designed to agitate."

"Well, that's quite a melodramatic way to describe every teacher's hope to have been a positive influence."

"Tell me about Bea Cherbourg."

"A brilliant student. She had an innate understanding of the language of cinema. She was extremely well-read. Shy, non-aggressive, but forceful of mind when it mattered."

"A good lover?" (All right, I was being a bit perverse here.)

Farber looked at me, trying to make up his mind. "Off the record?"

"Certainly."

"Yes, she was an exceptional lover. She had a lovely need to please."

"Do you have affairs with all your female students?"

"No. I pick one a year. One of the special ones. Passion intensifies intellectual transference. It's a teaching technique."

"You know the time will come when age will catch up with you despite your charm and passion, and 18-to-22-year-olds will no longer be attracted."

"Yes, I'm aware of that."

"What will you be left with then?"

"Just my memories."

"Well, I suppose those and an active imagination should see you through."

"I'm counting on it."

"You contacted Sara Hutton and recommended Bea, didn't you?"

"Yes."

"You taught Sara Hutton?"

"She was a student of mine. She couldn't be taught."

"Tell me about her."

"A privileged child."

"Yes, of a clown."

"Still privileged."

"Do you think this affected her?"

"Well, when she came here as a freshman, her major was sociology."

"Ah."

"Yes, the cliché major of freshman girls."

"She wanted to be of used to people."

"Yes, to help them."

"But she changed majors."

"Yes."

"Why?"

"I think she discovered that she didn't much like people, or, at least, certain people. The certain people that we are now referring to as the underclass."

"Poor people."

"Poor. Ignorant. Uncultured. Simple. In her view, at least."

"So she became a film major?"

"No. She became a philosophy major."

"A philosophy major?"

"Became somewhat enamored with Plato's Republic."

"Society divided into natural classes."

"One of the great things about Yale is that we are very community-oriented, especially through Dwight Hall. I would guess that well over half of our undergraduates actively serve the community in efforts to fight poverty, hunger, and homelessness. They help the elderly and disabled."

"You have your share of all that here in New Haven?"

"More than. You may have noticed on the drive to the campus."

"And Dwight Hall?"

'An independent service organization. Been helping people since 1886."

"Yet you still have more than your share of the underclass."

"Well, yes, but not way more than our share."

"So Sara Hutton, first-year sociology major, jumped right in and volunteered, through Dwight Hall, to single-handedly solve the ills of New Haven."

"Yes, she did, and then found the waters much too cold and jumped right out."

"How did you wind up having her in your class? She took it as an easy-A elective?"

"Well, one, it's not an easy-A elective. And she took it, I understand, at the suggestion of Max."

"Max who?"

"I never got his last name."

"Another student?"

"No. She knew him from somewhere else. I think they flew together."

"Flew?"

"In airplanes."

"Yes, I assumed something mechanical was required."

"She had learned when she was quite young. Ten, twelve, something like that. She probably meant this Max at the airstrip where she kept her plane. I never met him, but I understand he was a bit of a philosopher himself and quite charismatic. They were lovers, of course."

"'Sara Hutton couldn't be taught.' Your words."

"Once she lost her emotional virginity and discovered that no real harm would come to her if she gave up caring what other people thought, her true nature came out."

"Which was?"

"Icy. Haughty. Superior. Condescending—no point could not be argued."

"Her mind was not compatible with yours."

"No, although I'll admit enjoying the sparring. I think we became friends."

"Lovers?"

"Not my type."

"Too ugly?"

"Well, I do have standards along that line, but it was more—"

"A total lack of influence on her thinking. Do you think she even likes movies?"

"Not the ones I like."

"Yet she's now the president of a major motion picture company."

"Interesting, isn't it?"

"Do you think she only entered the industry because nepotism made it an easy job to get?"

"Riding in on the back of a clown? I'm sure it helped, but she entered at the suggestion of Max."

"He's in the industry?"

"I don't know, but that's what she told me on graduation day eight years ago. 'Max thinks it's a good idea if I get into the movies, so I guess I'm going to go to Hollywood,' is how she put it."

"Ever hear of the Golden Arse? And the kissing thereof?"

"No, I don't think so. Sounds very Greek, though, doesn't it?"

"You referring to sodomy?"

"No. Sororities. In this case, anyway."

"Gamma Phi Epsilon?"

"That's right. You do your research, don't you?"

"A film-themed sorority that Sara Hutton was the president of."

"Yes, in her senior year. This was Max's idea again, I think."

"How come you know so much about Max?"

"I don't. One just got to know a lot about Sara. People talked about her. She talked a lot about herself. She was like a continuing story you couldn't help but follow."

"What do you think Sara Hutton's influence on the American film has been?"

"It's not so much what it has been as what it could become. I mean, she hasn't been there that long, has she? The movies she makes at Olympic are essentially the equivalent in art of the original paperback novel trade. Cheap entertainment made for a cheap crowd. Only these films are anything but cheap. The crowd hasn't changed much, though."

"So who do you blame? Sara Hutton or the crowd?"

Sam Farber smiled. "It's such a symbiotic relationship that I wouldn't know how to divide it."

xx

An apt alliteration to call him an arrogant academic, I thought as I left Sam Farber's office. How arrogant? When we discussed Bea Cherbourg's death, there was no hint of emotion and certainly no indication of grief. But then, despite being lovers, she had not been a person to him but, rather, a conduit of his ideas. As far as I knew, he had not impregnated her in any biological way, but he certainly felt he had in an intellectual way, giving her a packet of, not genes, but memes, as Dawkins might declare. Is it a cause of grief if such a "mother" dies in "childbirth"? That would be antithetical to the rational basis of the conceit. Casual regret is the best one should expect.

Yet, there is something very red meat about the lack of survival of these memes compared to those that Sara Hutton propagates. Had the contest been fair? Had the fittest indeed survived? Had...?

It must have been strolling along York Street into the campus proper that affected me. Something about the grand gothic architecture forming hallowed halls. And the bricks, the oh-so-serious bricks. The bastard had balled her and propagandized his thoughts into her head, then sent her off near defenseless to Hollywood to effect changes he never had the guts to try to do himself. Those were the hard facts. I didn't much care for Sam Farber, but he had given me some valuable information. There is nothing like philosophy to get you into trouble.

8

QUALITY CRAFTED IN THE USA

I continued to walk deeper into the campus, but at a quicker pace, allowing the brisk air inhaled to stimulate the senses and add a little snap to my brain. I turned right at one point, ending up at a corner in sight of what I assumed was Harkness Tower, judging by the sign pointing its way. Across the street, I could see an open area leading to a square surrounded by the Old Campus, the generative core of the university. I jaywalked and went there to look for a comfortable place to alight and do some hard thinking. Unfortunately, as starkly beautiful as the square was with its snow-covered ground; tall, bare, frost-covered oak and elm trees; and deeply European feel to the surrounding buildings, I found not one place to sit to take this all in. Not one bench. Not even a fountain with a convenient ledge. When the snow did not cover the ground, the lawn now hidden underneath must be the only cushion for the young bodies housing the young minds expanding with Ivy League enlightenment. But that is age-old for the young, who don't worry about the effects of Nature on clothing and spinal columns. I, on the other hand, even when young, always somehow found it demeaning—"demeaning" may be too strong of a word, of course, but it's close to the meaning—to sit, squat, and sprawl like a primitive man who had not yet invented the improvement of the chair. To do so for reasons of stealth was another matter, but when no professional impediment to comfort is required, I require comfort. Given the limited resources, I leaned up against a tree.

In my search, I had made my way across the two acres of the square and was now facing the extent of it, looking across it directly towards Harkness Tower. Very Gothic, very natural looking, framed by the skeletal trees in winter starkness, very Old World.

This was the area where the freshman came to live, I recalled from my quick research. I imagined an 18-year-old Sara Hutton sitting here surrounded by this old brick womb of best-and-brightest nurturing, dealing with her newfound revulsion for the Underclass. I thought of her staring at the beauty of these buildings, their Gothic Revival and Romanesque styles seeming to speak of just what wonders Man has built, and I thought of her comparing that with the blight of the urban decay surrounding the campus. Who did the building? Who caused the decay? Natural questions. It's her answers that may have been unnatural.

I took my cell phone out of my pocket, called Roee, and had him patch me through the secure line to Petey.

"Fixxer! Where are you? I hear bells!" Petey came through, as always, loud and clear.

"Bells?"

"Yeah, you know, of the ding-dong variety!"

I stopped to listen. Petey was right. The crisp air was alive with the successive tones of striking clappers beating out music unfamiliar to me. Having been deep in thought, I hadn't noticed.

"I'm on the Yale campus in New Haven. There's a big Gothic tower in front of me. I guess it's coming from there."

"Yeah, but what's that music? I know that?"

"I don't know. Listen, I want—"

"Sure you do. You've got to know it. Everybody knows it!"

"Well, assuming you're a part of everybody, Petey, you tell me."

"I just can't think of it right now, but I know I know it."

I listened for another second. "Well, it's innocuous and inane. Does that help?"

"No. So many things are these days. Oh well. Yale, uh? What could they possibly teach you?"

"I haven't decided on a major yet. I need your help, Petey. You anywhere near the computer?"

"Sure, I just happen to have been poking around in it when you called."

"Can you check the database on airfields in this area? Not Tweed-New Haven, or any other commercial field. I'm looking for some small, most likely private fields."

"Well, let's see what we got." There was a moment's pause during which I could hear Petey humming the inane music that the bells had been playing, accompanied by the clack of computer keys. "Well, we got three private fields. One's connected to a big wholesale distributor out in East Haven."

"No, that wouldn't be it."

"One's a private flying club."

"Give me the details on—"

"Oh, this is interesting."

"What?"

"There's a file on one out in Mom's Cove with a stop sign on it."

"Really? You don't have that level of security clearance, do you?"

"Well—not so you would notice, Fixx, but I've always preferred going in the back door anyway. After all, I am but a servant of the State. Here we go. Oh wow! You'll never guess. The field is owned by—"

"Max somebody."

"Hey, don't bruise my lines by stepping on them. Not just Max somebody. Maxwellton James!"

A bell rang. Not one of the ones in Harkness Tower. "Why do I know that name?"

"Well, you and I never worked with him."

"He was a gun runner."

"That's right!"

"Central America."

"Lot of frequent flyer miles to Honduras."

"How did we compensate him?"

"Well, according to this, we didn't."

"What was he, one of Reagan's new George Washingtons?"

"Nope. It seems we allowed him to transport certain illicit drugs back up here."

"Not, I would assume, for private consumption."

"Not unless he took an occasional toot for quality control."

"And this airfield?"

"Just never seen by the good old blind eye of Uncle Sam. Nor, it seems, were the airfields he owns in Texas, Central California, and—"

"Nome, Alaska."

"Yeah! Just outside of."

"And his current activities?"

"None listed here. I guess he's retired."

"A rich man?"

"Well, he's got an expensive hobby."

"What's that?"

"He collects and refurbishes antique planes. You know, World War One, World War Two war birds, that sort of stuff. Rents them to movies. He's a big deal at air shows. Very respect—*The Monkees!*"

"What?"

"That's what the bells were tolling. The theme from The Monkees!"

"Oh. Ask not for whom the bell tolls, the bell tolls for cultural kitsch."

"Yeah! *Hey, hey, we're the—*"

"Petey?"

"What?"

"May I have the address of the airfield?"

"Oh, yeah, sure, Fixxer!"

XX

I returned to my car, which I had left in a parking lot on York, across from the 305 Crown Street building. It was a rented Ford Taurus painted a bizarre nightmare version of green. Just what I thought a freelance journalist on a limited expense account would be forced to rent. I drove out of the central city to the area known as Mom's Cove, which sat on the wide mouth of the Quinnipiac River, where it merged with Long Island Sound. The airfield was not hard to find. It was a desolate plot of land surrounded by one of the tallest chain-link fences I had ever seen. A narrow road with muddy, snow-slush tire ruts leads to the gate that had a dirty white sign on it that read in red letters:

PRIVATE AIRFIELD.
TRESPASSES WILL BE PROSECUTED
(If They Survive Their Wounds.)

I parked the Ford and got out, and went to the gate. It was locked with a new keypad system that was all shiny and sleek compared to the fence, which had had a long acquaintance with the various faces of weather. I looked through the fence. The property ran to the river's edge. Between the fence and the shore was one lone runway, running perpendicular to the river's edge; a large, two-story hangar, much larger than one would think a field this size would need; and a small one-story building, most likely the office, attached to the side of the hangar. There were no planes on the runway and no other activity that I could tell. There was one car parked by the hangar, a bright yellow Corvette.

I decided, despite the sign, to make my way in. I went to the trunk of the car and pulled out the Bag o' Tricks, a case slightly larger than a standard attaché that held an incredible variety of little tools lovingly created by Roee. I pulled from it the little device Roee was most proud of lately, which he had dubbed "Fingers Malloy." Looking like a one-button remote control, it housed various electronic this-and-thats, including a little microchip that had stored on it every possible combination a keypad was capable of. Attached to the side of a keypad and the button pushed, Fingers Malloy tried every combination with astonishing rapidity until a match was found. Then it displayed the proper number sequence on a little screen. Unfortunately, there are many combinations possible, so the amount of time one must wait varies from a minute or two to twenty. That's its only drawback. It could keep you rooted in the illicit act longer than you felt comfortable doing so. In the dead of night, under cover, that may not be a problem—especially if you have a good book and a tiny flashlight to kill time with. But in broad daylight with nothing to hide behind, it gave you a feeling reminiscent of the one you get with the classic reoccurring nightmare where you show up for school with no shirt on.

I did not have to be shirtless long. Fingers Malloy cracked it within a minute. It was an easy combination for an easygoing mind: 7-4-76.

I opened the gate and walked in. I stood for a second surveying the scene. The road with the ruts continued to the hangar. Except for the runway, the ground was covered with dirty snow and pieces of litter that had blown over the high fence. A bright blue winter sky was overhead, looking as crisp as the air felt. I walked in the ruts, avoiding the deeper puddles, not wanting to chance a noisy slip on the old snow. When I got to the tarmac, I quietly walked and came around to the opening of the hangar. A snowplow hidden from the road stood at the side of the hangar. Next to it was a weathered, burnt orange Clarke airplane tug with its fifteen-foot lashed-together tow bars jutting out from under its nose. Essentially a boxy little motorized muscle on wheels, the tug pulls airplanes in and out of hangers. Compared to the much larger snowplow, it was close to being cute, especially with the end of the tow bars resting on the little wheels that allow the driver to maneuver the bar as he drives.

Inside the hangar, two old C-23 transport planes stood towards the back. Not recently used, one had the feeling, but there was still magnificence to them as they stood there, their noses pointing slightly up in the natural snobbery of things that can fly. The rest of the hangar was empty except for assorted tools and equipment that lay about haphazardly and except for a man sitting on a chair, bent over the engine of a tiny airplane that, like the tug, was also in danger of being cute. It was sleek—but things built to be aerodynamic often are—and all white except for some black trim. It couldn't have been more than fifteen feet from prop to tail, with a wingspan of about the same length. The cockpit was only about four feet off the ground. The plane couldn't have weighed more than 500 pounds. It looked like a large-scale model or a serious toy.

The man was dressed in exceedingly wrinkled gray coveralls. If they had been washed anytime this decade, it must have been using the short cycle and with a brand of detergent that hadn't engendered much customer satisfaction. His hair, what there was of it, was short-cropped and gray. I walked into the hangar, making no noise, and came right up behind him.

"Nice airfield," I said by way of getting his attention.

There was no jolt of surprise. He just stopped working on the engine and turned to face me. The eyes were gray also, not to mention his general complexion. He slowly twisted his body in a follow-through as he stood up before me, scanning my particulars. "Who the fuck are you?"

"And with such a friendly staff." I countered.

"This is a private airfield. How the hell did you get in?"

"The gate was open."

"It was not."

"Look for yourself."

The man quick-paced out of the hangar and looked towards the entrance. He saw the gate swung wide open. "Damn!" I heard him say. He turned around and returned to me. "Why didn't you just drive in then instead of sneaking up?"

"Well, I did read your sign."

"So?"

"I didn't want you to take a shot at the car. It's rented, and I didn't take out the damage insurance."

"Got coverage on yourself?"

"Look, I'm a journalist..."

"That's hardly impressive."

"A freelance journalist. I'm doing a story on Sara Hutton."

"Who?"

"Sara Hutton. She's the president and CEO of Olympic Pictures."

"I can see why you don't have a steady job."

"Why?"

"You're not very good, are you? Look around. No movie studios here."

"Yes, I've noticed, but Sara Hutton went to school at Yale, and she's a pilot. I

understand she kept her plane here."

"Well, I wouldn't know about that. I haven't been here that long. Only been here about three months."

"Oh, really? That surprises me."

"Why?"

"You look so—" I considered the overalls again. "Settled in."

"I'd ask you nicely to leave, but I'm not a nice guy. So, if you don't, I'll kick the crap out of you."

"Seen Max lately?"

"Who?"

"Well, maybe you have been here a short time. Maxwellton James. He owns this field."

"How do you know that?"

"I used to buy all my drugs from him."

Mr. Gray took a hard look at me. I had finally cracked him. "Yeah, asshole, I'm a bad guy, just like you, and it was a pretty sweet deal when I used to get all my supplies from Max, and you know, I was sitting around the other day getting all nostalgic about it and realized how much I miss Max. Though he and I could talk about a reunion."

"Max is retired."

"Retired? What's the matter? He doesn't like money anymore?"

"Max has got plenty of money."

"Oh. Well, I hope he saved some for his old age."

"Hey, wait a minute, what's this bullshit about being a reporter and doing a story on Sara Hutton. What do you know about Sara Hutton?"

"Send a message to Max for me. Tell him we've been real disappointed since he Went Hollywood, and we're determined to bring him back into the family. Can you deliver that message, asshole?"

"Sure, I can get it to Max."

"Good. Business concluded. Now tell me about the toy airplane."

"That's not a toy. That's a Cassutt racer."

"Oh, it actually flies."

"Yeah, it flies. About 300 miles an hour."

"Not much room for your luggage, though."

"I said it was a racer!"

"You're very serious about this plane, aren't you?"

"Yeah, going to take it up right now. So why don't you leave." He started to walk out of the hangar, making it clear I should follow.

"Sure, why not? You got the message, and I'm sure you'll deliver it. Now, listen, I'll be back for the answer in one week."

Once out of the hangar, he jumped into the seat of the tug and started the engine. "Hey, wait a minute," he shouted, stopping me.

I turned around. He gestured for me to get closer to hear him over the engine. I assumed he was going to ask me my name. I had been expecting it and was prepared to tell him that Max would know who I was, but he had something different in mind. Just as I was in range, he suddenly lurched the tug to the left, causing the tow bars to swing on their tiny wheels swiftly to the right, sweeping me, unromantically, off my feet. I landed hard on the ground, then found myself oppressed by the full weight of his body landing on me, knocking the air out in a gasp. I would have lodged a formal protest if he hadn't, at that point, grabbed my head and slammed it onto the pavement. After that, I was in no condition for the paperwork.

xx

There are times when pain simply defines existence. Especially when you are coming out of a deep, unnaturally induced sleep and the pain is lodged in and around your head where the natural assumption declares existence lies. It is interesting how, when you begin to regain consciousness, you start to delineate the pain, separating that which is within the cranium from that which is without. The tactile pain of bruised and abraded flesh without from the amorphous, seemingly non-corporeal, pain within. Then, of course, there is the decision-making process: "Should I move and possibly intensify the pain? Should I open my eyes? Do I really want to see where I am?"

The first sense to poke out beyond the pain was my hearing. The high-pitched whine of an engine that seemed very far away made itself known through the disturbance of air. I didn't care. I couldn't muster concern for the very far away. Then an awareness that I was not lying as one would have expected, but seemed to be sitting upright, so upright I was stiff-necked, piqued my curiosity. I tried to move my head forward. I couldn't; something cut deep into my forehead when I tried. A rope, most likely, as I had just realized that my hands were tied behind my back. I dispassionately deduced that the rope around my head was probably linked to the rope around my wrists. Enough clear thinking had now invaded my head that I had no choice but to open my eyes to see the glimmer of the sun on the white wings of a faraway airplane that seemed to be coming directly at me from over the Quinnipiac River. It didn't take a second to realize that I sat in the middle of the runway, tied to a chair.

I appreciate the surreal as much as the next intellectually discriminating person, but having a plane land on my lap was not quite irrationally odd enough to tolerate. I began to struggle with the loosely tied knots, assuming I had plenty of—

No, not far away! Just small! That damn Cassutt racer and the tip of its right wing was just about to intersect with my neck!

I lunged to my left and fell hard onto my side as the tiny Cassutt roared its small but deadly, doppler-effected roar over my painful head. It was pain I luxuriated in. It meant my head was still attached to the rest of me.

I quickly got out of my loose bonds—Mr. Gray did not tie me up for security, but just for the better positioning of my head, like a golf ball on a tee—and scrambled to my feet. The Cassutt was banking a hairpin bank, obviously intending to give chase. I looked around me. There was no conceivable place to take cover except the hangar, but it was too far away; I knew I couldn't outrace the plane to make it there. I thought of running to the gate and the car, but that was also quite a distance, plus I noticed that the gate had been shut again. Outside of a disarming wit, I had no weapon on me, but I didn't think the plane could take a joke. I looked over the snow-covered ground beyond the runway. It was not entirely smooth. That might provide something. I ran, landing my feet flat to try to grip the snow and keep from sliding until I wanted to. I could hear the subtle change in the sound of the Cassutt, which meant it was following. I had to use that sound to gauge how close it was getting, as I didn't want to take my eyes away from the landscape I was weaving through and the task of spotting advantageous gullies and bumps. Still, the desire to turn my head was intense, but as you don't want to look down during a high climb, I knew not to face this potential death by RPMs.

I only needed to feel a millisecond of agitated air at my back to know it was the time. I saw and aimed for a little gully running perpendicular to the direction I was coming from. I leaped for it, twisting my body to land on my back. The Cassutt's prop kicked up snow as its underbelly passed over me in a blur.

Then my cell phone rang.

As the only one who could call me was Roee, I figured I could get back to him, but the phone seemed insistent. Roee will always hang up after three rings and try again. On the fifth, I felt compelled to answer. "Roee, sorry, just a bit busy at—"

"It's Petey. You better listen," I heard Roee say quickly.

"Fixxer, wow! That was a close shave!"

"Petey, how do you know that?"

"I've been watching you on the satellite."

"The satellite?"

"Yeah."

"And a hardy hello to you too, Fixx!"

"They've improved it since I was there."

"Yes, I have."

"Well, by any chance, does that satellite have a laser cannon that could beam down and zap this bastard?"

Petey laughed at the thought. "Oh, Fixx! You're such a fantasist! But, if you go about twenty yards to the north, you'll find a long stick, or something, just at the edge of the runway. Sorry, but that's the best I can do finding you a weapon."

"A stick?"

"That's right."

"No laser?"

"Not today, nope, sorry. Oops, head down!"

The Cassutt roared past again.

"Ooowwee, that sounded close."

I was still thinking of the stick. "Slingshot, by any chance?"

"Sorry, David. Stand up, and I'll point you in the right direction."

I did.

"Turn a little to the right—a little more—a little more. Run!"

I ran back to the runway as the Cassutt made a lazy bank. Mr. Gray had probably decided that cat and mouse wasn't a bad game and wanted to play it out. As Petey had said, I found a long, blond, rounded piece of wood poking out of a small snowbank on the edge of the runway. It looked like a broom handle. I grabbed it and pulled it out of the bank. It was a broom handle; it was a large push broom with a broad head with dull, colorless bristles. It was probably used to clear the runway of litter and little piles of snow, but what the hell could I use it for? I turned and found that the Cassutt was heading over the runway towards me, descending to a position level with my chest. What could I do? I took a stance, planted my feet as solidly as possible, and held the broom like a baseball bat, its head an unwelcome counterweight at the bottom. Timing, of course, would be everything. I fixed my eye on the plane and wondered what his plan was. Slicing me through the middle with one of the wings, my top half getting kicked up into the air to spin a while before plopping back down to the ground; my bottom half remaining standing, half the man I used to be? Or to hit me straight on, letting the prop mince the meat that was me? Either way, he was probably looking at me—a desperate man challenging him with nothing but a broom—and laughing uproariously. Yes, I could see that. He was now close enough to see. He was laughing uproariously.

It was good to know I had the talent to amuse.

The timing was absolute—

I simultaneously fell on my back while sliding my hands to the end of the broom handle, keeping it balanced as I swung the head around. As the Cassutt flew a bare five feet overhead, I pushed hard, ramming the broad broom head up against the tip of the right wing, causing the plane to suddenly flip 90 degrees and fly sideways for just a second before its left wing scraped the surface of the tarmac, causing the little Cassutt to cartwheel down the runway. I thought I heard a bloodcurdling scream from the cramped little cockpit—but that may have just been wishful thinking. After about the fourth cartwheel, one of the wings broke off, and the fuselage slammed into the ground, exploding upon impact. Then the fiery mess slid along the runway until it slid into the Quinnipiac River, becoming a small floating island of flame.

I stood up. I looked at the broom. On it was a label that read: "Quality crafted in the USA." I was glad of that.

The phone rang. It had fallen out of my pocket and was sitting on the pavement. I picked it up. It was Petey.

"Well, it looks like you tipped the scales!"

Then he laughed—a much sweeter laugh to my ears than Mr. Gray's.

9
WINKLE WATER

U sing the Spirit of '76, I got out of the gate, into the car, and back onto the road before anyone showed up to investigate the crash at the airfield. About twenty miles out, I saw a small, comfortable-looking inn. I stopped, checked in quickly, and went to my room to give myself some first aid. Besides the usual bumps and bruises from playing in the snow, I had a large knot on my forehead, which the check-in clerk, if he had noticed, failed to mention anything about, even when I asked him to get an ice pack to my room ASAP. Professional discretion? He just didn't give a damn? Didn't matter. I was happy not to have to make up a story.

When I got to the room, out of my clothes, and into the thick white terry cloth robe they provided, I noticed that I also had an ugly, cherry-black bruise on my right shin where the tow bars had caught me. It was amazingly sore now that I didn't need that leg to aid in my escape from death. The ice pack arrived, and I gave the porter a quick and straightforward room service meal order. The most enormous meat and potatoes meal on their menu; a bottle of vodka, Absolute if possible; a bottle of tonic water; two buckets of ice. And a good portion of freshly peeled lemon twists. I promised him $100 if he got the meal to me quicker than humanly possible and the booze even faster. He announced that his name was

Andrew and that he would not fail me. There's something about a financial reward that makes people real personable.

I got on the hotel phone and changed my plane reservations for the following day. I also upgraded to first class. I was in no mood for further discomfiture. I called Roee on my cell phone, gave him a brief report, and asked him to prepare specific computer files for my review when I got home.

"An unexpected bit of violence," Roee said.

"Yes."

"As I've always said, you should never go out unarmed. A Browning Hi-Power automatic would have done more than adequate damage to that toy."

"Yes, silly me, not to assume I would be chased by a puny yet pugnacious plane."

"A mistake that should not be made again."

"True. Bodily harm seems to be second nature to these people. We'll have to keep that in mind as we find a way to stop them."

"Stop them from doing what?"

"Not quite sure, but whatever it is, I'm sure it's worth being stopped."

I then asked Roee to connect with Petey and see if we could figure out just who Mr. Gray really was between our files and the ones he could access. I've always felt that if you are forced to kill someone, even in self-defense, you should damn well know just who that someone was. It tends to put the experience into perspective. Roee disagrees with me, but he said he would get on it.

As I hung up, I remembered a phone number tucked away in my pants pocket. I grabbed my pants and retrieved it. It was of a man in the area who I had been told might have some information on Gilgamesh Paul. I called him, introduced myself as J. W. Crick, the reporter, and stated, "I'm trying to find a Gilgamesh Paul."

"I don't like the mundane. In people or in problems," he replied.

"Then I apologize for bothering you."

"No, that's a quote from Gilgamesh Paul. The only one I can remember. I was never a big fan of his."

"So you wouldn't...?"

"No. I wouldn't. Plenty of others, but not Gilgamesh Paul."

I hung up, disappointed. Finding a lead to Gilgamesh Paul might have just rescued the day.

I drank my vodka tonics. I ate my meat and potatoes. I went to bed.

XX

The next day, when I got home, I went straight to the library, where Roee had conveniently placed the files I wanted to review on the computer screen desktop. First, I opened the file I had been reading through before the trip. I wanted to confirm my basic understanding of Olympic Pictures' financial situation. It was still carrying a large debt, but Olympic had recently released enough successful films to gather some positive business press portraying the company in a financial turnaround. The rumors that Sveriges Riksbank was ready to find a buyer were probably true. I decided to call an old source of mine on Wall Street. For a quick digital cash transfer to an offshore account of his, he was happy to reveal that, indeed, there would be an announcement in two weeks by Sveriges Riksbank that they would start accepting bids. He already knew who was waiting in the wings to make the bids. At least three of the other major studios would be interested. It would give them Olympic's current library of films. Not the fat one that had already been sold off, but some good, contemporary product for the simple amusements mill you could hear grinding twenty-four hours a day. Some well-financed independent suppliers of films would certainly make bids. They would love to have their own distribution set up rather than having to tow some major's line. Then there were some foreign media giants that, rich as they were, weren't making "American" films, so they had an inferiority complex.

"What do you think Sara Hutton's fate in all this will be?" I asked.

"Well, she helped pull the studio back from the precipice, but...."

"But?"

"She's very young. It was a fluke that she got this job. I can't see any of these players—all run by very powerful, very egocentric men—I can't see any of them making this investment and keeping her completely in charge. Of course, they'll keep her as president. But with a much smaller power base. They'll put a CEO over her and a CFO handling business strategy, diluting her greenlighting ability. She won't be happy. She'll probably quit, which would not be unwelcome."

"Despite her track record?"

"Maybe because of it. Motion pictures depend on emotions to communicate. You know, 'Make 'em laugh; make 'em cry.' What few understand is that the business is run through emotions as well. In all the years I've been following the motion picture business, I could count on my right hand the times I've seen cool, dispassionate logic be the basis for a business decision, and, as you may remember, Fixx, I lost two fingers in Iran."

"You were lucky not to have lost your head."

"Not luck. Roee. How is he, by the way?"

"Cool and dispassionate."

"I would expect no less."

"I assume Sara Hutton herself has sent out some feelers."

"For a management buy? Yeah, you assume correctly."

"And...?"

"No takers."

"Why?"

"Same reasons."

"Okay. Goodbye, Ivan."

"You kidder, you."

I next turned to a file I maintain of interesting personalities in the business. These are people just a little bit off from today's norm of the powers that be. Not the slick MBAs; the ironically well-suited lawyers and agents having love affairs with cigars; the Ivy League grads who "intellectually" dissect every script in development down to the sinews and bones, then don't have a clue how to put it all back together again. Instead, I was interested in people with at least a hint of the old show biz pizzazz, the gut instinct razzle-dazzle that makes them not necessarily better people but far more amusing. I had a role in mind that had to be played. I needed the right combination of personality and much liquid capital.

While searching, Roee came in with information on Mr. Gray.

"His name was Ronald Berger. Flew transport in Viet Nam. Until a drug habit grounded him."

"What was he using?"

"Not using; selling—the normal stuff, plus stolen goods from field hospitals. Had a whole network, I guess. Dishonorable Discharge. Pissed him off. Went on a rampage. Was stopped by an MP who hit him a bit too hard on the head. Been sort of surly ever since. Back home, he flew for small cargo companies. Drifted to Central America. You can imagine what he got involved in there. Met up with Maxwellton James. Went to work for him. Chief pilot, mechanic, restorer of old planes. Until James seemed to retire from his illegal yet sanctioned activities. James is now based on the West Coast. Berger stayed where he was. He liked to tinker with planes and race that little Cassutt."

"Had he ever attempted murder before?"

"Attempted and succeeded, it seems. Nasty business in a Honduran jungle. Nothing else is recorded, but it's probably safe to assume—"

"Wife?"

"No."

"Children?"

"Probably quite a few from what I can gather. Some Vietnamese. All abandoned—same story in Central America. No family values here."

"Okay, fine," I said, returning to the computer screen.

Roee did not move. I could tell he was staring at me.

"Fixx," he finally said. "It was self-defense."

"I think I've found a candidate," I said, ignoring his comment.

There was a beat of silence. Then Roee, interested in what I had found, sat down.

"Lydia Corfu," I announced. "Owns the top-rated TV channel in Greece, husband owns ships. Used to be an actress, then—"

"Became a director of B-movies for her own company here in the States." Roee had finished my sentence from his memory, which his closed eyes and concentrated brow indicated he was accessing. "First came to attention starring in an international coproduction—which she put together the financing for—as a Greek opera diva who has an affair with an American president. It was only a moderate hit here, but enough of one for her to come here and start producing. Of course, the locals wouldn't let her in the club for several reasons, none particularly attractive. All she could get going here were B- movies heavy on sex and violence financed by her profits from the Greek diva film. She then sold her films herself to the world at the film markets, mainly MIFED in Milan. Took the profits and put it right into her next film. Then she continued repeating the process through most of the 80s."

"Seems she was the kind of person who had to throw her own party because no one would invite her to theirs."

"That's right. Has a rather abrasive personality. Likes to sue people, but then, that's a Greek national sport. In 1989 when Greece privatized television, she married Konstantinos Metaxsa, the quintessential Greek shipping tycoon, giving her the money to start a TV channel. It's been hugely successful."

"How much money does she have?"

"How much money do you need?"

"Enough to buy Olympic Pictures."

"She doesn't have that much."

"That's okay. We can make it look as if she does or, at least, has access to it."

"Oh, sure." Roee smiled. "We're good at that."

I thought for a moment. Then I said, "If I recall, she's not bad looking."

"Well, she continued to star in her films. Providing the sex part."

"And the violence?"

"She kicked one or two groins in each picture."

I thought again. I went over everything that had happened since the night I met Bea Cherbourg. I had been doing this since my conversation with Farber at Yale. I was doing it one last time to see if the mental chart I had in my head still made sense. It did—too much sense.

I turned to Roee and said, "I think I have an idea of what's been going on. If I'm right, then two people have died for no reason at all, or for a reason that is, at once, so nefarious it ranks in the top ten percent of evil, and yet, so absurd and just plain silly, it supports the contention that all evil is, in essence, mundane. I need confirmation of my theory, and think I know how to get it. Why don't you call Norton and tell him I would appreciate it if he could set up a call between me and Larry Lapham."

xx

"What do you want?" Lapham said with little friendliness, understandable given our "connection," but since Lapham wasn't known for friendliness, I didn't let it bother me. He probably wears a Medic Alert bracelet warning any potential healthcare professional that his average temperature is not 98.6 but 68.9, and not to assume he was dead—just that he was a cold bastard.

"I see where *War of the Wimps* has opened big, and congratulations on the full-page reprint of Robert Jordan's review in the *Times* today."

"I sent the two million. Norton confirms he received the two million. So what do we have to talk about?"

"I need a favor."

"Two million dollars is not favor enough?"

"That wasn't a favor. That was commerce. You'll be doing me favors for years to come."

"Jesus! Talk about a pact with the Devil."

"If you're going to travel along the circles of Hell, you've got to expect to meet a devil now and then."

"All right. What is it?"

"I want you to throw a party."

"Throw a party? What the fuck for?"

"That's up to you. You could celebrate your new car, your recent vasectomy, or the fact that you're rich and other people aren't. I don't care, but I can suggest that a party celebrating the huge opening of *War of the Wimps* would not be illogical."

"And at what trendy and expensive venue am I supposed to throw this party?"

"You will throw the party in the lobby of your building."

"In the lobby?"

"It will be far less expensive."

"True. Whom do I invite?"

"Whomever you want, but added to the list will be me under the name of Tom McCabe—and Don Gulden."

"Who the fuck is Don Gulden?"

"He's been described to me as 'this little shit VP' at Olympic Pictures."

"I don't invite little shit VPs to my parties."

"You will this time—and won't he be pleased?"

I told Lapham when I wanted the party to be held and gave him other precise instructions, including getting back to Norton when all the details were set. Then I called Roee back into the library. He had been making his phone calls to get the most up-to-date information on Lydia Corfu, plus contacting Hamo Thronycroft, an old friend of ours in London.

"Hamo agrees," Roee said upon entering the room. "More than happy to help."

"Fine. Listen, do you remember that gunk Petey made up when we needed to layup that delegate to the World Population Council?"

"That stuff we put in his first aid kit in a bottle of Bactine?"

"Yes, then we put an exceptionally dull blade in his safety razor."

"He had a four-week snooze in the hospital. Did him some good. Lost some excess fat. Trimmed up nicely, then stayed in shape. Got rid of his old mistress, took on a much younger one."

"Mistress?"

"Well, a priest can't have a wife."

"Oh, yeah, that's right. Well, see if Petey can supply some. Don't pay more than two thousand. I only need a drop."

"I take it you've got a master plan in the works."

"Yes—we're going to be lawyers."

Roee gave a sideways glance, considering the idea. "Oh, wouldn't my mother be proud."

xx

Four days later, I attended Larry Lapham's party as Tom McCabe, non-entity. At least, that was the only designation anyone could put on me after a cursory glance brought no recognition. I wore a not-very-stylish business suit—real business, not show business—had a not-suitable mustache on my upper lip, and wore an ugly tie. I felt like Claude Rains in *The Invisible Man*. I moved among the masses unseen. I did have on an attractive tie-tack, however. Of course, it concealed a hidden microphone.

Lapham had done an excellent job throwing together the party. The stars of *War of the Wimps* were there. Studio executives were there. Well-groomed guys and nicely turned-out gals were there who were probably agents. You could tell because they looked uncomfortable in the suits that made them "Suits"—a designation partly descriptive, partly a curse. You knew that strategizing for their futures included costume considerations: "If I move from the agency to a studio, I'm still in a suit and a 'suit.' However, if I become a producer, it's jeans, maybe khakis, and a pullover." Their hair was also a giveaway, especially for the guys, who all had close-cropped bottom cuts that stretched from temple to temple, making them look like modern SS Storm Troopers in civvies.

As I milled about, not being invited to mingle, a snatch or two of conversation would rise above the din of what once was "cocktail chatter" and now could only be referred to as wine-walla.

"Hollywood is sick of paying the Stallones, the Willises, the Carreys. That's got to be the push behind animated features. I mean, does anyone really want to work on fucking fairy tales?" said a producer who used to be a studio head, who used to be an agent, who used to be written about.

"His problem is he wears his heart on his sleeve," said one well-groomed guy fingering an unlit cigar.

"That's not his heart. That's snot from wiping his nose," said another well-groomed guy.

111

Just beyond them, I saw the big hulking frame of Bernie Green. His name had been Greenblatt, but he had changed it in college in a horrible case of misdirection—it's his first name he should have changed. Bernie was the president of production for Brookman & Bloom, a company that had started in personal management, moved into TV production for their clients, primarily hot comics, and was now becoming a burgeoning force in feature films. Bernie had once called me, through Norton, about a job. I met with him and found him particularly stupid and the job he wanted me to do particularly vile. I turned him down, which agitated him greatly. He started screaming that he would put the word out on me, and then he threatened me with, "You'll never work in this town again!" Then I slugged him very hard in his big, squishy stomach. He doubled up. I clasped my hands together, and pile drove them down onto his bowed head. I used as my excuse that I hate clichés and told him so as he sprawled, groaning, on the floor.

I thought getting near Bernie and seeing if he recognized me through my disguise would be amusing.

"Did you hear about the bombing in Kansas City?" Bernie was saying to a group as I got close. "How many dead? Hundreds? That's how the country is going, one tragedy after another. But you know, for us, it's good because we make comedies, and people will want escapism. I mean, you really should buy stock in our company."

"Can I shoot him?" Roee's voice came in over the tiny earphone I was wearing.

"He's gay, you know," I quietly said

"I don't care."

"And Jewish, I believe."

"Yes, I know exactly who and what he is. Brings no credit to either my race, my religion, or my sexual preference. Can I shoot him?"

"Not tonight. Maybe later."

"Promise?"

"If you're good and eat all your pork. Oh, this looks interesting." I had noticed a tall, neatly bearded man about forty-five, a charitable contributor to the future of Italian tailoring, in an intense discussion with a beautiful woman in her twenties whose body demanded to be heard behind the preshrunk cotton. I passed close enough to catch:

"But I don't want to come between you and your wife," she said.

"Hey, you can't come between us if I only have you on the side," he responded.

I thought it best to move on to a group where a young man was pitching an idea.

"I want to make a film about a serial killer killing all the great people in Hollywood."

"Must be a short film," Roee editorialized.

"Must be a short film," I said, popping my head into the group.

"Hey! That was my line!"

The group looked at me, unamused. I quickly passed. "You can have it," I quietly said to Roee. "What a stinker."

"It wasn't the joke. It was the delivery."

Off in a corner, standing in front of a massive poster for *War of the Wimps*, George Christy was interviewing Larry Lapham for his "Great Life" column in *The Hollywood Reporter*. One of the last entertainment reporters with an old-fashioned sense of show biz, Christy was going on about the reassessment of Lapham's work by Robert Jordan, obviously willing to spread the word. Lapham did not seem displeased and stood there smiling, which, unfortunately, emphasized his overbite. "HEE-YUK!" I could almost hear Goofy exclaim.

Moving on, I soon overheard: "The only way you could get him to sit down and read a script is if he had diarrhea for three days running."

"Yeah, but then he would probably wipe himself with pages from it."

I passed that one quickly, finding myself close by Bernie Green again, who was now talking about a major radio personality just moving into film.

"He'll never be a big movie star because he has admitted over the air to having a small penis."

I moved between Bernie and the two-story glass window before

Roee could get off a shot.

Then the elevator doors opened, and Don Gulden arrived. He was about 5'7' and thin in a way that angered anyone who wasn't. He wore a dark gray suit that leaned towards Armani but not far enough to hide its fake Italian discount store origins. His hair was longish and combed straight back, but with the sides falling forward just enough to allow him the occasional brush back with his hand that he probably thought was sexy. He had no facial hair showing. Whether from meticulous shaving or insubstantial hormones, it was hard to tell.

Gulden gave his invitation to the attractive Lapham assistant, who sat at a table right by the elevator. He looked both cocky and nervous at the same time. Getting the invitation must have been a surprise. He handed it over to the assistant as if he believed it had been forged and he would be caught at any moment. But she just gave it a cursory look, smiled, and waved him into the lobby. He moved cautiously at first, looking and looking to be seen. He and a young female agent caught each other's eyes. They love-danced towards each other and came together, the female going to kiss him but stopped by Gulden, who then allowed her to kiss his cheeks. He did not return the kiss. She was not insulted by this; indeed, she displayed quick compassion—and not a little admiration—as she stared at his lips.

I wanted to watch him for a while before I made contact. What I knew about him from the digital text on the computer was typical. Twenty-seven, a graduate of an Ivy League college, started five years ago as an assistant to a director-actor based in New York, with a snobbish pride in all that. He considered himself somewhat literary, although his natural tastes tend towards alternative comic books—many balloon boobs, much graphic violence. He came to Hollywood when Sara Hutton offered him a VP position in development. She had difficulty staffing Olympic, as most people felt it was on its way out. It was an offer too good to pass up, so he came. He had a reputation for being eager to please his bosses—as it is nicely put—and for trying to build a reputation as "Artist Friendly." He was not succeeding in the latter, but he was trying.

Gulden moved on from the female agent and was standing with

Bernie Green. They probably knew each other well as Brookman & Bloom had a first-look deal at Olympic Pictures. I moved closer to hear what Gulden had to say.

"Look, Bernie, the writer hasn't cracked *Chimp's Holiday* yet. I mean, think of *The Iliad*, think of Ulysses traveling around the sea there for all those years, trying to get home, but he keeps getting waylaid, but he learns from that, doesn't he? So there's got to be something there we can use for *Chimp's Holiday*. I mean, when a man is turned into a monkey, what does he learn from that? What does being a monkey, living in the essence of monkey-ness, teach him?"

"Yeah! Yeah! That's the question, what does he learn? I mean, what's his simian arc?"

Gulden took a quick, deep breath, started to talk, raised his right finger to point out the what, then froze for a beat before saying, "I don't know. I'll get back to you on that."

Gulden had an affected accent, a careful, drawn-out style of enunciation like he was in a bad play about the old guard upper crust in upstate New York, or maybe it was just a carefulness imposed on him by the pain from two small, not quite healed sores on his lips. This explained his no-kissing policy—at least, no kissing at the moment.

As Green and Gulden separated, I approached Gulden.

"Mr. Gulden?" I said in a soft voice with just a hint of a twang in it.

"Yes?" He was, of course, confused. I did not look like anyone he needed to know.

"My name is Tom McCabe from McCabe & Wilde. Have you heard of us?"

"No, sorry. Are you a lawyer?"

"No. We're an executive recruitment firm. Headhunters. We work quietly but place about 45% of all executives in the motion picture business."

"Oh." His interest had been piqued.

"Now, I know you're happy right now at Olympic, but—"

"I could be happier," he said with all the drooling-tongue eagerness of a neophyte canine when the Puppy Chow is opened.

"Well, then, I really would like a few minutes of your time. If we could move over to those chairs." I pointed to two unoccupied chairs at one end of the lobby facing the floor-to-ceiling glass window affording a view across Washington Boulevard to the Sony lot. Lapham had been instructed to place the two chairs there and keep the party's flow focused on the opposite end. He had done a good job. No one was in that area. I walked Gulden over, offering him the closest chair. He sat. Then I naturally crossed behind him to get to the other chair. As I did, I casually and slowly brushed his hair with my right hand, twirling a lock of it around my forefinger. He felt something and started to react, but I placed my left hand down hard on his left shoulder and pinched with force while quickly tightening the twirl around my finger, pulling hard as I leaned down and whispered, resonant and raspy, into his ear, "Don't even say, 'Ouch,' or you'll be dead in a flash."

"What the—?"

I yanked on the lock of hair, pulling his head back. "Look! Over there, across the street, what do you see? What do you see on top of the Sony billboards?"

Gulden looked but said nothing at first. I pulled harder. "Ah—ah—a man."

"That's right. There's a man up there. A good friend of mine. He's got something in his hands. Do you see that? Can you see what it is?"

Between sweat and tears, he managed to make it out. "A—a rifle?" Gulden was reluctant to admit it.

"That is correct. It is a Galil Sniping Rifle with a telescopic scope. His father gave it to him. He loves that rifle. He's very good with it. You might notice he's aiming it this way. If you could look through the scope—you would see your sweating self. Now let me tell you what will happen if you make any sudden moves, make any noise I don't like, or refuse to answer my questions. My friend, who, by the way, can hear everything we're saying, my friend will pull the trigger on his beloved Galil Sniping Rifle, and a round—known to you amateurs as a bullet—a round will leave its nineteen brothers in the magazine, spin through the rifled barrel, leave the muzzle at a velocity of 2,674 feet per second, shatter this wonderful plate glass window in front of us and slam into your chest, bursting your heart."

"Why—why are you doing this?" Gulden's fear was intense and pungent.

"Why do any of us do what we do for amusement? I mean, why do people watch reruns of *Gilligan's Island?* There's a modicum of pleasure in it, I suppose." I tugged on his lock again. "Now, keep your eyes on my friend across the street and answer my questions. What's it called?"

"Wha—wha—what's what called?"

"It! It! The most important 'It' in your life right now, right? What's it called, Gulden? Is it the Order of the Golden Arse? The Union of the Golden Arse? The Golden Arse Association? Maybe the Society of the Golden Arse? The League of the Golden Arse? The Fellowship of the Golden Arse? The Federation of the Golden Arse? The Golden Arse Guild? The Benevolent And Protective Order of the Golden Arse? What the fuck is it called?"

"H—h—how did you know...?"

"I know a lot. What I don't know, you're going to fill in the gaps! Now what is it called?"

"Th—the Communion—the Communion of the Golden Arse."

"The Communion of the Golden Arse," I repeated. "Sounds inviting. By the look of your lips, you've just been initiated into this communion of—like thinkers."

"Yes."

"So you've kissed the Golden Arse?"

"Yes."

"When did Sara Hutton start this little club?"

"I—I—"

"My guess is at Yale. Good guess?"

"Yeah."

"So, how big is it now? Lots of industry people, not just Olympic employees?" There was a hint of reluctance. I tightened the twirl. Something close to a whimper came out. "I almost heard that," I said. "I hope the microphone didn't pick it up. How many?"

117

"About—about twenty."

"Any heads of other studios?"

"No, just some VPs and other development and production executives. Some agents and readers. There are about five or six readers."

"Up-and-comers with futures?"

"Yeah?"

"How does Max figure into the Communion of the Golden Arse?"

There was just that one-second beat before he answered. That one-second of a flash thought, silent, yet so loud. "Who?"

"Max!" I whispered a scream in Gulden's ear while I yanked the twirl.

"Ow!" Gulden said, cutting it short.

"Are you still looking at my friend? He heard that. It upset him. Hell, I can feel his finger itch from here! Maxwellton James!"

"He—he pays for—he pays—"

"Finances the group?"

"Yeah, and—and—"

"Helps shape the philosophy. Because you're little communion does have—doesn't it?—a philosophy?"

"Yeah. Philosophy."

"This industry retreat Sara Hutton hosted a while back. It was a meeting of the Communion of the Golden Arse, wasn't it?"

"Yes."

"That's when you were initiated, wasn't it?"

"Yes."

"And is that where Bea Cherbourg died?"

Silence.

"Are you looking at my friend?" I pulled down on his hair, raising his eyes again.

"Ye—yes."

"He's not hearing you. Is that where Bea Cherbourg died?"

Silence. A stream of sweat.

"You are an accessory to murder, Don Gulden."

"No!"

"Yes!"

"She died there, but she...."

"She what?"

"She wasn't murdered."

"Do you really think Sara will reward you if you cover up—"

"Sara didn't kill her!"

It was stated too emphatically to be a lie. "Max?"

"No."

"Gulden, we keep talking about death in the past tense. It will be present tense momentarily if you don't tell me who killed Bea Cherbourg."

"No one killed her. She killed herself!"

This was shocking. It was an incredible thing to have heard. "She killed herself?"

"She—she—she wouldn't let go. I mean, she couldn't let go of the Golden Arse. She couldn't stop kissing it!"

What an image was coming to mind, a confused and horrible image.

"Electricity, was it?"

"Yeah, yeah, but normally not, you know. I did it just before her, but—but, she must—she grabbed the button away from Sara and wouldn't stop pushing. Weird bitch!"

I yanked hard on the plug of hair with a grit of my teeth and, through that grit, said, "Where did this retreat take place?"

"San Simeon."

"Where in San Simeon?"

"The castle."

"The castle?"

"Hearst's Castle! They're always at Hearst's Castle!"

Hearst Castle? A state-run public attraction. It didn't make sense, but it made less sense that he could make this up on the spot. In my consternation, I must have increased the force of my pull on Gulden's hair, for he suddenly whispered between clenched teeth:

"Stop! Please stop! You're going to pull my hair out!"

"Yes, you're right, Gulden. I *am* going to pull your hair out, and it will hurt, but the conditions are the same. Any noise or indication you are in pain, my friend will pull the trigger. Do you understand?"

"Ye—yes."

"Good. Then prepare yourself."

The twirl of hair was now very tight around my finger. I pulled it with concentrated force; pulled against the resistance of the roots; pulled until my arm shook from the effort; pulled hard until the blessed relief of release came when the lock of hair separated from Gulden's scalp with a jerk, leaving behind a small patch of slightly bleeding scalp. True to the deal, Gulden made no vocalization of pain. He had only added to it by biting clean through his lower lip, right through the middle of the old sore, his badge of induction into the Communion of the Golden Arse.

"You did very well," I said as Gulden swallowed blood and blinked away sweat and tears. "Now, don't worry about infection. I have something for it." I took a little plastic tube of clear liquid out of my pocket and unscrewed the lid. "Of course, it will also put you into a coma for quite a while. My friend who invented it, not the friend who still has you in his sights. I have many friends with various talents— anyway, this friend amusingly calls this stuff Winkle Water, as in Van Winkle. I'm going to assume you get the literary allusion. Don't worry, you won't sleep for twenty years, only for about four weeks or so. When you awake, the Communion of the Golden Arse will be no more, and you will be under arrest."

I squeezed the contents of the little tube into the bloody patch on his head, then leaned down and quietly said, "And by the way, Ulysses' travels were recounted in *The Odyssey,* not *The Iliad.*" He looked at me with wide-eyed wonder. Then the eyes began to droop. "I would wish you sweet dreams, but that would be dishonest of me." His eyes shut. His breathing became slow but steady. I felt his pulse. It was stable as well. I positioned him on the chair so that he would not slump.

As I was leaving the party, not wanting to overstay my welcome, and as I passed the caterer's well-laid-out table of popular delicacies, I deposited the lock of Gulden's hair with the thin slice of scalp hanging from it right in the middle of a plate of precisely arranged long chunks of fried zucchini.

I hate zucchini

10
LYDIA, OH LYDIA

The next day Roee and I took Virgin Atlantic flight 008 to London. It's a good airline, attentive to customer service, and with an uncommon sense of humor. At least, I assume that calling its best seats Upper Class instead of First Class was done with a sly wink, even with an understanding of the obvious snob appeal. And the nose art icon painted on each plane, a sort of flying cousin to Rita Hayworth in her heyday, speaks of many things, but none of them are virginal.

We were traveling as Elsworth Henderson (me) and Charles W. Pinsker (Roee) of the law firm of Humboldt, Henderson & Pinsker. If you had researched this law firm, you would have discovered that they are a boutique, New York-based firm that deals exclusively with corporate mergers and buyouts. They were old-fashioned and unassuming. They never sought publicity and, indeed, discouraged it. Yet everybody on Wall Street knew about them. Not one person could claim an actual association with this firm, but everyone seemed to know someone who knew someone who could. It's the power of the rumor.

We sat comfortably in our matching Brooks Brothers suits, shirts, and ties, with our matching leather briefcases under the seats ahead of us, and we talked in matching low, serious tones about some arcane particulars of Security and Exchange Commission regulations—or so the surrounding passengers might have assumed.

"You don't think he either urinated or defecated?" Roee asked.

"I didn't notice anything."

"He was scared enough to. You should have seen the beads of sweat form and roll down his face."

"He's a man of admirable self-control."

"Or just anal-retentive."

"You know what's going to happen now, of course?"

"What?"

"The doctors won't be able to explain it, so rumors of a mysterious new disease will start. Of course, they won't last long because they'll be no second occurrence, but as long as they do, Lapham's guests will be pretty nervous."

"They'll wonder if it was the wine or the food," Roee guessed

"No. They'll wonder if it is sexually transmitted."

"Ah, yes. Would have been amusing to stay and watch it all."

"Sorry, Roee. Duty calls."

"Duty to what, exactly?"

I took a moment to think and a quick breath to fuel the process. "I don't know. I'll

get back to you on that," I said, quoting our sleeping beauty.

"Do you believe the suicide story?" Roee suddenly asked, in his irritating way of finding the flesh.

"It's hard to imagine Gulden being able to make that up while under that pressure."

"Yes, but—"

"And it does make a kind of sense."

"Sense?"

"How else could Bea Cherbourg harm Sara Hutton?"

"She was going to 'find out something about her.'"

"And do what with the knowledge? Turn it over to the police? It would have to be something illegal for that to cause Sara Hutton any harm. I don't think Sara Hutton is doing anything illegal."

"Well, an association with Maxwellton James...."

"No, I do believe he is 'retired' from all that. I think something far worse than the illegal is going on. I think something ideological is going on, and as much as we might dislike and distrust ideology, it is not, in America, illegal. Otherwise, America wouldn't be America, would it? So Bea found nothing useful. Just probably something that disgusted her. She was, unfortunately, prone to that. So a situation came up where she saw an opportunity to cause Sara Hutton much grief. It would mean her death, but—"

I stopped. There hadn't been much time to think this through, but now, making the thoughts solid and hearing them expressed, I could see that my preliminary conclusions were not logical. "It was an accidental death," I stated with a finality that Roee knew to take seriously.

"What's the track?" he asked.

"Bea, in the middle of the retreat, in the middle of the meeting of the Communion of the Golden Arse, saw that, although it was weird and awful, it was not much more than embarrassing for Sara Hutton—if anybody on the outside could see what was going on. That, at least, was something, but how do you call attention to a secret meeting of a secret society? An accident. A medical emergency that they would have to deal with might do it. Whatever 'fire' they were playing with, Bea thought she could handle and control the damage. She was wrong. She was naïve, romantic, idealistic—and wrong. So she died. Tragically fulfilling her goal far beyond any of her romantic revenge fantasies."

"So it was accidental. So where does your duty lie?"

"I misspoke. Not duty. Pleasure."

xx

We arrived at Heathrow Airport at noon and were picked up by a limo arranged by Hamo Thronycroft. It was part of a commercial fleet that companies within the City, London's financial district, used almost exclusively. Hamo assured us that the driver had requested was known for the occasional verbal indiscretion. We had no interest in hearing anything he had to say. We planned to do the talking.

"The meeting is set for what time?" I, as Elsworth Henderson, asked Roee as Charles W. Pinsker as the limo pulled out of the airport.

"Three pm."

"Well, I think she'll be happy. All the ducks seem to be in a row."

"I talked to her yesterday. She seemed very happy indeed. This would be quite a big leap for her. To go from owning a Greek TV station to ownership of Olympic Pictures."

"Do you think we have completely talked her out of putting this funding into the European Satellite business?"

"Lydia Corfu has a passion for the product. Always has had. She's involved herself in the delivery systems only to allow her to have a hand in the product. If she builds Olympic like she plans, getting into satellite down the road will be no problem."

"She buys that?"

"Her heart buys it—and that woman is all heart."

"Ah, the passionate Greeks."

xx

The limo took us directly to the Savoy Hotel on the Strand. As it pulled up to the front of the hotel, we could see Hamo Thronycroft standing by the curb. Short and thin, Hamo stood there in the cold in a long sleeve—but with the sleeves rolled up— solid blue silk shirt and rather wrinkled black slacks. He gave a little wave as we stepped out of the car, saying quietly, "Hello, Fixx. Hi, Roee." He was not necessarily being discreet. He rarely spoke above a hushed tone.

I gave him a good look. His light blond hair had thinned to nonexistent at the top since I had last seen him but maintained a fuzzy presence around the ears. His narrow face was ruddy, as always, but now possibly more so from the cold. His deportment was nervousness—I have never seen it any other way—which always gave him the impression of a man wanting to get on with it, get it over with, and get back to the comfort of a home and hearth not open to guests. Yet I have never met a kinder soul— genuinely kind. The nervousness, if that is what it was, probably derived from the sure knowledge that the world does not treat the kind in kind, that it often smears them to nothing but a slightly moist smudge, as one can easily do to various small harmless insects. Watching out for the giant thumb of indifferent evil can give one the aspect of the timid and shy.

"Hamo?" I greeted my friend with a question in my voice.

"Yes, Fixx?"

"You're not wearing a coat and tie."

Hamo looked down at himself, confirming that I was correct. "I never do."

"Well, that's somewhat of an inconvenience as this is the Savoy, and it is forbidden, at this establishment, even to use the public loo without the required accouterments. What if I had decided to take you into the Thames Foyer for high tea?"

"Wouldn't have gone. Only go to low tea."

"I see. Well, the other concern might be, as it is probably in the 40s— Fahrenheit, of course—aren't you cold?"

"Probably, but it was warm in the taxi coming over; it'll be warm in the hotel and in the taxi going back. A coat would just have to be put on and taken off. Waste of time when you're in a hurry."

"But you've been waiting for us here in the cold?"

"Ah, yes, but the thought of you, Fixxer, kept me warm."

"I'm touched."

"I'm freezing," Roee grumbled. "And I've got on a coat and an overcoat and a muffler and gloves. So can we go inside, please?" He pushed past us to lead the way.

"Born and bred in a hot and arid land," I said to Hamo by way of explanation as we followed Roee in.

"It's a pity. It truly is," Hamo said.

xx

We first met Hamo in Syria in the late Eighties, where he was producing and directing a documentary for BBC2 on tapping the Euphrates River for irrigation. Despite the dry subject matter, it turned out to be a good and fascinating film, especially given the fact that, while he was making the film, Hamo was also in the secret employ of British Intelligence, spending time looking into reports of a major terrorist training camp in the area. He found the camp, "stumbling" upon it while trying to get to just the right spot for an establishing shot of the Euphrates as it dropped out of the Taurus Mountains by the Turkish border. The instructors and students at "Hafez al-Assad U," as Hamo called it, were unhappy with the intrusion. Hamo swears he was a millisecond from death by various blows when "The light emanating from my harmless demeanor shone upon them and illuminated what was left of the good in their nature." They spared him but ripped all the film out of his cameras. Then they invited him and his crew to lunch. As they ate, the well-concealed video and sound recorders in their film equipment boxes, set down seemingly haphazardly, documented the camp in many of its particulars. After a long afternoon of passable food and political prattle, all in a friendly atmosphere, Hamo and his crew picked up their equipment boxes, made their goodbyes, and left to continue the excellent work of immortalizing the Syrian effort to bring paradise to Earth through irrigation.

Hamo had provided such services to British Intelligence for many years, traveling to many exciting locations and making several award-winning documentaries. Lately, though, he had forsaken self-sacrificing service to Queen and Country and kept the cameras rolling only for CNN, Sky News, and, occasionally, me. The pay is decidedly better—especially when he works for me.

He is kind. Not stupid.

xx

After we checked in, we went up to our suite for a quick report from Hamo before moving on to his offices. The suite was very Astaire & Rodgers in design, if not in scope. Reality has never been able to compete with the Hollywood of the 1930s, which leads to disappointment with reality at times. Good view of the Thames, however.

Roee gave Hamo a beer, fixed me a vodka tonic, and passed on any refreshment for himself.

"Roee tells me you have everything in place."

"Absolutely. The plan worked like a charm. She took the bait without a second thought."

"What did you tell her?"

"Well, of course, I had no problem with my credentials. In fact, I think a couple of my old documentaries have run on her station. Inexpensive programming. So, I just told her that I happened to luck into some information on certain members of the Greek Parliament that she's very opposed to. She's been trying to get something on them for a long time. The station gave her a power base in Greece, and she's using it to brilliant advantage."

"Sort of like a hobby."

"More like a passion. I told her that I had recently done a film in Athens and inadvertently got some information I thought she would be interested in, but that I did not intend to return to Athens to show it to her, that I didn't feel safe there. So she had better come here and meet me in London. She had no problem with conceding to that request."

"And you arranged for her pickup at Heathrow?"

"Yes, early this morning, with the same driver you had. So when you mentioned Lydia Corfu, I'm sure it made the proper impression. The name would have been fresh in his mind. He's probably already made a few phone calls and received a few fat gratuities for the effort."

"And the rest of it?"

"All set. We'll be meeting her in just a little while at the building. If all goes well, we'll head to The Pavilion in Finsbury Circus for drinks."

xx

The building was Hamo's, recently bought to house his First & Foremost Films. It was not on Wardour Street in Soho, where most of the London film community housed itself, but in the City, within sight and sound of St. Paul's. No 2 Wardrobe Place was built in 1680, part of the rebuilding of London after the Great Fire of 1666. It was in a location that, before the fire, used to be the King's Wardrobe—literally the area where the King's possessions were stored. It was much in Hamo's character to prefer the shadows of this historical ground to the bright lights of Soho, and it was much to my advantage. The financial world is often the only world that matters. It was good to have Hamo's ear to this particular ground.

The buildings that made up Wardrobe Place were off Carter Lane, arranged in a rectangle forming an open quadrangle, by which the buildings were entered through narrow seventeenth-century doors. The quad was all hard and blunt, brick and cobblestones, except for three old London Plane trees that had grown tall enough to snatch some sun at their tops. A genuinely urban tree (it's rarely found outside of London anymore), slightly older than the surrounding buildings, the London Plane had thrived in the sooty atmosphere of the old city. It had something to do with the soot aiding how the tree naturally exfoliated, shedding its bark in patches. The irony now was that with modern pollution controls, the trees were somewhat anemic compared to their robust past.

Five stories in all, including a basement with an old and creepy vault that Hamo used for a wine cellar, Hamo's building was registered with the English Heritage Commission, which would allow nothing to be done to alter its seventeenth-century look. This was fine by Hamo. He had restored it as close to its original condition as possible, even finding some charming naïve wall paintings buried under plaster and paper. Hamo, no longer utterly loyal to the England that is, was highly dedicated to the England that was.

We gathered in Hamo's office on the ground floor and sat around the small marble fireplace to wait for Lydia Corfu. Soon we heard a disturbance outside in the reception area, as if a force of nature had blown open the door and pushed all obstacles aside. Out of the ensuing cacophony, a female voice arose. It was a voice unlike any I have ever heard. Radio static able to articulate was my first and continuing impression.

"Tea? Don't want any fucking tea! Water perhaps—with ice— plenty of ice. What the fuck do I care if it's cold outside? You English ought to drink more iced water. It would stimulate your blood flow! Is this where I go?"

The door to Hamo's office opened, and Lydia Corfu, wrapped in a pure white ankle-length fur coat, walked in, stopped, and stared at us, one after the other. "You must be Thronycroft," she informed Hamo when she got to him.

"Yes, how did you know?"

"You look so typically English." Then she looked again at Roee and me as if we not only expected the scrutiny; but welcomed it. "And you two look like lawyers, but you're not. Lawyers all smell alike. It has something to do with what they secrete. You don't have that smell. Not that you don't smell. You just don't smell like lawyers."

She took in a deep breath, testing our scent. "It's a dangerous smell, though. Who the hell are you?"

Despite the challenge, she quickly removed her coat, revealing a short-skirted purple suit made of a quilted material covered in a rash of Dalmatian-like black spots. It clung closely to her body, which held up beautifully under the cling. Matching ankle-high boots, black leggings, black gloves, and a black mock turtleneck pullover completed the outfit. She sat in the fourth chair provided for her and made herself comfortable as she waited for a reply.

"That's a lovely Rena Lange you're wearing," was the only one I would give.

She snorted a refusal to be impressed with my knowledge of haute couture as she turned to Roee. "Jew!"

Roee was startled. Not something he was used to. "Yes—proudly so."

"Don't get defensive. Wasn't an accusation, just a point of fact." She dismissed Roee and turned to me, "And you're an American."

"Why does everybody always assume I'm an American?" I innocently asked Hamo.

"Must be your rugged good looks," he replied. ,Very cowboy."

"Oh, yeah. I forgot."

Lydia Corfu laughed and got up and put her coat back on.

"Please resume your seat, Ms. Corfu," I instructed.

"I would if I thought I was going to like you enough. I came for information on two dangerous assholes in the Greek parliament.

Do you have it or not?"

"We do not."

"Then goodbye."

"We have something possibly far more interesting to offer."

"Fine, take out an ad in the Sunday Times. I'm going to Harvey Nichols. As long as I'm here, I might as well spend some money."

She started to leave.

I started to sing.

"Lydia, oh Lydia/ Say, have you met Lydia?/ Lydia the tattooed lady."

She stopped. She turned around. "How did you know I have a tattoo?"

"More important, how did I know you named yourself after that song? Your real name is Iphigeneia Venizelos. You come from the island of Corfu, the only daughter of a fig farmer. You went to Athens as a young woman with pretensions of rising high, which caused you to imply to anyone of interest that you were of a stock somewhat higher than a peasant. After a song in an old Marx Brothers movie, you renamed yourself Lydia and chose Corfu because, I suppose, you can take the girl out of the island, but you can't take the island out of the girl?"

"How do you know these things?"

"I paid close attention in school when they taught us how to research."

"So? What? You're applying for a position as an investigative reporter on my station?"

"There's a rumor starting to circulate that you're planning to make a bid for Olympic Pictures in Hollywood."

"What?" She was genuinely stunned.

"Makes sense in a way. A Greek founded Olympic, and it's now in the hands of the cold Swedes trying to unload it."

"I have not thought much about Olympic Pictures since they passed on a brilliant film I wanted to make."

"Not *Noontime Nightmare*?" I said with mock umbrage. "How many groins did you kick in that one?"

Lydia Corfu took her coat off again, threw it on Hamo's desk, and sat down; then, very opened-faced, she smiled at me. It was a fantastic face. Beautiful in the way a woman can be beautiful and a girl never can. She had black, thick, bold eyebrows that arched over black marble eyes that picked up and reflected all available light. Her nose was strong and long and no-nonsense. Her cheeks were high and full of color. Her lips were full, sensual, painted in a subtle, natural red. Her teeth were even and white. Her hair was thick and long, although now piled on her head and pinned in place. It was mostly black but with shameless individual and discrete strands of gray throughout. There was something very sexy about those strands of gray flowing in a black sea. She was officially forty-three years old. I decided it was no standard female-actress lie. This woman would look grand at ninety and take every possible credit for doing so.

"Tell me, this rumor, how did it get started?"

"I started it."

"And do you have the billion dollars I would need to buy Olympic? Because as rich as I deserve to be, I do not."

"So you are aware of the situation with Olympic?"

"I am aware of everything!"

"I know the feeling. Would you want to buy Olympic if you had a billion dollars?"

Lydia looked up into a heaven of her design. She smiled again. "I could do much with it."

"You own the most successful TV station in Greece."

"Yes, I am huge in Greece. I am a star, a celebrity, a national icon."

"But...?"

"You are a man who understands the human soul. I like that. I deserve the world; all I have is a once glorious corner of it. It satisfies on alternate Tuesdays. Otherwise, I am unfulfilled." She leaned in my direction and shot her black marbles at me. "What have you got to fill me with?"

I took a moment to run the obstacle course of possible answers, then explained the story of Bea Cherbourg and how her employment at Olympic Pictures had led to her death. I talked about Sara Hutton, whom Lydia had never met, but knew much about. I detailed the history and assumed involvement of Maxwellton James, and she seemed genuinely shocked that such a person would become involved with Hollywood in any way other than as a drug supplier. When I told her of the Communion of the Golden Arse and what exactly I thought it was all about, what I assumed was its *raison d'être*, she not only understood—she applauded.

"I will be honest. It is sad about this, Bea, but I do not necessarily see this Communion of the Golden Arse as evil."

"Yes, I thought you might not."

"Nefarious perhaps and uniquely well thought out, but not necessarily evil. I might well want to join this Communion of the Golden Arse myself. Sincerely!"

"Yes, I thought you might, and that sincerity is key to my plan."

"Your plan? Why should I subscribe to your plan?"

"Because of what I can offer you. Although we will portray you—and backup that portrait—as someone able to marshal the billion dollars plus it would take to buy Olympic Pictures, it will be a fake. We cannot offer you Olympic. I am, though, determined to destroy the Communion of the Golden Arse and—"

"Why?" She again challenged quickly and fiercely. It demanded an answer, but the answer was complex—complex in its simplicity.

"Because I choose to. Choice is freedom. I am a free man."

"Oh, and I thought maybe you had been in love with this girl Bea."

"I hardly knew her."

"Love can happen in an instant. Although lust is more likely." She had caused a crack, and she knew it. "You know, no one has answered my first question. Who the hell are you? Not lawyers. Obviously, not the government, as this seems a personal vendetta. Organized crime? No. I do not see that in your eyes. Yet you are not casual in what you are doing. I mean, you are not amateurs. This is most fascinating. You are most fascinating. Even beyond your 'Rugged good looks.' Answer my question, cowboy, and we can continue to talk."

"For those who need to address me, I am called Fixxer.'

"Fixer? She asked with no hint of real wonder or surprise in her voice. "Just that? Not Bob Fixer or Joe Fixer?"

"No. Just, Fixxer. With two X's, when it is written down, which it rarely is."

"With two Xs?" She smiled, chuckled, and shook her head. "Boys!"

"Will be boys—yes. Mystery has its advantages."

"Hey, you don't have to tell a woman that!"

Had I made a mistake? A part of me, a several million-year-old part of me, wanted to walk away, traverse the savannas of the Great Rift Valley, and find some other female, big of breast, but with a more compliant will. But the part of me that could laugh at more than just the misfortunes of others wanted to start all over, to take another tact—but it was too late for that.

"Maybe we should concentrate on the advantages to you in this endeavor," I said.

"Ah, but I was trying to get at the advantages to you. I've heard of you, of course, Fixxer! I think I once threatened somebody with you. I had to; my lawyer was out of town, but I thought you were like Santa Claus. The one who knows when you were naughty, not the one who knows when you are nice."

It became apparent that I had to tell her something that would fit within her sentiment of rationally. "I eventually will reap a great reward for this endeavor."

"Filthy lucre?"

"The filthiest."

"Good. Now that I know what kind of man I am dealing with, what are you offering me?'

"Despite any attraction that you might have to the Communion of the Golden Arse, I think you would agree with me what a damn silly enterprise it is—even outside of it causing the death of a young woman. Who, as fragile as she may have been, had no business skipping out of the joys and pains of a full life. Now, if the sophisticated likes of you and I can see the absurdity, how would the general population react? Especially given the death of Bea Cherbourg. It could be scandalous, depending on how well the media milks it, making it potent commercial stuff. Help us with my plan, follow my instructions exactly, and I am prepared to give you all the credit for our eventual success. My associates and I never seek publicity. You can have it all and the celebrity that will come with it, and nothing, as you know Lydia, is as powerful in America as Celebrity. Then you build on it. You produce exclusive reports on the matter and sell them worldwide. More important, you fashion a feature film version. You star in it as yourself, as Lydia Corfu, a crusader for the right. Hollywood would be afraid not to make the movie. If it's a hit, the Hollywood that once snubbed you will suddenly be yours—for as long as you can keep it charmed."

11
SOFT, NOT WHIPPED

At every decent pub and wine bar in London, shortly after five pm Monday through Friday, crowds of eager drinkers flow in, fill up, and overflow with incredible speed and urgency. It is a phenomenon dictated by the human need for social interaction, the effects of alcohol on bloodstreams uncomfortable without it, and a government-mandated early closing hour. As London is a city geographically well-defined by its various professional pursuits, such establishments often take on the dominant occupation's character crowding their page of the A to Zed. Without, of course, ever losing their essential character as traditional English watering holes.

In certain pubs and bars in the West End, for example, the walls fairly reek—or smell sweet, depending on your attitude—of several hundred years of English theatrical tradition, even as their dark wood paneling and posters of shows long gone play host to the modern heirs of that tradition. Men and women of considerable talent and immeasurable pride in their profession who, over pints and G&T's and French wines and the occasional rebellious glass of California wine, discuss the theater with a certain sense of jaundiced awe, mention radio dramas they were not ashamed to have been a part of, complain about the lowering standards of British television, and the near nonexistence of British cinema. And, of course, almost every evening, Hollywood is disparaged without qualification.

Just to the northwest, in trendy bars that often gleam from glass and chrome, film, television, and radio producers, directors, editors, lighting cameramen, harried executives, and legions of young attractive women working their way up, gather in a communal spirit, wave and kiss and shake hands and agree over everything wrong in their industry. At the same time, they drink hurriedly so they can quickly get back to "it" for some "bloody sod" on their staff did an absolute "cock-up" today, and they'll have to spend the rest of the evening making it right. And, of course, almost every evening, Hollywood is disparaged without qualification—while still being eagerly looked to for coproduction coin.

Then off to the West, by the Inns of Court, barristers, solicitors, and judges (and probably the occasional criminal) gather within walls more staid and sober than not to relax their guards, their guards being a slightly irritating burden to maintain—but, considering they uphold the traditions of English common law, a reasonable one.

Then, back around the Houses of Parliament, politicians and bureaucrats gather in green lamp-shaded rooms of whispers to lubricate compromise—and to try to ignore the existence of the United States of America.

In the City, dark-suited but happy men and women get together in places such as The Pavilion in Finsbury Circus, places with an innate respect for the Good Life, and speak of little but money while thinking of little but sex. For, unlike theater, which can produce art; film, radio, and television, which can disseminate information and entertainment; law, which can deliver justice; and politics, which can create legislation, regulation, and confusion, these dark-suited men and women produce nothing but wealth— and wealth is sexy. They are happy little warriors having fun watching money move through their computers like digital sperm from one end of the world to another and back again, returning the proud parents of a bundle—of joy. Of course, as Adam Smith had pointed out, the wealth of a nation is far more than just its cash reserves, but that is too arcane for these dark-suited men and women.

Into this dark-suited and misty (almost everyone was smoking) island of joy, the sudden appearance of stark white fur, and the flash entrance of quilted and spotted purple as Lydia Corfu took off that fur, made an impact not undesirable to my immediate goals. Everybody noticed us, which caused a minute slowing of agitated drinking and a momentary diminution of decibels. Once all was normal again, we went through the crowd, noise, and smoke to a large booth Hamo had assured us would be reserved, even though The Pavilion did not take reservations.

It was a neat trick: The group from Hamo's office, occupying the booth, quickly downed their drinks, said their goodbyes, and vacated just as we were in claiming distance.

"Very nice," I said to Hamo.

"English accommodation is the best in the world."

"I'll recommend you to my friends."

"Thank you, sir. It has been my pleasure."

Roee, Lydia, and I sat as Hamo, uncomfortable in the coat and tie I had insisted he wear, went to the bar to order our drinks and to talk to the management. Lydia was already in the role, laughing at Roee's witticisms and telling me that she thought my report had been slightly sloppy but adequate. She called us rather loudly by our names of "Henderson" and "Pinsker." Her unique frequency of voice just added to the spectrum.

Hamo returned with a pint for himself, Bordeaux for Roee, a vodka tonic for me, and scotch rocks for Lydia. He also brought a big bowl of peanuts, which Lydia attacked voraciously, which surprised me. Although it shouldn't have, for she wasn't smoking. A European woman of power not smoking? Ah—she was trying to quit. After that reflection, I turned to Hamo. He nodded his head—just slightly. This was the signal that the management had confirmed that the party in the booth next to us was indeed from Leatherbarrow & Boyle, Ltd., the investment bank that Sara Hutton had secretly (or so she had thought) contracted to quietly search out possible international financing for her management bid to buy Olympic Pictures.

I knew, and Sara Hutton didn't, that Leatherbarrow and Boyle had "come a cropper," finding few interested institutions willing to back her. They hadn't told her yet. They were still commiserating among themselves over the loss of fees, probably at that moment.

It was my turn to nod, which I did to Lydia. She launched into the script in a fantastic demonstration of quick study memory.

"So," she raised her glass, "here's to Olympic Pictures and its return to Greek ownership."

Roee and I both looked concerned. I began to speak in a cautionary way. "Well, actually, Ms. Corfu, as you know, George Pangalos was an American citizen."

"A Greek is always a Greek!" she declared and dismissed. "Besides, today, the whole world is practically American. We are all practically American citizens."

"Ah, a very uptight Pinsker felt compelled to point out, "spiritually, or something, that may be the case, but legally—"

"Yeah, yeah, I know. That's why you want me to keep this Sara Hutton."

"Unless you pull an Engstrand or a Murdoch and become an American citizen," Roee put on the table.

"That I cannot do. My husband is very patriotic. He is still upset about the ascendancy of Rome. He would divorce me."

"Do you love him that much?" I asked.

"Ahaa, he satisfies me on alternate Tuesdays! But let's be honest, as Humboldt, Henderson, and Pinsker have pointed out to me more than once—he is my collateral."

"So," Roee reiterated, "backing Sara Hutton's management bid, letting her side retain majority control to comply with FCC rules, allows Olympic Pictures to buy one of the American TV networks eventually. That will give you an incredible basis for a global media company—films, television, cable, and satellite, all delivering company-generated and controlled products. Then you have it all. The medium, the message—"

"And the ability to massage it in," I said, finishing the point.

"First, explain to me again how I control Sara Hutton if Sara Hutton controls the company."

"Ms. Corfu, there's an old American saying that he who controls the purse strings... No one else in the financial community is going to back this woman. You'll give her what she wants today and control the cash flow tomorrow. As for your profits, the salary and bonuses we will negotiate for you will more than make up for any loss on paper. After all, it will not be a public company. Scrutiny will be at a minimum. It will be your company in all but the paperwork name. Furthermore, don't discount Sara Hutton's abilities. She has known success. And, on another hand, we hear from one of our sources that she has attitudes you might find yourself comfortable to be around."

"Attitudes?"

"Of a somewhat—social/economic bent."

"Okay. So, when do we make the approach?"

"When we get to Los Angeles. I will call her. I will set up a meeting."

"Good."

Lydia looked down at the bowl. It was empty of peanuts. "Hamo?" She smiled sweetly at our quiet friend. "Would you be the dear lamb I know you are and get me some more peanuts?"

xx

Were we overheard? According to Hamo's friend in management, the Leatherbarrow & Boyle group got the message. Their conversation had ceased twice. Once when we had entered and made our way towards them, boldly claiming the neighboring booth (I confirmed that. I had made a quick scan of them when we passed), and then, later, when the cumulative effect of the words Corfu, Henderson, Pinsker, Hutton, and Olympic had their impact, and one of the L&B group hushed the others, and they all strained to hear. After we left, that one, Robert Pye, had made a not-so-discreet inquiry of the management regarding our identities. As he had been well paid to do, the management was happy to inform him of our particulars, Henderson and Pinsker being old customers of The Pavilion, especially in the heady days of the Greed is Good Eighties. "Haven't seen them much lately, though," he lamented.

We learned all this by a report the management gave Hamo over his cell phone as we took a limo to Southwark through the flamboyantly Victorian Tower Bridge. We were heading towards a new posh and trendy restaurant on the bankside of the Thames, known for its stunning night view of this bridge, all lit up and shouting: London! This is usually why tourists mistake it for London Bridge, which it is not—London Bridge, the utilitarian-only bridge just to the West, is about as flamboyant as a plank over a creek.

We sat down to dinner and, in hush tones (Lydia was surprisingly good at this), discussed our triumph.

"As slick as picking figs," she said—and she would know.

"Often, disseminating information is as rewarding as gathering it," I said as I cut into a near-perfect rack of lamb.

"You mean mind-fuck a person?" Lydia asked—or accused?

"Well...."

"Not as much fun as a body-fuck, surely," Hamo slipped in quietly. We all stopped and stared at him.

"Dissimilar pleasures, to say the least," Roee finally added.

"But it was fun!" Lydia declared. "Better than acting. Like acting, of course, but better. The audience as victims!"

"That's a positive?" I asked.

Lydia Corfu smiled, deciding to keep her answer behind the smile. Then she asked, "Okay. Now. What did we buy with our little performance?"

"Legitimacy. I expect to be contacted by Robert Pye. Leatherbarrow & Boyle will ask for an invitation to the party. If we give it to them, their good judgment will probably lapse, and they will convince Sara Hutton that we are sincere prospects. We might have been able to do that on our own, but as our sincerity is anything but good, word of mouth can't hurt. It is, after all, the basis of all marketing."

"We do this why? So we can get invited to this Communion of the Golden Arse?"

"Can't get the evidence against them if we don't."

"Is it going to be dangerous? This Max guy...?"

"We plan to get in. Document what we can. See if we can find evidence of Bea Cherbourg having been there and of her fate. Then we get out. You then take the material and use it as you see fit."

"Good plan, but...."

"Yes, things don't always go according to plan. There is potential for violence, but I seriously doubt it."

"Well, if it comes to it, I have used many types of weapons."

"In movies," I felt the need to remind her.

"Yes, sadly, only blanks, but I am a method actress. I was always in the moment and always believed. So, I have killed—" She did a quick calculation. "Maybe 200-300 men."

"Make-believe massacre, my sweet Greek, can never stand beside the real thing."

She was about to follow with a joke when I'm sure she saw something in my eyes. I hadn't meant for them to reveal, but lamb and vodka often pacify me. She tried to look deep—a surprising revelation of her own—but I had recovered by then.

xx

The dinner was long and very European, with many courses. Hamo dug in. Roee was not unimpressed. Lydia consumed with visible passion. I savored. After dessert and coffee, we all sat back rather pleased with ourselves. A meal much more extensive than one should consume at a single sitting, and the crammed condition of your insides that follow, is a perverse pleasure. It is essentially a pleasure in avoiding the common hungry fate of much of mankind, but take pleasure in it we did. Guilt and shame could come later. Assuming any of us were susceptible to them.

We left the restaurant and got into our limo. I asked Lydia, "What hotel are you staying at?"

"The Hyde Park on Knightsbridge."

"Ah."

"You know it?"

"Very well. It's very, British Empire."

"Yes, very Masterpiece Theater. I love it. Do you love it?"

"I am—fond of it."

"Good. Because you are coming up to my room."

"Well, that's very kind of you," Roee said, ,but it's late and—"

"Not all of you. Just him," Lydia said, indicating me. "We have more to discuss."

"Do we?" I asked. "Tomorrow is not soon enough?"

"It is tomorrow."

Hamo looked at his watch. "She's right, you know." He had a twinkle in his eyes, which was pretty disconcerting.

"Even so...."

"You will not refuse my offer of a nightcap." It was a statement of fact.

"Well, seeing how you would like to take me back into the grand old days of the British Empire, and as you are offering me something so retro as a nightcap, I suppose I shouldn't refuse. It would be much like turning down a free trip to Disneyland."

"Disney World is more like it," Roee said.

"No. Euro Disney, definitely," Hamo had his say.

"You equate my offer to cultural imperialism?" Lydia said with mock offense.

"Are you baring any gifts?"

"You'll see exactly what I'll bare."

Hamo giggled, which was not very British of him.

We went north over Waterloo Bridge, then onto the Strand, merging into The Mall. We circled Buckingham Palace, went along Constitution Hill, then got onto Knightsbridge. The doorman was right there when we pulled up in front of the hotel. Lydia got out of the limo, turned, and stared at me. I turned to Roee and Hamo. "Once more unto the breach, dear friends," I said pointedly. Roee nodded, and I could see that Hamo was already on his cell phone as I, once out of the limo, turned to say goodnight.

Lydia and I entered the hotel and ascended the immediate, short staircase that brings one up into the Hyde Park's dark marbled entrance hall. The hotel doesn't have much of a lobby, having been built in 1892 as "residential chambers for gentlemen," but this gives it its charm of intimacy. A large mirror greets you with yourself as you reach the top of the stairs. The reception area is off in a small room beyond an open arched doorway to the left. The concierge is behind a large built-in desk to the right. Lydia quickly passed both, bearing to the left to go down a connecting hallway to the elevators. Soon we were up in her suite.

"Sit," she said, indicating one of two couches facing each other under a sparkling chandelier. I chose the one closest to and facing away from the three tall windows I knew looked out over Hyde Park. Since it was dark, there was no need to angle for a view. Besides, at the moment, the room itself was the view, eye enchanting with its generous volume provided by a high ceiling; with the antique wingback chairs and other furniture of the Edwardian period, the marble fireplace, and the general warmth exuded by the well-placed lamps spreading light against cream colored walls.

Lydia Corfu was a bit of a view herself. She had taken off the fur and draped it over the couch opposite me. She moved in purple grace to the fireplace and turned the control to spark the gas jets into action. Then she moved to the bar. "Vodka tonic seems to be your drink, but may I recommend a quite wonderful brandy I have here?"

"You may."

She turned to me and smiled. Then she turned back to the bar and fixed the drinks. Once done with that, she walked over and handed me mine. "Cheers," she said as she stood before me, and we tinged the crystal, and each took a sip. She then moved to the opposite couch and put her drink on the center table. Still standing, she slowly unbuttoned the three buttons of her suit coat while keeping her eyes on me. Then she reached up to her hair, pulled some clever device out, and shook her head. Her hair fell around her shoulders in a cascade of black sprinkled with lovely silver filaments. Then she sat, leaned back on some pillows on the couch, took another sip of brandy, and said, "I will call you Nico."

"Why?"

"Because it is ludicrous to call you Fixxer."

"I haven't even given you permission to call me that."

Greek fire lit her eyes. "Do I need your permission to call you Idiot?"

"I suppose that's not really in my control."

"Exactly. Nor is my calling you Fixxer if I want to—or not if I don't. Or Nico."

"Why Nico?"

"It was the name of my first lover."

"A fig farmer?"

"No! Not a fig farmer! He was a fisherman on Corfu. He was all bronze and brine—and taciturn, which was fine because I like doing all the talking. He was strong—very strong—and stubborn. He wanted me to stay in Corfu and be a fisherman's wife. He could not see beyond the island of Corfu, much less the horizon. To him, that was the world. He was stubborn—and he broke my heart. My next lover was a young, liberal academic in Athens. He was so happy to have such a stunningly beautiful lover; he was a whimpering lap dog to me. I broke his heart. Ever since then, I have preferred men somewhere in between."

"Somewhere in between?"

"Yes—I like my men like I like my cream cheese: soft, but not whipped."

"That's interesting. Because I like my women like I like my bagels. Hot, round, and with a hole in the middle."

Lydia took a beat to take it in—then she threw her head back and gave a full and throaty laugh, suddenly stopping to focus a questioning eye on me. "How round?"

"Well—round in all the right places."

"Ha! You are no cream cheese! Okay, so what? For once will let down my guard and be happy—just for tonight—to be one of your many bagels."

"What makes you think I have many?"

Lydia Corfu smiled seductively and said, Two, maybe three million years of human evolution."

"Oh. You have quite a grounding in science."

"Yes," she said, standing up. "I am very scientific."

Lydia removed her jacket and slipped out of her short, tight skirt. She now stood in her purple ankle-high boots, all black in leggings and a pullover. She kicked the boots off. She pulled the pullover off over her head and tossed it away. Then she reached behind with one hand, unhooked her bra, and let it drop. Only self-control kept me from gasping. With delight, I should add. She sat and pulled off the leggings in a smooth move. There was nothing left as she stood up again.

"Not Aphrodite," she said, "I know that. Aphrodite, to me, has always been a blonde—and perpetually in her twenties—but certainly Artemis, and, on occasion, when I am feeling most secure, I imagine myself as Athena."

"Weren't both those goddesses fairly chaste?"

Lydia silently questioned herself on that point. Then reached down for her brandy, brought it up, and finished it. She looked at me again when she had the simple answer. "Times change."

She walked over to me and sat down very close. She was all warm and scented. She moved her left hand to the back of my head and melded her fingers with my hair, giving her great control. She used it to guide me to a warm, deep, moist kiss. Her right hand went in another direction. Not uncharted. Not unwelcomed.

"Oh, my sweet Greek," I said when she had finally allowed me some air.

XX

At 3:30 in the morning, Lydia kicked me out of bed and told me to go home. It was not said with anger, just a recognition of the fact that she preferred to sleep alone when actual sleep was on the agenda. I told her it would be difficult to find a taxi this early in the morning. She said that shouldn't be a problem for a man of my resourcefulness. I couldn't argue the point, so I got up and dressed.

She watched me—intensely. Then she asked, "Why do you do what you do?"

"What do I do?"

"Ah, that's the question to answer first, I suppose. But do I need to answer it? You know what you do. I know what you do. Why do you do what you do?"

"I'm good at it."

"Why are you good at it?"

"I've been well trained."

"And who trained you?"

"People who were also good at it."

"Okay. Why Hollywood? As opposed to, say, the world stage?"

"I'm addicted to glamour?"

"Not good enough."

I shrugged my shoulders. "Why does a farmer till fertile soil?"

"Please, metaphors, I do not need."

"Do you know that famous quote from Fred Allen?"

"Who?"

"Fred Allen. He was an American radio and film comedian of the 1940s."

"Before my time."

"Ever heard of history?"

"Please, I'm Greek. We have history. You only have notes from the recent past."

"Well, in the recent past, he was known for making some highly quotable and cogent statements."

"I'm sorry, I'm still busy going through stacks of quotable and cogent statements from Socrates, Plato, Aristotle, Aristophanes, and Euripides. What time do I have for your Allen Fred?"

"Fred Allen."

"Aaa, there are still only two sides to that coin."

"Well, Fred Allen once said, 'You can take all the sincerity in Hollywood, place it in the navel of a fruit fly, and still have room enough for three caraway seeds and a producer's heart.'"

Lydia brayed a big laugh full of recognition. Whether there was any self-recognition in it or not, I'm not sure. "So?" she finally asked.

"So substitute intelligence, modesty, ethics, and a sense of fair play for sincerity in a four-to-one swap, and you could double the excess volume."

"Ah. Fertile soil for your subterfuges."

"Yes, and it also seems that no one is so susceptible to make-believe as the merchants of it."

"Easy marks?"

"Easy marks, indeed."

"So it was a business decision."

"Isn't everything?"

"Oh, I hope not." Lydia smiled. I was now fully dressed. "Nico, you are a damn handsome man."

"Yes, I know. I blame Mom and Dad."

"You know, now that you have made love to a Greek woman, you are no longer a virgin."

It was an idea that caused a chuckle. "How do you know I have not previously made love to a Greek woman?"

"Because if you had, you would have asked me to bed instead of the other way around."

"Oh, but I did. I just used—subterfuge—to make you do the actual asking." I kissed her on the top of her head. "Pleasant dreams, my sweet Greek."

xx

The night concierge was reading a battered old paperback of a novel by Angus Wilson when I got to the entrance hall. He agreed with me that a taxi would be hard to find but offered to call for a minicab. He was beginning to dial when a voice behind me said, "Where ya headed?"

I turned to face a middle-aged and mid-sized bulky man in a worn and unbuttoned overcoat covering a brown suit. He was smiling a big one, being very open-faced and friendly.

"Because I got a car out there. Can I give you a lift? I mean, it's the least a fellow American can do."

"Thank you. I'm staying at the Savoy but wouldn't want to trouble you."

"Well, I'm also staying at the Savoy, so it's hardly any trouble. I've read about those minicabs; they can really take you for a ride. I mean—" He laughed at his inadvertent joke. "Well, you know what I mean. Come on, the car's right outside. The company provided it. I'm not even paying for it."

From the Midwest, I guessed. Not formally educated, but smart. Street smart, as they used to say. He probably worked for a medium size company with something of international appeal, possibly something agricultural, some new farm implement, or something. This guy was perhaps their top salesman back home, being given a shot at Europe, or he was the inventor, here to demonstrate it—some kind of American success story.

He could also be an evil bastard, and this was a trap. I considered the possibilities. I had yet to make enemies on this little adventure. Why would it be a trap? Who knew I was here? Not that I had not made enemies in the past, but that was me or other various personas I've adapted, not Elsworth Henderson. Still, Elsworth was just a stiff version of me. Had I been recognized?

We're getting too damn paranoid as this century dizzyingly spins to an end, I chastised myself. He's just a fellow traveler offering a good-natured lift.

Then again...

Well—there was only one way to find out.

"All right then. Offer accepted."

"Great!"

He started to button his overcoat as we moved towards the stairs. Halfway down, he stopped me, leaned close, in conspiracy, and half whispered, "Mine was a Duchess. I mean, really. I met her on the plane. A bit horsy looking, but, wow, not bad in the particulars. What about yours?"

I whispered back, "A fig farmer from Greece."

He looked alarmed.

"A female fig farmer," I added with the proper haste.

He seemed much relieved as we started for the door.

There in front of the hotel, was a black limo. A perfectly proper chauffeur jumped out of the car and opened the back door for us.

"Picked up another American out having a good time, George. He's also staying at the Savoy. Thought we might give him a lift."

"Very good, sir," George said, somewhat too properly. It was, after all, almost four in the morning. As I got into the car, I took a good look at George. It was a pale, broad British face with a curiously long, skinny nose. He had blue eyes, somewhat too small, giving that double peep holes look as if the real George was inside this shell, looking out and ducking every time you tried to look in. His hair, once blond, was now prematurely gray and fell a little onto his forehead.

A nag raised hairs at the back of my neck—recognition? But nothing solid formed. Maybe it was just the old training.

Once we were settled, the limo took off down Knightsbridge and then made the proper turns to pass by Green Park. My traveling companion, a natural conversationalist, asked, "This your first trip to London?"

"No. Been here quite often."

"It's mine. I arrived just today, in fact, I haven't even been to the hotel yet and checked in. Thank God for American Express reservations. That Duchess was very insistent. We came straight from the airport. My god! What's that?" He pointed, stretching his arm across my face. I followed it to the right to confirm that he was seeing Buckingham Palace for the first time. I was just about to turn to him to report this fact when I felt a sharp sting on the back of my neck.

Right where that nag had been.

I snapped to see his smiling face and the small hypodermic needle he held.

"It causes a terrific headache, but other than that, you'll be fine," he said as I faded and slumped toward him. A sniff of his cologne—cheap, of course—was the last thing I remembered.

HOLLYWOOD
IS AN ALL-VOLUNTEER ARMY

12
A CLOSE SHAVE

The American had been correct. It was a terrific headache. The kind one associates with a hangover, a body's revenge kind of headache. Compounding its discomfort was stinging heat along my back and on my hands, which were tied together behind me. My legs were also tied to the legs of the hardback kitchen chair I sat in. I looked up. A flickering golden light provided the only illumination, making shadows dance around a small and narrow room, including the large shadow cast by myself, which covered in darkness a man sitting on a plush couch directly before me. He was so close that our knees were practically touching. Behind him were drawn heavy brown drapes. The subtle early morning light was sneaking in just where they came together. The man sat there, relaxed, considering me. We were in a house, I guessed, in the country. It was quiet. There was none of the traffic sounds of London.

The room was unexceptional. There were tables with lamps, pictures on the wall, knickknack shelves to my right, and a stereo on a low table to my left. Also, to my left and in front of me was a doorway leading into a hall. The front door to the outside was probably at the other end of that hall. Flowing in with the subtle morning light was the pleasant chirping of early birds. It was a much too benign setting to be feeling pain and sweating to heat.

"He awake?" The voice behind me was familiar and American.

"Yes, but I don't think he's quite warm enough," the man in my shadow said. ‚Why don't you throw some more logs on the fire."

I could feel the presence of the man behind me stoking the fire. The new wood intensified the crackle of the fire as it did the illumination in the room, beating back a bit of the dark and revealing the man before me to be the chauffeur.

"Better?" the chauffeur asked in such a way, with such a natural sense of authority, that I was sure he was no chauffeur. That nag was at the back of my neck again, fighting for breath in the moist heat. I looked deeply into the face before me. The small eyes looked past the long sharp nose; the wispy gray hair. Ah—in The Pavilion! He had been sitting in the Leatherbarrow & Boyle booth. I had given them a quick scan as we had made our way past. He had been there along with a young blonde woman, sexy despite being in a dark business suit, and two other men, one who needed a haircut, one who needed to lose weight (or a new suit, one size larger). The man before me was Robert Pye. I was sure of it. But such astute intelligence, I did not need to reveal.

"Wh—what are you doing? Are you going to rob me?" As Henderson, I asked the logical question, achieving an appropriate fear of the immediate future.

"I hadn't thought of it," he said. "Although I suppose if we are going to kill you, it can't hurt." He turned slightly to his right and went through a pile of things on the couch. They were my things. Coins, billfold, loose papers, a fax from Charles Humboldt of Humboldt, Henderson & Pinsker in New York addressed to Elsworth Henderson at the Savoy Hotel, London, covering the final details of a small real estate buy the partnership was going to make. It's called a cover plant, a small innocuous item that lends credence. He looked into the billfold and pulled out the 200 pounds I had in there. He looked up at me. "Housekeeping money," he said as he folded the bills and tucked them partway under a lamp on the table to his left.

"I don't understand," I said.

"Yes, I know you don't, Mr. Henderson. Let's just say you're my competition, and I, like the good capitalist I am, intend to eliminate my competition."

"Competition? I—I'm a lawyer."

"Okay. Then why don't I kill you because Shakespeare said to?"

"Look, 200 pounds is peanuts." I felt it was best to be desperate. "I can get you a lot more money than that if you just let me go."

"Sorry, not really an option, I'm afraid. Let me explain things. A man shouldn't go to his death confused. My name is Robert Pye. I'm an investment banker with Leatherbarrow & Boyle. Sara Hutton is my client. For about a year now, I've been working very diligently, if quietly, trying to secure the financing for Ms. Hutton to make a management bid for Olympic Pictures. So far, I have not been able to secure that financing. I have some preliminary commitments, but not all I need. Sara Hutton does not understand why, and she is screaming at me. I have come to understand that Screaming is the preferred mode of communication in Hollywood. My superiors are also not happy with the situation. Although they would never scream, their recent withering looks have accused me of putting the good name and reputation of Leatherbarrow & Boyle at risk. I would be upset if I thought I had failed, but I haven't. The Money doesn't want to get into bed with Sara Hutton. It is as simple as that. I was about ready to call it quits when I was lucky enough to overhear you in conversation with Lydia Corfu at The Pavilion. Although I'm sure that luck had nothing to do with it. You planned that, didn't you? How you found out we are representing Sara Hutton, I cannot guess, but it was quite clever of you—brilliant, actually, quite brilliant. You expected me to come at you with my tongue hanging out, hoping to get any piece of the action I could to save my face. But why would you need me at all? I suspect it's because, despite what you may have told Lydia Corfu, you don't have a hundred percent of the financing secured either. You have some. I suspect, just like I have some, but you're not having any more luck getting the Money in bed with Lydia Corfu than I have had with Sara Hutton—but now, ah! A *ménage à trois*. There is something—what else can I say?—sexy about that. You wanted me to come to you, though, didn't you? You wanted me to be the junior partner? No, that won't do; that won't do at all. So, thanks for the setup, but I'll take over from here."

"I—I thought English bankers were supposed to be gentlemen."

"Not these days, I'm afraid. Especially competing with you

Americans. You get nowhere, nowhere at all—" He suddenly raised his right hand to my face; a knife was in it. "Unless you have the cutting-edge." He ran the tip of the knife down my left cheek. I could feel the blood gather—then drip.

"George," Pye said to the man behind me. "I'm going to ask Mr. Henderson here a series of questions. If he doesn't answer them to my satisfaction, find ways to hurt him."

"Wait! Wait a minute. This is ridiculous. We can do business. You don't have to kill me."

"Oh yes, I do. Because you will tell me exactly what you have lined up, all the details, then you will die in an unfortunate mugging on the streets of London. What were you thinking, being out at four in the morning? Your tragic death will, of course, throw your whole effort into disarray. Then I will pick up the pieces and make it happen."

"I—I could strike a deal with you. We could cut you in on it."

"Why should I have some of it when I could get all? No, no, this is best, plus there is, of course, the consideration that if I were to backtrack now, accepting your kind offer, then your resentment over the way I have treated you this morning might eventually fester, and you might find some way to do me harm. No, self-preservation dictates that you must die. Now it can be easy and painless—or not. That is your choice. It's the only thing left in the whole world that you have any control over. Now, start telling me the sources of financing you have lined up."

I said nothing. Pye was visibly disappointed.

"It's absurd for you not to cooperate. It's not like I'm asking you to reveal state secrets. It is only business."

I said nothing. Pye waited a moment. Which was damn decent of him, but still, I said nothing. He shook his head, probably wondering why it had to be difficult when the outcome was obvious. There was an element of pity in his voice when he finally said:

"George?"

George walked over to me, raised his right hand to my face, and tucked his forefinger under his thumb. Like something from an old Three Stooges movie, I thought he would snap me on the nose. If this was their idea of torture, I thought I might as well nap.

Then he snapped.

Not my nose.

But my right eye.

It was so fast that I couldn't even blink in defense. The combination of shock, disbelief, and pain made me howl. Then he brought his arm up and swung it down, giving me a blow with the back of his hand that threw my head hard to the left, twisting my neck and destroying my equilibrium.

"The sources of financing you have lined up, please," came a strong and reverberating voice.

I shook my head straight. My right eye stung with a unique pain, and a flood of tears, maybe some blood, had welled up and overflowed. My left eye, in sympathy, I suppose, was a bit moist as well.

"That hurt!" I said with all the naive disbelief and surprise I could fake. It wasn't hard.

"Did it? Good, I'm glad," said Pye as he nodded at George.

I expected another broadside to the head and had prepared for it, but George had a creative moment. George gave me a swift kick to my left shin with, it was much too apparent, a steel-toed shoe. The surprise almost hurt worse than the strike.

"The sources of financing you have lined up, please?"

I opened my eyes. They had squeezed tightly shut in deference to my shin. I looked around the room while I tried to blink away all the involuntary tears. I noticed a framed 8x10 photo on one of the knick-knack shelves. It was of Pye in a sunny clime in a white linen shirt, delighted to be holding onto a beautiful and sensuous blonde, the blonde in the dark suit that I had seen him within The Pavilion. She wore no dark suit here. She wore a loose and revealing sundress. They both looked like people thrilled to be getting away with it. I instantly realized that Pye had a wife in a spacious Georgian in Kensington, dealing with the children and the charity work that would eventually help get him a knighthood. This torture chamber I was in was, I was sure, a romantic hideaway for him and the blonde. Small, nondescript, mundane, but with satin bed sheets and a stock of pornographic tapes for the VCR—

what a dumb place to die in!

Pye sighed with impatience. "George."

George slugged me—a good, old-fashioned right cross to the jaw. I and the chair, as one piece, flew straight back and down, my head landing hard against the marble hearth of the fireplace, then bouncing a short distance into the inner hearth, the flames immediately licking at the back of my head, right at that place where that nag had been. Hot vibrant light and searing pain were suddenly all of existence. Panic was unavoidable, but I managed not to scream out. Not that there was much time as George almost immediately snatched me out, set me up, and slapped the flames out of my hair. Diligent in this task, he slapped very hard.

Pye watched all this unmoved, probably not wanting to get emotionally involved.

"I'm going to ask you one last time to name the sources of financing you've lined up for Lydia Corfu. If you don't answer me, George will slug you again and again, and you will fall in the fireplace again. This time, though, George will not pick you up, and I will be happy to sit here to watch the flesh burn off your face until I can see the skull underneath. As I don't care for the scent of burning flesh, I would appreciate it, please, if you would name the sources of financing you have lined up."

"Excuse me, but that is proprietary information."

Hamo's voice—an unarguably sweet sound— came from behind my right shoulder.

"Who the fuck—" George was suddenly on the ground jerking with uncontrollable spasms. Pye was up on his feet, swinging up a pistol, when I heard another sweet sound: the voice of Roee.

"Don't! Your friend has just been stunned with a Taser. He'll recover nicely due to the pacifistic tendencies of my friend, but me, I don't mind killing for a good cause."

I assumed by the look on Pye's face that Roee was holding a formidable weapon, something more intensely phallic than the little pistol that Pye now tossed aside.

"Good. Now untie Mr. Henderson here."

Pye moved cautiously, but he did a swift job of freeing me. Then he stood back. I stood up. We were face-to-face. My "Damn handsome" yet somewhat battered face to his beady-eyed, long, sharp nose face. I gave him a quick uppercut, and he flew back and fell unconscious on the couch.

I turned to Roee and Hamo. "While dramatically thrilling, your timing seems just a little off."

"I'm afraid I have to take responsibility for that, Fixxer," Hamo said. "We put the tail on you—the 'Breach' as you coded—but, well, the young man I chose, I'm afraid, got bored waiting in the car outside the hotel. You were in there for an awfully long time."

"I was just trying to consummate our business relationship, Hamo."

"Oh, understood. Even the Inland Revenue wouldn't have a problem with it, I'm sure, but my man, Tim's his name, by the way, he got a bit bored, not to mention cold, so he decided to call up his girlfriend on the cell phone."

"So he was busily engaged in a conversation and didn't notice when I came out of the hotel?"

"No, no, he had finished long before that."

"So, he was no longer on the phone?"

"That's right. He was a hundred percent on duty, saw you come out of the hotel, get into the limo with—" Hamo looked down at the unconscious American. "This git here and dutifully began tailing you at a discreet distance."

"And then, didn't he dutifully call you to inform you that I was riding in a strange limo with a strange man?"

"Well, he tried, of course. I've trained him well. But, you see, that's where the problem comes in. I'm afraid the battery in the cell phone was depleted."

"Oh. He didn't have —"

"A spare or a car battery cord? No, I think he rushed out so fast when I called him that he forgot those usually indispensable items."

"He doesn't keep them in his car?"

"He was driving his girlfriend's."

"Whom he was with—"

"When I called him, yes."

"And they were in the middle of—"

"Not quite to the middle yet, I believe."

"So, in the car, bored and cold, he called her up to—"

"Continue with a perfectly natural part of modern romance, yes. Although separated by a certain distance, they seem to have made do."

"And this took a sufficient amount of time to deplete the battery?"

"Premature ejaculation does not seem to be one of Tim's problems."

"I hope you've noted that in his file."

"He's a good boy, he is. He knew he had to stay on your tail, no matter what. And he did, finally calling from a call box once the limo came to this location. I immediately called Roee, of course, and we got up here just as quick as we could."

"And where is here?"

"Hertfordshire," Roee answered. "Little village called Welwyn. Nice little house, white, two-story, probably only ten years old. A couple of acres in the back, mostly lawn and some woods. Neighbor next door has horses. Very pleasant."

"Would you like me to buy it?"

"It seems restful."

"Speak for yourself."

George groaned.

"Stuff something in his mouth and tie him up, would you?"

Roee and Hamo did so as they asked me what all this was about.

"I'm not sure. Except it seems that the banking business in England has taken a bit of a thuggish turn. What do you know about this guy, Hamo?"

"Pye? He's a top man at L&B—highly competitive, of course. Married Boyle's daughter, but I suppose that was to be expected. Has worked aggressively to make L&B an international concern, obtaining influence for the bank outside the UK. Known to make rather outrageous promises and claims but often delivers. Gotten much press here, magazine covers, and major profiles. We, meaning the British, both love and hate him, as we often do the successful. Consummate snob, but of a new sort. Comes from a middle-class family. Dad was the manager of a cinema in Birmingham. Mom was a nurse working for National Health. So, he has, I suppose, earned the right rather than just inherited it. If you don't count his marriage into inherited wealth."

"Ever been rumored that he had connections with characters like this one?" I asked, indicating the American.

"No. That comes as a bit of a surprise."

"Any hint of illegal activities? Insider trading, anything like that?"

"No. Known as a good citizen."

"Well," Pye was undoubtedly a man to muse on, "I suppose he just saw too many gangster movies at his dad's cinema as a child. It seems he wanted the Corfu-Olympic deal all to himself. So he wanted to get our sources of financing out of me, kill me, and pick up the pieces in the disarray. Does that sound logical?" I asked Roee.

Roee thought for a second. "Seems extreme. There's an ulterior motive in there somewhere. Maybe he had a large personal commission riding on setting it all up. Maybe it was pride? He was on the verge of failure."

"Yes," Hamo said, "he hasn't failed too often. If it had gotten out, it would have been, I suppose, a bit of tarnish on the family silver. Reputation may mean a lot to him."

It was Pye's time to groan. He regained consciousness and opened his eyes. The little blue beads reflected fear as they stared at the three of us. "How—"

"Shut up!" I shouted down to him. "I've heard enough from you." I turned to Roee and Hamo." Now the question is, what are we going to do with these two?"

"I suppose we can't kill them?" Roee asked.

"Hamo and I would vote against you on that idea."

"Two against one," Hamo said.

"But he was going to kill you," Roee protested.

"A momentary lapse in his basic ethics, I'm sure, due to the negative influence of the dream of wealth. We are all probably susceptible to it. There but for the grace of Goddamn-good-sense go I. But it is a problem. We certainly don't want him reporting to

Sara Hutton that we are lawyers with defenses beyond litigation."

"Well, the git here," Hamo said, "we can return to London and dump in an alley in Soho. I'll bet you he's nothing but a thug for hire Pye picked up. Probably doesn't know too much about the rest. He'll know I'll keep my eye on him, so I think that neutralizes him."

I turned to Pye. "Does that sound good to you, Pye? Don't answer. Just nod your head." Pye did so. I sat on the kitchen chair, bringing myself down to his level. "Now, what about you? You know, the proper blow to your head, a blow along the strictest of scientific methods, could fairly incapacitate you without killing you. Just the proper amount of brain damage, and you could still function, but you would have very little memory left—and absolutely no sense of self. Which has benefits as your self is not one I would think one would want much of a sense of."

"Look—"

"Shut up!" I screamed it into Pye's face, spraying spit. "Do not speak to me! I'm angry. Have some Goddamn sensitivity to that fact!"

I stood up and calmed myself. "Sorry, gentlemen. Some errant protein in my brain, I suppose. Well, I'm at a loss. Do you have any suggestions?"

Roee and Hamo considered the matter, both studying Pye intensely, which fairly unnerved him. Finally, Hamo gave up with a gesture of defeat, but Roee stroked Pye's face and said, "He looks like he needs a shave."

I looked and confirmed the fact. "Yes, he does, but I'm not really concerned about his appearance right now."

"Nevertheless," Roee said as he picked up Pye, put him on his feet, pulled his right arm around his back, and yanked it up. Pye grunted and squealed simultaneously. "He's going to have a shave. Where's the bathroom?"

Pye said nothing, his lips being sealed with fear.

"Would you please give him permission to speak?" Roee requested.

"Speak, Pye."

"Upstairs," Pye squeaked.

Roee roughly pushed Pye out of the room into the hall and up the stairs.

Hamo and I followed. When we all got into the bathroom, Roee let Pye go and then trained his Browning Hi-Power 9mm automatic at him. "Get out of your clothes. Except for underwear," Roee said.

Pye did so. He wore boxer shorts with real boxers on them.

"Shave," Roee said.

Pye reached onto a shelf and brought down an electric razor.

"Oh, no," Roee said, slapping the electric razor out of Pye's hand with the Browning, startling Pye. "No electrics. Real men don't use electrics. Don't you have a real razor?"

"You—you mean a straight razor?" Pye asked in confusion.

"No, a safety razor will do. I'll grant you that."

"No, I don't use one. But—uh, but my, my..."

"Paramour." I filled in the gap.

"He has a paramour?" Hamo asked, delighted over the idea.

"That's what he uses this place for."

"Oh," Hamo said. "You know you get a discount with a paramour."

We had to stop and stare at Hamo again. We just had to.

"She probably has one for her legs. In the tub."

Indeed she did. Hamo retrieved the disposable pink, slick-looking instrument and handed it to Pye.

"I—I don't have any shaving cream."

"Be a man," Roee instructed. "Shave without it."

Pye looked at him but then started to do as he had been told. He turned on the hot water.

"No water!" Roee made it clear.

"What?"

"Shave!"

Pye began to shave. It could have been smoother going. Roee moved close to observe. As Pye scraped the razor down his right cheek, Roee bumped heavily into his arm.

"Ouch!" Pye exclaimed. There was a small, bloody slice on his right cheek.

"Oh, I'm sorry," Roee said. "Here, I've got something for that."
He brought a little plastic tube of clear liquid out of his pocket.

"Winkle Water!" I exclaimed.

"Winkle Water," Roee confirmed. "I happened to have gotten
to Petey just when he was having a two-for-one sale. Thought it
might come in handy."

"Very prescient of you."

"Thank you."

"What is that stuff?" Hamo asked.

"The stuff that dreams are made upon," I said as Roee applied
the Winkle Water to Pye's cheek. Pye looked at all of us with
disbelief firmly lodged in his beady eyes. I suppose it had all gotten
a bit surreal. Then he collapsed.

Roee and Hamo grabbed him as he fell to ensure he didn't hit
his head on the basin.

"Another instance of the mysterious disease," I said.

"One in L.A. One in London."

"This will keep them up late at the Center for Disease Control."
,Think we ought to have Petey give them a call.'

"Probably wouldn't hurt. They're a bit busy with other matters
right now. Wouldn't want to divert their resources."

"Would someone explain Winkle Water to me, please?" Hamo
asked.

We did, as we went about the house, straightening things up.

"Who do you think will discover him?" Hamo finally asked.

"Well, when he doesn't show up at the office, I think his
paramour might think to look out here. Other than that, let's hope
he has a housecleaner or a nosy neighbor. There's not much more
we can do."

"And he'll be out for four weeks?"

"About that."

"Being found here in this love nest is going to be great fodder
for the tabloids," Hamo said. "Probably ruin his career."

"Good," I said. "I'm glad."

Then we stuffed George in the boot of Hamo's car and drove
the A1M back to London.

13
CAST YOUR FETA TO THE WIND

"When you left my bed last night, you were more handsome than when you entered it. Now look at you."

In a black velvet suit over a stark white blouse with shockingly large collars and cuffs, Lydia Corfu stood in front of me in Hamo Thronycroft's office examining the various "Badges of Courage" I had been awarded early that morning. A swollen and split lip, now nicely stitched thanks to Roee's battlefield first aid skills; a rather nasty bruised area around my right cheek; a scratch down my left, unfortunately not bad enough to someday become a romantic scar, and the somewhat ragged and singed condition of my hair at the back of my head.

"A banker did this to you?" Lydia said incredulously.

"I never could get a firm grasp on Economics."

"If a banker is going to do this to you, what happens when we face an ex-gunrunner and drug dealer?"

"You have every right to pull out."

"What? You think I'm one of your American women?" The examination over, she sat and sipped from a hot cup of coffee and attacked a bowl of peanuts Hamo had conscientiously provided.

"American women can be very tough."

"Yeah, yeah, back in the pioneer days. Plowing the north forty while pregnant. Pulling the wagon train themselves when the mule died. Yeah, I read all that, but your modern American woman. She spends all her days reading nothing but self-help books, books that tell her either how to be more feminine so she can catch a man or more feminist so she can slice his balls off. She prostrates in front of guru books trying to figure out how to get self-esteem, or she covers herself with crystals while howling and running like a wolf while trying to get in touch with some universal consciousness, which probably doesn't have a decent thought in its head anyway. No, no, no! Life sits there before you, beautiful and ugly; wonderful and awful; comforting and frightening. You do not need self-help. You only need to help yourself! Anybody who has to read a self-help book has very little self and is way beyond help."

"So you want to stay in the game?" Roee asked. He and Hamo were in the room with us.

"Sure, why not? But it looks to me like we can't play it right away. Do you think I want to be represented by a lawyer that looks like shit?"

Roee and Hamo both turned toward me. "He is not a pleasant sight at the moment, that's true," Roee said.

"Scary looking. I wouldn't expose him to pregnant women," Hamo added.

"Well, I have put us on a tight schedule," I reminded.

"How much time do you think we could spare?" Roee asked.

I thought about that. Don Gulden and Robert Pye would both be out for about four weeks. I was comfortable with that. We needed to get to Sara Hutton, get her comfortable with us, and hope for an invite into the Communion of the Golden Arse. Anything less than four weeks meant rushing the process. Unless...

"I suppose I could take a week off to heal up a little if you go in as an advance guard," I said to Roee.

"Make the first foray. Contact Sara Hutton, explain the situation, and tell her I'm there on a preliminary basis to judge her interest. If she's interested, then it will be worth our time to bring my partner and Lydia Corfu to Los Angeles."

"Exactly. Meanwhile, I'll convalesce at home, taking it easy and—"

"You will convalesce at my villa on Corfu. You can't go to Los

Angeles. Los Angeles is about wounds, not healing. You need the Mediterranean sun on your face. You'll heal much faster."

The suggestion had an immediate appeal.

"Will you be my nurse, bucking up my spirit with your compassion and giving me a reason to live?"

"No, but I have a seventy-seven-year-old housekeeper who does wonders with Aloe Vera. She has no compassion, however. Do not do as she asks, and she spits at you."

"I've always been an excellent patient. Haven't I, Roee?"

"My religion cautions me from bearing false witness."

"Really?" Hamo said. "My religion cautions me from witnessing false bears."

To look at Hamo and wonder was all that we could do.

"Well, a week in Corfu sounds wonderful. If you'll be there," I said to Lydia.

"I do have a TV station to run, Nico."

"Nico?" Roee wondered.

"Nickname," I said by way of answer.

"No," Lydia said, a smile carved from evil delight on her lips, "Pet name."

xx

Earlier that day, we had gotten back to the Savoy at about eight am. I was exhausted—more than I had been for quite a while. I had wanted to go straight to bed and sleep, forgetting about my wounds, but Roee, of course, would have none of that. He nursed me—more than competently. Then he made me take a scalding hot bath and threw three slugs of Dewar's down my gullet. Only then did he allow me to climb into bed, making me put on a pair of his cotton pajamas first—I usually sleep in only a tee shirt.

"You need to pamper yourself; feel like a little boy home sick from school. Consider it a form of homeopathic medicine."

"My mother never gave me whisky when I was home sick. You've improved upon Mother."

"Thank you."

Of course, now that I was in bed, I didn't feel sleepy. I felt talkative. "Should I allow myself to feel like an idiot?"

"Why?"

"I walked into a trap."

"It happens."

"Can't let it happen too often, or we could be out of business."

"Let it be a lesson to you then."

"Possibly."

The intoxicating warmth was beginning to spread out from my stomach, making me feel like I could defy gravity. That must have been Roee's intention. He wanted me to float off into dreamland. I was beginning to like the idea, even the sense of vulnerability that came with it, when, in the middle of closing the drapes, Roee was stopped by a thought. "I'm also wondering if there are no other things to learn here," he said.

"Such as?"

"Pye. If he's this tough on competitors, what must he be like if you're late on your credit card bill?"

"You think there's something more there?"

"I wouldn't be surprised, but I can't figure out what. The cover seems to have held. He was going to murder Elsworth Henderson, not The Fixxer. That much seems clear, but a banker murdering? After all, it's just business."

I seemed to have been tethered to the ground for suddenly, although still floating, I was yanked back and couldn't go any higher. I was still high, but... "He said that too."

"Who? Said what?"

"'It's just business.' Pye said that when he was requesting our sources of financing. He said something about it not being like he was asking me to reveal something important, like, 'state secrets.' It was 'just business.' You know, it occurs to me, Roee, that that's probably the most pernicious phrase in the English language. It's used to excuse so much, isn't it?"

"Is it?"

"Of course it is. Roee, what binds society together?"

"Fixx, you need your sleep."

"Answer my question. What binds society together? What has always bound society together? At least for the last ten to twelve thousand years or so?"

"I don't know. Common beliefs. Religion, on occasion."

"Roee, no disrespect to your own, but religion only binds the like-minded. I mean all of society, all of society in the mundane, the real. Nothing exulted."

"A sense of community, then."

"But where does the sense of community come from?"

Roee shrugged. "Common needs. Common aspirations. Common desires."

"Well, as most individual needs, aspirations, and desires often clash with one another, the most common one, I suppose, is the need to live well, to prosper, maybe something as basic as feeding yourself, and your family, if you have one. Hard to do that all by yourself unless you're lucky enough to be the sole occupant of an island with plenty of exploitable flora and fauna."

"How about political systems?"

"Same problem as religion, Roee. If anybody ought to know that it's you and me."

"I'm at a loss, then. Why don't I give this some thought while you get some sleep."

"It's business, Roee! Business binds society together; trade and commerce. It binds us because I cannot, or do not choose to make my own—" I looked for inspiration. I found I was lying under it. "Blanket, for example. So I paid somebody to provide this blanket to me, and he paid somebody to ship it to him, and he paid someone to weave it, and he paid someone for the wool from which to weave it."

"Your narration reminds me of those wonderful 16mm films we used to watch in school on the kibbutz—although we did try to be fairly self-sufficient."

"You obviously did not pay attention."

"No. I think I was passing mash notes to Teddy. He was cute."

"Business, Roee. The good old profit motive. Individual, selfish needs that, paradoxically, bind everybody together in a society. Not family, not a sense of community, not religion, not political systems, not kingdoms, not nations, nothing like that at all. But 'just business.' The simple day-to-day trading of basic needs for civilized existence. That is what separates us from anarchy. It is the core, the essence of human society. Yet we have talked ourselves into believing that business is somehow exempt from the natural human considerations of fair play. We demand that our children learn the—what?—the rules of the road. We demand values in our families, morality among our religions, and ethics among our politicians, but when it comes to business, everything's fair game instead of fair play. It's competition; it's not personal; it's just business. And yet, if business is the binding element of society, then nowhere else should basic morality be in evidence in sentiment—and in fact. Especially nowadays."

"Fixxer, haven't you always told me, much to my protest, that the universe is amoral."

"Yes, Roee, the universe is amoral. But that doesn't mean we have to be."

"Maybe you should stick to vodka," Roee said.

"So, this takes us back to the original question. Could a banker, in the heat of spirited competition, murder to further his goals? I can't find an argument denying all possibility of such an occurrence. Can you?"

"Sad to say—no."

That settled my body demanded its due. "Damn, I'm tired."

"Mental exertion, Fixx. It's the most exhausting kind." Roee said as he finished closing the drapes, tucked me in, and turned out the lights.

xx

Of the seven days I spent at Lydia's villa in Kassiópi on the island of Corfu, the Mediterranean sun, whose healing properties I was supposedly there for, made an appearance on only three, one more than Lydia made. Her TV station kept Lydia away, as she had predicted. It was the fact that Corfu is the wettest location in Greece, with not much less yearly rainfall than London, and that it was midwinter that seemed to have deterred the sun. I wasn't that disappointed. The sunshine as an exception, rather than a rule, has always been my preference.

Kassiópi—a holiday town without being a tourist trap—looks out across the Ionian Sea towards Albania. It's a favorite spot to build villas. Lydia's was a wedding present from her shipping tycoon husband, who himself had never been to the place. It was all white, sleek, and modern, with every possible convenience, luxury, and extravagance. It was built on a hill just above the town. It was a long, narrow building with large windows, a generous terrace facing the sea to the Northeast, and duplicate features on the opposite side facing the ascent of Mount Pantokrator to the Southwest. The views were of the blue or grey of the sea and the green of the land; the white and dusty red of the town buildings and their roofs, and the now and then rolling black of rain clouds, those coming in from the sea and those gathered to huddle around the peak of the mountain. The spikes of cypress trees appeared everywhere, tall and straight, as if on duty.

It was restful. The problem was that I didn't particularly want to rest. Helen, though, gave me no other choice. Helen, Lydia's seventy-seven-year-old housekeeper, known for her ways with Aloe Vera, took me in hand—she had a very tight grip—and ran my days. Lydia had been right; she had no compassion and very little patience. I was spat upon several times. Helen spoke no English and yet communicated precisely. She was about five feet ten, built like a bull, and dressed all in black. She moved like a bank of storm clouds through the sleek white of the villa. She was the near antithesis of her namesake; her face would not sink a thousand ships, but I did not doubt that it would take the wind out of their sails.

I had to moderate these views after I sat down to the first dinner she prepared. It was a local specialty called sofríto, a veal casserole in a white sauce of onions, peppers, wine vinegar, and garlic. I ate it with her homemade bread, alone on the terrace overlooking the Ionian Sea, watching the progress of the black clouds that would bring that night's rainfall. The combination of this expansive view of the Earth in its living parts—sea, sky, wind, land, flora, and fauna—and the wonders of tastes skillfully combined into something somewhat akin to ecstasy, if ecstasy existed, made me quite tolerant of being but a vassal in Helen's hands—at least until she started spreading Aloe Vera on my face again.

During the days when there were breaks in the rain, Helen would send me off on walks, slapping a hand-drawn map in front of me, handing me the proper attire, and booting me out of the villa. Each day a different walk, each walk stunning. It's as if she wanted me to see and intimately know the land she lived in. I assumed she wanted me to return and assure her that her land was as close to paradise as possible. Loyalty to one's land often causes the assumption that it is somehow more divine than all other lands, which never rise above the mundane of their dirt. I was happy to assure her as best as possible in the English she couldn't understand. She would snort in response, turn her head to the right, and spit. I took it that meant that she was pleased.

Of course, one cannot walk without thinking, and the thinking can take as many turns and directions as the walk. I kept getting onto narrow trails into my past. I would quickly backtrack, but there seemed to be many trails to my past. My parents' convictions, sad idealists that they were, kept popping up in the landscape; features one could view as noble from one angle, laughable from another. I kept tripping over my crudely forged double childhood so steeped in the "Importance of It All," yet, by necessity, so conveyed as sunny normal, or, rather, sunny Norman. The dead approached me on the walks—not unusual during a Greek odyssey—but I have little to say to the dead. They are not great companions, the dead, not many laughs.

On occasion, despite all this, even as it threatened to rain again, I realized how good life can be and marveled over the paradox.

When I returned, Helen, the nurse, would administer to me again and then disappear to prepare dinner. I would fix myself a drink and thumb through the many fashion magazines Lydia had about. Then Helen would serve me dinner. Afterward, it was time to go to work. Greece is ten hours ahead of L.A. Now was the time to call.

"Talk," Roee said, miles away.

"It's me."

"How's the vacation?"

"It's raining."

"Ah."

"Lydia's in Athens."

"Ah."

"Too much time alone."

"Ah."

"Talk to me, Roee. Tell me of progress."

"Charles W. Pinsker has made contact with Sara Hutton. I had a lovely lunch with her today in her private dining room. Ate from the finest china. Drank out of Waterford crystal. I think we hit it off quite well. I was conspiratorial in my general aspect and demeanor. I think she appreciated that. She is most interested in meeting Lydia Corfu and talking turkey. Not the country, of course."

"Of course."

"We will meet her next Saturday at her house."

"Good."

"Are you healing?"

"I seem to be. If you're referring to my recent wounds."

xx

I had Roee patch me into Petey.

"Petey."

"Fixxer!" The blare of Petey's voice was clear and, unfortunately, loud. "How are ya? Where are ya?"

"I'm on the Greek island of Corfu."

"Jeez, Fixxer! What am I doing wrong? I'm sitting in a goddamn basement of a gray building cut off from all things natural, and you're on the Greek island of Corfu!"

"Well, Petey, if you insist on being a civil servant."

"I'm just a slave to duty! So what can I do you for, and how will it profit me?"

"I need some quick information. Do you remember when you got the dope sheet on Maxwellton James, you mentioned he had other airfields, including one in Central California? That wouldn't specifically be in San Simeon, would it?"

"Well, I don't remember. Let me get into the computer and

check it out."

The tapping of computer keys came across the wire, accompanied by Petey's quiet humming. Quiet until he broke into song.

"*Hey, hey, we're the Monkees!* You know I haven't been able to get that out of my head since that day."

"Oh, by the way, did you get the thank you gift I sent you?"

"Sure did! And she was swell! Real nice girl! That was a page in the Kama Sutra I hadn't gotten to yet!"

"You know, she's probably the best in your local area. Has a hell of a client list."

"Yeah, I got that idea when she started humming 'Hail to the Chief' in the middle of it."

"Better than Eleanor?"

"Well, younger, at least. Okay, here it is. Ah—umm—that's interesting."

"What's that?"

"Well, not only is the airfield in San Simeon, it's part of that whole Hearst Castle thing they got there."

"Tell me more."

"Well, old man Hearst used to have a private airfield on the land. It went into disuse when the place became a State Park, but several years ago, Maxwellton James persuaded the state to give him a license to take over the airfield and turn it into an air museum. So that's where he's got most of his old airplanes. It's now part of the attraction."

"Interesting. Okay, Petey. Thanks a lot."

"Thank you, Fixx! Always good talking to you!"

Roee, of course, was still on the line. "Easy access to an airplane for a quick flight up to Alaska," he stated.

"Obviously."

"But why dump her on the frozen Bering Sea? Almost in plain sight?"

"I don't think it was planned that way."

"Ah. Then what was the plan, and why wasn't it carried out?"

"Questions we can't answer right now."

I thought for a second, giving something a bit of consideration.

I talked it over with Roee. He agreed with my conclusion, with his usual reservations, but, as I requested, he patched me into Newsstand Mike.

"Sherman Oaks Newsstand." It was Mike, stating a fact. Previously, that statement had always been clothed in a bright cloth. Not today.

"Mike, it's me."

I could hear him draw in a quick breath. He had never known me to call him direct before. I usually let Norton Macbeth do the communicating.

"Fixxer. Hello, sir, how are you?"

It was the first time I had known him to call me "Sir." I wondered how many strange places his head had been since I last talked to him. "You tell me first."

"Oh, I'm okay. Just working. Sorry, I don't have any interesting tidbits. Haven't really been paying attention lately, but, you know, I'll snap back."

"I need your help, Mike."

"For—for what?"

"Mike, Sara Hutton was involved in Bea Cherbourg's death, but I don't believe it was premeditative murder."

"Well, what—what does that mean? Does that mean she can't be arrested?"

"No, not at all. Assuming the truth can get out, there are charges of manslaughter, obstruction, and evidence tampering. There's a laundry list of counts a DA could charge her with."

"But none of them is going to get her the juice."

"You mean through a lethal injection?"

"Yeah."

"It's doubtful."

"So, what's the use?"

"Mike, you're assuming death is worse than a ruined life. You ought not to do that."

"Then you can fix her?" He asked with anticipation daring to be enthusiastic.

"I am in the midst of doing that now, Mike."

"Bless you, Fixx, bless you."

"Were that you had that power, Mike."

"Okay, so what can I do?"

"Have you ever visited Hearst Castle?"

"No—what?—that thing up the coast? No. I don't get away much."

"I want you to take a few days off from the newsstand. Go up to San Simeon. Take the tour of the Castle. Look around. Get a sense of the place for me. Do you have a camera?"

"Just an old Kodak."

"Call Norton. He'll arrange for a camera and a quick course in its use. I want you to take many pictures. Be the consummate tourist. Also, take a side trip to the air museum on the grounds. I want pictures of every airplane on display, each from several angles. While you're doing all this, keep your eyes and ears open. I want to know the mood of the place. Let me know if something seems wrong, even if you can't put your finger on it. Even if it is nothing more than the slight raising of the hair on the back of your neck, note it and report it. Never ignore the slight raising of the hair on the back of your neck, Mike. Can you do all this for me?"

"Of course, Fixx, I can do anything for you."

"Don't take this the wrong way, Mike, but there might be something here bigger than just the death of Bea, as tragic as that was. I want you to take this commission from me seriously and do a good job."

"Fixx, I'll—I'll come through for you. You know that. If you do Sara Hutton, if you get rid of that bitch, Fixx, I'm yours. You'll own me."

"Mike, I'm not sure I'm ready for the responsibility of ownership. Just let me have the right of first negotiation, and we'll call it square. Mike, I know you're still in a state because of what happened to Bea, but I need you to drop emotion as much as possible. Clear your mind. Clear your eye."

"Okay, Fixx. I'll call Norton right away."

"He'll also give you the funds for the trip and something for your time."

"Okay, thanks."

"Be bold, Mike, but be careful. There might be danger."

"What the fuck do I care?"

"Mike!" I said it with a snap. "Do me a favor. Care. Even if just a little."

After Mike hung up, I instructed Roee to call Norton and give him the details. Then I hung up.

Now, with nothing to do but think, I wanted to relax to some music.

Unfortunately, Lydia's taste ran to the current, the pop, the obvious, and the awful. She had not one CD I was interested in. I tried the radio and managed to get the BBC World Service. The discussion of orchids was slightly interesting but not really what I was in the mood for. Then I heard Helen in the kitchen. She was singing what I took to be an old Greek folk song. Her voice was that of an old woman. It cracked and even gurgled, but the song was sincere, evocative. I quietly opened doors and moved a chair as close to the kitchen as possible. I didn't let her know I was listening. I thought it might embarrass her or, if not, change the purity of her performance. I sat, rested my legs on a small table, and listened. The song melded with the sounds of wind and rain and the distant sounds of the ocean butting up against the beach. Now and then, a human voice floated up from the town, but the center was always Helen's song.

I mused on the Pleasant, one of the strangest creatures. Frail—yet a survivor.

At about 11:30, Helen was shocked to find me asleep yet not in my bed. She scolded me in words I will never know but will always feel. She rushed me into my room and slammed the door behind her as she left, her continuing tirade trailing off as she retired to her room.

XX

In the morning, I was woken by the whuup-whuup sound of a helicopter and the bright sun that seemed to crash through my window. The whuup-whuup got closer, and I knew the copter was landing on the roof.

A burst of competing sound came through the whuup-whuup.

It was the sharp, spiky voice of Lydia Corfu speaking rapidly in Greek. I assumed she was bidding farewell to the pilot and shouting orders to Helen. I could hear her progress through the villa—for she seemed to pass not one room without commenting—a progress that ended when the door to my bedroom swung open.

"Nico, I am here, and I have brought the sun with me!" she declared as she stood in retro bright yellow Capri slacks and a daisy-splattered blouse tied up to show off her midriff.

"Oh." I sat up in bed to face her. "Do you have the local concession?"

"I own the Sun! I own the Moon!" She rushed over to me, threw off my blankets, revealing all there was to show, then kissed me before I could protest. Not that I had been planning on it.

"A false statement, of course," she said after the kiss, "but one so glorious to declare. Now let me look at your ugly mug." She grabbed me under the chin and took control. "Aaa! It is repairing itself back to handsome."

She turned and spoke in Greek to Helen. Helen, taking one quick, sly look my way, left.

"Up! Shower! Dress! We will take a boat to a little hidden bay. Helen is preparing us much food. We will spend the day there."

"Will she pack feta cheese?"

"Large chunks of it!"

"Olives?"

"Handpicked and cured by herself."

"Bread and cold lamb?"

"Do you doubt it?"

"Wine?"

"Of course."

"I don't care much for wine."

"No problem. I know how to intoxicate."

"Well, given how you brought me here to recuperate, maybe I ought to stay in bed."

"Fool! There is no better bed in the world than the sands of a Greek beach!"

xx

We took a small yet tidy sailboat, which Lydia captained, making me the crew of one. Luckily, I've had some sailing experience, so I didn't embarrass myself under her harsh command. The barking of orders was as natural to her as the cooing of a dove, although the quality of her voice was far on the other end of the scale of aural pleasures. Despite this, she was never less than a "Woman," whatever that means as we end the twentieth century. As she went about the business to make the sailboat sail with a beauty and grace that matched the environment, her breasts, bringing great dimension to the field of daises, were a two-point statement of extreme confidence in being, and the curves that defined female were as glorious as a gibbous moon in daylight; round and firm and solid, and yet seemingly ethereal against the bright blue sky. Her smile was a life-beaming smile. If you caught the waves, you felt the frequency and wanted only to tune in, free of static. Her eyes oversaw all, darting to exactly where they needed to look to take in and tell what needed to be told. They, too, had a strong hand at the tiller.

Soon we rounded a sharp protrusion in the shore's landscape, and she shouted out and pointed, "Look! My bay!"

There, nestled between that protrusion and the next one up, was a small but brilliant patch of Cheshire Cat grin beach backed by a steep, tall cypress-covered hill of no paths. It was utterly deserted.

She edged the boat into the bay and dropped the anchor. She then stripped quickly and without warning, squealed in delight, and dove into the water so smoothly that there was hardly a splash. She stayed under an inordinate amount of time, but the water was clear, and I could see her darting from here to there, twirling, doing underwater somersaults. It was joy made corporeal. Then her head emerged from the sea, crystal runs of water streaming down her face, glistening in the sun. "Do you believe in mermaids?" she asked me.

"I do now, "I said.

"Strip," she commanded. "Don't let one inch of your body

avoid this sun."

I did as she asked, then joined her in the sea. There we swam, on and below the surface, splashed and chased each other like kids, giggled without shame, and coupled just as boldly.

Finally, exhausted, we made our way to the shore. The great Greek sands she had promoted were actually pebbles. Small and fine as pebbles go, but pebbles, nevertheless. "Lydia, I think this bed is going to be lumpy."

"Huh! Weak, pampered American!"

"You keep making that assumption."

"What assumption?"

"That I'm an American."

She looked me over. "Of course you are."

"Why do you say that?"

"Only an American these days would set himself up as a Knight-errant."

"Lydia, I work for money. I work for gain."

"So did the Knights. It was only in their fantasies that they were romantic."

"Well, even so, I hope you brought something to lay on."

"I have the most luxuriant cushions in the boat and our lunch. Why don't you get them while I lie on the beach?" With that, she laid down on the hot pebbles, beads of seawater evaporating off her naked form, as she brought her right leg up to a comfortable position and placed her right arm across her eyes to shield them from the sun.

I retrieved everything from the boat in two trips. In the first one, I brought the cushion.

"Thank god!" Lydia said. "You know, these pebbles are hard!" She smiled at me as she took the cushion, positioned it, and laid back down. "Now go get the lunch, please. I'm starving."

We feasted on feta, olives, bread, and cold, tender lamb strips. She drank her wine, and I drank the vodka she was kind enough to bring. Then we made love again in ways I will not describe, as some memories are not for sharing. Then we napped in each other's arms.

When we awoke, the sun was diminished but still brilliant, and the sounds in our private bay were of the sea lapping the pebbles, the wind through the cypresses, and birds informing the air of their presence.

Lydia turned to me and said, "Nico, I enjoy being rich."

"I'm glad."

"It's not the same as a religion for me."

"No, that would be disconcerting."

"But I am devoted to it."

"How so?"

"It is the condition of my life that I will protect fiercely."

"Understood."

"You are not against the rich, are you?"

"I would not be ashamed to be called rich myself."

"Then you are not for the redistribution of wealth."

"Oh, I'm sure we are all for the redistribution of wealth at one time or another. As long as it's not our wealth."

"So this little adventure we are on...."

"Has rewards for both of us. Not the least being the adventure itself."

"Something money can't buy."

"That's right. Chaos is free."

Lydia looked out to sea. I followed her gaze. Was she watching the simplicity of her boat bobbing in the bay or the complexity of an oncoming bank of clouds? Did they hold rain—or would they pass, magnificent ships of the sky, both craft and sail, graceful and haughty? Uncertainty. Certain people relished it.

She turned to me, and I turned to face her. "I have done as you asked. The information is in my files. Also, my husband's bankers are informed, paid, and will cooperate."

"And your husband?"

"I do not need to ask him. He grants me anything I want. He is an ugly little toad of a man but deeply generous."

"Do you, by any chance, love him?"

"Aaa, he satisfies on—"

"Alternate Tuesdays. Yes, I know, but that was not my question."

She looked out to sea again. A simple smile crossed her face, and she stated, as a simple fact, "He is dear to me."

"Will you ever show him that?"

"Aaa, probably not. He has too much power as it is." She stood up quickly and started to gather things up. "Nico, the sun tells us it is time to go." I stood up and began to help her.

"There is a little bit of cheese left. Do you want it?" she asked.

"No, thank you. I am quite satiated."

She grabbed the chunk of cheese. "Then let us cast our feta to the wind!" She crumbled the cheese in her hand and then tossed it up for a short flight before raining back down on us. We laughed again.

"Not quite your usual libation to the Gods," I said as I brushed some off my shoulders, "but I like it, my sweet Greek."

Lydia grabbed me and kissed me. Then I returned the compliment.

14
SIRED TO KILL

The next day was a day spent in Kassiópi proper, wandering around in the town, joining the local inhabitants enjoying the sun.

Lydia was greeted by many with smiles and shouts. She was a star here but also a well-liked neighbor. "I have been a benefactor to this town," she said by way of explanation.

"Did you grow up around here?" I asked.

"No. Down south in Kyvos. I couldn't spend time there. There I am still Iphigeneia Venizelos. It is a typical story. Nothing to speak of."

"I see."

"And where are you still somebody not named The Fixxer?" She tried to slip it in.

"Is this a good place for lunch?" I asked, closing the chink.

It was. Excellent seafood. We sat at an outdoor table overlooking the bay of fishing boats. I discussed the schedule for the coming week and what we would have to be prepared to discuss. Lydia listened carefully and took it all in—very serious, very professional.

The helicopter arrived that afternoon and took Lydia away. I decided to get one more full day of rest. Then, the helicopter would return to fetch me. I eventually would meet Lydia in Athens, from where we would start our trip to Los Angeles. "Evidence" would be left behind confirming that Elsworth Henderson spent the week in Athens conferring with his client.

xx

That evening I called Hamo in London.

"Well, is Robert Pye a rotting corpse, or was he found?" I asked.

"Oh, yes, he was found—rotten if not rotting. He's currently a guest of our National Health Service and a daily feature in our tabloids. He and the woman are being called 'The Bank & Bunk Mates.' As we had hoped, she went looking for him at the house when he did not arrive for work. She thought, or so the tabloids have indicated, that he might have been there with another woman."

"You mean, besides his wife?"

"Yes, she went looking for evidence of uber adultery."

"Uber adultery?"

"That's what I call it when you cheat on the woman you are cheating on your wife with."

"Did you just make that up?"

"No, I coined the term in 1981 during unfortunate self-analysis. You must understand, Fixxer, I was younger then and full of excess energy."

"Since dissipated, I trust."

"Long gone, I'm afraid. Only enough juice left for proper morals. Anyway, she found him cute as a bug curled up on the bathroom floor, snoring away. When she couldn't wake him, she panicked and called in the emergency people. Of course, after that, there was nothing to hide behind."

"And the mysterious disease?"

"Well, that's getting a little play, yes, but it's just not as sexy as sex, you see."

"Well, what is? Any press connection with Pye's ailment and a similar one suffered by a minor motion picture executive in Hollywood, California?"

"Not a word, but I'm keeping my eye on that."

"And George?"

"Well...."

There was a disquieting pause.

"Hamo? Talk to me."

"George has disappeared."

"Disappeared?"

"Off the face of the Earth, I'm afraid. Sorry, Fixxer, I had assumed he would be easy to keep track of. Several of these American thugs are working here, a bit of an expat community they've got for themselves. They're not hard to keep tabs on, but no one has seen him. Actually, no one even knows of him. I think he was new to the area. I think Pye had been his only employer, probably imported George, not wanting a connection with the local thugs, bad for his image, and all that. I guess George is back home in America."

"America's a big place."

"Yes, sorry about that."

"Well, I would have loved to have kept him in our viewfinder, but... How about the briefcases?"

"Done. They'll be waiting for you at Heathrow. The cameras are digital and fitted inside the shell of the cases. As are the batteries. The whole thing is camouflaged against prying eyes and x-rays."

"The lens?"

"Micro, of course, looks out of one of the twin holes on the lock where the key goes in."

"And the transmitter?"

"It's one whole side of the case, also camouflaged."

"All right. Fine."

"As to the last thing you requested...."

"Yes?"

"Sorry. Drew a blank. Couldn't find this Gilgamesh Paul anywhere. Don't know if he ever made it over to this side of the Atlantic."

"Too bad."

"Been on the hunt long?"

"Long enough."

"Maybe there are times when one should just give it up."

"You sound like Roee."

"Well, Fixxer, an obsession—"

"It is not an obsession."

"Okay. Sorry."

"Your efforts are appreciated, nonetheless, Hamo. Thanks for everything."

"My pleasure, Fixxer. Always has been, you know. Always will be."

xx

I spent the next day in various forms of sleep. Lazy napping in the sun, of course, but also the deep relaxation sleep I use as the ultimate restorative. It bothered the hell out of Helen. I think she thought something mystical was going on.

I woke up early the next day. Helen prepared a hot breakfast and took one last look at my head and face. She spat satisfaction in her healing; only a minimal trace of my banking problems was evident. The helicopter came, and Helen walked me up to the roof, carrying my bags at her insistence. I said goodbye in the little Greek I had managed to pick up. Suddenly she burst into tears, grabbed me, and started wailing. I had no way to assure her that my leaving was not quite the tragedy she was making it out to be, so I shed a few tears myself—a natural talent I have—and lamented enough to make her feel good. She continued to wave from the roof of the villa for a good long time as the helicopter ascended and Corfu dropped away.

xx

I met Lydia in Athens, and we took the ten am flight to London to catch Virgin Atlantic flight 007 to Los Angeles. At Heathrow, I retrieved the briefcases from baggage claim using the claim tickets Hamo had jet-packed to Lydia. I made her carry one, which she was not happy about. I picked up some copies of the tabloids that still featured stories about "The Bank & Bunk Mates" for the amusement of Roee, and we boarded the plane.

I maintained the presence of Elsworth Henderson throughout the flight, which very much annoyed Lydia. A stiff, humorless east coast lawyer whose vision was attuned mainly to numbers that crunched and added up, who was precise in his movements, neat in his habits, and whose contractual mind had managed to allow just enough room for the love of family, and a passion for golf, was not her ideal traveling companion. She tried her best to break me, like an American tourist trying to get a smile from a guard at St. James Palace, but to no avail. Finally, she groped me using the ruse of grabbing for a magazine. Elsworth, quite rightly, enumerated the sexual harassment laws in America and asked her, in a whisper, to keep her filthy little Greek hands to herself. Lydia exploded in laughter, startling passengers, attendants, and, most likely, the pilot, for, I swear, the plane took a dip. She opened the magazine, vowing to get back at me. In my last whisper, I told her I looked forward to it.

We arrived at LAX just after three. Roee, as Pinsker in his Brooks Brothers suit, was there to greet us with the limo. We took it to the Hotel Bel-Air, where Pinsker had been staying for the last week and where we now checked in. Pinsker and Henderson shared a garden suite; Lydia had one to herself. We unpacked, showered, then left for a planned dinner out on the town, but, of course, Roee and I took Lydia home so that we could speak in more private surroundings.

"Newsstand Mike is waiting for us," Roee announced on the way. "He has a report."

"Couldn't we have met him somewhere else? Was it wise to have him at home?"

"Fixxer, you made him part of the team. I trust him. I restricted his access to certain rooms, of course."

"Of course."

"Plus, he got a bit roughed up on the assignment. I felt he was owed a little care."

"How bad?"

"A broken arm and a cracked rib. I've got him resting comfortably. He'll be okay. Norton sent over Dr. Stone."

"What about his report?"

"You'll find it more than interesting," Roee said as the limo pulled into our building on Wilshire.

xx

"Fixxer, I didn't want to stay here. Roee made me," was the greeting we got from Mike as we entered. He moved stiffly, and his arm was in a cast and sling. "I could have done fine at my apartment. I didn't want to impose."

"Mike, Roee has a proclivity for charity, among other dangerous traits. By allowing him to indulge in it, you are simply extending him a kindness, which I thank you for. How much of my booze have you drunk?"

"Uh—well, Roee said—"

"You were welcome to it, Mike. A broken arm and a cracked rib call for a few drinks," I said.

"Oh, thanks, Fixx. You have a well-stocked bar."

"Yes, I suppose so. Roee tells me our wine cellar—if one can have a wine cellar on the fifteenth floor—is quite a marvel, but I wouldn't know about that. I am not a refined drinker. Now, Mike, just a note: If you ever reveal to anyone the location of my home, I will gut you like a fish. Is that clear?"

Such a slippery slope I had put Mike on. There's a small pleasure in it.

"Yeah, Fixx, of course. You know me."

"Yes, Mike, yes, I do. Now I would like you to meet Lydia Corfu."

The recognition in Mike's eyes was immediate. "Oh, Lydia Corfu! Sired to Kill, right?"

"That's right. You have seen it?" Lydia inquired, a small smile crossing her lips.

"Of course."

"When?"

"It was during the early days of cable before they could get good movies. I mean, well, actually, um, yeah, it was okay."

"Thank you. *I* thought so." Lydia became somewhat chilly.

"I've seen all your movies. I've always thought that with just a little bit

better stories—"

"I wrote the stories," Lydia said with her words now encased in ice.

"Doesn't change my criticism," Mike said. "If you can show me the reviews and the box office to change my mind, I'll consider it."

"He's an insulting little man," Lydia complained to me.

"Well, Mike loves movies," was the only explanation I could offer.

"And what about my acting?" Lydia asked Mike. I admired Lydia's courage.

"Well, um, you don't have to study with Stella Adler to kick men in the groin convincingly.

"Something I still know how to do," Lydia made clear.

"Ah." Mike looked up at her with soulful eyes. "You wouldn't reach that low, would you?"

"Americans!" Lydia said, explaining it all to herself.

"The wonders of chemistry," I said to Roee. "You never know when bringing together two seemingly harmless substances will lead to something volatile."

"I am not harmless!" Lydia declared.

"Does that mean you're harmful?" Roee asked, following the logic.

"Well, no, I meant...." Lydia had not fully considered the antithesis.

"Shall we go into the library?" I said, coming to the rescue. "I believe Mike has a report for me."

xx

We walked into the library, which Mike took little notice of, but Lydia was impressed, mainly because the books were in categorical and alphabetical order. She also noticed what few do. For many titles, I have two copies. She wanted to know why.

"One would be a first edition or collectible for one reason or another. The other is a good reading copy," I said.

"How clever," she said.

"More practical than clever. Now, if you will all sit." They all did. "Mike, what happened?"

"Well, I went up there like you said—it's a great drive, by the way, I hadn't realized—uh, anyway, I took the tour, which was, uh, fascinating, you know, amazing. Talk about overweening pride! Hearst built this thing over, like, years and years. Did you know a girl architect designed it?"

"Uh, Mike...." Roee darted his eyes to Lydia.

"Oh, sorry, *woman* architect," Mike corrected.

"Bet you she was still a girl," Lydia said.

"Uh, yeah, well...."

Poor Mike.

"Go on, Mike, but please tell me things relevant to your assignment. I can take the tour myself later for the color. Tell me your feelings while on the tour."

"You mean, besides envy of the super-rich?"

"Yes, besides that."

"Well, you know, it was like going through a museum, a look-but-don't-touch sort of a thing. The tour guide was good—too good when I tried to break away a little bit to take some interesting pictures, she called me right back. It's very controlled, but then, I guess you would expect that."

"Anything else?"

"Well—this is where I got that hair at the back of the neck thing you wanted me to pay attention to; it turned out to be a damn good indicator," he said, indicating his arm in the sling.

"And what exactly elevated the filaments?"

"Well, the State Park and Recreation Service runs the place."

"Is it big government that frightens you?"

"No, but those State Park Rangers weren't really what I would have expected."

"Rangers?" Roee questioned. "At a place like Hearst Castle? They couldn't have been Rangers. Usually, in this kind of attraction, the State has tour guides, not Rangers, who are essentially a police force."

"Oh, they had tour guides, all right, and ticket sellers and all that, but I'm talking about Rangers. You know, the guys in the Smokey the Bear hats who wear guns and mace and nightsticks."

"Sounds like Rangers, "Roee said.

"How many were there?" I asked.

"Enough. They were peppered all over the place."

"What bothered you about them?"

"Well, I mean, Park Rangers, you'd expect them to be like Boy Scouts grown up, guns or no guns, but these guys seemed more like your neighborhood bullies grown up."

"How so?"

"Well, and this was just a feeling, you see, but it was not just that they were unfriendly. They just were not friendly. You know what I mean? This was a real contrast with the tour guides without the guns, who were friendly, but why should there be a difference? I mean, there's this State Park I go up to in the Tujunga area, no tour guides, just Rangers, and the Rangers there are really friendly and helpful. They seem to care, even if they do wear guns, but these guys, they had a whole different attitude. I mean, that became, uh, painfully clear when I took that other tour to the air museum."

"What happened?" I asked.

"Well, I was taking the tour, snapping a lot of pictures like you asked me. Made myself out to be a real airplane buff. Then I saw this hanger. Not the one with the planes on display but, you know, a working one, I assumed. But it was closed, and without any signs up or anything, it just had a feeling of 'Keep Out' about it. Well, I figured that's exactly what you would be interested in. So I left the group when the guide was pointing out some boring stuff on the bottom of a plane and slipped into the hangar, and it was, you know, just an airplane hangar. You saw airplanes in there. Some were under repair; some were being rebuilt, but then I saw this big pile covered by a bunch of canvases, and, you know, I got the hair thing again, Fixx, so I went over to it and lifted a corner of the canvas. Now I was never in the service or anything, but we got plenty of magazines about this at the newsstand, and I'm pretty sure it was a huge pile of ammo. Boxes and boxes of it."

"What kind of ammo?"

"I don't know. Except it wasn't for handguns or rifles or stuff like that; these were big, serious metal boxes."

"Any markings on the box?"

"The only thing I remember is Browning 303 because, you know, I recognized the name Browning and, well, 303 is an easy number to remember."

Roee looked at me. I shot him an eyebrow acknowledging that I shared his thoughts. Then Roee turned to Mike. "Did you look inside these boxes? Did you see rounds of ammo?" he asked.

"Didn't get a chance. I was about to when this Ranger came up behind me, grabbed my arm, and twisted it up around my back, asking me what the fuck I was doing there. Oh, excuse the language, Lydia."

"Don't give it another fucking thought," she said.

"Oh, okay. So he asked me what the fuck I was doing there, and I said, well, I was just curious, so I thought I would look, and that's when he pushed me into the ammo, and I fell hard on my arm on the boxes, and it broke, and my rib cracked against the edge of one of the boxes. Then he threw that old saying at me about the cat, curiosity, and killing, then told me to get the fuck out. So I, um, I did. So I got back to the tour, back to the parking lot, and into my car, and I drove home—non-stop. I got to tell you, that ain't easy with a cracked rib and a broken arm, but I think fear took my mind off the pain."

"It will do that," I said.

"When Mike got home," Roee said, "he called Norton. Norton connected with me. I went out to see him, saw the injuries, and that he was in pain. I brought him here, and Norton sent Dr. Stone over. Mike's been here ever since."

"Interesting," I said. "Now, what about the photographs?"

"Oh, I got 'em. I think the Ranger would like to have taken the camera away, but I convinced him I was just a dumb tourist airplane nut who got off the track."

"I've got the photos over here." Roee got up and led us to my desk. Photos were laid out of the castle and the air museum. Those of the castle revealed little outside of the mock Italian grandeur of it all. However, one shot that featured one of the Rangers gave credence to Mike's impression. The pointed campaign hat that he wore, the kind not only worn by Smokey the Bear but by Canadian Mounties on parade, put his face into shadow, but you could still tell it was a hard face. Normal humans shouldn't hold that against him—but we took the license.

Mike had done an excellent job on the photos of the planes. There was a P-38 Lightning, an A-26, a B-29, a Japanese Zero, a Mustang P-51, even an old Northrop prototype of the Flying Wing, and, in an intriguing display, two Messerschmitt Bf 109s stood on the tarmac facing off two Supermarine Spitfires, the main mechanical combatants of the Battle of Britain.

"They're beautiful!" Lydia said, genuinely impressed.

"Yes, they are," I said. "Despite being powerful engines of destruction."

"That was just their function, at a time when that function was necessary," Roee said, "but that is not their essence."

"They are so much more elegant than modern planes," Lydia said.

As we scanned the photos, admiring an elegance of a past era, my eye was suddenly taken by someone in the background of one of the pictures. It was one of the Rangers, hat off, just having finished wiping his brow. He was a bulky individual of possibly medium height, although it was hard to tell as he stood away from the tourists, alone on the tarmac with nothing close by for reference. But there was something about him. Something that nagged at the back of my neck. I grabbed my magnifying glass and took a closer look. The nag had been right. "Roee," I said, "take a look at this Ranger."

"That's the one that got me in the hangar!" Mike said, "Ugly bastard, ain't he?"

Roee took the glass and, bending down, gave the man the scrutiny he deserved. When he rose back up, he was sure. "George," he said.

"George," I confirmed.

xx

After dinner, we gave Mike the painkiller prescribed by Dr.

Stone and sent him off to bed. Then we took Lydia, not to mention Henderson and Pinsker, back to the Hotel Bel-Air. We made much noise in the lobby when we arrived (Pinsker really can't hold his liquor) just in case Sara Hutton had a "friend" hanging out. Once in our suite, Roee and I changed out of our East Coast formality into casual, although I assure you, quite stylish clothes, and quietly exited by our private garden entrances and left the hotel by a back way.

On the drive home in the Porsche, we considered the matter.

Roee said, "So, things may not be so simple."

"I suppose you're right. I'm always hoping they are, and I'm always disappointed."

"George in London. A thug for banker Pye. George in California. A not very friendly State Park Ranger who breaks arms at Hearst Castle."

· "Specifically, the air museum."

"Which is run by Maxwellton James."

"An ex-gun runner and drug dealer who seems to have a, at least, philosophical relationship with film executive Sara Hutton."

"Who had secretly employed London banker Pye to secure financing for a management takeover of Olympic Pictures." Roee turned to me. "I don't suppose we can chalk any of this up to coincidence?"

"No, I don't suppose we can."

"So we have to assume...."

"We have to assume it's an even more dangerous game than it's been so far and that the trap I'm trying to lay for them could turn around and be a trap for us."

"So do we pull out, having no real financial stake in the matter?"

"Oh, I'd hate to do that. Wouldn't you?"

"I don't know if I would hate to, but—"

"Good."

"That's not to say that caution is not advised."

"Understood. We should call the Captain in the morning. We might need his services."

"That is certainly not beyond the realm of possibility."

After a moment, I asked Roee, "Do you remember Petey's

sound cubes?"

"Oh, yeah. They're cool."

"Cool? They're cold."

"Well, apparently so, anyway."

"Have him ship two or three overnight to us."

"Okay."

"Have him ship them out with, oh, let's say, some frozen ham steaks from that favorite butcher shop of his."

"Must they be ham?"

"Lamb cutlets, then."

"Thank you."

"You're welcome, and I think it might be advisable to get ourselves out to Chino tomorrow, see Maloney, and put a few hours in the air. Agreed?"

"Couldn't hurt," Roee agreed. "Whereas so many other things could."

XX

When I got home and climbed into my bed for the first time in several days, my head on the pillow filled with thoughts of Lydia and the situation I was putting her in. She had not balked at the potential of danger, indeed, she seemed to have welcomed it, but that was all just dramatic flair. A proclivity of hers I was taking advantage of. Given the new information, it was my decision whether to continue taking advantage of it. She was not a naïve woman. Without discussing the peripatetic George in front of her and Mike, she still, I believed, got the connection and knew that the stakes had been raised.

Nevertheless, she did not make a move to question. Of course, what I offered her in exchange for her participation in my little ruse was too good for her to pass up: The Hollywood fame she could milk out of our success and the addition to her fortune that would come from it. Mostly the Hollywood fame. It's different from other fame; it's Mount Olympus fame instead of just fame in the agora or the assembly. It's the kind of fame that allows you to eat ambrosia and commune with the gods in the clouds. It is also fame as mythic as ambrosia and the gods. And as insubstantial as the clouds. But that only adds to, does not diminish its allure. It is fame not so much for doing—although many do much—it is fame for just being.

All attention to the essence that is I.

What possible greater satisfaction in yourself could there be?

Worth the risk of your life? For some, yes. Maybe for most. But most rarely get the chance.

So a fair bargain had been struck between Lydia Corfu and The Fixxer.

I turned the pillow, which had grown warm under my head, to its cool side for what comfort I could find there. Soon, I was asleep.

15
FRESHLY SQUEEZED

Two days later, on a quiet Saturday morning of bright blue sky and wind-washed air, our limo took Lydia Corfu and her two lawyers to Sara Hutton's house on the corner of Delfern and Faring in the Holmby Hills section of the Bel-Air Estates. Her house, seemingly a transplant from the plantation at Tara (sans the Civil War and its messy deprivations), was huge, white, pillared, and impressive. As Roee stepped out of the car, he quietly said, "Mmm, Sara Hutton must be a romantic."

"Aren't all girls?" I added.

"Boys!" Lydia admonished.

Having announced ourselves through the intercom at the driveway wrought iron security gate, the front door was already open, and standing in the doorway was not an old family retainer of African-American ancestry in the elaborate livery of the main house butler—I admit, I half expected such—but a middle-aged Latina in a simple gray dress and apron. She looked work weary as she squinted at the bright morning sun.

"This way, please? Miss Sara is in the living room."

She escorted us through a grand entrance hall with a liquid-looking floor, past a sweeping staircase, and through a set of tall double doors. There, in a large room filled with sunlight pouring in from tall windows that overlooked an extensive, lush backyard, Sara Hutton sat cross-legged on an oversized, comfortable couch surrounded by film scripts.

"Miss Sara, the guests are here," the Latina announced.

Sara Hutton put the script she had been intently reading down and stood to greet us. She was about five foot seven and wore black jeans and a white ribbed cotton tank top covered by an unbuttoned man's black and white checkered shirt. Her brown hair was one inch short of shoulder length and as straight and shapeless as her body, its only significant feature being bangs. She was barefoot. She was all comfort.

"Thank you, Josephina," she said to the Latina, who turned around and left. She then turned to Roee, whom she knew as Pinsker. "It's good to see you again, Mr. Pinsker. Thank you for coming to my home."

"Ms. Hutton," Roee began the introductions, "may I introduce Ms. Lydia Corfu and my partner Mr. Elsworth Henderson." To us, he introduced "Ms. Sara Hutton."

"Good to meet you, but as this has become such an informal first-name world, why don't I call you Lydia and Elsworth?"

Lydia, who was wearing a simple Giorgio Armani outfit of gray slacks, a light gray cashmere sweater, and a charcoal gray blazer cut somewhat like a riding coat, and who had her hair down in stunning waves of black highlighted by gray strands, opened her face with a wide smile. "Of course, you can call me Lydia, but it is dangerous to call lawyers by their first names. It only gives them license to become much too familiar. Keep them in their place, I say. Besides, how often do you want to have to say Elsworth? No, the boys here, I think, must remain Mr. Henderson and Mr. Pinsker."

"Okay, Lydia. We'll keep the bonding among us girls. Please be seated. Should we have something to drink? Coffee? Water? Juice?"

"Do you have fresh squeezed orange juice? I truly miss the fresh orange juice in California. In Europe, it is, I'm afraid, not so good."

"Of course—and you, gentlemen?"

"Orange juice would be fine," I said, pleased that Lydia followed the script. Roee nodded his assent as well.

"Josephina!" Sara yelled, bringing her forth in short order.

"Yes, Miss Sara?"

"Would you bring out a big pitcher of orange juice and three glasses? I'll have coffee."

"Yes, Miss Sara."

"Oh, and," Lydia said, "could we have many ice cubes in the juice? I like it very, very cold. You have no objections, do you, boys?"

"That will be fine," I said dryly.

The amenities over, Sara's long and narrow face dropped from the introductory smile and welcoming eyes to the slight slit mouth, haughty eyes aspect so well known by the Hollywood select. She placed those eyes on Lydia and moved them over hills and valleys.

"So, Lydia, what do you find so appealing about me? What are my qualities that turn you on?"

Lydia stared at Sara and did not flinch. Then she raised her dark, slash eyebrows. "I love a woman with small firm tits."

Sara pursed her lips before they broke to speak. "You misunderstand me. I meant in a business way."

"Oh, business. I thought you had confused my name. I thought maybe you thought my name was Lydia Lesbos."

"No. That is not the kind of mistake I would make."

"Good. Business?" Lydia sat up very straight and leaned towards Sara, displaying the extent and quality of her breasts well. Then she took in a deep breath through her nostrils. "You have the scent of success about you." She took another breath. "And the scent of determination. The two, of course, mingle well." She breathed again, "I smell that good pungent smell of smarts, hard smarts." Lydia breathed deeply one last time, "And there is nothing rank in your scent. Like the rotten sweet smell of the sentimental."

There was just the tiniest bit of admiration in Sara's eyes. "How very animalistic of you. Do you let your nostrils make all your business assessments?"

"My nostrils are simply reporters. My brain writes the story."

"I almost feel like I should turn my tail towards you and let you get the real essence of me."

"That will not be necessary."

Sara Hutton gave Roee and me a glance. "Gentlemen, I hope you will remember all this as the basis for future negotiations."

"One could hardly forget it," Charles W. Pinsker said.

"Okay, let's cut the cute crap." Sara grabbed back control of the meeting. "Are you seriously here to tell me that an ex-direct-to-video film femme fatale with pretensions that she's a writer and producer can fund—maybe to the extent of a billion dollars—my bid to buy a major motion picture company?"

"Ms. Hutton!" I spoke up sharply. "That is a completely unfair assessment of Ms. Corfu. Although she once had a very successful career as a non-studio Hollywood filmmaker of highly programmable products in the domestic video and foreign distribution markets, she is currently the sole owner of the highest-rated TV station in Greece, which brings in advertising revenues 43.264% greater than her nearest competitor. She also has become a major player in providing coproduction funding for various European-based TV and film products. Because of this, she has become a highly respected businesswoman in Europe, who fields, every day of every week, solicitations by major European and Asian banking institutions interested in providing the wherewithal to allow her to expand her interests. They are interested in her pursuing one of two areas. The worldwide satellite business, which we have advised her against currently, or the American media industry, which they admit is the best, strongest, and most profitable in the world. Added to this is her relationship with Konstantinos Metaxsa, arguably the wealthiest man in the world. I am speaking here of her business, not marital or conjugal relationship, of course. So to answer your question, are we serious? Yes. You already believed that to be true, or you would not have invited us to your home, away from prying eyes and ears in your office."

Sara assessed it all. Then she said. "She still used to earn her living kicking men in the groin."

"I can't think of a better qualification for a business partner," Roee stated.

Sara snorted out a laugh just as Josephina returned carrying a large tray with a crystal pitcher of orange juice, the ice cubes clicking happily against the side; three tall crystal glasses, each with their wondrous ice cubes, and a small glass carafe of coffee and a china cup from which to drink it.

Sara allowed Josephina to set the tray on the cocktail table before us and leave without being thanked. "Help yourself," she said to us as she began to pour her coffee. It smelled wonderful. Guatemalan, I was sure. From the Huehuetenango region, I suspected, because of its spicy aroma. I would have loved to have had some, but a plan is a plan, and I thanked Roee properly when he handed me my orange juice.

Sara sat back on the couch with a sly smile and sipped coffee. Lydia watched her like a cat preparing to pounce. Which she did the moment she saw Sara start to speak.

"Well—"

"Sara, have you ever spent a dime of your own money in this business?"

"Of course not. That's something my father taught me. Never spend your own money."

"Really? My father might have advised the same if he had ever had any excess money, but he would always put what little he had back into the farm. 'Back into the land,' he always said. Which was not a business to him, a way of life, yes, a way to live, yes, but not a business. He died poor but—"

"But a rich man inside, I'm sure," Sara said, more than sure she had gotten the irony across.

"No, not at all. He was a mean, petty, ignorant man who hardly said three words of love to his wife and none to his children. Sadly satisfied, I was going to say. For the life he led was all that he required. That doesn't make him 'rich in spirit' or some such silly excuse for financial failure. Just undemanding. Well, I, his daughter, have demanded more. But the technique remained the same. Put the money back into the land, back into the life. So I invested my own money into my own projects time and time again. I never hesitated to invest in myself. I funded my movies so that I could write and act because that's the life I wanted—"

"Vanity productions, Lydia. Simple, silly vanity productions. Instead of swimming with the sharks, you created a safe little pond for yourself. Why should I respect you for that?"

"Because the productions may have been vain, but they were not done in vain. I sold my movies at the film markets, MIFED and AFM, always achieving at least twice my costs, often more. I would take that money, fund my next film with a 10% increase in the budget, and pocket the rest. Then I would sell that movie, again getting at least double my costs. Again, the next movie, a 10% increase in budget, the balance into my pocket. I did this over and over and over until I built up a substantial personal fortune. The bulk of that money did not come from America. I could never sell beyond direct-to-video here in America. I was locked out of theatrical distribution in this country."

"You weren't locked out, Lydia. Your movies just weren't good enough. No stars, simple plots. You had okay production value, but otherwise—"

"Aaa, you head towards my point. If I did not make my money in America, where did I make it? In what you call the foreign market. Europe, Asia, and South America. My films sold well there. You see, I made my films for the teaming masses. And Europe and Asia and South America, especially, are where the teaming masses team. This is something Hollywood did not get back then. They did not understand the power that a simple, yet visceral, diversion had on the minds of the mundane poor bastards that most people are. Your snotty, well-fed American teenagers of the time liked to act oh so blasé and say, 'Life's a bitch, and then you die.' Remember? They had no idea how much life, for most of humanity, really is a bitch, and they were all looking for something to take their minds away from that. The mundane masses. There are billions of them out there, and that's much demand allowing us to keep the ticket prices low, making our product completely inclusive. It was a simple formula. Then the world changed, as it too often does. Hollywood got it! Started to understand and exploit the international market that it used to look down its nose at, and it started profiting by that understanding. Profit Hollywood never invited me to share. So when Greece privatized television, I said, to hell with Hollywood, I will go home where I'm appreciated. Where I'm a star. But the world has become so fucking small. Watching Hollywood grow on a formula I developed never ceased to gall me. Watching Hollywood make my kind of movies, but with the big stars only it could afford, and with expensive special effects and production values, pissed me off. Are the stories any more complex than the simple ones you accused me of telling? If you answer yes, you are either a liar or completely self-deluded. So I'm back. With financial wherewithal, and if you think I was good at kicking groin—wait till you see me kick ass."

Sara, who had sat blank-faced through much of this, threw her arms up, said, "Wow!" and laughed, then continued, "What a performance! From the heart, though, I can tell, and I like people who are pissed, who feel there are several pounds of flesh owed them. It's a solid motivation. All right. Maybe we can be in business together. I guess I will have to overcome the embarrassment of an alignment with an ex-producer of schlock B-movies. But, what the hell, that's all Sam Arkoff and Roger Corman have ever made, and now they do tributes to them. Okay, so, talk to me. What are the deal points?"

Roee and I, dry, dull, and precise, laid out the deal as we saw it. It couldn't help but appeal to Sara Hutton, as she remained the nominal power. As to dancing on occasion to Lydia's tune, she saw quickly that that would become music made by her relationship with Lydia. You could see the plan forming behind her eyes to form that relationship—in any way necessary. Still, Sara Hutton was Sara Hutton.

"I suppose if we align with you," she said, "we will produce and distribute epics starring Lydia Corfu."

"Of course! Why not! I want to see if a major studio's marketing department can make me an American star. As to Foreign, I still have a following."

"And you have a love for your audience."

"Aaa, they don't even satisfy me every other Tuesday."

"A respect then?"

"No! What respect? I respect the jingle in their pockets that should be in mine. Aaa, let's do this deal and do the world a favor. We'll anesthetize the teaming masses with good solid, simple entertainment. Ha! If nothing else, it will keep them off the streets!" Lydia laughed at her excellent joke.

"An admirable goal," Sara said, the slit splitting into a smile.

As we stood up to say our goodbyes, I coughed a few raspy

coughs and quickly poured more orange juice into my glass to moisten my dry throat. As Sara had her attention on Lydia, I slipped the sound cube I had palmed into the nearly full glass of orange juice. I sipped, then set the glass on the tray, feeling much better.

Sara saw us out, saying that one of her lawyers would be in touch with us at the Bel-Air on Monday. She closed the door to Tara, excited, I hoped, about tomorrow.

Back in the limo, as we pulled out of the driveway, I turned to Lydia and remarked, "You didn't drink much of your orange juice."

"Oh, do you think she noticed?" She said, displaying quick, professional concern. "But I told you, I hate orange juice—and that coffee!"

"Yes, I know. Sorry, but it was necessary."

"Why?"

"I needed an amplifier for the microphone."

"Nico, I know you will eventually make sense out of this, but if you must play your games—"

"I needed a glass of orange juice, well iced, to slip a bug into."

"A bug?"

"Yes."

"You mean, of course, a concealed listening device, not an insect."

"Of course. Look."

I pulled out of my pocket one of Petey's sound cubes. It looked exactly like an ice cube, clear except for the frosted fractured area in the center. I handed it to Lydia.

"A plastic ice cube? I don't understand."

"It's a microphone and transmitter built by a friend of ours. The clear encasement is made from a special slow-dissolving polymer. The guts of the piece are disguised as the opaque section in the center, including a microplastic battery, a tiny sliver of plastic made up of an electrolyte sandwiched by positive and negative electrodes. It has just enough juice to power the transmitter. The mic is at the tip of the fracture. You can see it extending from the center to the cube's surface. As it sits in your hand, the mic is not very good, but submerged in liquid, with the liquid amplifying sound waves, it is perfectly adequate.

"It was designed to be used briefly, leaving no trace of itself. When the polymer encasement completely dissolves, the center guts break up into little pieces of plastic that look exactly like orange or lemon pulp and get, we assume, washed down the drain. Total security."

By this time, Roee had instructed the driver to pull over and stop the limo behind a parked van on Baroda, a street not far from Sara Hutton's house.

"But why bug her now?" asked Lydia.

"Come on, let's get out."

We exited and dismissed the limo. Then Roee opened the rear door of the van.

In a pair of headphones, Newsstand Mike sat at a set of instruments. We jumped in with him, and Roee closed the door.

"We are bugging her to catch any quick conversations that may happen before Josephina clears away the tray," I said, now answering Lydia's question.

"A conversation among who? Sara and her servant?"

"No. Sara and Maxwellton James."

"I've got something," Mike said as he hit a switch.

"So, what do you think?" Sara Hutton was saying.

"An exciting prospect, obviously."

It was the voice of a man. It was a voice right down the middle. Neither too high, stretched, wispy, wimpy, or an itchy irritant. Nor a too deep, malevolently macho slug to your ears. It was a smooth, calm, calming slide of a voice, textured just enough to be interesting. It was a crooner's voice. A voice that made love. All forms of love. Especially the kind that blinds—and binds.

"We've done well placing you at Olympic, Sara, but that placement is under threat. This could give us exactly what we need."

"Still, she's going to want to call the shots."

"Oh, Sara, I think you're man enough to deal with that."

"I'm not so sure. My contract must be rock solid."

"Of course, but you've got lawyers to see to that. We should concern ourselves with the expansion Lydia Corfu could buy us. Think of the spread of our influence."

"Yes, it's tempting."

"Plus...."

"What?"

"I think we ought to invite her to the Castle for the next get-together."

"Are you kidding? It will kill the deal if she is totally against it."

"I don't think so. Did you hear the things she said?"

"Yeah, yeah, fine. Put down the masses. We all do it in casual conversation. The masses are asses; the leaders are peters, and there's a whole lot of sodomy going on. So what?"

"I'm willing to take the chance that she's not being frivolous. That there's some deep thinking going on there. If you want control of Olympic, and all our other ambitions, invite Lydia Corfu to become a member of the Communion. Then there will always be higher objectives we can call on if we come to a dispute."

"I'm not so sure."

"Sara, just do it. Do it for me. Call them up and invite them."

"Okay, but I'm going to want a lot from you if this blows my chance to buy out Olympic."

"That's no problem, Sara. You know I'm a giver."

"Josephina! Come and clear this tray!"

I nodded to Mike, and he turned the receiver off.

"We're in," Lydia seemed pleased.

"Yes," I said. "So it seems." I quickly looked at Roee. His eyes told me he agreed with me. We were in. But if Maxwellton James had expected us to leave a bug behind, which he was now possibly—and fruitlessly—looking for, then what we had just heard may have been nothing but playacting to snare us in. Which was a whole different quality of "In." Outside of precautions, though, what could I do?

It was not so much that the game was afoot—as that it was just unfinished.

16
LABOR INTENSIVE

Sleep was not my friend that night. I had expected to spend most of the next day giving some thought to the kind and quality of precautions I could take, but sometimes the brain has a more demanding work ethic than the essentially lazy body. It's one of the drawbacks of sentience. Around 12:30, I almost went into the library to sit down to some music and a view of the twinkles from the windows of Bel-Air mansions, but somehow, I knew that was too sedentary for this assignment. So I quickly dressed, went downstairs, grabbed the Porsche, and drove up to Sunset Boulevard, turning left to take it to the beach. The curves of Sunset, taken at a certain speed, cause one to metronome to a particular rhythm, which sets up a useful meditative state.

Bea. Her desires. Her naiveté. Her controlled beauty. Her outrage. Her death. Mike and his devotion. The arrogance of Sam Farber. The snobbery of Sara Hutton. The murderous pilot. The murderous banker. George.

Max.

Maxwellton.

Maxwellton James.

Warbirds and the Battle of Britain.

Never has so much been owed by so many to so few.

At the end of Sunset, I turned right onto Pacific Coast Highway and started moving up the coast, past Malibu, to a little restaurant I knew hidden in a cove—hidden except for its reputation and the massive sign on PCH that pointed the way. The Sailfish Bar and Grill has been a well-known coastline eating and drinking establishment since the Nineteen-forties. Patrick Dumphy, one of the classic Hollywood supporting players of the Thirties and Forties, founded it. Its patrons for its first years were mainly the Hollywood crowd, especially those with homes in Malibu. The place saw many enjoyable evenings packed with the faces and personalities of the oversize big screen best buddies, sweetest gals, sexiest vamps, and toughest guys, who were all near daily "acquaintances" of every man, woman, and child in America, but who were known by none of them. There was no sign on PCH pointing the way in those days, and the restaurant was a comfortable hideaway for these people. Patrick Dumphy was one of them. Every night it was like inviting his friends home for dinner. The stars could be "real" here, relax and enjoy themselves, have fights and have affairs, drink too much, and practice an honesty that was not allowed at other times and in other places. It was the Clubhouse, unofficially members only, and so, very exclusive.

Once Patrick Dumphy's crowd passed from the scene, by death or death of career, he was forced to open the restaurant to the plebes. His acting career was gone, and this was now the sole source of his income. Luckily newspaper columnists had made the place legendary, so once the sign went up on PCH, it wasn't hard to get the crowds to flock. Occasionally some of the old crowd did pop in during the late 50s and early 60s, but they were now just stars of nostalgia going there to be nostalgic. None of the "New Brats"—Dean and Hudson; Brando and Wood—as Patrick Dumphy called them would ever deign to go there. So the tourist trade paid the bills, and Patrick Dumphy drank up the profits.

When Patrick Dumphy died in the late 60s, his son, Patrick Jr., took over. He liked the tourists, and he milked them and bilked them, offering not very palatable food and dusty proximity to a glamour gone but not allowed to be forgotten. The Sailfish Bar and Grill became a bit of a joke—but never to Patrick Dumphy the

Third, who was essentially raised there, revered the memory of his grandfather and hated what his father did to the place. As sons often do, he rebelled against his father, leaving home young to become an adventurer, to become the kind of character his grandfather had portrayed in the movies.

I met Pat3, as almost everyone called him, in South Africa, where he had put together a group of mercenaries to storm Robben Island and break Nelson Mandela out of jail. This was Pat3's idea and Pat3's adventure. No one else wanted him to do it. Not even we knew Mandela, who had significant doubts about their eventual success, and some concern for his health if the operation were to happen. But Pat3, being a big-hearted Irishman who hates injustice and took it upon himself. It was a stupid idea. I was charged with stopping it and getting Pat3 out of the country, which I did with extreme efficiency. He hated me at first, but once things were explained to him, especially after he had read a personal letter to him from Mandela, thanking him for his concern but expressing the belief that there would eventually be a political solution to his problem and any rash action now could jeopardize that, he came around, and we became friends. As a friend, I suggested he stop trying to turn movies into reality and return home. This idea was abhorrent to him, but he said he would consider it.

Later, upon his father's death—which he heard about while trying to ferret a politically-minded Buddhist monk out of Tibet—he inherited the Sailfish Bar and Grill. He returned to it to find it in a desolate state serving horrible food to more than awful customers. Because of his left-leaning, big-hearted, liberal attitude, he quickly made friends with the New Hollywood. He shut down the Sailfish, restored it to its Forties seedy grandeur, got an incredible chef from the Carlyle Hotel in Manhattan, and reopened with a flare of fanfare. It quickly became the place for all the power players in Hollywood: Stars, directors, executives, lawyers, and agents, as well as the high-priced hairdressers, physical trainers, yoga gurus, and nattily attired sailor-Scientologists that were now so much a part of the landscape.

I turned left off PCH onto the steep little road leading to

Heaven's Cove and the Sailfish Bar and Grill. The one-story building sat right on the beach, backed by a large parking lot extended to the left to accommodate daytime beachgoers. To the right was a sheer rocky cliff, on top of which was a mobile home park. Moonlight bathed the cove, assisted by the incandescence of the restaurant and parking lot lights. There were only a few cars left. The last of the bar crowd was just going. The sound of them— loud drunk voices informing the world of their presence—and the sound of the ocean were all there was to be heard.

I pulled up close to the back of the building, by the kitchen door. Pat3 was standing there having a smoke. He greeted me as I got out of the car.

"Hey, Fixxer! How's tricks? And I do mean that literally."

I came up and shook his offered hand. "Tricks, in general, are fine, Pat3. It's certain tricks in particular that I'm having a problem with."

"Well, I'd give you a good meal, but we've shut down the kitchen. Got plenty of vodka, though."

"Don't need food; don't need a drink. What I need is some good honest labor."

"Ah. Well, we still have a load of the dishes from the last shift."

"Send your crew home. I'll get them done."

"You sure?"

"I need the work. I need solitude. Send them all home, and don't dock their pay. I'll leave a little bonus for them. Make sure they get that as well."

"Okay, Fixx, whatever you want, but do a complete and good job, will ya? I got a hell of a lot of Sunday Brunch reservations."

Pat3 entered the kitchen, and I went to the car to retrieve a CD boom box and some CDs. When I reached the kitchen door, three Latino men came out and clasped me around the shoulders with cheers and thanks. I had been this strange benefactor to them on several previous occasions. They never understood it, but they loved me for it, and if they had known my name, I'm sure they each would have had a child who answered to it.

As I walked into the kitchen, I momentarily regretted my actions. There were piles of dirty pots, pans, crystal, and china.

Pat3 had his coat on. The lights in the restaurant proper were out.

"The front's all locked up. You know how to lock the back and turn on the alarm." Pat3 started to leave, then stopped. "Say, should I be asking to see your Green Card?"

"You're almost as funny as your grandfather in *Hail of Bullets*."

"Ah, yeah, I liked that one. Well, good night, Fixx. Enjoy your weird hobby."

It wasn't a hobby. It was a simple technique. Occupy the body—free the mind. Work had practically been a religion to my father. All kinds, but especially menial labor. It was not so much the labor as the laborer he worshipped, "The poor bent backs of the poor," as he liked to say. He was, of course, a romantic. Unfortunately, his romance extended to participating in the labor to feel closer to the laborers. He would go out every summer and work on work crews, join assembly lines, dig deep in mines—and wash dishes at local greasy spoons. The fact that he was an academic and wrote a major work on the American Working Man never quite forgave him, in my mind, for dragging me along on many of his forays into the workaday world. In his mind, he was giving me "lessons no school could teach you." That was fine, but the bumps, bruises, calluses, strained muscles, aching back, pounding head, and withered soul still hurt. There was nothing I could do about the physical pains, but my soul I protected with my mind. I found that repetitious manual labor, taking up only the mechanically inclined areas of the brain, left free the more abstract loving gray glob to roam over thoughts, puzzles, problems, dreams, fantasies, and plans. I found manual labor to be oddly meditative. This is assuming, of course, that you had something interesting to meditate on. Although a comfortable chair, a stimulating drink, and exciting music are usually my preference when I wish to meditate, there are times when only a return to the days of my father-controlled youth will suffice. This was one of those times.

It should not be surprising to note that my current love of luxury also stems from those days.

I set the CD boom box down and plugged it in. I took out a CD, some works by David Diamond, a twentieth-century

American symphonist, a Copland without the chaps. I turned the volume up high and started his Symphony No. 1. The orchestra with bell began pounding out in a broad romantic sweep engulfing the room of stainless-steel sinks, copper kettles, and filthy china. I started the water running hot. I breathed in the steam. I was free with the soap. Suds dominated. I threw my hands into the clean infernal. The water burnt like hell. I loved it. I took a deep breath and started cleaning off the residue muck of expensive tastes, carefully getting each plate perfectly clean as Diamond transported me to a place far beyond this wet and soapy battleground.

Going over facts, I saw the future—or at least a reasonable facsimile. I started to change it, doing this to get that, arranging that to avoid this. It became a whole for me. If I dropped a pebble in at this end, I could see where the ripple landed at that end. I gathered my pebbles. I mapped out where I would drop them. Control of the ripples, that's what I was after.

Three hours later, just after five am, I was done. The kitchen looked great. I took a moment to be pleased, to be satisfied with a good night's work. Besides Diamond, the Duke had kept me company, with Gershwin and Porter chiming in at the end once most of my thinking was done. I gathered up the boom box and the CDs and left the building, securing it with its alarm. I put the boom box and CDs in the Porsche, grabbed my cell phone, and walked to the beach. It was cold and damp and dark, but I did not care; I had on a heavy long coat. I walked until I found a convenient spot against the cliff wall and sat on the sand. I set my watch alarm. I deep breathed myself into a special sleep for one hour.

xx

When I woke up, it was the start of dawn. I gave myself a moment to sit and watch the waves, which were silver in the gray light, and listen to the joyful cries of seagulls, happy that another day of feeding had arrived. Then I picked up the cell phone and called Roee.

"Talk."

"It's me."

"I figured. Norton usually takes Sunday off."

"I'm sitting on a beach."

"Yes, I can hear the seagulls. Is this beach, by any chance, in the continental United States?"

"I'm here by the Sailfish."

"Oh, and how is Pat3?"

"Prosperous by the number of dishes I've washed."

"Can't you burn incense and speak mantras like everybody else?"

"Sorry, but it's our peculiarities that make us endearing."

"And endearing you are, Fixxer. I take it there are marching orders."

"Yeah. Let's put in some phone calls."

"Can't this wait until you get back?"

"No. I like to talk when I'm ready to talk."

"It is fairly early on a Sunday morning."

"What are you worried about? It's not your Sabbath."

"Simple common courtesy."

"I try never to go in for anything common. Not to mention simple. First call: the Captain."

xx

"Fixxer, how are you?"

The Captain came on the line much more cheerful than I had expected.

"You sound almost happy to hear from me so early on a Sunday morning."

"Why not? You didn't wake me up. I'm showered and waiting for a pal to pick me up for some early morning golf. Eighteen holes; breakfast at the Country Club. It's how I like to spend my Sundays."

"Well, I need but a few moments of your time."

"Regarding what?"

"Bea Cherbourg."

"I knew you couldn't stay away."

"Indeed. You willing to help?"

"You make the calls, and I'll make the shots."

"Good. First, I'd like you to check out something for me."

"What's that?"

"Find out when the state started assigning Park Rangers to Hearst Castle, as opposed to just the normal tour guides. Then see if there is anything unusual about the people hired to fill the positions. Do a background check on them. Don't just take what's in their state files. You'll be looking for things hidden from or ignored by the state."

"What's up with Hearst Castle?"

"I'll have to explain that later, but I wouldn't be surprised if you'll find that these Rangers have somewhat less than admirable backgrounds."

"What do you want me to do when I get the goods? Have them arrested?"

"No. At least not yet. What I want you to do is look for a weak link. I want you to find one of the Rangers—outside of a guy possibly named George, Roee will supply a picture—find one of the Rangers with a past awful enough so that we can exploit it and force him onto our payroll."

"Okay. What else?"

"Just be available to take some time off. I also have some rather detailed instructions, but I'll give them to you tomorrow."

"Right."

"Things may get a bit—elaborate. If you would like, I'll happily add a bonus for this one."

"Hey! Didn't I offer to help? Just for helping's sake. Don't ever assume my word's not my bond."

"You have my admiration for that."

"Yeah, I know, but can I frame it and put it on the wall?"

"How's Mrs. Captain?"

"Grumbling like the golf widow she is, but otherwise doing fine."

"Good. We'll be talking."

"I look forward to it."

xx

The next call was to Petey.

"So you wanted to spend a couple of days in California?" I greeted him.

"Sure! Love to! When?"

"Soon, but first, that new and improved satellite of yours...?"

"Yes?"

"Can you hook into it from a laptop?"

"Tricky!"

"Twenty-five grand?"

"But then, so am I!"

"Roee will call you back with the details and a list of other supplies and needs."

"All right, Fixx! See ya soon!"

xx

Then we called Maloney in Chino.

"Roee and I want to come and talk to you about some particular flying conditions. Any hints you have would be appreciated."

xx

Next was Mike.

"Mike, I've got more work for you."

"Fine. Whatever. I'm yours."

"Contact Roee and have him update you on Henderson and Pinsker. Then, when I tell you, you will meet Henderson and Pinsker at the Hotel Bel-Air. While there, you will endeavor to make yourself conspicuous—nothing too loud and obnoxious, just something obvious. Roee will give you the complete scenario. Call him later today through Norton. As always, I will need you to do a very good job, but you'll do it by being incompetent."

xx

Finally, I called Lydia.

"I need you to take your performance from a nomination to a win."

"What?" she said in a groggy voice. "I was asleep."

"Well, of course, you were. Have room service send up a pot of coffee blend 32A. Usually, they only make it for me, but I'll be pleased to share it. What I have in mind for your performance will take a little rehearsal."

"I never rehearse!"

"For this performance, you will, my sweet Greek."

xx

The calls done; I looked up to see early morning joggers on the beach. They all looked happy and relatively carefree. They couldn't have been, of course. No one is.

xx

When I got home, Roee had a hot breakfast waiting for me. A cubed lamb omelet seasoned with rosemary; his unique hash browns made from small new potatoes; homemade sourdough bread, toasted to my standards, butter nicely displayed in a silver bowl, marmalade he had brought back from London filling the volume of a matching silver bowl, and, of course, a pot of black hot coffee. He joined me, and I discussed the details of the immediate future and how I would seek to control it to our advantage.

After breakfast, we left for the Hotel Bel-Air, sneaking back into our suite. A room service breakfast had been ordered for us and devoured by a couple of loyal employees I have on the hotel staff. We put the cart of leftovers out in the hallway. We then dressed in Henderson and Pinsker casual clothes, well-pressed slacks, pink Izod short-sleeve pullovers, and loafers with tassels. Then I called Lydia to invite her out for the day. When she heard our plans, she passed, declaring a day on Rodeo Drive in Beverly Hills more to her liking.

We left our room, went into the lobby, and received directions from the concierge to Santa Monica and the Museum of Flying. Then we got into our rented Town Car and headed in that direction.

It was not hard picking out the tail. He was good, but not good enough. We wondered if he was Sara's boy or Max's or working for both. It didn't matter. The information we wanted to impart was being imparted. Henderson and Pinsker were plane buffs. The tail joined us inside the museum, a very slick display of historic aircraft, and was treated to a boy-like enthusiasm rarely seen on the faces of these two usually much more dour legal professionals.

HOLLYWOOD
IS AN ALL-VOLUNTEER ARMY

17
THE BAD GUYS

We sat at the Hotel Bel-Air the next day, waiting for Sara Hutton's lawyer to call. At around two-thirty, she did. A cool, efficient woman, she confirmed from us the basics of the deal we were offering, as it had been explained to her by Sara, and set a time on Wednesday for us all to meet her in her office in Century City to discuss the matter in more detail. Up to that time, we had spent the day in small talk and going over specific financial arrangements, all of which bored Lydia considerably. She made outrageous faces as we read the mundane chit-chat from a script I had prepared, rolling her eyes; dislocating her jaw; sticking her tongue out farther than I would have guessed it could go—if I had ever been asked.

We knew the rooms were bugged. I had allowed it. It had been done on Saturday while we were at Sara Hutton's. A man had bribed a porter to let him into our suite, where he placed a series of bugs. All of which we later found and greatly admired but kept firmly planted. The porter, of course, belongs to me more than he belongs to the Bel-Air, and would normally have protected the sanctity of my room with his life, or, at least, to the extent of a good, solid beating. But I wanted the room bugged. I wanted Max and Sara to hear the mundane reality of Wall Street lawyers at work and play. I figured it would confuse them, especially if they suspected us. I suspected they did, but I didn't know to what extent, and I didn't know exactly what they imagined, but all that I was now doing was in preparation for the worse in both cases.

After the call had come in, we—Lydia and her two lawyers—left the hotel for an early supper somewhere. As we passed through the lobby, Pinsker and Henderson told Lydia all about the neat planes they had seen the day before. She was not impressed.

We got into the Town Car and quickly shook off the tail. Then we drove home to relax and drop the playacting, which, after a while, does grow weary.

That is, Roee and I dropped the playacting. I'm afraid Lydia had to put in some more hours as I made her rehearse a small but vital part of her upcoming performance that I was convinced she would be called upon to play. There wasn't much to memorize. Indeed there were no lines at all, but the acting had to be saturated with verisimilitude. When she satisfied my exacting demands, I told her she could quit and poured her a large brandy. She drank it somewhat crudely, forfeiting the delights of savoring for the joy of buzz.

"Ah!" she said with pleasure. Then she looked hard at me. "Nico, do you have any peanuts?"

I had no idea if I did or not. I turned to call Roee, but he was already entering the library with a bowl of the requested edible.

"Ah, bless you my child," Lydia said as she grabbed a handful. "So, now what?"

"I'm expecting a visitor, who you are welcome to meet as he may become critical to you. I believe he will be willing to stay for dinner, assuming, Roee, that you are grilling swordfish."

"I am. It's his favorite."

"And who is this visitor?"

"The Captain."

"Captain who?"

"Just the Captain."

"Oh. Like you are just The Fixxer."

"Yes, somewhat. He's my main—uh, contact—in local law enforcement. I find him useful on occasion."

"He's a policeman you have bribed," Lydia stated, reading through my euphemism.

"Are you shocked?"

"Please, I do not shock easily."

"Let's hope so. For we're betting on that, aren't we?"

xx

The Captain arrived at six o'clock and was happy to accept our invitation to dinner, although he said Mrs. Captain would probably be upset. But he would deal with that later. Besides, he preferred her meatloaf cold and in a sandwich with plenty of ketchup. He was quite taken by Lydia, whom, I'm sure, he found exotic. The Captain is like many American cops of his age: a Marine out of uniform, somewhat uncomfortable with changes in the country, and usually empathetic only with things Anglo-Saxon, even if they are not. The Captain, I should add for clarification, is six-foot-two, naturally thin, but just now taking on the bulk of middle age, with light brown hair that was probably blonde when he was a child, cut in the typical police-military style. The Captain is a man sold on the stated mandate of law enforcement. He is also a man who damn well knows that administration, bureaucracy, and the subtle-to-blatant intolerant bent of many attracted to police work muddies the waters of that mandate. He also thinks the pay stinks—and that he is worth much more—an attitude I exploited with my original offer of secret employment. I suppose this makes him a corrupt cop, except in this: I employed him not so much because I knew he could be bought but because I knew he had a charmingly childlike love of Justice, a concept not often made concrete in the officialdom of law enforcement. This "good" quality about him is more valuable to me and more malleable than any other quality he may have lacked in the standard norms of integrity.

After the introduction to Lydia and the pouring of drinks—the Captain and Lydia bonded over a blended malt whisky—we sat comfortably in the library as I gave the Captain a short overview of the pertinent past events, then sketched in my plan to bring Sara Hutton and Maxwellton James down, detailing Lydia's role in the proceedings. The Captain was impressed. Not the least by what Lydia had volunteered to do.

"But look," the Captain said, "I feel it's only right to warn you that, given what I've found out today, this thing is not free from danger. People involved in this have some violent records."

"Hey, it's drama! Real drama! Meat, not vegetables. I love it. Couldn't keep me away," Lydia declared with a straight back, high head, and uplifted—pride."

"Captain, you have to understand," I said, "this is the 'True Story' the film will be based on."

"What?"

"It's probably too Hollywood to explain. Why don't you go on with your report?"

"Well, I've had a hell of a day. I ran into some local roadblocks on this Ranger situation at Hearst Castle, but I managed to get to the right people and get the info out of them. Ten years in Internal Affairs gives you a real knack for interviewing civil servants. They got a real prominent sweat button you can push. Anyway, the story expanded into a federal connection. So, through Roee, I tapped into Petey to follow that up, which wasn't easy either, but I think we eventually tracked down the story. It's pretty incredible. Here's what we believe happened.

"About a year and a half ago, the state officials directly in charge of Hearst Castle received a threat in the mail. It came from some outfit that referred to itself as the Underclass Avengers. The threat was to blow up Hearst Castle. No reason was stated, no timeframe was mentioned, and no political statement was made. Well, you know, governments receive these kinds of letters constantly. It was turned over to the local San Simeon police, and they came in after hours and did a bomb sweep. Nothing was found."

"Why after-hours?"

"The people running the Castle didn't want to upset the tourists. That place makes money for the state, you know, which is ironic because the state almost turned down the Hearst family when they offered it to them. The state thought it was going to be a white elephant. Hugely expensive to keep up, and not enough interest from the public— especially seeing how it was so remote from any major tourist city, like San Francisco or L.A., but they took it, and the crowds flooded in from day one. It seems the common man loves to see how the elite live."

"Except for the common men in the Underclass Avengers," I said.

"Oh, yeah. Except for them. Anyway, no bomb was found, so they chalked it up to a nut case. Then a second letter arrived. This one was more specific. It outlined exactly the kind of bomb it would use—aluminum nitrate—and why Hearst Castle was the target. It seems the Underclass Avengers see it as the perfect symbol of the evils of what they call " The Overclass.""

"Can't have an Underclass without an Overclass," I reminded him.

"Don't get philosophical on me here, Fixxer; I'm trying to give a report."

"Sorry."

"Well, again, the matter was turned over to the local police, another bomb sweep, nothing was found, they still considered it as no serious threat, but then, somehow, this State Senator from that area, Joe Skinner, heard about it and got involved, made himself a pest, and demanded action. He wanted armed men on guard 24 hours a day. He wanted metal detectors and bag searches. Well, the Castle people were dead set against it, of course, saying it would ruin the whole experience of going to the Castle. Yeah, ruin the ticket sales they meant. They refused, end of story. Then a third letter arrived declaring that the Underclass Avengers were still planning to blow up Hearst Castle, but they hadn't yet decided if they would do it at night, with little loss of life, or during the day in high tourist season, with many lives lost. This was getting scary. Even the Castle people were ready to do something but didn't want to turn Hearst Castle into an armed camp. So Skinner gave them a palatable option. He offered to contact certain Federal authorities he knew who were well versed in terrorist activities and see if they would lend some men from this extremely secret anti-terrorist group that worked for, but somewhat independently of, both the CIA and the FBI. These were supposedly the best-trained men in this field. They were trained to operate subtly, without metal detectors, bag searches, that sort of thing. They would conduct hourly bomb sweeps very inconspicuously and, through hidden video cameras and just good old eye contact, they would keep monitoring for terrorists. Anybody suspicious, they would cut from the heard, so to speak, and gently question. They know the personality type so well, it was claimed, that no one could get past them. And—here was the beauty of the whole idea—Skinner suggested putting them in Park Ranger uniforms. It's a State Park facility, after all, and it shouldn't seem that unusual for a few Rangers to be around, and they can carry weapons. But they're Rangers, the weapons, to the public, seem almost ceremonial, just part of the uniform. This, Skinner said, would be far better than normal police or a bunch of guys in dark suits, sunglasses, and little earphones. Well, the Castle people bought it. It seemed to answer all their needs. So suddenly one day, boom, they've got these Guardian Angel Rangers hanging around making them feel secure."

"What's this Federal group they supposedly came from?" I asked.

"Well, this is where I had to use Petey. He tapped into the Fed computers and had to break through several encryption codes, he told me, to get the info. It seems these men weren't really a part of any anti-terrorist group. Still, they were, occasionally, individually and as a group, temporary and secret government employees, used for what one secret memo Petey found called 'crummy covert' operations. Real illegal stuff. When they were used this way, they were under the direct command of some guy named Stanley Sands."

"Stanley," I said, turning to Roee. He nodded in agreement with me that things were becoming apparent.

"Petey tells me he was murdered about a year ago," the Captain added.

"That's right," I said. "In a case that has never been solved."

"Nor does anyone seem eager to solve it," Roee added.

"Why not? One of our own?"

"'Our' has become a plastic concept at the agencies. Stanley was very much a stand-alone. Useful during a certain period in our history. Increasingly an embarrassment to more modern sensibilities. Stanley wasn't murdered as much as he was executed."

"Oh."

It was becoming an intriguing story. Lydia had gotten caught up in it. "This is exciting," she said.

"These are facts not for your amusement, Lydia, but for your edification." I'm afraid I snapped a bit too harshly. I turned to the Captain before registering Lydia's reaction and said, "Go on."

"Petey tells me that you'll find this interesting: Stanley Sands was the man who ran a Maxwellton James when James was running guns down to Central America and the man who afforded James protection for dealing the drugs he brought back up in exchange."

"Interesting," I said.

"Petey told me to make sure I told you this too: This Max James took over the old Hearst airfield about a year and a half ago. State Senator Skinner sponsored and godfathered the deal. This was just before the first letter from the Underclass Avengers arrived."

"Not surprising. For I'm sure, Maxwellton James is the Underclass Avengers. Although somewhat ironically so. He sent the letters to set up the proper paranoid atmosphere that allowed him to implement his plans. And Joe Skinner probably owes some allegiance to Max. Either financial or philosophical. It doesn't matter which. The results are the same. He helped Max 'storm' Hearst Castle without firing one arrow or battering with one ram. I think we'll eventually find that Max has unpacked his bags and sleeps there in the very bed once used by William Randolph Hearst himself. Once we know Max, that action will seem perfectly appropriate to his personality. But be that as it may, were you able to get anything on the individual Rangers?"

"Oh, yeah, and a lovely bunch they are too."

"How many?"

"Twelve."

"Interesting number. Involved with James during the gun running-drug dealing?"

"Yeah, most of them."

"But government commissions have been rare of late, I assume."

"Dried up completely. Sands had been ordered about two years ago to cut them all off. The agencies were trying to cover up this part of their past and limit the bad press and the embarrassment. Computer files, though, are computer files—somehow, they never get erased. Sands, of course, insisted on their continuing usefulness, but, uh, as he himself was pegged as old hat, no one was willing to listen to him. Maxwellton James had pulled out of all this quite a while before; once there were no guns to run to places, he felt good about running them to. Then he quit the drug situation to concentrate—ostensibly—on his antique plane hobby. Then a little over a year and a half ago, while Sands was sitting around finishing his time before retirement, James contacted him with a proposition. Organize the old gang; give them the false identity of a super-secret antiterrorist group within the government and front the lending of that group to the State of California, as long as California would pick up their expenses. A price was negotiated; Sands arranged all the paperwork. As far as California knew, as far as they still know, those Rangers at Hearst Castle are Federal antiterrorist experts protecting their little cash cow castle."

"And Maxwellton James got himself a twelve-man palace guard paid for by the State of California," I said.

"So it seems."

"Someone in the agencies has figured all this out, right?" Roee asked.

"Yeah. Too much internal housecleaning going on to hide it. It was discovered right after Sands retired and just before his death. I guess he had threatened to write a book."

"Damn dangerous things, "I said.

"What?"

"Books."

"Oh, yeah."

"No one on the Federal level has bothered to inform the State of California about any of this, right?" Roee asked, again displaying insight.

"That's right. They think it is dirty laundry better left in the hamper. That's why there were so many encryption codes Petey had to work his way through. Oh, uh, by the way," the Captain took a folded piece of paper out of his shirt pocket and handed it to me, "that's Petey's price for helping me out."

I unfolded the paper and looked at the figure. Much like Petey himself, it was too loud. I smiled. "Petey has always been a bit of a fantasist."

"Well, he said the codes were very complex."

"Yeah, and he probably broke them soon after they were installed. Believe me, Petey's hardest work on this was to punch a button and read the screen. I think this figure is negotiable." I slipped the paper into my coat pocket. "So give us the details on the twelve, Captain."

"Well, they all seem to be well-trained, paranoid mercenary fanatics on the ego trip that their efforts, no matter how illegal, not to say immoral, have the purifying goal of saving Western Civilization."

"Which, on the surface, is not a bad goal," I said.

"No, I suppose not," said the Captain.

"But one fairly superfluous and open to corruption if Western Civilization is actually in no need of saving."

"A debatable point," Roee said.

"Is it?" I challenged.

"But," Lydia asked somewhat perplexed, "they're bad guys, right?"

"Oh yes, they're bad guys," I said. "But then, aren't we all on occasion?"

"Fixxer!" Frustration had gotten to her.

"They have all, I assume, murdered; they lie incessantly; they have stolen; I'm sure they cheat at cards and with women; they have extorted, assaulted, agitated, and hooked very young people on drugs, and it is more than likely that they no longer honor their mothers and fathers if they ever did. If all this makes them bad guys in your book, Lydia, then they're bad guys. That is not germane to our actions, however. For us, they are the enemy, good or bad, and we have elected to oppose them, so we will. Effectively, I'm sure." I turned back to the Captain. "What did you get on our George?"

"George Alonzo. He's what's known as a utility man, a human

tool. Use him for the odd jobs. Always freelance. Done everything from simple rough stuff to hits. From protection services to being a surrogate avenging angel. Crazy, of course, but crafty. He's a bit of an artist in his way. He's considered creative."

"Yes, I said, rubbing my right eye, "I can attest to that."

"Given the history you've explained, I assume he won't be in plain sight when you get up there."

"That's what I expect too."

"But he'll be around. You know that. Bit of a wild card."

"Understood. Now, our turncoat? Have you got a candidate?"

"Yeah. Barnes. Sheila Barnes."

"A woman?"

"Doesn't stop her from being a bad guy. Sheila Barnes was a Marine Sergeant dishonorably discharged for sexual harassment."

"Lesbian?"

"Hell no. It was her very male Major, a Medal of Honor Vietnam Vet, who was the—uh—victim. I think she had overweening pride regarding the power of her pussy—Ah, sorry if that was too crude of a way to put it, Miss Corfu."

"That's okay. I have not a little pride in my own."

"Ah—oh—okay. Well, anyway, a few good men were too few for Sheila Barnes. She came out disgruntled. Hooked up with this group, I suspect, to try to recapture that old fraternal feeling."

"So what do we have on her to get her on our side?" Roee asked. "Murder? Extortion? Drug dealing?"

"No. Her children."

"Children?" Lydia questioned.

"Well, the odds were against her, weren't they? Even with the Pill. She has two. A boy and a girl. They're both in a private boarding school in England. By all accounts, she's a good mother."

"What are you suggesting?"

The Captain looked at me. It wasn't an easy look. "Have them kidnapped."

"What?" Lydia was outraged.

The Captain continued. "We would never hurt them, of course, but Sheila Barnes doesn't know that."

There was pleading in Lydia's voice. "Nico, this is getting—"

There was a hardness in mine. "You know what we need this woman for. It's your scene. She's essential for its success, and her being a woman is perfect for it. I told you, my sweet Greek: Aren't we all on occasion."

I turned to Roee. "Call Hamo. See if he would be willing to attend to this."

xx

The Captain detailed the ten others: They were all variations on the theme of tough guy rationalizing a basic antisocial bent by claiming that the curve was just a detour to a better society. After he had wrapped up, we entered the dining room and enjoyed Roee's swordfish dinner. It was, of course, delicious, that hardly needs to be noted, but by reporting it, I relive it—satisfaction times one and a half.

xx

At five am the following day, Roee and I drove to Chino to the Planes of the Past Air Museum to meet with Bagwell. This had been the first permanent air museum in the country. It was founded in 1957, only twelve years by the calendar since the end of World War II. In those bright days of Eisenhower-the-president-looking-like-a-gray- grandfatherly-small-town-banker in his suit, as opposed to Eisenhower-the-warrior in his medal-bedecked uniform, that last romantic war must have seemed ages ago. The planes that had helped win that war were probably scoffed at as museum pieces in the then 'now' of the jet-age-becoming-the-rocket-age. Ed Bagwell didn't take it as an insult but as inspiration. So, out east of Los Angeles, just east of Pomona, right in the middle of dairyland, he started taking rusty old "tin birds" and restoring them to their former glory.

Our Bagwell was his son, a sibling to war birds. His expertise in them was beyond intelligence and had become instinctual.

It was a fast, early morning drive out the Pomona Freeway to the Chino Airport, where the museum was located. An appropriate place. It had been one of the first training fields when the war broke out. The old barracks were still standing. We arrived just after six am. Petey had already arrived and was setting up his equipment. Bagwell was fascinated by the equipment but couldn't understand what it was all about. We took him aside and explained that we needed to fly his two Spitfires again today, but under particular, indeed, peculiar conditions which we would simulate. He was shocked by our proposal and was on the verge of refusing when I opened a canvas bag I had been carrying. In it was two million dollars in cash. One million for each plane in the unlikely—we hoped—event of tragedy striking us. Or, more to the point, of us striking tragedy.

Finally, Bagwell agreed when we added that two-and-a-half percent of the bag's contents would be donated to the air museum if all went well.

He and a crew got the Spitfires ready as we helped Petey adjust his satellite dish. Once contact was made, we changed into flight suits and helmets and climbed into the planes. Despite the insurance in the canvas bag, I could see Bagwell grit his teeth and grimace when Roee and I started taping the heavy black construction paper to the inside of the plane's bubble-shaped canopies, cutting off all view of the outside world. We checked our radio link with Petey. It was strong and clear. Then we both, completely blind, taxied onto the runway and took off into the early morning sky.

There were some nervous moments, but, on the whole, our trial flights were successful.

But then, of course, no one was shooting at us.

xx

We were finished by ten o'clock. We thanked Bagwell and gave him the $50,000. I told him he should take some of it and have a complete physical. We may have done some damage to his heart. As we helped Petey pack up, he explained the arrangements he had secured. They all seemed fine. Then he gave us the package for Lydia, part of the order of supplies Roee had put in. We opened it.

Petey took out the particulars and explained the use of each one.

"You're sure this is going to work?" I demanded to know.

"Hey! What? I developed it myself!"

"If it doesn't—"

"Yeah, yeah, I know! You'll slit my throat, reach down my gullet and yank out my heart!"

"I'll be angry enough to."

"If it doesn't work, I'll give you the knife! Okay?"

"Okay."

We drove back to L.A., watching the clouds gather overhead, clouds predicted to bring light showers by that evening. We went straight to the Bel-Air Hotel, parked on the little used side street where we kept the Porsche, and entered the grounds through a well-camouflaged gate and our suite through the private garden entrance. I turned off the direction-specific digital player that had been pumping out morning sounds of Henderson and Pinsker waking up; showering; making phone calls to the office in New York; ordering breakfast from room service and eating it; discussing the fact that we had no appointments that day, so it was, essentially a free day. Subterfuge aided and abetted by our confidants in the Hotel.

It was now near noon. Pinsker suggested we go for a swim. I protested, saying there was some paperwork. Pinsker insisted. So we got into bathing trunks, went to the pool, swam, then gratefully fell asleep on the lounge chairs by the oval pool.

The hotel staff quietly covered us with thick, long terrycloth robes, not wanting to disturb us, for it was just a little cool.

HOLLYWOOD
IS AN ALL-VOLUNTEER ARMY

18
NOSTRILS OF A SNAKE

We met with Sara Hutton's lawyer on Wednesday. Anne Barnett was a humorless professional who took seriously the fact that her job was to look after the interests of her clients. She was not a Hollywood lawyer. She was a corporate lawyer with many dealings in the international world of finance. Her office had been decorator designed and was attractive and comfortable but void of personality. Her desk was organized and uncluttered. She spoke to her staff courteously, but each request was a demand. She asked very tough questions and probed intensely the deal we were offering. I believe we satisfied her—just.

As the meeting was wrapping up, a call came in from Sara Hutton. Anne Barnett put it on the speakerphone.

"So you've worked it all out, all the deal points are set, and we're ready to roll, right?"

Everybody laughed, for everybody knew she expected it.

"Pretty near, Sara, pretty near, but you know how these things are," Anne Barnett said. "We have more discussions and some due diligence to do yet. On both our sides, I would think."

"Yes, I agree," Pinsker said.

"But, in the main," Anne Barnett continued, "the basis is there for negotiations."

"Good, good, but we all know how long that will take, don't we?" I asked. "I hope, Anne, you'll not tie Lydia up too long. She's got a TV station to run back in Athens."

"Well, certainly, the attorneys can handle most things. But I would like Lydia to meet my partners, who will also be heavily involved. Unfortunately, they won't be back until next week. Can you extend your stay until then?" she asked Lydia.

"Well—" Lydia started.

"Oh, sure she can. Look, Lydia, I'll keep you entertained. In fact, we should spend some time together. We're contemplating a marriage here. We shouldn't just leave it up to the yentas. Let's get to know each other. Got any plans for this weekend?"

"I haven't seen my husband for a while. I was going to go home to Athens and jump into our conjugal bed."

"Oh. Well, would he be disappointed if you didn't?"

"Wouldn't you be?"

"Well...."

"But business is business. I can stay."

"Good. Uh, Anne, I don't want to take up your precious time or bore you with the mundane here. Perhaps you have something to do while I finish talking with Lydia?"

Anne was happy to take the hint and excused herself. Once the door had shut, Sara spoke:

"Lydia, do you like flying?"

"It depends whether you're talking a private jet or commercial. If commercial, then whether you're talking First Class, Middle Management, or Steerage."

"No, no, I mean, do you like airplanes; the history of flight?"

"Not particularly. Why should I? Unless I owned an airline, of course. Even then, what's the past got to do with shipping bodies today? The boys here seem to, though, they were bothering me about some old planes they saw just the other day."

"Ah. Mr. Henderson and Mr. Pinsker. I almost forgot you were there."

"A good lawyer knows when not to be a mouthpiece," I said.

"Really? Like negative space in art, I suppose. But you're into airplanes, uh?"

"We both fly, yes," Pinsker said. "And we have quite a collection of aviation art."

"Well then, you should be excited about this, and Lydia, believe me, you'll enjoy this. I'm a pilot also, have been since I was a teenager, and I have a real passion for old classic airplanes. It's the romantic in me, I guess. I got introduced to them while I was at college by a man who has become a particularly good friend of mine. Well, he's now operating the San Simeon Air Museum, and we try to get together about once a month to fly these old warbirds from World War II. We're doing that again this weekend. Now what I like to do, is invite some people from the industry up, executives both here at Olympic and from other companies around town, give them a bit of an air show, then that night we get together for some general discussion about the state of our industry. Sort of like a retreat."

Lydia was aghast. "Sara, you get together with your competitors?"

"Sure, Lydia. As you know, it's a small industry; we hardly have secrets from each other anyway. So why not foster a communal spirit? That said, I must say I very carefully handpick the participants. It's considered quite an honor, among the know, to attend one of my retreats."

"Really? Then, of course, I must go."

"Good, good, I think you will find it illuminating, Lydia. We get pretty—well—deep in our discussions about the industry. It's not all just glamour and glitz for some of us; we're very serious about this business, and all seem to share a particular outlook. In getting to know you, I feel that you may think along the same lines."

"If the lines lead to money, I do."

"Lydia, you're a deeper thinker on the subject than you're giving yourself credit for, I'm sure of that, but we are all so used to portraying the bottom line as the only line because we think that's what's expected of us. Among the groups I put together, we can be comfortable and drop that—let's face it, Lydia—stupidly macho stance and concentrate on the true social aspects of what we do. It's refreshing. I'm sure you'll find it so as well, and, in any case, if we have a marriage, you'll need to know where I'm coming from. It would be unethical of me not to reveal it to you."

"Sure, sure, I appreciate that."

"And bring along the boys. I hate for them to miss the planes."

"That's very kind of you, Ms. Hutton," Pinsker said.

"Think nothing of it. Now, I can provide a limo if you would like."

"Well, where is this place?" Lydia asked.

"Uh," I broke in. "It's up the coast. About halfway between here and San

Francisco."

"You know it then?"

"Oh, yes. Quite well. I was going to suggest to Ms. Corfu that we should drive up that way if we had the time. I thought she would enjoy seeing the coast."

"Henderson, I grew up on an island. I've seen many coasts."

"Oh, but he's right. The California coast is special."

"What I would like to suggest, Lydia, is that we drive up the day before in the Town Car. That way, I can show you some of the highlights. San Simeon has some perfectly comfortable motels to stay at that night."

"Motels?" Lydia said, wondering if their walls would be slimy to the touch.

"Oh, come on, Lydia, don't be such a snob. It sounds like fun, and don't worry about a motel for Saturday night. You'll be my guests at an extraordinary place I'm sure you'll like. I'll have my office fax all the details to your hotel. The Bel-Air, right?"

"That's right," Pinsker confirmed.

"Fine. Lydia, this will be great fun, you'll see. I've got to run now; I've got New York on the other line. Bye."

The line clicked off. We all looked at each other. Lydia took a deep breath and then let it out. I think she had just, for the first time, truly realized that the game was going forward, but then she smiled. To reassure us. Which was more than I could do for her.

xx

Around nine-thirty the following day, we received a visit from

Mike at the Hotel Bel-Air. He came in wearing some old, faded, slightly torn jeans; a sweatshirt extolling the virtues of Prescott, Arizona; an old Army fatigue jacket and his well-soiled Sherman Oaks Newsstand baseball cap. He went to the front desk and asked for Henderson and Pinsker in a voice not subtle. The more-than-subtle desk clerk directed him to the white house phones. Mike went to them, gaping at the lobby as he had been instructed to, and called us.

Pinsker went out to collect him and escort him to our garden suite. The previous Monday, Roee had thoroughly briefed Mike on the plan, who Henderson and Pinsker were, and what was expected of him. When he arrived in our suite, he was definitely, "in the moment," looking furtive and giving furtive glances.

"This is Mr. Henderson," Pinsker introduced me. I also was in the moment. I stood ramrod straight in the middle of the living room on the thick, florid rug that defined the area and laid on the suite's highly polished wood floor. Mike headed toward me with his hand stretched out but stopped as he reached the rug, wondering if he should tramp on it with his much-scuffed, probably not well-wiped work shoes. As I made no move, he had no choice but to suffer the pang of trespass and slam his thick, heavy soles onto the delicate pale pink flowers weaved into the rug. None of this could be heard through the small microphones of the well-placed bugs, of course, but the atmosphere all this generated, I was betting, could be felt.

"Uh, hello, Mr. Henderson. I'm Mike—"

"No last name!" I sharply cut him off. "I don't care to know it. Is Mike your real first name?"

"Yes."

"A pity."

"Sorry."

"It wasn't your fault, I'm sure. Sit down. Help yourself to coffee, juice, or Coke if you want." I pointed to a tray of refreshments on the glass-top table before the couch.

Mike looked around. "Got any beer?"

"It's a bit early, isn't it?"

"Not when someone else is paying."

"If you must, then. In the refrigerator."

Pinsker directed Mike to the refrigerator in the kitchen area. He opened it up and was delighted to see bottles of Corona. He grabbed one, twisted off the top, and returned to the living room.

"Sit," I commanded as I sat on an ornate armchair with a back straight enough to keep my posture formidable.

Mike sat dead center on the fat, luxurious couch, somewhat sinking into it. He took a long drawl of the beer and then let out a breath of pleasure as if to say, "Thanks." He looked around the suite while he waited for me to speak. Which I didn't do immediately, so he finally spoke up.

"This is really a nice hotel room."

"It's not a room. It's a suite."

"A suite?"

"Yes."

"*Sweeet.*"

"Oh. Do you really think so?"

"Yeah, sure." There was a tinge of surprise in his answer as if he had not expected me to continue the small talk.

"I find it too feminine," I said. "I find the decoration of most hotel rooms, especially the costlier ones, to lean far too much to the feminine. Don't you?"

"Well...."

"That painting behind you, for example."

Mike twisted to look up at a tapestry-like painting of five stylized swans on stylized water.

"Is that something any man—you, for example—would ever choose to look at if it weren't forced upon you?"

"Uh, no, I guess not, but then, you know, my idea of art is movie posters."

"Movie posters?"

"I like movies."

"Well, yes. Who doesn't?"

"No, I mean, I *really* like movies. Anybody can tell you that about me."

"Anybody?"

"Yeah, sure."

"Say, the Pope, for example?"

"Well...."

"Or the Chairman of the Joint Chiefs of Staff?"

"No, you know, what I—"

"Or any one of the stars of any one of your favorite movies of the last five years? Could they tell me that you *really* like movies? Or would they answer any inquiry by me with, 'Mike who?' indicating that they not only can't tell me that about you but that there is no you to them, that you do not exist to them, even to the extent of insignificance? Do you think that could be the case?"

"Uh, well—"

"From now on, Mike, speak when spoken to, and do not intrude your biography into the proceedings. Okay?"

"O—okay."

"Mike, our friends here in L.A. tell me you're usually willing to do odd jobs for cash, no questions asked."

"Yeah, sure! You don't earn much money working a—"

"Mike!"

"Oh, okay, sorry."

"Would $5,000 for three days of work be sufficient?"

"Yeah, sure! I mean, just barely, but okay."

"Do you mind an element of danger?"

"Fuck no! Makes life more interesting."

"It could make life more dead."

"Well," Mike said with a nonchalance he had rehearsed. "It's not like I have a family who would grieve."

"Right. Here's the situation. Mr. Pinsker and I are doing business with an important person in this town. We are going to be this person's guests this weekend. Now when Mr. Pinsker and I do business with important people, especially when we take out time to socialize, we always like to document the proceedings."

"How do you do that?" Mike asked in all innocence.

"Through our briefcases."

Mike snorted out a laugh.

"Mike—you seem to be a fairly useless member of society. Laughter at your betters is not really in your purview."

"Sorry, Mr. Henderson, I wasn't really laughing at you. I—"

"Remember the five thousand, Mike. Hold that as a goal in your puny little mind, then shut up and listen to me."

"Yeah, right, okay."

"Obviously, these are not normal briefcases. We have gone to quite a bit of expense to improve them. Each one is a self-contained digital video camera and short-range transmitter."

"Really?" The boy in Mike popped up. "You're kidding?"

"Don't question me, Mike. I find it irritating. Go open up one of the briefcases." Mike got up awkwardly out of the plush, clutching his Corona, spilling a bit on the couch. ,Oh, shit! Sorry."

"Mike, maybe you're not the right man for this job."

"No, no, look, I can do it, whatever it is. I'm just nervous, that's all."

"What do you have to be nervous about?"

"You."

"Me?"

"Look, don't take this as an insult, but you're a scary bastard."

I laughed a laugh tinged with as much evil as possible without lapsing into melodrama. This was calculated, of course, as I was playing to the particular crowd of two that I assumed was listening in, basing the direction of my performance on the old saw, "It takes one to know one."

"Open the briefcase," Pinsker re-instructed Mike with impatience.

Mike moved over to a small, round dining table on which the two briefcases stood. He opened one. Inside was the usual complement of files, legal pads, an electronic notebook, pens, pencils, etc.

"I'm sorry. I don't see it," Mike said, perplexed.

"That's the point, isn't it?" I said, "But I guarantee you that, built into the shell of the case are all the electronics that we need, laid out in the same pattern as the tartan cloth that lines the cases. It helps to confuse the X-ray machines. Super thin batteries power the unit."

"But—but where's the camera?" Mike asked, inspecting the case closely.

"Mr. Pinsker?" Henderson said by way of instruction.

Pinsker walked over to the briefcases. He pointed to the small, rounded brass lock in the center of the unopened case. It was not a combination lock, digital lock, or anything high-tech, but a good, old-fashioned key lock with two small holes, looking somewhat like the nostrils of a snake, sitting in anticipation of a small two-pronged key. Pinsker pulled out of his pocket the key for the unit and showed it to Mike, pointing out that, instead of two prongs, it had only one on one side, the other having been removed. This was noticeable only if one took a good look. Pinsker then inserted the key in the lock and turned it. He pulled the key out and very subtly twisted the dome-like lock, pointing the snake nostrils at Mike. He then pointed out a small monitor that sat on a side table.

"Oh my god!" Mike exclaimed as he looked at the clear black & white image of himself on the monitor.

"It's a micro snorkel camera," I said, "built into the lock with the lens positioned to view out of one of the holes of the lock. The other hole accepts the one-pronged key. When you turn it, it unlocks the briefcase and turns on the unit. The lock is on a swivel base, so you can position both the case and it to get precisely the shot you want. The images the digital camera picks up are transmitted to the receiver-monitor. The unit can transmit within a radius of five miles.

"Now your job is going to be to sit in a motel room just a few miles from where we are going to be and monitor our transmissions and record them on digital videotape. You will get two feeds from the two briefcases, so you will have a double receiving unit. When we are all done, if all goes well, we will meet you at a prearranged location close to your motel, collect the equipment, and pay you your five thousand. If, while you are monitoring, you see either of us come to harm or if we do not show up at the prearranged meeting place, you will have instructions on where to send the tapes. Within days a customer at the newsstand will buy a copy of Le Figaro from you for five thousand dollars and change. Do you understand all this?"

"Yeah, sure."

"Good. Mr. Pinsker will give you a short course in operating the receiver unit and the recorders. Then you will aid him in packing it up. A bellhop will then take it out to your car. Tomorrow you will drive up to San Simeon. Do you know where that is?"

"Yeah, sure. Where the castle is."

"That's right. You will drive up there immediately upon leaving us. You did pack a bag as instructed."

"Yeah."

"Good. Just south of where the castle is, there is a row of motels on Highway One. Check into one of them. I don't care which, as long as it isn't the Cavalier. Set up your equipment, then lie low. Do not—I repeat for emphasis—do not call attention to yourself while there. The transmissions will start coming in sometime on Saturday, so be at your post non-stop during that day—lay in a store of food and drink. Nonalcoholic, I must insist. If you happen to see Pinsker or me late tomorrow in the general area, do not acknowledge us. Is that understood?"

"Yeah, sure, but what about my upfront expenses? You know, gas, food, the room."

I sighed. It was a wonderfully world-weary and piqued sigh. "I suppose a $250 per diem would be adequate?"

"A per what?"

"I will pay you $250 daily for three days to cover expenses."

"Really? 750 bucks? You mean beyond the five grand?"

"Yes, beyond that."

"Cool."

xx

Later, after we had left the hotel and snuck home, we celebrated our performance at a gathering of the troops: Mike, Lydia, the Captain, Petey, and Hamo on the speakerphone from London. Mike was laughing, somewhat uncontrollably, as he explained how I had managed to really "scare the shit" out of him even though he knew I was just playing a part. Everybody else was smiling, enjoying Mike's nervous pleasure. I was not.

"People!" I sharply called everybody to order. "It was a necessary charade. Part of a calculated subterfuge to send mixed signals to James and Hutton. Are we sincere? Or are we not? Are we—from their point of view—evil? Or are we not? If we are evil—is our evil contrary to theirs, or complementary, just good old-fashioned commercial evil, self-contained in our desire for profit and power, therefore evil they can co-opt? Is it evil that would find their evil attractive? I am convinced that our original game of getting them to accept Lydia as a serious buyer of Olympic Pictures has been found out. They know something more than that is involved, but I'm just as convinced they don't truly know what our game is. Therefore they continue to play. They can't afford not to. They must know. Our advantage is that they would never suspect that we would ever go to all this trouble just to avenge the death of Bea Cherbourg, an incident that has faded into insignificance for them, I'm sure. They would never expect a motive as pure as that, as—"

"Wait a minute," Lydia interrupted, looking at me as a wife might if I had just inadvertently told her of a dalliance with another woman. "What happened to the filthy lucre you would realize from this?"

"Lydia, my sweet Greek, there is nothing so filthy as the coin of revenge."

"You just said the motivation was pure."

"Ah, well—"

"I hate pure motivations. I don't trust them. They lull people into the fantasy that they must win because their story must have a happy ending, so they don't stay on guard. They don't work hard or pay attention to what they are doing. You know, like fatalistic cultures that never learn how to drive cars properly because, what the hell, their day and time are already set down anyway, so it's fucking crash, bang, boom, all fucking day long! I mean, have you ever taken a taxi in Taiwan? Who was this fucking Bea to you anyway?"

"She was nobody to me," I said calmly as Lydia fought the urge to hyperventilate. "She was Mike's special friend."

Mike blushed and lowered his eyes.

Lydia gaped for a second. Then she said, "Aaa, you Americans! You're such fucking cowboys!"

"I told you!" Hamo's voice came over the speakerphone.

"So, where's your reward going to be? In heaven?" Lydia asked with some anger.

"What do you care? Yours will most decidedly be here on Earth."

"If I'm not killed!"

"True. If you're not killed."

Mike spoke up. "Look, Lydia—"

"Don't talk to me, you lovesick little man!"

"Well, if it makes you feel any better!" Petey loudly chimed in. "I'm doing it just for the filthy lucre!"

"Then you are to me like a god." Lydia grabbed Petey's face and kissed it.

"Yeah, that fits!" Petey said, delighted after he had been let go.

"Lydia," Roee said dispassionately. "I fully expect the Fixxer to profit from this endeavor."

"You do?" I asked, bemused and not a little confused.

"I took it upon myself, with the aid of Norton Macbeth, to contact Jim Duncan."

"Used to be president of Universal."

"Yeah, left during a shake-up to 'form his own production company.' He hates producing. He finds it too—too real, I suppose. It's tough work, you know. Duncan misses the power of being a studio head, of dealing only with peppering out a few Yeses into a vast field of Nos, the fantasy of budgets, the evenings out with stars he's tried to take advantage of during the day. I asked him what it was worth to him if we could arrange Sara Hutton's fall from grace and his ascendancy to the presidency of Olympic Pictures. We agreed on one and a half million. I figured it couldn't hurt to have a side game going."

"Roee, that's a fine initiate, especially as Sara's fall is already in the works," I said. "But Duncan's ascension?"

"Haven't quite got that figured out yet, but I assumed, you, being such a clever boy, that you would think of a way."

"Your faith in me is awe-inspiring."

"Plus, he's a Duncan. You know, like the yo-yo. Give him a little jerk, and I'm sure he'll spin back up."

"I'm not sure he isn't a little jerk himself, but I get your point.

So, Lydia, I am rescued from do-goodness. Are you pleased?"

"Well...." She scowled. It's a look I had not previously seen on her. It would have been unattractive save for the tinge of the little girl that was included. "Maybe on alternate Tuesdays."

"Good. Then let's move on. Mike, I think you're all set. Any last questions?"

"No. I should leave. I was supposed to have left a couple of hours ago."

"You didn't because you've already blown some of the $750."

"I have?"

"Yes, on not inexpensive liquor."

"And you'll show up late and a little drunk," Roee said.

"No. A lot drunk, I think. At least, apparently so. Not, I caution you, Mike, in reality."

"Okay."

"Max's men will be on the outlook for you. They will just about have given up when you pull in. Very conspicuously. They won't be able to miss you."

"What about George?" the Captain asked. "He might recognize Mike as the snooper at the air museum. Supposedly Mike's never been up there."

"I doubt if George is the kind of talent Max would put on simple surveillance. As you pointed out, George will stay in the background. Mike, you know your motel?"

"The Silver Surf. Room 11."

"All right. Good luck."

Mike shook hands all around and left.

"Captain, you all set?" I asked.

"Yes, I've got personnel up there and down here."

"And the replacements?"

"I got them."

"Are they pilots?"

"You bet."

"Good. Petey?"

"I'm as ready as a bitch in heat!"

The Captain, who always finds Petey amusing, chuckled. "Petey, I've said it before, and I'll say it again—you are one sick puppy."

"I meant Joan Collins!"

"Hamo?"

"I've got the kids."

"Their condition?"

"Having the time of their lives. Not sure Euro Disney will survive, though."

"Captain, has Sheila Barnes been informed that we are holding her children?"

"She has, and she is ours."

"Okay. Good."

I noticed that Lydia had not been paying attention. Her focus was somewhere else. "Lydia, if you want to back out, this is the time."

She came to. She looked at me. At the others. Back to me. "Aaa, what for? You're my cowboy hero. You'll protect me."

"That's right, and you'll forget about me when you become the Queen of Hollywood."

"That's okay. I think you would rather ride off into the sunset anyway."

"Could be you've discovered the true me."

I turned my attention to the whole group. "Let's have a pleasant drive up the coast tomorrow. Everybody should enjoy it and relax. Saturday will be eventful and possibly nonstop. With any luck, we will rest on Sunday without having to nurse too many wounds."

19
"I ONLY FEEL NAKED WITHOUT CLOTHES"

We spent the night at the Bel-Air and, early in the morning, packed up the Town Car and took off, taking Sunset to PCH, turning right to head up the coast. I drove, Lydia sat in the front passenger seat, and Roee sat in the back. Despite the pleasure of driving along the California coast, an activity that engenders breezy chatting, Lydia was unusually quiet, setting the tone for the drive. Without admitting it, she was having butterflies about more than just her performance. I had given her plenty of opportunities to quit, but she had turned down each one.

I usually would admire such resolve, but I was unsure about hers. Often, we can act against our instincts if other forces intrude—hungers, desires, irrational wants. Was she still in the game because of the rewards she expected, ignoring that the potential of danger had intensified since that first afternoon in Hamo's office when it all seemed like a profitable lark? Or was a long-buried, rarely-admitted integrity forcing her to keep this contract? Integrity she may hardly have recognized, thus found confusing. Possibly it was just a silly bravado. She did not want to be seen as a quitter. Lydia was of that generation of women who had forced themselves into what traditionally were men's territories, who never got used to not proving themselves. There was no rest for the weary feminists of her type. Then again, it may have been something more profound and, quite frankly, more disturbing than any of these. Was she concluding that she was fighting on the wrong side, more that she knew, because of my unfortunate slip, that this was a battle of opposites? This worried me the most. She was not incapable of private scheming. Would I find her more of a liability than an asset when we were in the thick of it?

It's never easy figuring out the true motivations of other people. Other people are always foreign to us. While, ironically, being native to our needs.

When we got to Santa Barbara, I decided to stop for an early lunch. As beautiful as most of Los Angeles is ugly, Santa Barbara is an almost too perfect Pacific comfort zone. Big houses; large ranches; fine and expensive hotels, all like jewels dropped into the setting of sea breeze polished brilliant precious blue and green metal. Anchored to Earth by thousands of palm tree plugs, Santa Barbara should be a floating island rising above the mundane; that would make sense. Roee and I have often talked of relocating there, but we worry that the lack of friction would too cool us to the harsh realities of humans, which we have found too amusing to forgo.

"When I lived in L.A. before, I never came up here." Lydia was talking again as we sat in a restaurant gifted with views of both the ocean Santa Barbara faced and the green hills it backed into. "I'd heard of it, of course, but I had no idea what a little paradise this was."

"Many people in the industry live here," Roee told her.

"Really?"

"It's not that far from Hollywood. Even for its new queen," I said. "Certainly closer than Corfu is from Athens. Especially by helicopter."

"Lot of money up here?" she asked, referring not to the actual coin but to those who hold it dear.

"Of course. Beauty is in the purse of the be-hoarder," I said.

Lydia looked at me and met my eyes for the first time that day. "You are a strange, if lovely man, Nico. I can't figure you out."

"A fruitless effort, believe me," Roee said with a smile.

"To be 'figured out.' What would that do to a person?" I asked. "Set him in stone, stopping his heart? That's no way to die."

"Yes, but at least you get a ready-made statue for your memorial." Roee winked at Lydia, encouraging her not to take me seriously.

Ignoring Roee's wink, Lydia said to me, "Knowledge is power."

"That's the old saying," I replied.

"No one has power over you."

It was a statement of fact. "Only Roee. But that's because he knows my palate."

"So I have learned at least a little about you."

"Yes, I can feel the stiffening begin."

"In the right part of your anatomy, I hope," Lydia said and smiled. It was good to have her back. There is nothing quite like a glimpse at what money can buy to charge the soul.

XX

For the rest of the drive, Lydia returned to her former, more gregarious self, commenting on the undulating hills, sensual in their flow to the coast, asking what they were like during Spring. Green and full of wildflowers, I told her. She was fascinated by the craggy shapes of the large old oak trees that stood everywhere on the hills, sometimes in clusters, often just one, starkly standing alone and more beautiful for that fact. The true symbol of California, I told her. She gasped at her first sight of the enormous rock that rockets out of Morro Bay. Had this been Greece, she said, there would have been a mythological story behind that rock, something to do with a god throwing it during a battle with another god or giving it as a gift to the Nymph of the bay. How did she know there wasn't such a myth among the Chumash Indians, I asked. Was there? She politely wanted to know. I told her if there was, I'm afraid I was unaware of it. We then made up our own myth about the rock, Roee adding some gruesome details of sea otter sacrifice.

She got silly when she saw herds of cattle on the hills, leaning out the window, mooing at them, hoping for a reply. Roee was quite embarrassed by this. I joined Lydia in laughing about it.

A little over two hours after we had left Santa Barbara, we pulled into the parking lot of the Cavalier Ocean Front Resort on the motel row of San Simeon. "Resort" was an optimistic name, but the establishment tried hard to earn it by operating like a hotel, with dining facilities, room service, and a courteous manner. It was indeed on the oceanfront if you booked the right rooms, which Roee had. They were three adjoining rooms in a separate building from the rest of the hotel that sat near the edge of a cliff, the shallow beach, and the Pacific Ocean directly below. The view was stunning—once the shore-hugging fog lifted. This was the Central California coast here, a real continent-falling-into-ocean kind of coast, not a bright beach ball, hot dogs and soda, lazy day in the sun kind of coast. This coast did not amuse you—it brought out the brooder in you.

The rooms, comfortable if not large, featured a small fireplace, the centerpiece image of their sales brochure. It went with the fog. Sex was as probable as it was possible in these rooms, but it was Romance that they were selling.

Roee went to his room to rest. I took Lydia down for a walk on the beach. It was strewed with rocks and driftwood, leftover timber, most likely from Northern California logging. As the sky was now overcast, the ocean was gray. The damp and cold sand was also gray as the tide came up high here. Surprisingly the Mediterranean in Lydia did not react against all this. She was, instead, drawn to the foreign. I liked that in her.

"So," she said after we had stood for a while just looking at the ocean, trying to catch a sight of a seal, "you will sleep with me tonight."

"Is that a request or an order?"

"Neither. It is a need. Sex, you know, is life. I very much wish to be alive tonight," she said, taking a deep breath of the ocean air.

"I am honored you chose me," I said with a cartoon-like flourish, trying for a lightness, probably failing.

Lydia looked at me with a quizzical eye. "Roee is unavailable."

"Not to me," I said brightly. Lydia chastised me with her eyes. I had no more retorts. As a last refuge, I kissed her on the gray beach.

xx

Sara Hutton's faxed instructions had said to come to the Visitor's Center for the Hearst Castle at ten am, and someone would meet us there. We checked out and left the Cavalier at nine-forty the next morning. It was a clear day. No fog. No overcast. Upon waking, I had been dismayed to discover this when I had gently slid out from under Lydia's arm, got up, opened the sliding glass door, and stepped onto the balcony. The air was clear, calm, and filled with the squeals of seagulls. The ocean pounded the shore, adding its agitated sounds into the air. The sky was light blue and featureless. There was no hint of clouds except the little black cloud forming directly over my head.

Henderson and Pinsker dressed in conservative casual: Loafers with tassels, well-pressed slacks, and sport coats over their Izods. Lydia, her hair up and secured against the sea breeze, wore a bright, tight Nicole Miller dress of large squares of color and a low sweeping neckline. Her cleavage greeted the day with a smile.

We pulled into the visitor's center at nine fifty-five and were approached by a State Ranger even before we exited the car. He was a big, hard, blunt man. Not a PR person's dream.

"Lydia Corfu, Mr. Henderson, Mr. Pinsker?" he demanded to know, almost standing at attention in his drab, light olive uniform, his "Smokey the Bear" hat, as Mike called it, giving him a no-nonsense air of a slightly absurd quality.

"Yes," I acknowledge.

"Follow me. I'll take you to your transportation to the air museum."

"Fine," I said, and we got out of the Town Car, Roee and I grabbing our briefcases. "You won't be needing those," Ranger Blunt said.

"That's okay. We don't mind carrying them," I said.

"No, I mean, I'll arrange to have all your luggage picked up for tonight's stay, your briefcases included. It's Sara Hutton's orders."

"Sara Hutton gives orders to State Rangers?" Pinsker wanted to know, coming up real close to the Ranger, almost face to face, to share the shade under the brim of his hat.

"Well, you know, her request. We're happy to oblige."

"That's fine for the bags, but we'll keep the briefcases."

"Well, you know, you'll just have to lug them around the—"

"What kind of gun is that?" Pinsker interrupted the man, pointing to his large gun in the holster at his side, almost touching it.

The Ranger backed up. "Uh? Well, it's a Smith & Wesson 629."

"Are you going to continue to carry it?"

"Of course, I'm, uh, you know, a police officer. It's my duty."

"Well, I'm a lawyer," Pinsker said as he held up his briefcase. "This is my weapon. It's full of ammunition. I never not carry it. Does that make sense to you?"

"Well, yeah, I guess. I was just trying to save you the inconvenience."

"Fulfilling my duty to my clients is never inconvenient, Ranger."

"Okay. Sure. Whatever you say. Follow me."

Despite what the Ranger said, we could tell he was disappointed.

He led us through the visitor's center, a cleanly designed modern structure in the California Spanish style of white stucco and red tile roof. As this is where tourists pick up the buses that take them up to the castle sitting on the hill Hearst thought of as enchanted, it was not surprising that it had the feel of a terminal with its very high ceiling and row of ticket windows, snack bar, and gift shops. The Ranger rapidly passed by all this, taking us back outside to the bus area, and ushered us into a white stretch limo, asking for our car keys so he could see to our luggage. Another Ranger was in the driver's seat, eyes forward, sitting at attention, the pointed Ranger hat grazing the limo's ceiling. When Ranger Blunt shut the door behind us, the limo moved forward immediately and started up the road toward the castle.

"Not too many State Rangers get to drive limos, I guess," I said.

"It's Sara Hutton's," the second Ranger said. That's when we knew she was a woman. When we knew it was Sheila Barnes. "She drives it up here herself, never has a chauffeur. She's real nice, real regular, you know? So I don't mind volunteering to drive her special guests to the air show. It's a neat car. Fun to drive. Love to take my kids to Disneyland in it someday."

The mention of Disneyland was the code word Hamo had given her. Hamo's sense of humor. We did not reply; there was no need to. The code signaled that she had talked to her children that morning and knew they were safe. It was an up-to-the-moment assurance that she was committed to working for me from now on.

Suddenly there was an incredible roar to our right. We looked. Two vintage warbirds were coming at us, very low. One was a Messerschmitt 109. One was a Spitfire. Side by side, they flew at us. Lydia screamed and ducked, but the planes passed overhead with plenty of space to spare, although it hadn't seemed they would, with the intense roar rattling the car and wiping out all other sounds for a second. Sheila did not flinch and slowed the car only to make a left turn onto a road that led to the airfield. Once we cleared some trees, we could see the field ahead of us as the two planes rose, did barrel rows, and fly off again.

"That was a greeting from Sara Hutton and Max James," Sheila Barnes explained.

Lydia rose. "A simple wave would have been fine."

"They're excellent flyers. We were never in any danger."

"Still, not very prudent," Pinsker said with some disapproval.

"They both have a lust for life, that's for sure," Sheila said.

"Listen, I know lust and life," Lydia said. "What just happened had very little of the attributes of either."

"Here we are."

Sheila pulled up outside of a new building matching the style of the Visitor's Center. The signage was large and grand gunmetal bolted over the white stucco entranceway: SAN SIMEON AIR MUSEUM. Tour buses were stopping, letting off people clutching their tickets to go in. A third Ranger came up to the car. Hatless, very blond, and muscular, he opened the door for us.

"Sara Hutton suggested I take you through the museum, then outside for the show."

"Fine," I said as we got out of the car, Roee and I still clutching onto our briefcases.

"You can leave those here if you want. Sheila will watch them."

"No, thank you," I said.

"Okay. You'll have to drag them along with you."

"That's quite all right," I said. "I feel naked without it."

"Really," the third Ranger said in a dry voice with no cracks. "I only feel naked without clothes—but then I'm the simple sort." He turned and marched toward the museum entrance. We quickly followed.

The museum was quite impressive and quite a contrast from the Chino Air Museum, which relied on donations and volunteers and housed itself in a corrugated metal hanger. This building had a vast three-story high interior with antique airplanes hanging in midair at various heights and the many planes on display on the ground floor. Second and third-floor mezzanines ringed the building's center interior, allowing you to view the hanging planes up close. There was an elevator-stairway area up against the left wall, and the right wall was all glass at the second and third levels, beyond which was a snack bar on the second floor and a restaurant on the third. Directly ahead was the vast space of open hangar doors and the field beyond.

A glance established the extent of the collection. A World War I F26 Bristol Bi-plane fighter hanging just overhead painted a shiny olive green and orange, while the Heinkel He 162A Salamander, a German Jet fighter, stood right before us. One of the very first jet fighters, produced in 1945, a bit too late to help Herr Hitler out, it stunned you with its look, its engine weirdly on its back, a big hump right behind the canopy. Weird, but "Cool," as the young kid in you wanted to say. There were French WWI Bi-plane fighters as well, and Boeing pre-WWII pursuit planes, still bi-winged, but also the Boeing "Peashooter," the first U.S. Army Air Corp "Monoplane," quite an innovation for its time, 1933. The "Peashooter" was rather garishly painted in red, white, and blue, with yellow added to the wings. Also up overhead hung a Horten IV German Flying Wing. There's the essence of flight—just a wing.

"This must have cost the State quite a bit," I said.

"Not a penny," the hatless Ranger said. "Max paid for everything. The building, the restaurants. The planes he already owned. He maintains everything at his cost. For the use of the land, the State gets a fat percentage of the ticket sales, the gift shop, and the food service. It's a good deal for them."

"It's interesting that all you Rangers are here at the airfield," Pinsker added. "I mean, I can understand you being up at the Castle, but—"

"We're only here during the air shows for crowd control. It's an off-duty assignment. We believe in the spirit of volunteerism." He said it in a way that left no room for argument. "You can look around here or join the others in the VIP seats outside," he informed us.

Already bored standing among the blunt realities of a boy's fantasies, Lydia said, "Let's go outside. It's a beautiful day to sit with other VIPs."

More planes were on display on the tarmac. Fighters; transports; bombers; another flying wing, the famous Northrop, painted in a bright yellow-orange. And beyond the tarmac, on a flat grassy plain, was a recreation of a WW II RAF airfield, complete with the simple brick and corrugated metal roof buildings, a bright yellow wind sock dancing on the end of a pole, and various chairs haphazardly placed about in front of the HQ for the nonchalant pilots to lazily while away the time in-between the battles that could very well take their lives. There were three Spitfires on the grassy field, two grouped and one quite far from them, and one Spitfire landing. The one that buzzed us, I assumed. When it came to a stop, the pilot jumped out, flight-suited and leather-helmeted. It was impossible with that and the distance to tell if this was Sara or Maxwellton James. The pilot went into one of the brick buildings, and my attention was taken by sound and movement overhead.

The sky was filled with planes. Four WW I biplanes flying in formation and, at a higher altitude, four Grumman "Cats": The F4F Wildcat; the F6F-5 Hellcat; the F7F-3N Tigercat; the F8F-2 Bearcat—or so the thunderous public address system blared out with love, pride, and adoration over the constant hot-engine roar that filled the air.

"So many letters, so many numbers," Lydia said, unhappy about it. "Why don't they just call them John, Paul, George, and Ringo?"

"Here we are," Hatless pointed to a set of plush, theater-like seats arranged in four ascending bleacher rows of six seats each. The whole affair was up against a hanger, rested on a raised platform, reached by a carpeted set of steps, and was covered with a canvas awning to provide shade. Next to it was a roped-off area where a chef was preparing food and a bartender prepared drinks. Four other Rangers were positioned at equidistant spots to the sides and in front of this VIP section.

"More volunteers," Roee whispered to me.

"I'm almost moved to tears," I replied.

Five people were in the seats, four men and one woman, all attractive. If not by their raw physical appearance, like models in magazines, then by how they were dressed, groomed, and self-appraised. They sat close together and had binoculars that they were all looking through. Oddly enough, the binoculars were not trained on the sky, looking at either the biplanes or the "Cats." They were, instead, trained parallel to the ground. They may have been trying to get a detailed view of the various planes on the tarmac. But as they were whispering to each other, giggling, and even snorting out short, snotty laughs, I had a feeling they were picking out and examining individual members of the hundreds of paying public that had come to the show and were now—still and video cameras at the ready—milling all around the tarmac getting good views of the planes, possibly thinking how they would fare as the pilots thereof.

It was an interesting cross-section of the population. As you would expect, there were older men, veterans of the Second World War, or of the times at least, most in plaid or striped short-sleeved shirts, not always ones of the right size, and baseball caps, some of which announced the military units they had been in. Was this trip necessary for nostalgia for the "Good War" when America was a solid monoculture, true blue (not to mention red and white) kind of country? When the loudspeaker announcer was not blaring, you could hear Glen Miller's music mixing with the rapid piston banging of flying engines above. Glen Miller's music always took you back, even, for some, back before they were born. Ah, the Good War! It had resonance. These men seemed to come in pairs, buddies remembering the Big One, or paired with their wives, gray-haired women not always enthusiastically trailing their husbands. They seemed to amuse the group of five, especially when the old warriors might sit in the middle of the tarmac on folding chairs they had carried, catching a breath and looking up to watch something roar overhead.

There were younger people too. Families with kids, mainly boys (two or three generations who missed the Good War), who wanted to see the neat planes, the kind they made models of. There were young t-shirted guys—boys again among the aircraft—who were also into fast racing cars; you could tell by their jackets, hats, and attitudes. And there were young women out to prove to their boyfriends that they could share a manly passion, so let me into that part of you.

They gawked well, all these people, at the romance of flight.

The crowd came in all shapes and sizes, but rounder shapes and larger sizes seemed to be the norm on the tarmac. Often those shapes and sizes were covered in unfortunate choices of clothes. Shorts stopping short of covering thighs like massive institutional bread dough, just kneaded. T-shirts tenting out over the bay of bellies, letting the breeze in underneath. I had a suspicion the five also found this amusing, like kids in school.

It has never seemed to me anything but apt that school rhymes with cruel.

"These are Sara's other guests," Hatless announced, then left us, leaving us to the introductions.

In a unified move, the five brought their binoculars away from their faces, turned their heads our way, then looked down at us. All five, including the woman, immediately registered a tiny twinkle in their eyes when they landed on Lydia, possibly nestling comfortably in her cleavage. I couldn't say I blamed them. Lydia's cleavage was very 1950s, especially in this dress, especially at the angle from which the five were viewing it.

"Hello!" Lydia said cheerfully as the five stood up. "I'm Lydia

Corfu. These boys are my lawyers, Henderson and Pinsker. You can ignore them."

"Hi," one of the men said. "Sara said you would be joining us. Come on up."

We marched up the little stairs that led to the platform. When we got there, face to face with the five, the man who had spoken said, "I'm Thad Darrow. This is—" He pointed to each one in turn. "Brooke Bloom, Nick Paulsen, Brett Korner, and Abbie White."

Thad was an eager young man with wispy, light brown hair over a sharp, focused face accented by his frameless glasses' small, round lenses. He was about five foot six.

Brooke was a tall woman, maybe twenty-eight, skinny in an elegant way, with long, straight ash blond hair, clear skin, bright eyes, and a mouth that closed into a line that was scary.

Nick had very close-cropped dark hair that would be gone in a short matter of years. His face was perfectly proportioned; there wasn't a thing you would change; thus, he had a naturally confident look. He wasn't handsome as much as he was just—right.

Brett was handsome. Wide grinned, joyfully so. Tall, well built, happy to be him, with a commanding head of dark gold hair combed in a chaos of swirls that nevertheless seemed to have a pattern.

Abbie was an intense, lanky, black-haired man with big teeth, a big nose, big hands, and—by the look of his shoes—big feet. To trip, to stumble, and to stutter seemed his immediate destiny. Yet when he moved, bending down from the third highest row of chairs, to shake our hands, he was nothing but control and grace as he said in a deep, well-modulated voice, "It's a pleasure to meet you."

Thad pointed to some seats, and we sat as Lydia said, "So, who's winning?"

They all laughed a knowing laugh.

"Actually, it's quite interesting," Thad said, "all these historical planes."

"Yeah, kind of neat," Brett said.

"They had a wing walker a moment ago," Brooke said. "About as stupid a thing to do as I can imagine. Standing up there, holding an American flag, flapping in the wind. Whoopee, I'm a Yankee Doodle Dandy. You should have seen the crowd point and Oooo! and Ahhh!"

"It's all part of the invite," Abbie said. "You don't get the evening without the day. That's what Don Gulden told me."

"How is he, by the way?" Brooke wanted to know. "Is he still in the coma?"

"Yeah, that's what I heard," Brett said.

"I'm glad I didn't go to that party," Thad added.

"You know, there are rumors that it was a hit," Brett said.

"Excuse me?" Brooke raised her eyebrows.

"Yeah. A new form of mob hit. You know, they reported there was a guy there that no one knew. Kind of creepy looking, people have told me."

"Why would the mob want to put Don in a coma?" Brooke was incredulous. She seemed to come naturally to the state.

"Oh, Don was really into gambling," Brett said. "Didn't you know that? It started at Harvard. He used to spend his weekends in Atlantic City, driving all night Friday to get there. He always told me he never did worse than break even, but who knows? And he loved Vegas."

"So you think he was into the mob for gambling debts?" asked Thad.

"I don't know, but, you know, let's not waste the thought. What do you think of it as the premise for a movie? Robert Downey, Jr. would be perfect."

"Yeah, sure. Do you think you could push it through at Tri-Star?"

"I don't know. Can you present the idea to Jim?"

"Is it a Jim kind of idea?"

"I don't know. Make 'em, uh, make 'em a government clerk at the CIA into the mob who witnesses—uh—who witnesses—the mob takes down an important agent, so he tries to blackmail the mob to get out of his debts, but things are even deeper and darker than he thinks, so now he's got the mob chasing him and the CIA chasing him, so he goes to a friend—a girlfriend—at the FBI for help, but, what he doesn't know, is she's involved as well, doesn't want to be. Still, for some reason, she is. So we have this moral dilemma when she has to turn him in."

"Who do you see playing the girl?"

"How about Gwyneth Paltrow?"

"I don't see her fucking Downey."

"Matthew McConaughey, then, of course, Matthew McConaughey."

"He wouldn't do a stupid movie like this."

"Then why would Gwyneth?"

"She's a girl; what choice does she have?"

"Hey!" Brooke slapped the back of Brett's head.

"Ouch! Well, Brooke, take over Hollywood and change things then."

"No, I accept the reality. I just think we shouldn't bandy it about."

"Ladies and gentlemen!" The loudspeaker suddenly announced. "The highlight of our show is about to commence. Return with us now to the glory-filled skies of the stalwart island of England, standing alone against the might of Hitler's hordes during the summer and fall of 1940. There, off in the distance. Do you see them? Three Messerschmitt bf 109s, the pride of the Luftwaffe, coming to strafe an RAF base, but into the air goes the greatest fighter plane of all time, the Supermarine Spitfire, the brilliant creation of Reginald J. Mitchell. What you are about to see, ladies and gentlemen, is a recreation of a classic World War Two dog fight among these two classic war birds. You will hear the guns fire and see explosions but don't worry; it's all just an amazing simulation created by the great special effects team at Olympic Pictures!"

The crowd scanned the sky with binoculars, camcorders, or hand-shaded eyes. Suddenly an arm extending with a pointing finger shot out while a cry shouted, "There!"

People turned, and more arms shot up and pointed. Off to the west, coming over the Pacific Ocean playing the part of the English Channel, came three Messerschmitt fighters flying in a triangular formation, their yellow noses bright in the sun. It was a formidable fear they engendered, coming in fast and low. When were the guns going to open? Your gut wanted to know.

"Scramble!" came over the loudspeaker, and off at the mock RAF field, four pilots ran like mad for their planes. The Messerschmitts began to strafe, small explosions chewing up the ground before them. One of the Spitfires that sat quite apart from the others exploded under the fire before its pilot could reach it— a brilliant special effect. The plane could be quickly put right and exploded over and over. The three Messerschmitts shot up into the sky. The three Spitfires followed. Then they put on a show. Flying lower than in actual battle, they mixed it up, pursuing each other, weaving, dodging, and "bouncing" on each other. Over the loudspeaker, we could hear the radio transmissions from the Spitfires, many "Tally Hos. rabbit leaders," and a few "Let's get those bloody Krauts!" kind of dialog, somewhat lacking in authenticity whenever Sara Hutton's female voice would shout out something like, "Wingman! Bandit Two 'o clock!"

The crowd loved it. They couldn't tell the good guys from the bad guys, but it didn't matter. They *OOOOOed* when a plane was "hit" and started to bomb its way down to the ground, a trail of black smoke streaming from it, and *AHHHHed* just as the plane always pulled up at what seemed the last minute to rejoin the fight.

It was—I must admit—somewhat grand. And Henderson and Pinsker expressed their delight in it. The five seemed to enjoy themselves, although I think Brooke might have liked it more if one of the planes had crashed. At least I detected a little breath of disappointment whenever the planes recovered from their fall. Lydia was captivated. Her mouth hung open. She called it "amazing" about four times. When the loudspeaker announced the end of the show and the planes formed into two groups and prepared to land, she led us all in vigorous applause.

The Messerschmitts landed on the tarmac, while the Spitfires landed on the grassy RAF field. One of the Messerschmitts, though, and one of the Spitfires broke off from their comrades of the sky and taxied over to the area directly in front of us, the sound of their engines growing louder and louder until they stopped and sputtered down into silence.

The pilots ejected themselves from their planes in smooth,

jaunty moves that saw them swing themselves out of the cockpits, land both feet on their wings, then cast themselves off, landing on the ground. Very romantic. They both were in costume. One was wearing an RAF flight officer's uniform and leather jacket—dashing by design. The other wore the uniform of a German fighter ace, a leather waist jacket, well-cut pants tapering down at the end and covered by high, well-polished boots. Of the two, the German uniform was the niftier. It often happens that way. Bad guys seem to have a better sense of design. British Redcoats: Very natty. Pirates: Eye patch, bandanna, and sash as defining accessories. Indians: Great use of feathers. Unless, of course, you consider the U.S. Cavalry to be the bad guys, but even they had nifty blue uniforms as opposed to the drab olive of today's army. Darth Vader: A symphony in basic black.

I could recognize Sara now; she was the pilot of the Spitfire. She took her leather flight cap off, smiled at us, and waved. The other pilot was a tall man, maybe six foot three, and bulky in build without being fat. When he took off his leather helmet, we could see that he had dusty red receding hair strangely piled on his head. Then he reached up, pulled out bobby pins, and his hair came tumbling down. It was very long—ending just above the small of his back—and narrowly falling between his shoulder blades. As he walked towards us, his hair blew up in the wind—it was that thin and light—glowing with sun highlights that pierced it.

The two walked up to us. "Hello, everybody! Hello Lydia, glad you could make it," Sara said, still breathless from the exhilaration of the flight and the fight. "I'd like you all to meet a very good friend of mine and a man you should all get to know very well, Maxwellton James."

Maxwellton James stood before us on the tarmac, the two warbirds back-dropping him. He smiled broadly. His eyes, which were a strange, muted green, glowed. His large forehead, partly an illusion from the receding hairline, was pink and freckled and icon-like. His hair, flowing back off his forehead, continued to wave in the wind.

20
GORGED WITH STYLE

"Hello—Hi—How are you?" Maxwellton James was up on the platform, greeting us, shaking hands. Like a skilled and masterful politician, he could look you straight in the eyes with the slightest tilt of his head to the right. Such a look could take you aback. People don't really look into each other's eyes, do they? But the slant of his head kept it from being disconcerting. Straight on, such a look pierced you naked. At an angle, it took in your protective cover and seduced it.

In his greetings, Max had something particular to say to each person; Sara had briefed him well. To Nick, for example, he talked ice hockey, knowing Nick was a fan, having played on championship teams in high school and college. To Brooke, he mentioned that he had managed to lay in a case of a little-known-in-America Irish beer. It was, of course, her favorite, only indulged in when she traveled to the UK. Lydia, he paid much attention to, thanking her for coming on such short notice, hoping she enjoyed the show, mentioning a particular bill under consideration in the Greek Parliament and how he hoped her efforts to defeat it would succeed, as it was detrimental to the media business in Greece.

Then he came to Henderson and Pinsker.

"Ah," he looked at us with his muted green eyes. "The lawyers. Briefcases in hand, ready to do business, I see. But we are doing no business here this weekend, gentlemen. Wouldn't you like to unload yourself of the burden of carrying them? I'm sure one of the Rangers would be happy—"

"They've already offered," I broke in. "Numerous times. Their concern for our comfort has been admirable."

Max was stopped. The Rangers' failure had most likely been reported to him as he flew high above in his Messerschmitt. "Leave it to me," he had probably sighed, regretting the incompetence of others. "There is nothing like a good public servant," Max said, a slightly different texture to his smile now.

"But as we explained to them," I continued, "we are far more comfortable hanging on to them. Goes back to law school, I suppose. I was always afraid of losing my homework."

"I see. Well, my duty as a host is to acquiesce to the desires of my guests. So suit yourself," Maxwellton James said in that same voice we had heard over the bug. That smooth voice. Not smooth and slick; smooth and soft. A pleasant wrap around your consciousness. His voice had no hint of irony or a lack of sincerity; it was plain without being bland, well-modulated, and direct. It was the voice of a pal, a buddy, a friend. It was not the voice of a dangerous man.

But it was a dangerous voice.

"You like airplanes, I understand." Max divided his attention between Pinsker and me.

"Very much," Pinsker said.

"Would you like a close look?" Max indicated the two warbirds with a quick dart of his head.

"Yes, that would be quite exciting," I said.

Max led us down to where the Messerschmitt and the Spitfire stood. Combatants. Fighters. Mechanized flying armor for twentieth-century knights.

Henderson and Pinsker showed their delight quite openly, their lawyer's reserve diminishing in front of the machines, which they walked around, touched, bent close to, inspecting details.

"What model Spit is this?" I had Henderson ask, abbreviating the name to sound like a member of the Brotherhood.

"It's a Mark II."

"One of the early ones," I said in awe.

"It actually fought in the Battle of Britain," Max proudly said. "It cost over a million dollars to return it to prime condition. Still got its original Rolls Royce Merlin XII engine."

"How about armaments?" Pinsker wanted to know.

Max looked at him, then challenged him. "Well, you tell me. You know this stuff, right?"

"Looks like 'B' wing to me. Four Browning machine guns; two 20 mm Hispano cannons."

"Exactly. See, you know your stuff."

"Only from pictures. We collect aviation art," Pinsker said.

"It's all we hang on our walls at the firm," added Henderson.

"But you fly, don't you? Sara told me—"

"Only Pipers and Cessna's," I answered. "We've never flown anything like this."

"You haven't flown until you've flown something like this," Max said with that superiority of the initiated. "Look at the Messerschmitt. It's a Bf109E-4. Magnificent machine. Built not just to conquer the air, but to use it, to turn it into a medium to express yourself." Max looked up at the dark gray plane, mottled for camouflage. "Your joy. Your delight." He then looked back down at us. "Your anger. Your righteous indignation." He paused to allow us to consider. "All other planes are— transport. Flying them is easy. Be powered. Control airflow. Exploit lift. Go from point A to point B. To pilot something like that is to be no more than a passenger."

"Well, still—"

"You want to take her up?"

"What? Now?" Henderson asked, amazed, teased, not daring to hope.

"No, of course not, not now. I don't gamble a million-dollar plane on someone who's only flown Pipers and Cessnas. I could put you through training. Rigorous training. Then you could have the experience."

"Unfortunately, we don't have the time to undergo rigorous training, but you made my heart jump there. I really would like to. You know, flying is flying. It's all the same principle. I could fly it."

"You think so?"

"Sure, but I would rather fly the Spit."

"The Spit?"

"It's the better plane, isn't it?"

Max sighed. "And it's the winners who write the history."

"What?"

"Did you know that in fighter vs. fighter losses during the Battle of Britain, 219 Spitfires were lost, but only 180 109s?"

"But I thought—"

"Yes, I know what you thought." Max smiled; he refused not to be my friend. "But the facts are what they are. Romantic visions of right fighting might don't ever change them. They might warm your heart and put a lump in your throat, but they don't ever affect reality."

"Well, yes, I guess that's so. But you must admit that the Spitfire is aesthetically the finer machine," I declared.

"I would argue—"

"You can't," I said. I was emphatic. "This also is a reality." I got close to the German fighter, pointed to each feature, and spoke with the dispassion of a lawyer ticking off the charges against the accused. "The Messerschmitt is all hard lines. A square, boxy canopy. A fat, brutish lump of a nose. The thick wings sort of just jammed into the fuselage. The tail is a straight, harsh 45-degree angle set against the fuselage. Now look at the Spit." I let passion creep in now. Not melodrama, but crazy love. I wanted to make Max uneasy. "Curves, everywhere curves. The canopy is rounded. The nose curves up gracefully. The wings are thin and delicate, and they curve onto—not into, that's important—onto the fuselage, as does the tail. Like organic parts of a whole body. Like the neck of a beautiful woman curving onto her shoulder."

"Henderson!" Lydia admonished. "Stop being poetic. It's unbecoming of a lawyer who is protecting my financial interests."

But Max was impressed. "Good points, Mr. Henderson. For someone who collects aviation art. Still, I prefer the Messerschmitt.

I prefer a blunt instrument." Max smiled at me again. This time it was nearly paternal and almost kind. Then he turned his attention to the group. "I believe the chef is preparing a delicious lunch for you all to enjoy as the rest of the show continues. Sara and I have more flying to do, but we'll join you when we gather later this afternoon. The Rangers will take excellent care of you and ensure you get to your destination on time."

"Which is where?" Thad feigned innocence but not well.

"That's a surprise, but I suspect you've already guessed. Most likely having been told in the strictest of confidence by someone who has preceded you."

Worry rammed Thad's guts. "Uh, no, really—"

"It's okay. I know you can keep a confidence. That's why you're here."

Max turned to Sara. "Shall we?"

"Absolutely," she said.

They climbed into their planes and started them, initial puffs of smoke expelling from the engines. Then they taxied away.

"Lunch."

It was Ranger Blunt, appearing suddenly. The five took little notice of this, but why should they have? We followed him to tables laid out with food, buffet style.

Max had been right; it was a delicious lunch. Beef, chicken, and salmon, cooked on an open grill with a selection of vegetables. Three types of salad were available, including a Greek, and the most wonderfully sour of sourdough bread, baked right there in a portable oven. There were drinks of every kind, of course, well-brewed coffee and three desserts. One heavy on chocolate, one heavy on fruit, and one a light pastry filled with a delicate cream.

Five Rangers stationed themselves around the area, warning off errant plebes and pointing out the van across the tarmac selling hot dogs, chips, and warm sodas.

Our conversation, at first, revolved around the food as we ate it as if talk of it not only spiced it but etched it on our palates for future reference and comparisons. Then, as the air show continued, the conversation moved on to other subjects, none relating to planes in the air. It was all Hollywood talk. Most of it was just chatty, some of it catty. Henderson and Pinsker did not partake, but Lydia got into it. She told stories of her past and of making B movies around Los Angeles and of all her cleverness in avoiding various obstructionist authorities, for she never got the proper film permits, dealt straight with the unions, and never paid off the Teamsters. She told how a Teamster official, at least he said he was a Teamster official, promised to break her legs. She told him, "Look, I'll make you a deal. Don't break my legs, and I'll suck your dick."

"What? He went for it?" Thad seemed excited.

"Wouldn't you?" Lydia held herself and her abilities up proudly.

"Well...." Thad blushed.

"Of course, afterward, the bastard still demanded a payoff."

"No!" Brooke was delighted to be shocked. "So you had to pay him?"

"No. I sued him. For sexual harassment!" Lydia loudly laughed.

The five laughed with her. They loved Lydia. She was a character—and they had been so little exposed to character.

Around two fifteen, the show was over, and the hatless Ranger came to us and suggested we spend some time in the museum proper while we waited until three PM when the limo would take us to our destination.

"Why do we have to wait until three?" The precise Pinsker wanted to know.

"Winter hours," was the hatless one's only answer.

We went into the museum, looking at the planes on display and reading the information about them on the little cards. Brooke, I noticed, started to hang close to Lydia. I think she was in love. The guys found most fascinating the old, yet operable, training guns, WW II versions of virtual reality, where you looked into a scope, saw a film of the enemy, sighted, and pushed the firing thumb button.

There were whoops as the enemy died.

At three o'clock, the Rangers came to us. They herded us into the white stretch limo, a congealed and happy unit of companions, except for Henderson and Pinsker, who sat squeezed together, clutching their briefcases in the same manner, dreaming of advantageously written contracts.

It didn't take anyone long to realize that we were heading up towards the castle on top of the Enchanted Hill, as Hearst had dubbed it, really the peak of the Santa Lucia Mountains. If it was enchanted, it was only because Hearst had paid for it to be so. We started winding slowly up the road, passing tour buses on their way down, but there were no tour buses in front of us or following behind. Winter hours.

As our caravan of the limo and two Ranger cars, one ahead, one behind, passed from the grassy coastal plain into the oak woodlands of the higher elevation, Abbie said, "I feel like we're in *Citizen Kane*."

"Why?" Brett asked.

"Because of the scene when they're traveling on Kane's Xanadu property."

It meant nothing to Brett. "I haven't seen it."

Abbie was shocked. "You've never seen *Citizen Kane*!"

"No, never got around to it."

"You didn't see it at Harvard?"

"I was an MBA," Brett said as if that explained it.

"Yeah, but, but—"

"I've never seen it," Brooke said.

"Me neither," Nick said.

"Me too. I mean neither, I guess," Thad added.

"The greatest film ever made," Abbie was trying to explain it to himself, "and you guys, film executives all, have never seen it?"

They shrugged in concert.

Abbie turned to Lydia. "Have you seen it?"

"Of course."

"And?"

"Overrated."

"Overrated!"

"Gorged with style. How clever! I like simple storytelling. Clean and direct."

"Yeah, direct to some guy's nuts!" Abbie said.

"Oh, you've seen my films!"

"I suffer from insomnia."

We came to the landscaped area that denoted the grounds of the Castle. There were pine and fir trees, fruit trees, and other plants exotic to this locale. Suddenly on a slight elevation above the road, you could make out part of a curved structure with Ionic columns, one of the marble colonnades that adorned the Neptune Pool, if my memory of research served. The cars stopped, and we got out of the limo and followed Ranger Blunt up some stairs to an area in front of La Casa del Mar. Fine enough to be a palatial home for just about anybody but the most ostentatious, it was here, on the hill, just one of three guest houses. The view was spectacular, which was not unexpected. Wealthy men like William Randolph Hearst did not spend thirty years building such homes without a breathtaking view—a view not just of beauty. Your eye followed the land downward, past the well-maintained landscaped area, to the oak woodlands, then onto the grassy coastal plain, finally picking up the ocean at the finely etched coastline. This ocean did not end abruptly at the far-off horizon but continued in a curve beyond it. This was a planet you were standing on! You felt that deeply. And if you had owned this land, it would not have been too challenging to allow yourself to feel like a god astride it.

"This way." Hatless and seven Ranges ushered us through the grounds of patios and gardens; of fountains; of ancient statues— an Egyptian that was probably over 3,000 years old—and of reproductions—Donatello's David high atop a three-tiered fountain casually standing nude over the severed head of Goliath, his exposed penis just as casual (nice to know the kid didn't get off on violence)—until we got to the front entrance of the main house, the actual Castle, as everyone calls it, La Casa Grande, Hearst called it, when he didn't just refer to it as the "Ranch House."

"Wow!" Brett said.

"Jesus Christ! It's like a fucking cathedral!" Brooke added as her eyes traveled from the gothic entrance full of sculpted limestone portraits of religious figures— including a Virgin and Child high over the massive, iron bar-covered doors—to the twin Spanish Renaissance bell towers. "This thing was built on purpose?" Brooke questioned. "I mean, like, in this century? For a home?"

The doors were now open, and in the doorway stood Sara

Hutton. She was still wearing her RAF pants but had the jacket off. The light blue shirt had been opened at the neck, and the black tie had been pulled down for relief. As the clothes had undoubtedly been tailored for her, she did not look odd, like a little girl playing daddy-dress-up, and yet she was not attractive enough as a female to make it a unisexual sexy fashion statement. It was just her uniform, and she wore it with authority.

"Brooke, my dear," Sara addressed the unbeliever, "William Randolph Hearst loved beauty. Wherever he found it in the world and could buy it, he did. If he couldn't buy it, he reproduced it. He wanted to be surrounded by beauty, so he built all this. Architecture, sculpture, nature, everything you're going to see inside. It's a beauty cocoon! What a fucking neat idea! If you can afford it."

"Yeah, but," Brooke's lip curled, Elvis-like, in mild disgust, "it's so—so—"

"When you build yours, Brooke, then you can decide on the beauty."

Sara then turned to all of us. "Welcome. You will be guests at La Casa Grande, a privilege long since faded into the past when the Hollywood elite was regularly called up here to keep company with Mr. Hearst. I hope you will find it a pleasurable and enlightening stay. The Rangers will take you to your rooms. Freshen yourselves up. Go for a swim in the Neptune Pool if you wish. Cocktails are being served in the Assembly Room at six sharp. Oh, and by the way, Lydia, we have put you in the Celestial Suite on the top floor. I certainly hope you don't mind being that close to heaven."

"I have no objections if heaven doesn't," Lydia said.

Sara smiled and stepped back into the house, closing the doors as she did so.

"This way," one of the Rangers, who had not yet spoken to us, said as he led us around the back of the house and had us enter by a narrow door. There various Rangers took control of us and led us to our bedrooms.

Sheila Barnes took Lydia off to the Celestial Suite while the hatless Ranger conducted Henderson and Pinsker to:

"The Della Robbia Suite," he stated the fact dryly.

It was like stepping into the early Italian Renaissance.

"Della Robbia?" I inquired of Hatless.

His eyes went hard. "I'm not a guide."

"Oh, sorry, thought you might—"

"I'm here for security."

"Security?"

"Valuable property. State park. Protecting it for all our citizens."

"How democratic of you. So this Max? What is he, first among equals?"

He seemed not to understand the question as his brow knitted tight.

"Never mind. Uh," I slapped my pockets, "I would give you a tip, but I'm all out of change."

An insult he could understand. Hatless snorted. "Enjoy your stay," he said in a tone so mono it truly stood alone. "I've been ordered to say that, but I don't mean it." He turned and left.

"He's honest in his insincerity," Roee said.

I gave Roee a look, one to remind both of us that we were probably being listened to. "Nice room," I said.

There were two beds, side by side, each a four-poster carved in walnut with massive headboards. Behind the beds was a tapestry of some happy maids. Over one window was a round wall plaque featuring stars, and over the fireplace was a base relief of a man and a child. Across the room was a large painting of a woman looking immaculate. On the floor was an oriental rug. On it was an octagon table with chairs. It was all dark and heavy and somewhat oppressive, as if we should, in this room, be planning the poisoning of some colorfully robed head of State.

"Well," I said to Pinsker, "should we get a little sun?"

xx

Henderson and Pinsker showed up at the Neptune Pool in the same clothes they had worn to the air show, carrying their briefcases. They came to a deck between a colonnade and the mock

Greek temple facade and sat stiffly in two patio chairs. They placed their briefcases on their laps, opened them, pulled out papers, and began to consult with each other.

We were the epitome of gray men.

It was about seventy-five degrees, but the five were in the pool. How could they not be? Three hundred and forty-five thousand gallons of pure, clear mountain spring water in a setting that would not look out of place on Mt. Olympus—I mean the home of the Gods, not the high-price residential district in Los Angeles, just off Laurel Canyon—is damn inviting, no matter what the weather.

Brooke was doing laps in an asexual one-piece suit you usually see on competition swimmers. Abbie was alternatively floating on his back, then doing backward underwater somersaults. Thad was clinging to the side of the pool by a grouping of statues of goddesses, mermaids, and cherubs, slowly kicking his legs, dreaming, still wearing his small round glasses. Brett, wearing tight trunks, kept getting out of the pool to dive back in, showing off the form of his not-unattractive body—the form and a particular protuberance thereof.

"Flaunt it, baby, flaunt it," Roee whispered.

"Hey!" Nick called from the deep end where he was treading water. "What are you guys doing there? Get your suits on! Come on in!"

"I'm sorry," I shouted across the pool, "we didn't pack any suits."

"So?" Brett said on the edge of a dive. "Skinny dip. We will, if you will."

"I think not," Pinsker said as Roee regretted.

"Ah, come on, join us," they all said encouragingly.

"Leave the boys alone!"

It was Lydia, suddenly there in a beige bikini. "Skimpy" was a word that hardly covered its briefness—as it hardly covered Lydia. Its flesh tone finished the dreamlike illusion. Maybe, after all, she was Venus.

"I do not pay my boys to have fun. Much less frolic in the water. I'm only comfortable when they have paperwork in front of their eyes, and I'm only comfortable when that paperwork includes projections of the profits they are helping me make. So please, don't splash around them or encourage them into frivolity."

With that, she ran towards the pool, leaped off the edge, and dived in with the grace of a Maxwell Parish sea nymph. Parish with a touch of Vargas.

"Well, I think I found something interesting about Della Robbia!"

It was Petey. Not quite whispering in my ear through the concealed earpiece. I could have answered through the micro-microphone well-camouflaged on my person, but I did not need to. Petey would know to give his report. Having heard the name mentioned while monitoring us earlier, he decided to look up Della Robbia. He checked guidebooks on Hearst Castle, and he checked into the history of art. He gave me the information. I noted it. Roee, on the same frequency, heard it as well. We would have shared a chuckle if we did not think it might have been inappropriate for two fully clothed lawyers sitting around the gorgeous pool of the gods to do.

When the five and Lydia had had their fill of swimming, they all got up on the deck and found spots surrounding Henderson and Pinsker to stretch out on and dry off.

"Do you know who has swum in this pool?" asked Abbie, the film buff.

"Robin Leach while he was doing a segment on *Lifestyles of the Rich and Famous*—the Deceased Edition," Brooke suggested.

"Yeah, well," Abbie said, "dead, but not forgotten. Charlie Chaplain. Cary Grant. Robert Montgomery—"

"Who?" Brett asked.

"Elizabeth Montgomery's father," Nick answered.

"Who?" Brett asked again.

"*Bewitched*," Thad stated.

"Oh, yeah. We're remaking that!" Brett was now happy. He understood.

"Greta Garbo," Abbie continued. "Buster Keaton. The Barrymores, John and Lionel. Irving Thalberg." The last name was said with some reverence. "They all used to come up here. Do you know how rarely anybody gets to swim in this pool anymore? Do you know what a privilege this is?"

"How do you know they all went for a swim?" Brett wanted to know.

"What?"

"All those old stars. How do you know they went for a swim just because they visited here? I mean, maybe they couldn't swim or didn't like to swim."

"That's not the point."

"Well, you asked, 'Do you know who swam in this pool?' So I thought—"

"Okay, then. Do you know who's been up here? Who has stayed at this place?"

"All those dead people you mentioned?"

Abbie was disgusted. "Yeah, all those dead people. Those dead people used to be the royalty of Hollywood."

"And now we are!" Brooke announced it, raising her hands as if accepting some appointment—or anointment.

"Yeah, like I said. It's a privilege for us to be invited up here."

"How did Sara pull it off," Thad wanted to know.

"Not Sara. It's Max," Abbie said. "He can make things like this happen. Don Gulden came up here. He said we are going to hear some very serious shit. Some important stuff. He said, 'Count yourself lucky to be included. Those who are will be the Hollywood of the future.' That's what he said."

Lydia laughed at the drama of it. "Wouldn't this Max be more impressive if he actually owned this place?"

"Hell, no!" Nick said. "That would only take money. Getting us in here took manipulation of the government. That's Power!"

Brooke gave a little shake and just the tiniest squeals at the word, power. The temperature had dropped a couple of degrees, and a cool breeze was rising, so it may have just been a shiver—or it just might have been the manifestation of a thrill over what the word represented. That would not have surprised the gods.

xx

At six pm, we all gathered in the Assembly Room on the ground floor of the Castle. A sitting room so large—2400 square feet, Petey lodged into my ear—that the grand piano in one corner was hardly noticeable. The room had been built to display four large tapestries that depicted the victory of Roman general Scipio Africanus Major over Hannibal at Zama in the year 202 BC—or Petey told me.

"Kind of feels like a museum," Henderson said to Pinsker.

"Yes," Pinsker said. "Wish I had one of those audio tour setups to find out what *absolutely* everything is in detail."

"You would?"

"I would."

"I wouldn't. No, I wouldn't like that at all. I would hate that. It would irritate me. Drive me to certain violence, I'm sure. Something gruesome. Bloody. Many body parts lying around, say like there was after the battle of Zama."

"All right, I'll shut up!" The Petey in our ears said. "I thought maybe a little edification would be welcomed, but if this is the way it's going to be appreciated, consider your tour at an end!"

"Small miracles, Mr. Pinsker," I quietly said to Roee, "are always the most welcomed."

After a closer look, I realized that the Assembly Room seemed less like a museum than the lobby of an ancient, never refurbished, Grand Hotel. Once the central meeting place of power in its city, now a quiet, if moldy, respite for those weary of the twentieth century and not looking forward to the twenty-first. There were groupings of overstuffed chairs around tables; a card table and chairs; the grand piano you had to look for; a sitting area anchored by a couch under the window; a long mahogany table in the center of the room with four substantial silver candlesticks on it, a massive, ornate French stone fireplace adorned with statues; several old and dark carved wood choir stalls ripped out of some gothic church. The choir stalls, which lined the walls under the tapestries, formed a row of uncomfortable-looking chairs with extremely tall backs—trying to reach heaven, I suppose, like the vaulted ceilings they would look best under. When you could see them, the walls were formed of large, light-colored bricks laid in an alternating pattern. The floor, seen where the oriental rugs were not, was teakwood done in a parquet design. The whole room was illuminated by thirty-two groupings of four naked light bulbs each, attached to a Renaissance ceiling of elaborately carved wood panels. It was not vaulted but was stratospheric enough not to matter.

Four of the Rangers were there, serving drinks, including Hatless and Blunt, now in civvies. I did not doubt they were still armed, and a brief accidental bumping against Hatless confirmed the fact. Nick, Brett, Abbie, and Thad were in suits, a small army of Armani (to be a walking cliché seemed admirable to these gentlemen), and Brooke was in a skintight, near fire engine red cocktail dress that ended mid-calf in a flare out of ruffles. Lydia's dress was stunning, deep azure blue emphasizing everything about Lydia that took so well to highlighting. She wore her hair down, allowing it to cascade on her shoulders. On her lips, she wore red-purple lipstick that sparkled.

Henderson and Pinsker? Brooks Brothers, of course.

Sara entered, grabbing our attention in an awfully (or wonderfully, depending on your perspective) short, simple black cocktail dress that left her arms, back, and legs bare (no stockings, I noticed). Her hair was gelled into style, making it almost a soft helmet, and she wore make-up, well applied and subtle, but giving her a glow of the face we had not seen before.

"Hello, how are you," she greeted us. "What are you having to drink?"

Almost everyone had a martini in large glasses of fine crystal with jade green steams and bases. Sara saw this and said, "Oh, I'll have one of those," to Ranger Blunt, who prepared it and brought it to her. Their eyes met as both their hands held the glass during the transference. It wasn't hard to sense that a connection was made.

Sara took a sip. "Isn't this a fabulous room?"

Everybody said yes, yes, and nodded in agreement.

"Did you enjoy your swim?"

"Yes," Thad said. "What a great pool."

"Well, the indoor pool, you know," Sara said, "which is like this huge Roman bath, is even better. Of course, that one is best used late at night." She turned to Lydia. "You should feel right at home, Lydia. Everything Hearst has here in the Castle was brought over from Europe or based on works from there."

"Yes, I suppose it could serve well as the parliament house for the European Union," Lydia answered.

"It would be marvelous as that, wouldn't it? If it was only in Europe, of course." She had apparently not understood the tone of Lydia's tuning-forked tongue.

"That's okay. Europeans love to travel."

"Well...." Sara had no idea where to take it. "So, Lydia, you've spent the day with my friends here, but let me play the good host and really introduce them to you."

She walked over to Thad and put her arm around his waist. "Thad here is an agent at William Morris. Young and aggressive, yet with a quiet, subtle method that, oddly enough, is bringing him much attention in the business. He's making his name by concentrating on new directors. His current star client is Jim Cruikshank, who made last year's big sci-fi epic, *Hell Planet*. Such a good picture Thad." She gave Thad an affectionate squeeze around his middle—as if he had made the film.

"Brett is a director of development at Tri-Star, just moved up from the story department." She moved over to him and grabbed his hand, like a girl clutching a boy's hand at the prom. "We're very proud of Brett."

"But you do not run Tri-Star. You run Olympic Pictures," Lydia said.

Sara took the accusation with an open face. "I'm trying to inject some magnanimousness into the industry." She looked up into Brett's face. "Keep up the good work, Brett." He leaned down and kissed her. It must have been expected, for she returned it promptly enough.

"Both Brett and Thad went to Harvard, by the way. Not as impressive as Yale, of course, but...."

Thad and Brett chuckled. They now thought of Sara as their alma mater.

"Abbie!" Sara gestured towards the lanky man. "NYU. Film Department. He's the VP, the only VP for producer-director Ira

Vollenberg. Ira makes great movies. Serious movies. Cinema at its best. He blows me away with his technique. Now, Abbie, if we could just find a movie for him that will gross more than thirty-three fucking cents at the box office, we would have a major player there."

"I'm working on it, Sara, but—"

"Abbie—we will find that project," Sara said as she walked over to Abbie and kissed him, on the cheek, like a loving sister.

"And Nick. Nick's an entertainment lawyer with Hungadunga, Hungadunga, Hungadunga, and McCormick."

"That's a Marx Brothers joke." Lydia pointed out.

"Yes, I never mention the name of his law firm because I hate the bastards, but Nick, I love. Nick has potential. Because he's an entertainment lawyer who really—don't you, Nick?—wants to be a game show host."

"I love game shows," Nick said with a real passion, dispelling any thought that Sara might be kidding.

"I know you do, Nick, but the influence of a game show host is about on the level of the influence of good sportsmanship on the National Hockey League. So, in your dreams, Nick, only in your dreams."

She turned and walked over to Brooke, who looked almost shy at Sara's approach. "Brooke, my love. Brooke runs the production company for Sara Hemmings. Not our greatest female star, but certainly programmable."

"Sara!" Brooke covered her ears as if to hear such a thing was sacrilegious.

"But Brooke is primed to be stolen away by some great diva. Aren't you Brooke?"

"I prefer working for women."

"That's lovely." They kissed. It was a long and passionate kiss. The men wanted to drop their mouths, but they knew they were just too damn sophisticated to do that—so they didn't.

When Sara was ready, she addressed Lydia again. "Every one of these five, Lydia, these are the kind of talented people in the industry I try to surround myself with. Truly, the up and coming."

"Up and coming? Sounds like premature ejaculation!"

Most broke into unsure laughter but stopped when they saw Sara hadn't. Sara was cold-eyed. "No, I don't think so."

Suddenly there was a burst of laughter coming from the fireplace. Then from a hidden panel on the left side of the fireplace, Maxwellton James appeared.

"I heard what you said just as I was coming out of the elevator, and, honestly, it took me a second to get it. Very witty, Lydia, very witty, indeed. Inappropriate, though, for these young people, I'm sure. Cream of the crop all, that's what Sara tells me, you're all cream-of-the-crop. I welcome you all to the home of William Randolph Hearst. Lately, for about thirty years or so, the property of the State of California. But we won't let that stop us from enjoying Mr. Hearst's hospitality."

21
SPITTING FLESH

Maxwellton James was oddly elegant, standing before the French fireplace in a loose-fitting black silk suit over a billowy white, collarless shirt. It was as if his large form had been draped to give it dignity. His high, broad, pink forehead reflected some of the light from the 128 naked bulbs in the ceiling above, as did, it seemed, his teeth, presented with the curtains drawn as he smiled upon us. His hair remained loose, flowing behind him, but now meticulously brushed smooth.

It was strange admiring a man for not putting his hair in a ponytail.

Hatless rushed over to him with a large, chilled glass of very dark beer, one-third of it a brilliant head of foam. Max took the frosted glass and downed the beer in three large, silent gulps. Without the slightest smack of his lips or any hint that he had enjoyed the drink, he returned the glass to Hatless, who handed Max a pressed, white cloth napkin in return. Max wiped the substantial foam mustache off his face and thoroughly dried his hands of moisture picked up from the chilled glass. Then he unfolded the napkin and blew his nose in a long, apparently successful fulmination. He neatly folded the soiled napkin and returned it to Hatless, then announced, "Dinner is being served in the Refectory. Would you follow me?"

We did, exiting the room through a door on the right side of the fireplace.

If King Arthur had had a long, skinny table instead of a round one, this is where he and his knights would have sat. The Refectory was a vast hall with a ceiling at least three stories high, covered with panels of life-sized, carved wood saints to watch over (and bless, one assumes) your meal. There was a fireplace you could walk into, inviting a couple of friends in to join you for the evening. There were more choir stalls along the walls. Hearst must have gotten a bulk deal. Colorful flags fluttered on high by the tall, gothic windows, and there were tapestries—of course—there were tapestries on the wall featuring selected moments in the Prophet Daniel's encounters with King Nebuchadnezzar, which Petey couldn't help but tell us all about. The power of space denotes power, with the added benefit of religious artifacts denoting Truth—or so one might like to believe.

The skinny dining table down the middle of the room comprised a series of narrow monastic tables positioned end to end. It's said that Hearst liked the up close and personal dining they afforded, or maybe he liked the tables for the slight humility they added to a grandiose room. Then again, perhaps they had just come free with his large order of choir stalls.

There were place settings for ten on the table, strangely laid out so that the last person on the right on both sides would have no one sitting directly across from them.

Max crossed the room to the center chair of the table's far side and began to hand out the seating assignments.

"Sara will sit on my left, with Thad to her left. Brett, you're on my right. Lydia, I have reserved you the seat across from me, with Brooke on your right and Nick on your left. Abbie, you're to the right of Brooke." Then, with a short pause to emphasize the afterthought: "The legal staff can take the end seats."

Henderson and Pinsker started to look for a place to set their briefcases, which they still carried. Max noticed this.

"I know you're attached to those cases, gentlemen, but surely you could have left them in your room. They would have been safe there."

"They brought them on my instructions," Lydia stated. "I never know when I'll want them to provide me with facts, figures, and information, and I am not tolerant of delay."

"Nothing wrong with being demanding of your underlings, Lydia," Max stated, underlining the underlings. "On the serving table behind you, then, would be the perfect spot, gentlemen. On either side of the model of the Titanic."

A bit of cat and mouse? We could not have picked better spots for full coverage. So, as instructed, we put our cases on the table on either side of a large glass display box with a model of the Titanic, steaming through the North Atlantic waters just moments before striking the iceberg, which was also modeled inside the box. Roee and I quickly took keys out, ostensibly unlocking the cases so they could easily be opened at Lydia's command, and surreptitiously positioned the snake nostrils. Mine I focused on Max. Roee, I was sure, set his to take in a good angle on Sara.

Max picked up a small silver bell and rang it. Rangers, including Sheila Barnes, all in tuxedos, brought out the dinner. It was seven courses of delicious food, well prepared and excellently presented. It was the kind of transcendent meal that could make one believe in—and practice—evil.

Max led all the dinner conversation in a thoroughly charming manner, paying the proper amount of attention to each of his guests (sans Henderson and Pinsker, of course, lost on either end) but paying the most attention to Lydia. He led with his eyes, cooing at her, smiling at her wit, laughing at her jokes, and complimenting her very being for its existence. Lydia gave back in like charm, meeting Max's eyes often, flashing her best smile just for him. The subjects of the conversation were insubstantial, typical polite dinner chat, but the orchestration was magnificent. The general air of privilege the five had already felt must have intensified to something equating to a refined heroin high.

"You know," Max said as we finished dessert, "when Hearst gave dinners here, it was always informal. Ketchup bottles and mustard jars on the table instead of the condiments served in fine, silver receptacles, as we have here for you tonight. He serviced Mr. and Mrs. America with his papers, magazines, and movies, so I suppose he thought it was the least he could do to feel close to them. The penance he paid to excuse himself for having the power, money, and good taste to surround himself with the best and finest of art from Europe?"

I'm afraid Henderson snorted as he tried to suppress a laugh. Max looked my way, displeased with the rowdy exile interrupting the beginning of what was the reason we had all been gathered, but that was okay. It was time to get under his skin again.

"Which one are you?" Max asked. "Frick or Frack? Muck or Meyer?"

"My name is Henderson, Mr. James, and excuse me, but Hearst may have bought a lot of stuff in Europe, but it was hardly all the best and finest."

"Is that a legal opinion?"

"I was an art history major before I turned to the law."

"Specializing in what? The history of aviation art?"

"No, that's just a hobby that came later with my interest in flying."

"You are obviously a complex person, Mr. Henderson. Why the switch from art history to law?"

"Not much money in art history."

"Oh, but there would have been so much more satisfaction. Especially for the soul."

"My soul is perfectly satisfied with money, thank you."

You could see Max make note of that, but you couldn't perceive his judgment as to its veracity.

"But it's not satisfied with Mr. Hearst's art collection," Max said.

"It has its merits, but much of the stuff is second-rate. For example, we've been put in the Della Robbia bedroom suite, named obviously because most of the artwork in there comes from the Della Robbia family. Well, Luca Della Robbia, the founder of the family, he was pretty good, close in talent to Donatello, but there's nothing of his in there. It's mostly glazed terra-cotta stuff churned out by his family's shop after his death. Made-to-order cheap church decorations. The kitsch of its time, but, you know, from Hearst's perspective, I suppose, a four-hundred-year-old Italian Madonna and Child is a four-hundred-year-old Italian Madonna and Child. He must have been impressed. I think, though, quite frankly, he was taken for a ride more often than not."

It was hushed when I had finished. Max stared impassively at me. Sara could not hide her feelings; she looked angry, her ugly face growling silently. The five sat and watched and anticipated. Lydia broke the thick calm.

"Well, it's better than collecting Lladró figurines!"

Brooke tittered.

"Yes, well," Max said as he picked up the silver bell and rang it, "cigars and brandy?"

Sheila Barnes came in rolling a silver and glass drinks cart on which sat a large decanter of brandy and ten crystal snifters.

"I think you'll enjoy this brandy," Max said as Sheila began to serve us. "It once belonged to Charles de Gaulle. It would have brought a rather hefty price at Sotheby's had it not been stolen the night before the scheduled auction. How it came into my hands is a great and rather amusing story—but not for tonight."

Ranger Blunt was in the Refectory now with a large humidor chest of inlaid woods, maple and mahogany among them, gleamed to a piano finish, which brilliantly picked up the light of the chandeliers overhead. He presented it to each one of us in turn, lifting the lid as if showing the wicked Queen her most fervent desire: The freshly retrieved heart of Snow White.

"The cigars are not Cuban," Max announced. "I happen to believe that Cuban cigars are highly overrated. Something to do with their being illegal." It was a very knowing statement. "Plus, I've always refused to do business with Castro—who is a pig. These are Dominican and as rare as Cuban, for they come from a factory with a very exclusive clientele."

The five went wide-eyed and near dizzy at the sight of the cigars. Fat, brown, round, each one was selected with a trembling tenderness as if to hold it too roughly would be to bruise and spoil it. Once selected, the cigar was handed over to Ranger Blunt, who prepared each one for lighting by making a precise V-cut to the ends. Then he would hand them back to the anticipating recipients. All, including Brooke, placed the cigars between their lips with deep satisfaction and gratefully accepted a light from Blunt— dreams of them and their cigars pictured on glossy magazine covers rolling off the presses in their heads, no doubt.

Henderson and Pinsker refused Ranger Blunt's offer. Max showed exaggerated surprise.

"Doctor's orders," Pinsker said. "Asthma runs in the family."

"My father died of mouth cancer," I said by way of my explanation. "It wasn't pretty, those last months, him spitting out flesh all the time."

We were instantly ignored.

Sara and Brooke were the most childlike in lighting up and appreciating the smoke and the most disappointed when Lydia refused to join them, feeling the blow to women's liberation.

"Oh, come on, Lydia," they urged, leaving the invite into the club unstated but gilt-edged, nonetheless.

"No thanks," Lydia said, her radio-static voice puncturing the air. "The next time I feel compelled to wrap my lips around something long, cylindrical, and brown—I'm going to want it to be Denzel Washington."

The five laughed, delighted to have their absurdities pointed out to them.

Abbie raised his long, brown, burning cylinder into the air and cried, "Surrogate cock suckers of the world, unite!" There was more laughter. The five felt fine, pleased with themselves, deeply and satisfied. It was a combination of setting—is this the power of Feng Shui?—sustenance, satiation, and smoke.

The preparation, now completed, Max got back onto the track. He raised his snifter. "Please join me in a toast." The tone of his voice indicated that things now were to be serious and not lighthearted. "To the twenty-first century!"

"To the twenty-first century!" everybody quickly repeated as they raised their snifters.

"It's going to be a bitch!" Max declared very pointedly, then took a sip of his brandy.

The rest were not quite sure what to do. Some joined in sipping, and some just sat and waited.

Then Lydia downed her brandy like a shot and said, "Well if it's going to be a bitch, may that bitch be me!"

22
THE 21ST-CENTURY BITCH

No one laughed. The look on Max's face did not allow for it. It was a stone. A stone with charm—if that can be imagined—but a stone, nonetheless. Solidity, rock solid, something substantial, and very appealing because we all want the teacher to tell us what's important and what's not.

A stone—with charm—and meaning.

And just a hint—possibly too slight for the others to perceive, but I was predisposed to—just a touch of madness in the two muted green eyes set in the pink stone of his face.

"They took the Future from me," Max started to speak. "The bright and shining Future. Do you remember it? It was laid out and portrayed in popular science magazines. At World Fairs. By Walt Disney. Cities. Bright, colorful cities of tall gleaming buildings. Cities clean and well-ordered. Interconnecting bridges between the buildings of moving sidewalks automatically covered during inclement weather by crystal-clear plastics, open to the sun on gorgeous days, of which there would be many. We would each have small flying cars to buzz around the city, jet packs, or personal ornithopters. Our clothes would never fade or soil. Robots would do the manufacturing in the factories, the paperwork in the office, the childcare at home. They would tote that barge and lift that bale. Meals would be delicious, plentiful, prepared by automatic cookers. There would be acres of parkland in the cities, lots of recreation and fun. Always something to do. They never even considered that one could be bored in the Future. Everyone was to be happy in the Future, and the Future was always called the twenty-first century."

He had been speaking to no one in particular; his eyes had been slightly lifted, concentrating on that bright, shining Future, but now he brought them back down and focused on Brooke.

"We're almost there, Brooke. The twenty-first century. What do you think? Did we make it? Did we get that Future?"

"Hardly," Brooke said with a sweet and sour snort.

"Hardly, indeed," Max said. "The twenty-first century will not be that bright, shiny future of colorfully illustrated magazine covers. It's going to be, I'm afraid, '...a series of jolts and jars and smashes in the social life of humanity...'" Not my words. Some writer in *The Economist* in 1930 wrote those words. He was sitting in London at the time. The depression had just started. Europe was rumbling with the festering forces that had been abated but not controlled at the end of World War I. So he knew that World War II was inevitable, so he wrote those words and was right. There were jolts, and there were jars, and there were smashes to the social life of humanity, but nothing compared to what's coming in the twenty-first century."

Max paused. The stone smiled.

"But why am I talking to you guys about this?" He put a loving hand on Brett's arm, turning to look past Sara to Thad, then crossing the table with his eyes to scan and acknowledge those of us on the other side, not so very far that his eyes could not achieve the same effect as a loving hand gently placed on a willing arm. "You makers of franchise entertainment, you makers of tent-pole movies to hang your global media corporate wishes on, you— Show Biz folks. Except for our lonely lawyers, of course, but you happen to be on this train, Muck and Meyer," Max made quick eye contact with Henderson and Pinsker, "so you're just going to have to make the stops with everybody else."

Then the subject returned to the objects.

"Why bring all this up? Especially after such a lovely day of fun—fun renewing the battles of yesteryear when we did manage, by the barest of margins, to recover from those jolts and jars and smashes. And fun swimming in the pool of privilege. The joy of an excellent dinner. Superb brandy. Wonderful cigars. Why must I be such a downer among you 'entertaining' folks?"

Max got up from the table. "Tunnels dank and dark are often the only conduits to the light. I will take you to the light. Even more exciting, I'll show you how you can be part of the light."

Brett and Abbie started to get up as well, thinking it was time to follow, but Max waved them down with his hand, assuring them that they could sit and relax; it wasn't time to march just yet. Then he moved around the table and crossed over to the large glass case on the serving table behind me—those of us who needed to shifted our positions in our chairs to face him.

He looked at the model of the Titanic moments before being jolted and jarred and smashed by the iceberg.

"This was not one of Mr. Hearst's treasures, by the way. This is mine. I built it myself. I love it. It's a great symbol. Of what? Of the whole history of humankind, a history that is about to take an unfortunate turn. Unless we work to prevent it, our civilization may be doomed. But, if it is inevitable—and there is plenty of evidence indicating that it is—unless we work to prevent the turn from being so sharp that we lose our purchase of the road, spin out of control, crash, and burn. The ride will still be wild, but maybe, just maybe, we will not be crushed in a total wreck."

Max turned to us, keeping the model to his side. "I'm sorry. I rather dry-docked my metaphor, didn't I? Well, returning to the perilous waves." He pointed to the Titanic. "It was called a Luxury Liner. The upper decks were beautifully appointed. Hand-carved woodwork, polished to a high shine. Marble staircases. Crystal chandeliers. The deepest, thickest, finest carpets. Great chefs working in the most modern of kitchens to create delicious meals for refined palates. Large, spacious staterooms. The most solicitous service ever, making the passage over the North Atlantic as comfortable as humanly possible for the elite, the privileged, the rich, the deserving, and the important people of the day who, quite frankly, ran the world to their specifications.

"It cost, as you can imagine, quite a bit of money to travel on the upper decks of a luxury liner. But the irony is that White Star, which built and operated the Titanic, did not profit from first-class passengers. As high as the ticket price was, it didn't go anywhere near covering the costs, much less pushing the books into profit. The money was made down here." Max pointed to the lower decks, "Steerage. Not very well appointed, of course. No great staterooms. Just a hole to cram them into. Who? Immigrants. Millions and millions of immigrants wanted to get from the old world, where they had been ground down into the pavement, to the New World, where the pavement, they believed, was made of gold. In 1905 the North Atlantic trade had its first million-passenger year, and there were millions more waiting at the ticket office. It was a numbers game, like everything else. A volume business. These ships weren't built big and impressive to impress the significant and special few. They were built for volume to carry the rank and oppressed many, carrying on their backs, so to speak, the significant and special few in the manner they were most accustomed to—the manner they quite rightly deserved. I'm not stating any of this as a criticism. I don't criticize the natural order of things. What fucking good would that do?

"The deserving—the smart, bright, crafty, talented deserving—have always ridden on the backs of the mass of humanity that weren't smart, bright, crafty, and talented, and so, of course, not at all deserving. There are more of them than us, though, more of them than us. A resource. A vast resource of little flesh pockets of muscles. Muscles to till the land, row the ships, build the Pyramids, and—yes—pick the cotton, take out the garbage, and pay for passage to the promised land with every last cent of their meager savings. Have you ever known it to be otherwise? The natural order of things. We all give to society what is ours to give. The deserving give intellectual/creative/cultural impetus. That is their true wealth to share. The mass provides what little wealth they have: their labor or the meager savings their labor has acquired. A pitiful pittance per individual but great, transferable wealth in mass quantities. The natural order of things.

"Not nature, but Man!" Max mocked a protest as he moved on toward the massive fireplace. "You might suggest that—" He stopped and looked down the long, narrow table at us. "Well, of course, none of *you* would suggest that I'm sure, but maybe some people with their emotions on their sleeves and their brains in storage might suggest that Man divided himself into the Haves and the Have-nots, not Nature. But man is as much a part of Nature as any old—oh—delicate dandelion, for example, or a plague of locusts, or the magnificent Big Horn Elk, or UV radiation, or a gorgeous sunset—caused by Man's pollution. So let's not deal with that old argument.

"Nature throws curves at us." He pointed down the room back to the Titanic display. "An iceberg. Upsetting the natural order of things. 2200 people. 1500 drowned. There weren't enough lifeboats. Proportionately, more from steerage drowned than those from the upper decks. Because there weren't enough lifeboats. The natural order of things. Oh, some millionaires died. John Jacob Astor. Benjamin Guggenheim. Isidor Straus. The rich make their sacrifices too. People seem to forget that."

Max returned to his chair, Sheila Barnes greeting him there with a fresh snifter of brandy. He thanked her sweetly and then sat.

"Twenty-first-century icebergs? There's going to be quite a few. First, I think you'll have to agree, overpopulation in the developing nations."

Max took a drag on his cigar and then blew the smoke up to the saints.

"That's a bit of PC nicety, isn't it? 'Developing nations?' We used to call them underdeveloped nations. Some did develop. Rather well. Japan. South Korea. Taiwan. Others, though, especially many in the southern hemisphere, have not, and they are not making great strides. Why? Because, with some atavistic notions of the cattle value of human life, they keep pumping out babies they cannot adequately feed, care for, or educate. Numbers add up, nevertheless. Volume is filled, regardless. Without any corresponding increase in resources, of course. So let's have some simple honesty with ourselves, shall we? They are not developing nations. They are non-developed nations. And they are not about to get developed anytime soon.

"Another iceberg? Environmental problems. Very real, I think you'll agree, and, yes, we in the developed nations caused a lot of it, but we are also the ones now cleaning up our act. But the non-developed countries, in their futile bid to catch up to us, industrializing with no sense of a world social conscience, burning and cutting down the rain forests for farmland to feed their creeping, crawling masses, or maybe to export fine beef, they are now the ones truly fouling the air with their stench, and they won't listen to reason. They refuse to learn from our mistakes. But then, why should they? When the Holy Grail image in their head is the clean, comfortable, luxury-appointed upper decks of the developed nations. Especially as portrayed in our film and television entertainment!

"Yes! The product of your endeavors. But let's put the guilt aside for a minute. I'm sure I'll remember to return to it later."

It was time for Brett and Thad, Nick, Brooke, and Abbie to throw and catch furtive glances at each other, so they did. Lydia kept her eyes on Max—fascinated.

"And yet another iceberg. Technology. We—" Max gestured to us all. "We love technology. No reason not to. It has done wonders for our world, but our world is the developed world that deserves the wonders of technology. The non-developed world, unfortunately, does not equate well to technology. An explosion of technology is, in fact, antithetical to an explosion of population, for technology is to relieve laborious burdens. That's why developed nations decrease their fertility rates. More technology, less need for human labor, fewer people to share the wonders of technology and its financial fruit. A proper balance is struck. People used to think technology dehumanized us. Of course, it doesn't—much the reverse. By relieving us of laborious burdens, it frees us to become more human. Technology lets us be people, not labor. Isn't that the natural way to equal the distance between the Haves and the Have-nots?

"Are you getting any of this? Are you understanding? The world is divided between the Haves and the Have-nots. Always has been—the natural order of things. The Haves used to need the Have-nots. To lift the bales, tote the barges, buy tickets in volume, and fill up steerage so the Haves could comfortably ride in first class. But less and less, the Haves are going to need the Have-nots. The Haves have learned to control their numbers, educate their young, and share the wealth—among the deserving. The Have-nots have learned nothing. They are pushing their resources beyond the limits, pushing their masses into our lands, pushing disaster.

"This is not a maybe. This is a certainty. The war between the Haves and the Have- nots is coming. It is not a class war. It goes beyond class. Beyond race. All Haves create themselves equally. All Have-nots stew in resentment equally. The battle is coming.

"I am here to recruit you into the army of the Haves."

xx

Max took a sip of his brandy, giving us a moment to digest what he had been saying. Another moment to reflect on it. He savored the drink with his eyes closed. The smallest of smiles moved across his lips. He looked contented. With the brandy? With his performance? He had a commanding charisma; there was no doubt about that. Influential in a one-on-one or small group situation like this. I suspected he might have been ineffective in a small crowd—too many people to make love to at one time, too much spreading of the wealth. A good politician is not always a good campaigner. A good campaigner is not always a good politician. The best of both are the ones who recognize it and concentrate effort where their strengths lie.

No one spoke. No questions. No quips. Just anticipation. All eyes were on Max. We were waiting for the intermission to end.

Max opened his eyes and took in everybody in one sweeping glance.

"Do you like statistics? Of course, you do. Everybody does. Some people think statistics are boring, but they're not, are they? They're fascinating. Like two-headed sheep and albino midgets. Look how perverse these are:

"In 1825, there were one billion people on this planet. One billion! Abbie, is that a lot? One billion?"

"Well," Abbie said, "I'd like just one dollar from each of them."

"Yes, I bet you would, and if I could arrange it, Abbie, it would be yours. A billion dollars! I would love to wrap it up neatly and hand it to you, but that's not my purpose—at this moment.

"1825—one billion people. A quarter of a century before, that great pessimist, Malthus, saw it coming. 'Whoa!' Malthus said. England alone is crawling with too many people. 'Look out!' he yelled. We're crawling all over ourselves, chasing the few loaves of bread available for the many; death and destruction, death and destruction is the only fate of mankind!"

Max had raised his voice here to a near shout, gesturing with both arms thrust into the air, his hands wide open to the saints above, not in supplication—the saints just happened to be in the way.

Max's arms came down slowly as his whole body settled comfortably in his chair. Then he quietly continued.

"Mankind fooled him, or rather, the smart, bright, crafty, and talented among mankind did. We found clever ways to draw out of the earth enough to feed on. We were happy. We prospered, and we were fruitful.

"So—1925: Two billion people. 1976: Four billion people. 1990: Five point three billion people. One dollar from each, yes, Abbie? One dollar from each? And in 2025, only a quarter of the way through the next century: Eight and a half billion people are projected. 2050? Ten to fourteen point five billion people!

"Malthus was right! Just premature.

"Here's another statistic. Between now and 2025, ninety-five percent of population growth will be in non-developed nations.

"Do you see the problem? The Haves really could have the twenty-first century of our dreams. The Haves have the intelligence, self-control, and ingenuity to build a bright and shining future. The Have-nots hardly have the wherewithal to build mud huts. The Haves, with a few exceptions, almost all live in the northern hemisphere. We used to call it Western Civilization. That which gave birth to you and me. Can't call it that now. The

Japanese, the South Koreans, who knows, maybe the Chinese, have joined us. Are the Russians far behind? But what is their key to membership? Adaptation of the principals of Western Civilization. Which is why Arabs, despite those with riches, may never be able to join."

His cigar flared upon inhalation. A billow of smoke followed.

"Have you ever heard the Tokyo String Quartet play Mozart, by the way? Marvelous!

"So now we are, the North, and we could have our lovely twenty-first century—"

The stone turned to steel. "If it wasn't for the South.

"One would love to see them pick themselves up by their bootstraps. Africa, South America, but they hardly have the boots for it.

"Billions of them down there. Would you like a dollar from each one of them, Abbie?"

Abbie knew not to answer. So Abbie didn't.

"That's not much more than what many make in a week. Lousy markets down there. Just lands of diminishing resources, crawling with people, both resentful and envious of us, streams of them flowing north, up from Africa into Europe, for example, or up Latin America into the good ol' U S of A. Not that there won't be plenty left behind to continue polluting the earth to death.

"You all know what I am talking about. You are bright, intelligent people. Jolts and jars and smashes in the social life of humanity are coming. They cannot be prevented. Two world wars in the twentieth century? The twenty-first will be nothing but world wars. The only question is, what kinds of wars? Armed conflicts: North against South? Islam against the rest of us? The Haves against the Have-nots? Environmental conflicts: Hole in the ozone layer, and yet too much ozone? No clean water? No fresh air? Global warming on top of all that? Natural conflicts: Nature against Man? Diseases against Man? The Elements against Man?

"Any one of these brings us close to Doomsday. Any two in combination practically assures it. In a whimper or a bang? Whatever! The twenty-first century is going to be a bitch!"

Max looked around at all of us. He smiled a great big, broad smile. "Hemlock, anyone?"

"No," Lydia spoke up. "But I would like some more brandy."

"Of course. Sheila?"

Sheila practically ran over to Lydia and refilled her glass. Everyone else offered up their snifters for more.

"And I would kill for a cigarette," Lydia complained.

"Sorry," Max said as he placed his cigar in his mouth. "Don't keep any around. Carcinogenic, you know. But I understand your meaning: What's the use? If the world is going to hell in a handbasket, why not indulge in every death-dealing but enjoyable vice we can afford? After all, it is only money. It is only life. Both fragile and ephemeral things at best."

The stone and steel returned.

"Unless we are vigilant in our protection of them."

Brett, who sat next to Max, seemed agitated. He had a jaw on a well-oiled hinge, so it's not surprising his had dropped the most. He spoke. "But—but, well, shouldn't the government do something about it—or the UN maybe?"

Max turned to Brett, disbelief prominent on his face. Then he broke out into a rapid-fire series of choppy laughs.

"Government! Governments are passé. Governments are useless. Governments have only two real functions. One is to collect taxes. The other is to fill in potholes. The first is a habit that needs to be controlled. The second is a duty they seem to ignore. Governments have national anthems but no real national purpose. Because there is no purpose to being a nation anymore—it's a borderless world. Haven't you heard? Twenty-four-hour electronic worldwide movement of currencies: Buy, sell, transfer. Worldwide trading on stock exchanges, twenty-four hours a day, the rise and fall of fortunes. Worldwide communication on the Internet, twenty-four hours a day, speech freer than ever, and all this zipping across borders as if borders didn't exist—because, for all practical purposes, they don't.

"There will soon be only three currencies that matter. The Dollar. The Yuan. The Euro. How soon after that will it come down to two? How soon after that will it be only one? Which one will be transcendent? Or all three might crash. Then will it be currency credits issued not from nations' banks but from stock exchanges? But no matter what you call it, it will still be Wealth, and in the final analysis, it will be issued by the wealthy to the wealthy for the wealthy.

"It's Wealth that runs the world, not nations, and right now, the world's wealth is controlled by globalized corporations. You know it, and I know it. You—" Max referred to the five. "All of you, in one form or another, work for such corporations, and they work for their stockholders, but their stockholders have put their trust in fund managers. Fund managers are the new representatives of the people, but only "the people" who hold stock. It's no longer One Man One Vote, folks. Whether that one man is a dictator whose one vote is the only vote that counts or whether that one man is one of many, each equal in their one vote. So don't tell me, Brett, that governments will solve the problems of the twenty-first century."

"Well, then," Brett was desperate for an answer, "the corporations should, uh, get together then and—"

"Corporations are faceless entities that compete. They share mutual interests, but none strong enough to get them to drop their single-minded Purpose of Profit to band together to solve any but their own localized problems. Like the fading governments, corporations are too visible to probing eyes attached to critical minds. Not to mention that often global corporations are headed up by egomaniacal, popinjay champions of self-aggrandizement, who are so busy jumping from spotlight to spotlight, they never really have time to peer into the dark corners of the future."

"I assume." It was time for Henderson to speak up. "That there is an organization that does peer into the dark corners and that you are a representative thereof."

Max cocked his head as he looked at me.

"You're very smart," he said, "for a man who spends all day in his briefs." Max laughed at his own poor joke. "You are, of course, correct."

Max paused as his smile dropped. He took a long breath through his nostrils and returned his concentration to the five plus Lydia, where his eyes often fell.

"There is a quiet crew of people who either all have wealth, work for wealth, or are sympathetic towards wealth as the protector of culture, who have banded together into The Enclave. That is what it is going to take to protect us. Some of these people may be heads of large corporations, but their loyalty is to The Enclave. Some of these people may be from our finest think tanks and universities, but they do their real thinking for The Enclave. Some of these people may be in politics, working with the ineffectual governments, but are actually working for The Enclave. Some may be in Law Enforcement. Some may be in—law infringement. There are the religious among us and the thoroughly pragmatic. We have representatives of Old Money, Recent Money, and Very, Very New Money.

"We call ourselves a quiet crew because none of us seek the limelight. All of us have decided to serve—and save—our civilization. All of us, each in our own way, are hugely influential within their sphere. Through our actions, agreed upon by all, we work to influence governments and corporations and other entities of power—power from the mild to the toxic—to make the right decisions; to take the right action that will help us prevent a disastrous turn of history or, as I said, at least diminished the impact of that turn. We are not Pollyannas. The jolts and jars and smashes are going to come. The question is, how virulent will they be? Not to Mankind. We don't give a shit about 'Mankind.' We care only about our civilization. The Enclave is dedicated to the preservation of our civilization.

"To succeed—we need your help."

Max was now looking directly into Lydia's eyes, and she was looking into his. "Yours, Lydia," he continued. "And yours, Brooke," he said, starting a survey, "and Abbie, yours too." He turned to his right and put his arm around Brett. "And Brett's, we will need Brett's help." Then he turned to look past Sara to Thad. "And Thad's, of course. Most definitely yours, Thad."

All thought about this for a second, with a solemnity not often found outside of monasteries in remote locations. Then Thad quietly stated:

"You know, I'm about ready to close a deal on a project in

which a mutated version of the AIDS virus, irradiated to the size of squirrels, attacks San Francisco, destroys it, then heads south towards Los Angeles. How exactly am I supposed to help preserve civilization?"

Max seemed delighted with the question.

"A better question than you might imagine, Thad. But first things first. Thad, in your climb up the show biz ladder, have you ever kissed ass?"

Thad's head moved back slightly, more shocked by this than by anything else he had heard all evening.

"I, well—"

"Come on. Honesty. I demand it."

"I, uh, on occasion, well, let's say on occasion that I've been nicer to certain people than I would have been had I been in control of the situation."

"So you've kissed much ass."

"Yeah, okay, I have butt hairs in my teeth."

"Fine. The first thing you can do to help preserve our civilization is to kiss just one more ass, but it will be the most important ass you'll ever kiss. Indeed, it will be the last ass you will ever need to kiss."

HOLLYWOOD
IS AN ALL-VOLUNTEER ARMY

23
TESTING THE TESTOSTERONE

Sara spoke with a particular delight:

"Yes, it's true, it's all true! You've heard about the kissing of the Golden Arse, haven't you? I know you have because I made sure the rumors spread specifically in your direction. Don Gulden—that poor boy, does anybody know how's he doing? Don was particularly good at spreading. You don't know the details, though, do you? You've just had to live off the rumors, and Lydia here, not to mention Frick and Frack, haven't even had the rumors to keep them warm. But now it's time to reveal all and end your breathless anticipation."

Sara turned to Lydia to address her comments. For it was Lydia she really had to sell, and Lydia who she leaned close to.

"Lydia, for some time now, the quiet yet rampant rumor of Hollywood has been that Sara Hutton was running a secret society. A very exclusive secret society. I made it a secret because Hollywood loves secrets. I made it exclusive so that everyone would want to join. I'm sure everyone thought it was just a lark, like male executives from various companies climbing mountains together or shooting white water rapids together. Testing the testosterone, I like to call it.

"Then, a name started to creep into the rumors. A strange

301

name. Golden Arse. Something to do with a Golden Arse. Intriguing. An animal from myth with meaning or the greatest and richest posterior of them all? Then, names got out, names of those who, it had been said, got to kiss the Golden Arse and become members of this secret society. Look at the list. The Buzz people, the people making names for themselves, the people getting closer to power, the people with the first blushes of power. People realized that to be asked by Sara Hutton to join her secret society was like an anointment. Have you heard she has retreats? Is that where she asks you to join? How can I get invited to one of her retreats?"

Sara leaned back now, comfortable that she had Lydia's, and everybody else's, full attention.

"It's satisfying to see your baby grow and be successful. You see, Lydia, I started the Communion of the Golden Arse in college at Yale. It was Max's idea. I was at loose ends about what to do with my life. Max was the pragmatic one who told me I would be stupid not to use my father's connections and get into the Industry. Important, he said, the Industry is becoming so very important. Its profound effect, Max pointed out to me its profound effect. 'But you've got to have a strength,' he said. 'Strength by association. Can't join the Old Boy's Network. Don't join the New Girls Network. Too limiting,' he told me. 'Form your own,' he said, 'now, don't wait.' Form it with whom? I asked. 'What?' Max said. 'People at Yale, other colleges in the Ivy League, they're not going to get well positioned?' So, using the base of Gamma Phi Epsilon, I formed the Communion of the Golden Arse and invited people interested in film and, more to the point, the Industry. We made a pact to help each other, to hold each other's hands as we entered the industry and had to bend over and kiss some grimy asses to get ahead, but we did it secure in the knowledge that the only ass that mattered was a much finer ass, was our ass, was the Golden Arse.

"You can't imagine what strength that knowledge gives you.

"It worked. Several of us hit Hollywood simultaneously, well-credentialed in education and contacts. That doesn't mean we didn't hit brick walls, but we were there to help each other over the walls. We would talk each other up, for example. Send out what I like to call Hot Flashes on each other so that our personal and collective value rose as the talk increased.

"We all did well.

"Then it was time to take the Communion of the Golden Arse to the next level. I've always consciously picked members that I knew needed success. Not just desired but needed. People whose sense of self-worth had much to do with their desire for self-wealth. Which is a great motivator; it centers people. But I also picked people who had a total view of life, who saw beyond their personal concerns and cared about what was going on in the world, cared about its future, cared about that which we have created, that which is fine and good—people who cared about our civilization. People who would be willing to help protect and defend that civilization. I presented the ideas to the charter members. I introduced them to Max. Max introduced them to the Enclave. Not one failed me.

"Now, as I bring in new members to the Communion. I am as choosy as I've ever been. The fact that all of you are sitting around this table with Max and me, you can take as the greatest compliment you will ever be given. To sit around this table is to be invited to join the Communion of the Golden Arse."

Five little thrills went up, waved in the air, shouted for joy, and dived down into their hosts—all without making a sound.

"Membership guarantees that you will be aligned with a group of people in the industry who have your interests as much as their own in their hearts. Suddenly you will be talked about around town. Hot Flashes will be sent out about you. Offers and opportunities will fall into place. That place being, of course—at your feet. Soon, power will be the door you walk through.

"My goal is to one day have each person on Premier Magazine's One Hundred Most Powerful People in Hollywood list be a secret member of the Communion of the Golden Arse.

"Then our real work will begin. Our service to the Enclave."

"In the twenty-first century," Max picked up the pitch without letting even a beat go by, "when the jolts and jars and smashes come, those people who are in power, many of whom will be members of the Enclave, will be formulating philosophies, making decisions, influencing the execution of actions that will be hard and harsh and, to weak minds, horrific.

"Wars will be fought. Certain governments will need military might—in techno-power and manpower—to fight and win those wars. Specific segments of society will need to be—prepared—to willingly give up their sons and daughters to be a part of those fights.

"There will be famines—in the South—heart-wrenching, human tragedy famines. There will be an essential job to do. Not stopping the famines—which would be, in any case, impossible— but stopping the hearts from wrenching.

"Plagues? Yes, but the task will be keeping them in the Southern Hemisphere. Do we want to waste our resources in any effort beyond containing them in the Southern Hemisphere? Absolutely not. Let Nature take its course. Why should we work against it? The planet cries to shed itself of the overburden of nonproductive peoples. Everything we do to prevent it causes the earth to cry even more violently.

"To save our civilization, the Enclave will work along Nature's course, helping Nature to do what Nature needs to do."

"The Communion of the Golden Arse," Sara picked up the thread, "has a vital role to play. In the twenty-first century, its members will be the power elite of all media. We will be in film, television, the Internet, news gathering, and dissemination. We will control the media's mighty influence, from big-budget action films to emotion-stirring dramas to the 'opinions' of pundits. An influence to spur people on to action or to pacify them into acceptance of the inevitable, the necessary, and the natural. It's a power that exists now. It is just not organized and dedicated to a common goal. The Communion of the Golden Arse, working as calmly and quietly as the Enclave does in other spheres of influence, will organize that power and dedicate it to preserving our civilization.

"As I see it, there is no greater calling you will ever be asked to answer; no more important task you will ever be asked to assume."

By the end of her speech, in the thickness of the atmosphere, Max's left hand was holding tight onto Sara's right. Max offered his free right hand to Brett, who took it and encouraged him to reach the short distance across the table to offer a hand to Nick. Nick took it. Sara offered her left hand to Thad. He hesitated only slightly, then took it, simultaneously offering his hand across the table to Abbie, who took it as Brooke took Abbie's other hand. Then Nick and Brooke offered their free hands to Lydia in a beautifully coordinated movement. Lydia slowly looked at each hand. Then she looked at Max and Sara. She was not smiling, her face was still with contemplation, but her eyes were alive with excitement. She raised both her hands and allowed them to hover for a second. Then she vigorously grabbed the hands of Nick and Brooke, completing the circle.

A circle Henderson and Pinsker were left outside of.

"Good. Excellent." Max said.

"Welcome to the Communion of the Golden Arse," Sara said with overweening pride hanging out for all to see.

"Welcome to service to the Enclave," Max added.

"Now," Sara stood up. "Follow me. Like all good secret societies, we must have our initiation ceremony."

Everyone stood, including Lydia. Lydia, who I no longer could tell if she was following my script—or if she had allowed Max and Sara to suspend her disbelief. It had always been the chance with Lydia. I had accepted that in recruiting her. It was just disconcerting that I could not, at this moment, tell where her loyalties lay. As we remained seated as all those around us stood, I caught Roee's eye. He communicated back the same concern.

"No, Lydia, stay," Max said. "Let them set up, and we'll join them in a minute." He turned to the others. "As Lydia is a visitor, I want to fill her in on the current lay- of-the-land in Hollywood." He smiled gracefully at the five. "Stuff you are well versed in. It won't take long."

The five didn't care. Sara shot a question at Max, but he nodded calmly. "It's okay." Sara led the eager others through the door at the other end of the long hall from where we came in.

Lydia and Max sat.

"Lydia. Gentlemen," Max said, acknowledging us for the first time in a while but not asking us to close any gap. Then he turned his full attention to Lydia. "Are you comfortable with this?"

Lydia smiled. "Comfortable? I am shocked! I am completely and thoroughly shocked. To hear Americans talk this way. So practical, so pragmatic, so real. Instead of the little fantasies of sunshine and lollipops you usually spew out. How utterly refreshing."

"Then we should work very hard for your deal with Sara regarding Olympic Pictures to come to fruition."

"Absolutely! We must be a player in media as big as any of them. So we can hold up our end—and profit greatly."

"And profit greatly, you will. But I am concerned now about any opinions the gentlemen to our sides may have."

Lydia looked with surprise towards us, then back to Max.

"Opinions? They're my lawyers. Their only opinions are the ones I pay them to have."

She did not give us away, she could have and didn't, but then she couldn't reveal our subterfuge without admitting she had been a part of it and struggling to convince Max that her conversion was genuine. She had very little time if she was looking for a way to do that. The do-or-die moment was just around the corner. Was her mind working furiously, trying to figure out a plan quickly? Her face, her attitude, revealed nothing to me.

Was I worried? I had a slight concern.

"Do you agree with that?" Max was asking Henderson and Pinsker.

"We act on our client's behalf," was my answer.

"Can I feel secure that you will keep confident all you have heard here tonight?"

"If we can close the Olympic deal to our client's satisfaction, we'd keep your laundry list confidential," Pinsker said.

"And there's a little thing called Attorney-Client Privilege. If they breach it, they are perfectly aware of my success rate in litigating against those who cross me."

"Yes, Lydia, we're well aware of that, and I assure you, it will never come to that," I said coldly.

"Good," Max said. "I will offer you my trust because your client is far more important to us than the other five. They are perfect candidates for the Communion; they will be willing soldiers of propaganda—but nothing more. Lydia, on the other hand, although soon to be a valued member of the Communion, is also, I believe, a worthy candidate for the Enclave, and with your permission, Lydia, I will be happy to nominate you at the earliest possible opportunity."

Lydia looked generally surprised and moved. Then in all apparently genuine humility, she said, "I—I would be honored."

My slight concern took on some heft.

xx

"Can I do a little retouching first?" Lydia asked as she took a tube of lipstick out of her small evening purse.

"Interesting shade," Max commented as he waited with the slight impatience men have similarly waited with for ages.

"Made especially for me?" Lydia finished, examining her accuracy in a compact mirror. "I love it!" She inserted the stick back in the tube and threw the compact into her purse. Then she stood up and joined Max.

As they were halfway out, Max turned to us just as I was about to say something. "Oh, you guys can come if you want. I told you I trust you. Don't forget your briefcases. I know how attached you are to them."

He turned and led Lydia out of the room. Henderson and Pinsker hurried to grab the briefcases and catch up.

xx

Max invited Lydia to follow him.

Max took us through the game room featuring two pool tables and another tapestry. This one depicted a none-too-successful stag hunt. Then we entered Hearst's private movie theater, a scaled-down version of the vast picture palaces that were its contemporaries. Scaled down but still a great space, ornately decorated, with a high ceiling and illumination provided by rows of mock caryatids, sculpted life-size women hanging on the walls,

307

holding lamps in their hands, standing at attention, standing guard. The walls between them were covered in the most luxurious red silk.

Five darkly hooded figures sat silent and still in the middle of the front row of the theater seats.

Max and Lydia walked to the front. Roee and I followed, he down one side and I the other. As Max and Lydia came before the hooded five, I stopped at the first seat on my side, and Roee did the same. We well positioned the briefcases on the seats.

Max handed a hooded black robe to Lydia, who immediately and enthusiastically put it on, then sat in the middle of the five, in the seat left vacant for her. Sara Hutton was nowhere to be seen, but on a stage in front of the screen was a little black altar, not much more than a three-foot-by-three-foot platform with a three-foot high post projecting up from the far end. A black box stood on top of the post, and three long black wires, two thin, one thicker, came out of the back, fell close to the floor, then looped back up, their ends attached in some manner to the top of the box. I looked carefully at the base of the platform. From my side angle, I could see a thick black cord run out of its back and disappear under the movie screen.

"Welcome, initiates," Max said, positioning himself on the stage before the altar. "Welcome to the Communion of the Golden Arse. A secret, and dare we say, sacred, communion of like-minded protectors and defenders of our civilization. But no long speeches now. Your duties and obligations to the Communion will soon be made known. The benefits, I think you already know. We are not a very formal organization. There will be no weekly or monthly meetings. No conventions. We will not have a float in the Hollywood Christmas Lane Parade. All that would be detrimental to our purpose. But we do take this opportunity when we welcome new members to seal our bargain with them. Seal it with a kiss. A kiss upon the Golden Arse."

Music came from somewhere, solemn music, and out from behind the movie screen came a slow-walking hooded figure, head bowed, hands clasped in front. The figure reached the altar and stepped up on the platform with its back to us. The figure raised its head to the expanse of the white screen before it and mumbled something that almost sounded Latin but almost assuredly was gibberish. Then the figure slowly turned around. From the side, I could not see the face, but from the suppressed tittering of Brooke, I was sure the five and Lydia could. Then in a grand gesture, the figure threw off its robe!

Standing before us, her arms stretched up in a hallelujah pose, was Sara Hutton, laughing with glee at the grand silliness of it all. A silliness incorporating the fact that she was standing there naked, displaying her shapeless body and pitiful breasts, not so much shamelessly as with absolutely no sense of aesthetic courtesy.

Naked, except for a pair of shiny golden panties that seemed to be made of Mylar. A Sonia Rykiel design, no doubt.

Sara turned around, took the two thin wires from the top of the black box, and plugged them into two small plastic pieces hanging from either side of the crotch of the golden panties. She took the third, thicker wire by its end, which was thicker still, and cupped it in her right palm. Then she turned around and faced the five and Lydia.

"Brooke Bloom, approach the altar of the sacred Golden Arse," Sara said.

Brooke got up, went to the steps at the side of the stage, ascended, then approached the altar.

"Step upon the altar."

Brooke stepped upon the platform and joined Sara.

"Remove your hood," Sara commanded.

Brooke did so. It was evident she struggled not to laugh, partly from the situation, partly from nervousness. The rumors had included this ordeal, as I knew from watching Don Gulden spread them with his sore lips, so Brooke's apprehension was well-founded.

"Are you ready to kiss the Golden Arse?" asked Sara.

"Can I kiss these first?" Not waiting for an answer, Brooke put her mouth upon Sara's and gave her a short kiss of some depth. Sara laughed after they parted. Brooke said, "And this?" Brooke leaned down the short distance to Sara's breasts and surrounded the nipple of the left one with her lips. Sara was momentarily delighted and then chastised Brooke.

"Initiate! This is not the time to kiss the luscious lips and the fleshy titties, but to kiss the Golden Arse. Are you ready to kiss the Golden Arse?"

"Okay, yeah, sure, I am."

Potent Brandy. And the exclusive Dominican cigars may have included a foreign leaf or two.

"On your knees then!" Sara ordered.

Brooke fell to her knees. Sara turned slowly, bringing her gold-enveloped ass before Brooke's face. Then she bent and spread the gold Mylar to a smooth surface across her buttocks with her hands.

"Wet your lips, Brooke Bloom," Sara commanded between her legs.

Brooke wet her lips.

"Kiss now the Golden Arse! Kiss now the Golden Arse," Max started to chant, encouraging the others to chant. Their voices rose to join Max's.

"Kiss now the Golden Arse! Kiss now the Golden Arse!"

Brooke leaned forward and gently placed her lips upon Sara's golden arse.

"Kiss it so I can feel it!" Sara screamed.

Brooke leaned in, applying more pressure.

Then Sara subtly took the wire in her right hand, placed her thumb over the button, and applied a half-second's pressure.

There was a considerable spark where Brooke's lips and Sara's ass met, then Brooke flew back, propelled with force, falling off the platform and onto her back on the stage. We all instinctively moved towards her, but Max yelled in a booming voice, "Stop!"

Everyone stopped. All we could do was look at Brooke. Tiny twin streams of smoke were drifting up off her lips. Her hair was frazzled. The very slight smell of burning flesh was evident.

Then Brooke began to laugh.

"Wow! What a trip!" she declared with very little originality.

Max went to her, picked her up, and hugged her.

"Congratulations! You are now a member in good standing of the Communion of the Golden Arse," he said as he led her off the stage and to her seat.

"Thad Darrow, approach the altar of the sacred Golden Arse," Sara stood upright again, facing forward.

Thad rose hesitantly, took the steps to the stage, and approached.

"Step upon the altar."

Thad stepped upon the platform and joined Sara.

"Remove your hood," Sara commanded.

Thad removed his hood, then, with a giggle, stepped back off the platform.

"Ah, can I go later?"

Brooke's 'shock' had sobered him up a bit.

"What?" Sara said with mock anger and umbrage. "Is the initiate balking?"

"Only for a moment or two. Just need some time to work up the—uh—uh—"

"Courage!" Brooke yelled it out, then whimpered a tiny ouch. It seemed that her lips were sore.

"Well, uh—"

"Hey, I did it. Come on!" Brooke said more carefully.

"Uh—"

"Initiate!" Sara called his attention. "Do not fear to test your testosterone. Step up upon the altar and prepare to—"

"Hey!" Lydia stood up. "Let me do it now if he hasn't got the balls."

"Is initiate Lydia Corfu claiming that she has got the balls?"

"Nope. Although most people I've dealt with in my career considered me just a bitch with balls. Well, they were wrong, and they were fools. It was estrogen all the way, baby, estrogen one hundred percent."

"Then Lydia Corfu of the estimable estrogen, approach the altar of the sacred Golden Arse."

Thad was immensely relieved as he hurried off the stage and sat down. Lydia stepped onto the stage, moved quickly to the platform, and stepped onto it.

"Remove your hood."

Lydia removed her hood.

"Initiate. Are you ready to kiss the Golden Arse?"

311

"Yes," Lydia said quite seriously.

"On your knees then!"

Lydia fell to her knees. Sara turned slowly around as before and brought her golden ass before Lydia's face. Then she bent and spread the gold Mylar to a smooth surface across her buttocks.

"Wet your lips, Lydia Corfu," Sara commanded.

Lydia wet her lips and made them sparkle even more.

"Kiss now, the Golden Arse! Kiss now the Golden Arse!" Max and the others chanted.

Lydia leaned forward and planted an enthusiastic smooch onto Sara's gilded tuchus.

Sara smiled in mad delight as she placed her thumb over the button and plunged it down.

Like a magnet, Lydia stuck to Sara's ass as the unbroken electrical current sparked and burned at her lips; her hair shot straight out, her body stiffened and shook with convulsions, and Sara laughed like a madwoman.

"Lydia!" I screamed as I ran and leaped upon the stage, but Ranger Blunt stepped out from behind the screen and jabbed an AK-47 into my ribs, stopping me. Roee, I could see, was being covered by Hatless.

Sara, with a flourish, finally removed her thumb from the button.

Lydia detached from Sara's ass and fell sideways onto the platform.

I pushed Blunt's AK-47 aside and ran to Lydia, falling to my knees and pulling her into my arms. She was a mess. "Lydia!" I cried. "Lydia!"

She opened her eyes—barely. She spoke in a whisper.

"At least I made it through—life—without once having read a—a self-help book."

Then her eyes closed, and she was gone.

I snapped my head up at the ugly, naked, grinning creature above me.

"You bitch! You stupid, fucking bitch!"

I moved towards Sara, hands outstretching to grab and rip at her throat, but the red, mad rage suddenly ceased as a large, heavy booted foot slammed into the side of my head.

It was, Roee later explained, a boot belonging to George.

HOLLYWOOD
IS AN ALL-VOLUNTEER ARMY

24
SLICING FLESH

"**D**o you think I'm fucking stupid?"

It was a calm, whispered question coming out of the black, accompanied by hot breath blowing in my right ear. I didn't, at that moment, have the imagination to pluck an answer out of my throbbing head. Just let it be black, I thought, and quiet, and then maybe the pain would go away.

Then the hot breath blew in soft puffs into my left ear.

"Do you think I'm fucking stupid?"

I did not want to think at all, much less have to determine the intelligence, or lack thereof, of a disembodied voice. What did I care? What was it to me?

"Do you think I'm fucking stupid?"

It was a furnace blast of hot breath and angry decibels directed dead center into my face. I winced. The wince made everything hurt even more. I still did not open my eyes. Black was my only friend.

"George," the voice said, not giving any specific command, but the implication was clear.

Suddenly a bright, harsh light flooded into my right eye as its lid was lifted and pulled up. I could feel a tear flood, and I looked through it to see the distorted image of an arm whose path led up to the impassive, backlit face of George. Then, into view, growing as it thrust towards me, blocking the harsh light, haloed by backlit glowing hair, was the face of Maxwellton James.

"Open your other eye," he said.

My other eye refused to follow the command.

"George."

George, my right eyelid between his thumb and forefinger, squeezed—squeezed very hard.

I could hear myself scream.

Then George added his sharp thumbnail to the squeeze.

Somehow it was like two of me screaming as nail sliced through flesh, and tears rolled uncontrollably down my cheek. My left eye popped open. I was now fully awake.

"It was just a simple kick in the head," Max said. "No need to get melodramatic about it."

George was still squeezing. All my instincts to lash back were discouraged by the fact that I seemed to be securely tied by all four limbs to a chair.

Chairs seemed to be my curse on this adventure.

"Could you ask George," I rasped out, "to let go of my eyelid?"

"Why?" Max played the innocent fool. He was not good at it.

"It's annoying."

"I'll bet. George, let go of the poor man's eyelid. Very clever, by the way, George. I like it."

"Thanks," George said, displaying no small amount of pride in his work.

"We now go back to my original question. Do you think I'm fucking stupid?"

Full memory was now mine. "Lydia!" I cried.

"Lydia is dead. You killed her. You killed her by involving her in some stupid plot to stop me."

"Where is she?"

"What does it matter? She's dead. The carcass has been carted away by one of my rangers. It will take a plane trip: the first stop will be Nome, Alaska. From there, a confederate of mine will fly it across the Bering Strait into Russia over to the Central Siberian Plateau, where it will eventually be buried in an unmarked grave, as will your carcass. You will be listed as missing by the authorities. Missing in Action, I assume, by your organization. What I want to know is, is it a criminal or a legal organization?"

"What are you talking about? I'm a lawyer. My name is Elsworth Henderson. I'm a partner in the law firm of Humboldt, Henderson & Pinsker. We specialize in buyouts and mergers."

"Then why did you come here with clever little video cameras built into your oh-so-precious briefcases?"

George held one of the briefcases up.

"Is George pointing the tiny lens correctly? Let's see, it is in one of these keyholes, right? Do you think it's still recording? Let's find out."

Max raised a walkie-talkie to his mouth. "Russell?"

"Yes, Sir."

"Are you still receiving us?"

"Yes, Sir."

"What do you see right now?"

"A hideous face, Sir. With a cut and swollen right eyelid."

"Very good. Give me your location again."

"Room 11 of the Silver Surf Motel, Sir."

"The previous occupant of this room? What was his name? Mike?"

"Yes, sir, that's right. He has been prepped and packaged for shipment to Russia, Sir."

"All right, Russell. Thank you for your fine work." Max put the walkie-talkie down. "Tell me the purpose of these recorders now, or I will have George slice your eyelid off completely."

A shiny, sharp steel blade switched open, not an inch from my eyes.

"Okay, but—but first, where am I?"

I was conscious enough now to have been trying to ascertain my situation. I knew I was tied to a chair. I was clothed, except for my suit coat, which had been removed, probably to tie my arms down better, but where were we? The light behind Max and George was bright enough to obscure vision. No clues there. The environment felt strange; for one thing, it was muggy and sound. I suddenly realized our voices, especially, had a hollow, echoing quality.

Max smiled. "Where are we, boys?"

The hollow sound of water being agitated somewhere below.

"Look down, just slightly behind you," Max said.

I did. I saw, directly behind and maybe fifteen feet below, illuminated clear water rippling over blue tiles featuring graphic gold sunburst images.

"You are in the indoor Roman pool room here at the Castle. Specifically, you are tied to a chair on the edge of the diving platform that bridges an alcove. This is quite a large pool, very elaborate, and about the size of two tennis courts. If you look to the sides a little, you will see that my men are almost all here below us, fully armed, some of them cooling their feet off in the pool, but then, who could pass up such an opportunity? You'll notice to your right, at the side of the pool, your Mr. Pinsker, being guarded by several of my men. You may address him if you like."

"Charles, are you okay?" I called down to Pinsker.

"More to the point," Roee as Pinsker said, "are you?"

"He's just fine, Mr. Pinsker." Max looked down on Roee—figuratively, I'm sure, as well as literally. "Worry not." Then he addressed me. "Why did you think it important to document the proceedings here tonight?"

"Look," I started, "we were involving our client in a complicated deal. She would provide the cash, but Sara Hutton would get all the company's control, which was necessary if we wanted growth into the broadcast area, so...."

"So?"

"So, we heard about the rumors. We checked it out. We thought if we could get invited, get something on tape that was—damaging, embarrassing, we would have that to control Sara with."

"Blackmail?"

"Why not?"

Max laughed his hearty laugh. "Bullshit!"

"It's the—"

"What were you doing at my airfield at Mom's Cove?"

"How—how did you know?"

"Yes, how did I know? Especially considering you splattered

poor Ronnie Berger all over the tarmac, so there were no actual witnesses to your visit. Except for the video surveillance system I set up during the old days and have maintained out of pure, perverse, but not altogether unwarranted, paranoia. You see, I have so many enemies. In the old days, when I used to import drugs, I dealt with many criminal elements. Also, in the old days, when I used to—patriotically—export guns, I had dealings with many elements from the secret world of government intelligence. These were concurrent associations, and I often had difficulty distinguishing between them. I guess I didn't have a program to tell the players apart."

He laughed a little bit over this joke,

"So which are you? You aren't anybody I ever sold drugs to. I don't forget such people. So what's the deal? You from the government?"

"I was just investigating Sara and doing a thorough job for my client. I talked to a teacher at Yale. He knew your name from when Sara was a student; he knew you flew together. I was in the area and thought I would check out the airfield. I played tough to your guy because he scared me; thought it was a good way to get out of there safe."

"Don't you guys hire private investigators anymore?"

"Lydia wouldn't let us, so we had to do it ourselves. We're obviously not very good at it."

"You were good enough to kill Ronnie Berger."

"Hey, he was trying to kill me! It's not my fault he crashed. He was doing all kinds of weird flying."

"Explain England to me. When Pye called me with your description, saying you were a lawyer snooping around the deal, I had an inspiration. I sent a video frame from the airfield tape over the computer. A good close-up of you. When he confirmed the ID, I told him to kill you. I had no idea who you were and why you were pushing into my business, but I also had no patience for such intrusions. So I told him to kill you and free me from the annoyance. Pye's greedy need to check you out and get some information seemed to have saved your life. How did Mr. Pinsker find you? George tells me it was an interesting rescue."

"We always have trailing bodyguards in Europe. We do work for Israeli companies. We're always afraid of Arab terrorists."

"Did you know your friend Hamo is ex-British Intelligence?"

"Of course. He's also my wife's cousin. That's why we hired him."

"You seem to have an answer for everything, Mr. Henderson."

"I'm telling you the truth."

"Are you? Not having a polygraph machine handy, how can I test that? There must be a clever way. Well, while I try to think of one, why don't you go for a swim?" Max moved to the side, allowing the light to blind me.

"George."

George blocked that light as he moved in, placed his heavy booted foot on the chair between my legs, and pushed.

It was a fifteen-foot free fall, which my stomach decided not to make. Sudden cold wetness accompanied the splash, and a surprisingly swift drift down to the bottom of the pool ended with a jolt as the chair landed perfectly upright.

Despite a groggy and now oxygen-deprived head, I had the presence of mind to realize that the legs of the chair must have been weighted for just this outcome.

Even through the water, I could hear a sudden, loud commotion. There was gunfire, a scream from Max not to fire, screaming about "damage to the tiles, you fucking idiots," and a splash, quickly following one another.

Roee, still fully suited in the best Brooks Brothers has to offer, was floating beside me, reaching for the ropes that bound me to the chair. I could see by the disconcertion on his brow that the ropes were not loosely tied.

Another splash. George—dressed down for the occasion—swam at Roee. I grunted a warning, but it was too late. George grabbed Roee around the neck with his left arm and pulled him away from the chair. His right arm went up, the switchblade protruding from his fist. Roee easily deflected the thrust, grabbing George's arm and holding it away. Weighted enough with shoes and wet clothes to have purchase on the pool's bottom, he bent his knees, then shot his legs straight, slamming the top of his head up under George's chin. Stunned, George let go of Roee and the knife. The knife floated to the bottom, Roee shot to the surface, did a dolphin, then dived down to me. I'm sure he could see I was close to passing out as he grabbed the two back legs of the chair, and with the combined wonders of adrenaline and buoyancy, he lifted the chair as high as he could.

My head broke the surface. I gasped for air, taking in as much as possible, then holding it as I went underwater again, falling and jolting onto the pool's bottom.

Roee went for more air, diving back down towards the abandoned knife. Unfortunately, George was back with us, and they met and grabbed the knife together.

I had a strange flashback—lack of oxygen will do that—of a comment Roee had made about Larry Lapham and Robert Jordan when they were flailing about, fighting on the floor of our fake TV studio ten gazillion years ago. He had compared them to the mating practices of a particular species of squid that fornicated in a frenzy of violent movement.

Somehow the memory seemed appropriate.

Blood started streaming from the area of the fight. A great deal of blood, bright red, diluting quickly to pink as it flowed outward.

The two were still. George's head was flipped back like the top of a PEZ candy dispenser. The slice had been that deep. Roee dropped him, shot to the surface, then returned to me and cut at the ropes with the switchblade.

I was free but with no strength. Roee grabbed me and dragged me to the surface.

We broke to the view of Max surrounded by several of the Rangers, all with their AK-47s pointed at us.

"Lethal hand-to-hand combat in adverse situations," Max said. "Such as underwater. Was this part of the New York State Bar exam?"

He gestured for two Rangers to pull us out of the pool. They sat us against the blue and gold tiled wall by the decking to the side of the alcove.

Max squatted down to face us and watched us struggle for fresh oxygen. Once our breathing became more regular, he nodded at

Ranger Blunt. In a swift move, Ranger Blunt brought the butt of his AK-47 down onto Roee's head. Roee collapsed into my lap. I could feel the warm blood from his scalp wound flow onto my legs and run into my crotch. I tore off my shirt and quickly used it to apply pressure on the wound to stop the bleeding. Max seemed to have no objections. His mind was elsewhere.

"Now you tell me exactly who you are and why you're really here, or by God, I'll kill you both in small, painful, ignoble increments. For the death of George alone, I should do that. But tell me the truth, and I'll spare you the ignobility."

I had stopped Roee's bleeding. He was still unconscious but breathing easily. I laid his head on the bunched-up bloody shirt and turned to Max, collapsing my body language into a whisper of complete surrender.

"His name," I said, referring to Roee, "is Roy Jenkins. My name is Gilgamesh Paul."

"Gilgamesh?" Max stood and stared down at me. "What kind of fucking name is that?"

"Sumerian. An old character from myth. The first hero. My parents were academics."

"Well, I suppose that explains it. Can I call you Gil?"

"I'd prefer if you didn't. Always sounded too—fish-like for me."

Max laughed. "Well, Gilgamesh, what are you doing here?"

"We're private investigators."

"Working for whom?"

"Working for the parents of Bea Cherbourg."

"Bea Cherbourg? That little bitch who killed herself?"

"You killed her. You and Sara Hutton. We know that. We were hired to get the evidence."

"All this was about that stupid little bitch? How did you get Lydia Corfu involved?"

We needed a way to get close to Sara Hutton and you. To be able to get up here. We read things in Bea's diary that made us think you were running a weird sex club up here. We thought, maybe that's how she died, through some weird erotic death thing, like those people who choke themselves for the intense ejaculation.

We promised Lydia all the material on the videotapes and exclusivity to break the story. Also, to sell the story back to Hollywood for a feature. Seemed poetic justice."

"Weird sex club?"

"Yeah."

"Unbelievable. Lydia's offer to buy Olympic was, of course, part of the ruse."

"Yes."

"We never took it seriously, you know. No matter what Robert Pye told you, we weren't desperate for money. The Enclave will provide the money. We just needed to make an elaborate effort to hide the tracks."

Max thought for a moment, then said. "I'm impressed. Moderately. I mean, I got on to you soon into the process, didn't I? Still, an elaborate scheme for a couple of private investigators in the pay of a not-well-to-do middle-class couple. What did they do? Mortgage the house?"

"No. This is a pro bono case."

"Oh really? Intrigue and amuse me some more."

"Bea Cherbourg was my niece."

"Ah. So it's personal. How long have you been a private investigator?"

"Ever since I retired from the FBI."

"No wonder you're incompetent. You were undercover?"

"Yes."

"And this Mike?"

"A civilian we recruited. He knew Bea. Had a crush on her. She had told him she was going on this retreat."

"Well, what an idiotic story—but idiotic in that oh-so-human way."

Max smiled a big grin. "I believe it. No reason not to, at this point, as you soon will all be dead and a bother to me no more."

"Why—why did you kill Bea?"

"We didn't. I told you. She killed herself. All we ever did in the initiations was put on a little show for effect, give the people a little jolt to the lips and wounds they could proudly show off. For some reason, Bea grabbed the switch out of Sara's hand and wouldn't

stop pushing the button. It was a shock—if I may use that term—
to all of us. Sara stood there screaming, 'Get this bitch off my ass!'
Our other initiates stood with their mouths hanging open, not
knowing if this was real—or part of the show. I had to pull the
plug behind the screen to stop the damn thing. By that time, your
none-too-bright niece was dead. And lipless.

"I had had a bad feeling about her all along, but Sara was being
ruled by lust. Did you know she fucked your niece, by the way? On
several occasions. The last one was a beach party where Sara
wanted to be called Annette. I had to be 'Frankie' and fuck your
niece, also. Sara is quite warped. But I allow her one now and then
to keep her lesbo libido under control. It helps keep her mind
focused.

"At first, I thought the damn thing was a disaster—the frying
of Bea. Until I saw its effect on the initiates, that now, suddenly,
they knew the Enclave's power. I could see it in their eyes. I've
always counted on greed for their loyalty, but this was an even
more powerful assurance. Fear. Very effective. I decided at that
moment that we would kill someone at each initiation. One of
Sara's lusts or some dispensable development executive. Plenty to
choose from. Then you guys came along and provided Lydia.
Couldn't have been more perfect."

"How are you going to account for all these missing people?"

"Certain people in this world are accountable for what they do,
and certain people aren't. We aren't. Do you understand? Even
when we have glitches, even when we make a lapse of judgment
and hire a hard-drinking Eskimo to do a simple job like transport
a body into Russia, and that hard-drinking Eskimo drinks hard and
thinks throwing the damn body into the Bering Sea would be just
as effective, forgetting, due to the hard drink, that it's Winter and
the Bering Strait is frozen over—even then, body discovered, we
will never be held accountable. The Enclave takes care of its own."

"What are you going to do with us?"

"I told you. You will rest in peace in Russia."

"Why Russia?"

"I have a bit of a hobby there. Mock dogfights are okay when
you're amusing hoi polloi, but when you really want to test your

skills, you've got to have live ammo. There are not many places around here where you can do that if you're not government-issued. But in the uncluttered skies over the great Central Siberian Plateau, there are not too many authorities around to bother you, and the few that are, are easily paid off. I've refurbished many old Culver PQ-14 radio-controlled target aircraft. It's a lot of fun shooting them down, but it's not the same joy as a real kill. Luckily, by turning a hobby into a profit, I've never found a lack of adventurers who will pay me to fight them—rich enthusiasts with their own warbirds who want to test their mettle and skill. They have very little compared to me, but they never realize that until it's too late. The high price of self-knowledge."

Roee groaned next to me and opened his eyes. The muzzle of an AK-47 was placed between them.

'I'm so happy you're all right, Mr. Jenkins. Tell me, do you really fly? Or was that just part of your ruse, which Mr. Paul has now thoroughly revealed?"

Roee, looking somewhat cross-eyed, answered. "No, we fly."

"Just Cessna's and Pipers?"

"No. We can fly anything."

"I thought as much. You guys just looked the type. I'm pleased. Then I will offer you a noble death instead of an ignoble death, which would be easy for me to arrange and extremely painful for you. The lovely Sara Hutton and I will challenge you two to a dogfight in the skies over San Simeon. It won't rouse suspicion; people will think it's part of another air show. It will be an unfortunate accident when the two of you finally crash and burn."

,You're not considering the possibility that we might shoot you down," I said.

"No chance of that. You see, Sara and I will have live ammo. You will have none. Not even blanks. You'll have to go, 'YAK-YAK-YAK-YAK,' just to get into the spirit of the thing."

"Not very sporting."

"I didn't say it would be sporting. I said it would be a noble death. You have caused me much trouble. I have no obligation to be sporting with you. I will give you a handicap, though."

"A handicap?"

"Yes, of a sort." Max turned to Ranger Blunt. "It will intensify the nobility if they have to fight through pain while flying, don't you think?"

"Yes, sir," Blunt said.

"Good." Max looked down at us. "We fly at dawn, gentlemen."

Then he left as Ranger Blunt and one other, under the cover and protection of their compatriots' AK-47s, picked us up, shoved us against the wall, and started pounding and tenderizing us for the battle ahead.

25
SPITTING FIRE

The ugly, grinning face of Sara Hutton greeted me with the dawn.

I was flat on my naked back on the tarmac of the airfield. I took a quick mental roll call of body parts and faculties, and nothing seemed AWOL, although I couldn't find a member of the ranks that wasn't in pain. Sara, squatting close to me, continued to look at me and grin like a not-too-bright primate cousin investigating a termite hole. Soon I realized she was playing with one of my nipples—a thought frightening enough to startle me and make me gasp.

I heard a moan. Painfully I moved my head to the left and saw Roee lying on the ground next to me, just moving into consciousness. His clothes were torn and bloodied, as was his face. I assumed I looked not too dissimilar. I turned back to Sara.

Her grin scrunched into launch mode, and she spat a relatively large quantity of phlegm onto my eyes, nose, and the right corner of my mouth.

It was warm moisture but turned cold rapidly as the temperature couldn't have been much over 50.

"Good morning, *Gil-ga-mesh*."

"Any chance of a rag to wipe my face?" I asked.

"Here," she said, violently pulling and ripping at Roee's shirt until a piece was torn off.

It must have helped bring clarity to his pain.

She threw the piece of shirt in my face. I sat up, wiping her gift away.

"Sorry, you missed the rest of the initiation. We had a fine time—once Sheila got rid of the barbecue, and everyone calmed down. Now they really know how important their task is and how our enemies surround us. I think they were awed and inspired by it all. All that remains is for them to see our enemies vanquished. So we've brought them here. Can you see them? They're in the bleachers."

I could see. They were all waiting for the show.

"Watching you die will bring real closure to this experience."

"Boy, you really do go for the cliché, don't you?"

Sara Hutton rammed her fist into my right eye.

She stood up, angry. She yelled at one of the Rangers, "Get them into flight suits. And into the Spits! You better get up there fast," she said, addressing me again. "Or we'll kill you on the ground."

Sara Hutton walked off and climbed into her waiting and running Messerschmitt 109. The plane then joined another piloted by Max for a short taxi to the runway, then a near "hand in hand" take off.

Rangers grabbed Roee and me and, none too gently, relieved us of what clothes we had left on. The Five, I noticed, had their binoculars trained on us, looking at our naked particulars, no doubt.

I hope we didn't disappoint.

Various orifices were quickly checked as they looked, poked, folded us in half, and probed to see if we were concealing anything that we could use to our advantage. Then we were thrown into flight suits, dragged to our Spitfires, and stuffed into the cockpits. We made like rag dolls during all of this. It seemed the best way. No resistance at all. Everything hurt like hell, nevertheless.

The Ranger who stuffed me in forced a leather flight helmet on my head and plugged it into the radio just as Max and Sara flew very low over our heads, screaming, "YAK-YAK-YAK-YAK" through the radio at us. The Ranger, ducking out of reflex, slipped off the wing and fell to the ground. He recovered quickly, jumped back up on the wing, slammed shut the cockpit flap door, and screamed at me over the rapid pounding piston engine noise, "Get moving, or next time it won't be just a sound effect!" Then he slid the bubble-bulged cockpit canopy into place over my head, jumped off the plane, and ran as far away from me as possible.

Fraught with life-or-death as the situation was, all I wanted to do was go to sleep. It seemed an excellent way to combat the pain; that was the only combat I was truly interested in.

Then a loud voice came into my head.

"Wisdom! Always remember the wisdom!"

Wisdom, I thought. Ah, yes, I have sought all my life for wisdom.

"The teeth, Fixx! Roee, don't forget the wisdom teeth!"

Ah, yes. Wisdom is in the manipulation of the tongue.

Mine reached back to the upper right wisdom tooth and found the tiny switch. My tongue pushed it in. The flap in the fake tooth opened, and the small but potent amount of Petey's unique and exclusive painkiller-stimulant formula flowed into the back of my mouth, and I struggled to move my throat into a swallow that would send it into my system. Once done, I repeated the action with my upper left wisdom tooth for a second dose but didn't have to struggle to swallow as the first dose of the medicine was already taking effect.

"Whoa! Petey! What is this stuff?" I heard Roee exclaim through my still concealed—and waterproof—earpiece.

"Oh, just a little recipe of my mother's!"

"I take it you're receiving us okay," I said.

"Yes, the fake nipple microphones are working beautifully! Although it was touch and go when Sara tried to turn you on, Fixx!"

"They itch," Roee said.

"That's because you got the application glue wet!"

"Not intentionally. Are you sure you can hear us okay over the engine noise? It's intense."

"Hey, my nipples are very sensitive!"

329

"So are mine, if it comes to that," Roee said. "But why did we have to have two?"

"I wanted to record you in Dolby Stereo, of course!"

"Not THX?" I asked.

"Nah. Lucas wouldn't give us the license. Listen, by the way, they are about to strafe you again, so I would get the hell up in the air."

Fully awake and feeling only muted pain, we didn't need any more prodding. We gave each other the thumbs up, taxied to the runway, boosted the planes, and hit the airfield's perimeter at well over 200 MPH. Once airborne, we stuck up our noses and climbed so steeply that the leading edge of my wing blanked out the horizon from my view.

"Oh, coming up after all?" Max came through the earpiece in the helmet. "Well, okay then. Now we can get things started."

"They're climbing fast and very vertical, but to the east. Probably trying to get way up above you to bounce at you from out of the sun," Petey reported.

"Keep a watch on them. We need a minute in these planes to get oriented," I said as Roee and I leveled out.

I looked around the cockpit and made a quick check. Everything seemed normal. The instruments were all reading. The plane was fully fueled. The control column responded well as I gripped its unique spade handle. I tried the gun-firing button on the handle. Nothing. Max was a man of his word.

Now I turned my attention to the sky. The bubble canopy on the Spitfire was great for visibility and headroom, helping to dispense any sense of claustrophobia. Indeed, you never felt "stuck in a can," as one might imagine. You felt one with your machine. That was comforting until you realized what a big target this extended body made of you.

Roee was flying to my right. He pointed south. I nodded. Let's get the chase going. We ended our climb at 5000 feet and gave the planes full throttle as if we were running home.

"Leaving us guys?" It was Sara. "That's not nice. You're killing the show for the others."

"They're coming at you from the east! They're going to bounce you! Don't look. You'll get sun in your eyes! I'll guide you!"

I had confidence in Petey and his satellite, but it was strange being the conduit of a remote control.

"They're coming! They're almost in range! Don't move yet. Don't give them any idea you're anything but sitting du—NOW! NOW!"

I pulled back on the throttle, jammed the flaps down, and jerked as the plane lost thrust and gave in to drag.

Roee's plane duplicated my movements.

The real YAK-YAK-YAK-YAK of Max and Sara's guns sounded, and they both bolted down at a 45-degree angle, not thirty feet before us.

"What the fuck!?" said Max, losing some of his equanimity.

Roee and I banked right in a coordinated movement and dove in pursuit of the two 109s, quickly getting on their tails as they eased out of their dives and leveled off.

I turned on the plane's transmitter and screamed, "YAK-YAK-YAK-YAK," as I came up behind Max's Messerschmitt, then immediately turned the transmitter off.

"Well, you're livelier than I thought you would be. Care to explain?"

I did not.

"All right. You and your buddy can fly. So fly, you bastards, fly!"

I could hear him switch off or switch to another channel as the two 109s rapidly climbed, and Roee and I shot forward.

They were out of our sight, but we weren't out of theirs. Real live YAK- YAK-YAK was followed by a series of THUD-THUMPS as I saw metal rip along my right wing. I immediately throttled back, flipped the flaps down, and brought the Spit down to about 79 MPH, causing it to stall.

There was a moment's grace, a sense of floating, of position in the heavens.

Then the plane started to flutter down like a falling leaf. Maloney had assured me such a trick would not throw the aircraft into a spin, which I would not have liked, but it gives, he had said, an excellent impression of a dead duck.

"He's just sitting up there watching you, Fixx," Petey said. "He's not pursuing at all."

"Good. Roee?"

"Giving Sara a merry chase and an erratic target. Uh, you are going to come out of this, aren't you?"

"Not until I see the foam of the whitecaps." I was right over the ocean, an ocean that twirled below me. I closed my eyes for just a second, just enough time to conquer the dizziness that was beginning. Then at the right moment, I did what I had to do to stabilize the craft and speed forward just a few feet above the shoreline, heading south.

"Oh, very fucking clever!" came the voice of Max into my ear. "But I see you, I'm on to you, and I'm right behind you."

"That's not quite accurate," Petey said. "But it's only moments away from being so."

I looked up. A rear-view mirror is attached to the top of the canopy on a Spitfire. It's good for checking the condition of your tail. I looked into it now, watched the California coast rapidly stream behind me, and waited for Max's 109 to come into view.

There he was! It was duck and weave time. I pulled left, got myself over solid ground, and started to fly very low, skirting the ground in an undulating pattern matching the undulating, cow-covered hills. Whenever I saw an outcropping of live oaks, I flew as close as I dared, hoping to make Max skittish, forcing him to pull up and take me out of sight. It didn't work. If Max knew fear, it wasn't the fear of slamming into a live oak. Suddenly the pasture was clear of trees if not cows, and Max fired his guns. I saw the fire spitting from his wing and cowling guns through the mirror. I hopped up, and dodged to the side. I checked the mirror. Cows were dropping.

I did a quick climb, not wanting to sacrifice any more innocent bovine bystanders. I flew into the sun and found Roee there at 15,000 feet.

"Welcome," he said over the nipple phone.

"It's good to see you. Any damage?"

"Well, my right boot is full of blood."

"Leg wound?"

"I guess, but with Mama Petey's Excellent Elixir, how can I tell?"

"Guys, if you want to give them a bounce, you're in the perfect position! They've lost you, and they're cursing at each other. Five thousand feet below you!"

Petey gave us the exact location, and we dove for it, taking advantage not only of the sun behind us but of a certain angle of attack that I was pretty sure would have us obscured, from their point of view, by one of the slats in the Messerschmitt's ugly, squarish canopy.

"YAK-YAK-YAK-YAK," we orally shot at them as we passed close by their heads, then turned south and sped on.

"You guys are truly foolish," Max said.

"We got you now," Sara added.

"Petey, is that your baby up ahead?"

"Yeah, can you see how it's progressively getting blacker? It's going to be a hell of a storm!"

"Well, keep pumping that seed in there."

"Exactly what do you mean by—"

I never heard the rest of Petey's statement as suddenly my plane violently lurched, my head shot forward—flying off the rest of me, I quickly imagined—and there was a white-hot point of pain in my back, then nothing.

xx

"Fixxer!" It was loud, and yet it seemed like a whisper.

"Fixxer!" It was less of a whisper and more of a shout. "Wake up!"

The sweet somethings in my ear had been Petey. He was screaming now, trying to pierce what he hoped was just a fog on my brain, not a shroud.

My eyes opened. A whole herd of cattle was gathered directly below, lazily munching on grass impervious to the utter (not to mention udder) destruction I was just about to rain on them. I grabbed the control column and pulled back—it was not too willing to give, but I was not too willing to give up. Soon the nose of the plane started to ascend, eventually became parallel with the horizon, and finally stuck itself up snobbishly, and I shot away from the hard, solid ground.

"Whew!"

"Thank you, Petey. I was trying to think of just the proper word. What's the action like?"

"Roee is just entering the storm. Sara seems mad enough to be following him in."

"Well, we counted on that, didn't we? Max?"

"Pretty much on your tail! So beat it the hell into the storm!"

I did so as I tried to settle back in my seat, but a hot protrusion was sticking into my back.

"You know what, Petey?"

"What?"

"I think one of Max's cannon shells almost pierced the armor plating behind my seat."

"Almost?"

"Well, if it had been more than almost, I doubt highly if I would be talking to you right now."

"Ouch!"

"Thank you, Petey. Your eloquence is always welcomed."

"He's almost within firing range!"

I pulled back on the control column, climbed right over on my back, then flew upside down toward Max. This disconcerted him enough that he failed to fire, and I gave him a jaunty wave and smiled as our canopies passed very close to each other. Then I dove, came right side up, and headed south into the storm.

Max probably would have followed me anyway, but this last challenge assured it.

xx

Clouds are mountains of moisture. Often white, fluffy, and benign, but no less majestic because of that. Especially when you approach them on their level, fly among them, watch them pass slowly, and view the aspects of their always interesting textured surfaces and the extent to which they rise above you and extend below you, massive in their lack of mass.

These were not that class of clouds that Roee and Sara had disappeared into and which I now entered. These now surrounding me were lead weights of clouds, black, cold, enveloping droplets that clung onto the canopy. There was no visibility except the flashes of lightning cracking quickly in and out of existence.

"You lucky sons-of-bitches!" It was Max. "But the storm won't hide you forever. Even if you get out and land somewhere, the Enclave will find you."

I snapped the transmitter on. "Assuming the Enclave even exists, Max."

"You doubt it?"

"I doubt many things, Max. Defines me as a twentieth-century man, don't you think?"

"I'll admit I'm impressed with your flying. Especially given the handicap I handed you."

"Max, do I sound like a man in pain?"

"No—no, you don't." There was anger in his voice.

"As for the storm, Max, luck had nothing to do with it. I arranged the storm."

Max laughed with genuine amusement. "There's a megalomania here I had not perceived before—Gilgamesh."

"A little white lie, Max. My name is not Gilgamesh Paul."

"I'm so relieved for you. Any chance you want to tell me your true name?"

"No chance at all, Max, but there are those—a few friends, some enemies—who refer to me as The Fixxer."

"What...?" It was Sara gasping.

"That means something to you, Sara?" Max demanded to know.

"Well—well—there are rumors."

"There are always rumors, Sara, but what do you know?"

"Just that he's someone you can use. Someone you can call on when you want to— to fix things."

"Oh. One of those. A thug for hire. What I don't understand, though, Fixxer, is who are you 'fixing' things for?"

"Myself, Max. In this case, myself. I don't like your attitude toward human life, Max. It's not conducive to a happy society."

"You're fucking joking! Who's paying you?"

"Not a soul, Max. Your destruction is on my ticket."

"Shit!" It was Sara.

"What?"

"That lightning was close. Can we get out of here?"

"No! Keep an eye out for them. The clouds will break! Fixxer, tell me the truth. Why? Who? You're no fucking white knight."

"Max, how can you say that? You hardly know me."

"I know humanity."

"Maybe I'm not human—or maybe I just can't get the image out of my head of a beautiful young woman, so sincere in her desire to create, so serious in her need to be vital. An image that keeps changing into a grotesque, frozen, lipless carcass—as I believe you refer to the dead."

"Moral outrage? Are you trying to fight me with moral outrage?"

"Well—outrage, at least."

"Too damn bad you've failed. Despite your elaborate campaign to bring me down, you have failed completely. Any rumors as to your effectiveness must be just that."

"Max, I just can't agree. Captain, are you, by any chance, monitoring these transmissions?"

"We've heard every word of them, Fixx."

"You see, Max, while Mike was in room 11 of the Silver Surf Motel receiving and recording the transmissions from our briefcases, the Captain, an official of law enforcement, I should add, was in the room directly above, doing the same thing. This was our backup in case our equipment was destroyed as the Captain and a few of his men engaged your people in battle, protecting, of course, the life of Mike. Captain, did Russell and gang put up much of a fight?"

"Nah, they're such pussies; they'll probably die of ovarian cancer. Won't you, Russell?"

There was no answer from Russell. Then there was the sound of a gunshot. "Yes, yes, I'm a pussy!" came the terrified, diminutive voice of Russell.

"Russell's positive report to you was a false one induced by the

Captain's persuasive manner."

"Oh, my God! They've got all those tapes!" Sara screamed.

"Get off the air, Sara!"

There was just a hint of agitation in Max's voice.

"It's over, Max. Your usefulness to the Enclave, if there really is such an organization, is over; if there isn't, your little malignant fantasy of behind-the-scenes power is over. So why don't we all drop out of these clouds and land? I believe we are quite close now to the Santa Monica Airport."

Petey had been in my ear this whole time, keeping me informed about our relative positions.

"Do you think the Enclave will be stopped simply because I may be? The Enclave is larger than any one man."

"I'm sure of it, Max. Will it be Santa Monica, or do we have to go to Long Beach?"

"Fixxer!" It was Roee over the nipple phone. "The clouds...."

But I could see for myself as I emerged into a canyon of clear sky surrounded by massive black thunderclouds. Roee was ahead of me. As was Sara, just above and behind Roee.

"Attack, Sara, while you can, now, now!"

Sara dived. Roee maneuvered an erratic pattern trying to stay out of her gun sights. She was firing nonstop, knowing she would eventually hit him as she got right on his tail. Then, just as he was slightly higher than Sara's Messerschmitt, Roee dropped his landing gear. The immediate drag threw his Spit back at the 109, and its right wheel connected with and smashed off Sara's canopy.

We could hear her scream through the radio as her plane spun and dropped into the black clouds below.

"Sara!" Max screamed and dived after her. Roee and I followed through the clouds, popping into the clear air and rain over Hawthorne.

"Bail out, Sara! Bail!" Max was screaming. His fear and concern were monumental and surprising.

Sara did not bail. She was most likely unconscious or dead, and her craft was in an angle of descent that would eventually see her crash into the middle of downtown Los Angeles.

"Roee, not that the community redevelopment might not be

welcomed, but even on a stormy Sunday, there might be a few people down there."

"The anniversary roadshow edition of Phantom of the Opera is playing a matinee at the Music Center," Roee informed.

"Ah, well, there would be a rather satisfying draining of some less than tasteful gene pools...."

"Nevertheless...?"

"Nevertheless."

Roee hit his throttle, shot off to the right, and then made a wide turn to his left to approach Sara's plane from her starboard side. From my position, it looked like he was heading straight toward her and would intersect, smashing her and himself to pieces, but I knew that wasn't the plan. The risk was immeasurable, however. Not only his speed, but his angle, his timing, everything had to be perfect. He just wanted to graze her at the rudder. If he could get the tip of his wing to nick the end of her rudder, he could force it left, thus causing the plane to yaw left. That would head the aircraft towards the Hollywood Hills. There were homes up there, but also some open, clear areas. There would not, then, necessarily be a loss of life.

They intersected.

There was no ball of fire.

Sara's plane turned.

It was now heading towards the Hollywood Hills, speeding towards the summit. If it passed over it, it would head towards Burbank, and Roee would have traded one mass destruction for another. But it suddenly lost enough altitude and crashed, finally, with a spectacular display of hot fire and bright light, right into the HOLLYWOOD sign.

"Well, that's a rather large contribution we're going to have to make to the Hollywood Chamber of Commerce," I said.

"Pay attention, guys; Max is on you!"

Max bounced on me from above, bullets and shells ripped through my plane, then flew off towards the crash site and did a victory roll over it.

"Goodbye, my love," came his soft, sweet, and tender tribute to one of the most vile and ugly women I had ever met.

"Fixx, are you okay?" It was a concerned Roee.

It was the question utmost in my mind, which had been taking a rapid inventory of my craft and myself.

"Well, I'm conscious, and despite some holes in the plane, and a rapidly decreasing fuel level, I'm flying, so I suspect so—for the moment."

"Good for you," Roee said.

"Bad for you!" was Max's opinion.

Max had come around and was on approaching directly toward me. I was in an actual "run but could not hide situation." I was at a dangerous disadvantage with gas spilling out of bullet holes. My thought was to get out over the ocean. If there were going to be another dropping of flaming hot metal from out of the sky, it would be best to be away from track homes and malls.

"Maxwellton James, this is Captain Skip Jones of the California Air National Guard. I order you to cease hostilities and land your unauthorized craft."

The sky was suddenly crowded. A Harrier jet hovered nearby, and three Huey Cobra helicopter gun-ships kept crisscrossing in front of and behind me.

Max broke off his attack and screamed into a climb.

"I miss the bugles," Roee said.

"What?"

"Of the Cavalry."

"Sorry, gentleman," came Captain Jones' voice. "But we have plenty of armament if that makes you feel any better."

"Just not the same," Roee complained.

"Oh, all right!" Then Captain Jones, not consistently accurate as to his notes, hummed out a vigorous rendition of "Charge" as the Harrier followed Max, somewhat leisurely, up into the storm clouds.

"Max, time to give up," I radioed to him.

The line was open, but there was nothing but silence from Max.

"The Enclave cannot protect you, but we can protect you from the Enclave." More silence.

"Sorry about Sara, but why should you—"

"I AM WITH THE STORM; THE STORM IS MY

339

BROTHER. I AM THE STORM, AND I SHALL BECLOUD
THE WORLD; THE STORM SHALL PROTECT ME. I AM
THE STORM, AND THE STORM IS—"

It was a horrible sound. The crack. The sizzle.

"He's falling in pieces," Petey reported.

"Where?"

"About a half-mile out over the Pacific."

"Hope he doesn't hit any whales."

"Time to land, I think, Fixxer," Roee advised.

"As the E looms on my gage, I can't find fault with the idea."

"I've got a problem, though."

"What's that?"

"When I removed Sara's canopy, I lost my right wheel."

"Really?"

"Really."

"Captain? Are you on Petey's line?"

"I'm here, Fixxer."

"It looks like we won't have to fake the emergency landing. Is
everything ready with our strip?"

"Traffic is being cleared now."

"You understand the situation?"

"Yeah, but what are you—"

"Just have about six of your fastest, strongest men available
near the end. Can't explain the plan now, but you'll get it when you
see what we're doing."

"We'll be ready for you."

"All right. Roee, match me for elevation and speed, and we'll
skip hand-in-hand along the boulevard."

Roee positioned his Spit as close to my port side as possible
then we flew in a coordinated pattern to position ourselves to
approach our landing area, coming in over Hancock Park and
Beverly Hills, all the while watching our relative positions to each
other as much as our airspeed or any other indication on the
instrument panel.

"This has got to be surgical," I said to Roee.

"You're the doctor," he replied.

As the ground grew in its immediate importance, we could see humanity and its structures whiz past below, start to pick out individual structures we knew well, and individual humans all, it seemed, pointing up at us. Then there were the flashing lights of the roadblock and the mass of black & white police cars. As we flew over their tops, I suddenly had a thought.

"Captain? The overhanging traffic lights?"

"They've been cut down. Certain officials none too happy."

"Christmas bonuses?"

"That's what I was thinking."

"Okay, Roee, this is it."

We touched down on Wilshire Boulevard side by side, the tip of my left wing placed just inches under the tip of Roee's right wing. When our wheels hit the pavement, gravity caused Roee's right wing to desire the ground and press hard on my wing, tilting my Spit down to the left, lifting its right side. For a moment, we each landed on one wheel. Our flaps were up, breaking our speed, and soon we were traveling relatively slowly. Six brave officers of the law came running out towards us, got behind us, and ran to the intersection of the wings. At the appropriate moment, I veered off right; Roee's wing fell and was caught by the six, running to keep pace, holding the wing up.

Soon we both stopped directly in front of the high-rise building in Westwood where we live.

We breathed easier. At least Roee and I did. I can't vouch for the six.

The whole area was deserted of traffic, but there were observers, most well back on the street or looking out of windows from the various high rises. More officers, including the Captain, surrounded us as we climbed down from our planes and disappeared among the confusion of men.

In a very few minutes, two soon-to-be-well-rewarded members of the LAPD were wearing our flight suits and Roee and I were wearing their uniforms. The Captain ordered us—now officers Saunders and Hough—to go into the building directly before us and take statements.

Roee and I gladly entered the building, but we did not take statements. Instead, we took the elevator to the fifteenth floor, our home, and entered its sanctuary of silence.

26

"DO YOU BELIEVE IN ANGELS?"

Immediate first aid was rendered to us within the crowd of police as we were changing clothes. Second through—at the very least—thirty-second aid was rendered by Dr. Stone, who, with two nurses and much portable medical equipment, was waiting for us on the 15th floor.

He was not happy with our raw meat conditions. I could tell by the shaking of his head and the little noises he made with his tongue. Dr. Stone is a man of few words but of many noises.

Roee had several contusions and bruises, plus a chunk of flesh torn out of his right leg. His right cheekbone was fractured, and he probably had a minor concussion due to the AK-47 butt.

I had many of the same injuries, but the most prominent was a weird-looking right eyelid.

Dr. Stone grunted a need for explanation.

"A very nasty man stuck his thumbnail through it," I answered his grunt.

"Nurse, penicillin."

I also had an unusual circular first-degree burn in the center of my back. Dr. Stone treated it, not wanting to know how it occurred.

Both Roee and I were exhausted. After the patching, Dr. Stone ordered us to bed, giving us something to help us sleep. We retired to our bedrooms; each assigned a nurse who would stay outside our doors with magazines and paperbacks to fill in the time.

It had all moved so quickly, precisely as I had planned it, that many questions I may have had didn't even occur to me to ask until dark and quiet and fading consciousness was the welcomed comfort that surrounded me.

I fell asleep with "Lydia" on my lips.

xx

It was that wonderful time coming out of sleep where you feel completely relaxed and all the metaphors you can grab for have to do with floating or flying or any state of affairs where you feel no pressure at all, including, and most importantly, the pressure of physical objects against your skin. It was a quality of time you wanted to experience deeply and hold entirely. Therefore you neither want to fall back into sleep, for then experience is deadened, nor to fully wake up, where experience is far too alive, especially to pressures, internal and external.

But you must go deep or surface; lovely limbo is not meant to be. I opened my eyes.

Lydia.

She smiled.

"Do you believe in angels?" she asked.

"I do now," I said.

xx

We had slept, thanks to Dr. Stone, for more than twenty-four hours, our wounds constantly being tended to by the nurses. During that time, all loose ends were wrapped up. Once we were fully awake and fed and feeling as fine as circumstances permitted, we were taken by our nurses into the library in wheelchairs. It was, they said, at Dr. Stone's insistence, but I didn't believe them. I think it was just glorious maternal instinct.

As we rolled into the library, our cast of characters greeted us with applause.

There was the Captain, of course, and Mike. Petey was there, as was Hamo Thronycroft, who had flown over from England with Sheila Barnes' boy and girl, who now sat close to their mother, who was keeping a tight hold on them.

And there was Lydia, looking gorgeous in a Bill Blass suit.

The nurses transferred us from wheelchairs to easy chairs, then excused themselves.

"First off," I started, "Sheila Barnes, my sincere apology for putting you through a hell no parent should go through, but I think you will agree that it was necessary. I assume your children have reported that they were never mistreated."

"Mistreated? They want me to adopt Mr. Thronycroft!"

There was laughter.

"Well, I can understand that. We have all wanted to adopt Hamo at once or another, but I'm afraid the upkeep would be beyond your means."

"Especially seeing how I'm out of a job now."

"Well, let's talk about that. But first, I think the children would be better entertained in another room where a video system for games and movies has been set up. They will also be fed."

Hamo led the children out and then quickly returned.

"Captain, please explain our arrangements for Sheila."

"Sure." In his blunt manner, the Captain laid it out. "You must testify against the other Rangers, all of whom we've captured. Not to mention the five—what should I call them...?"

"Industry types will suffice," I said.

"Yeah, those five, and then there are the 'Industry types' who were present when Bea Cherbourg was killed. You will have to testify against them."

"Do I get immunity for this?"

"Immunity, a new identification, relocation for you and your children, the whole works," the Captain said.

"Can I trust the government on this?"

"You don't have to," I said. I am arranging it, and I will guarantee it." She looked at me. All questioning left her face. She accepted the situation.

"A job will be found for you," I continued, "that fits your particular skills. On occasion, I may have freelance work for you. Private schools for your children, I think, to keep up the kind of education you've established for them. Also, if you wish, we can arrange someone for you to talk to about your somewhat out-of-control sexual needs. Mind you, I'm not opposed to the quantity of sex you may desire, but, rather, the quality of men, which that desire, uncontrolled, leads to. If you disagree with me that that is a problem, you are free not to accept the offer. However, if I ever discover that your children are suffering because of it, I will take any measure I see fit to correct the situation. Is that understood?"

"Yes, but why are you helping me at all? I'm as guilty as the others."

"Without you, I could not have saved Lydia's life. I put a value on that."

"I only did what I was instructed to do, and I did it under duress."

"Yet you did it, and a life I consciously put in jeopardy was saved. I will explain no more."

"Except maybe—could you explain how you did it?"

"Petey?"

"Well, it was very simple, actually," Petey began. "We knew the electrocution happened by contact with the lips. That was obvious from the autopsy report on Bea Cherbourg and Fixxer's observation of Don Gulden showing off his burnt lips at Larry Lapham's party. So I prepared a lipstick compound for Lydia with thousands of near-microscopic glass beads. Glass, of course, will not conduct electricity. So, as long as she allowed only her lips to contact the hot item—in this case, one hot ass—"

"Petey," I admonished.

"Sorry. In this case, a gold-colored, electrified Mylar pair of panties covering the buttocks of one Sara Hutton—then she was perfectly safe. As an added protection, though, just in case the altar had been electrified, I provided Lydia with a pair of stockings made from a sheer, super-thin rubber."

"They were extremely uncomfortable," Lydia said. "I would

have been willing to die just to get out of them."

"Yes, well, rubber, you see, doesn't breathe," Petey explained.

"You're telling me. I was sweating like a Turk!"

"Lydia!" I admonished.

"What? Oh. Sweating like a turkey, then. On the night before Thanksgiving. Passive, American PC enough for you?"

"For all except the poultry lobby."

"Well," Sheila Barnes said, not quite appreciating our banter, "she sure acted like she'd been electrocuted."

"'Acted' is the keyword," I said. "She plays Medea next week." Sheila didn't understand this, but Lydia smiled.

"Thank you. I had a good director."

"But—but her hair...?"

"Oh, just a little electromagnetic device," Petey explained, "in the form of a hairpin. Hit the remote-control switch, and it really frizzes out the hair. Roee had the switch in his pocket. Get the timing right, and who's to know?"

"Well, it was really convincing."

"But it wouldn't have been upon scrutiny of—of the remains," I said. "That's where we needed you, and you did an admirable job."

"As I said, I just did what I was told. I got to her first, before the other Rangers, and dragged her off behind the screen. Max and Sara were more concerned with calming everybody down and with you guys. Then I just told them I had everything under control regarding getting the body ready for shipment to Alaska. They didn't particularly want to pay their last respects."

"She's being modest," Lydia said. Once she got me behind the screen, she checked to make sure I was alive, made sure I was comfortable and kept a very diligent eye out for others. Then she hid me in a safe place in one of the guesthouses. You will always have my deep gratitude, Sheila."

"What did you replace Lydia with?" asked Roee. "You had to deliver something to the Russia-bound plane."

"A calf from one of the local ranches. Dislocate its limbs correctly, and, in a bag, it's just another body.'

"You stole it; I take it?" I asked.

347

"Well...."

"Roee, get the name of the ranch. We'll make a reimbursement."

"What about all those cows Max shot down?"

"Oh, yeah. Maybe it's the same rancher. In any case, everybody gets reimbursed. Now, Sheila, I think you should join your children for lunch. Later the Captain will come and fetch you and take care of everything from there."

Sheila nodded and left the room.

I turned to Lydia. "I can't tell you how relieved I was when you gave me the code words."

"I was thinking of not doing it. To see if you would cry."

"Oh, I would have cried."

"What code words?" Petey demanded to know.

"Lydia and I arranged for her to have a dying statement. If it included 'self-help book,' I would know she was all right."

"Wait a minute!" Petey exclaimed. "What did you need that for? Didn't you think my stuff would work?"

"Petey, I always have full confidence in you; it was just—well, call it an emotional need for reassurance. Truly a character fault in me, and I apologize for it."

"Oh, that's okay! Actually, I wasn't sure it was going to work!"

"What?" Lydia turned to Petey.

"Well, theoretically, but how often do you have to protect someone from kissing an electrified golden ass?"

"Which brings up the question, Fixxer," the Captain said. "How did you know they would try to kill Lydia? Especially in this way?"

"I knew that although our cover had not been penetrated, our sincerity had. Maxwellton James knew we were enemies of some sort, but he didn't know what sort. He was the kind of personality who would have to know. That's why I allowed him to overhear our plans with the briefcases. They were too intriguing for him not to want to get his hands on them. I was sure he was also sufficiently egoistic to want to have the candid, historical record of his actions. So I knew he would let them operate to the very last moment."

"Like Nixon keeping the tapes," The Captain suggested.

"I suppose. The only way to satisfy all his needs was to invite us in. Once in, he couldn't let us out. So murder was always his plan. As to knowing they would use the Golden Arse as the murder weapon for Lydia. It's perverse. So were Max and Sara. It fit."

It was time to move on.

"Captain, you got wonderful cooperation from the State," I said.

"You bet. Once I explained how Max and State Senator Joe Skinner had duped them. It was going to be embarrassing for them, no matter what. Only a full-out effort to support us could take the focus off that embarrassment."

"And Joe Skinner is...?"

"In custody."

"Ouch!" It was Roee, suddenly unbuttoning his shirt and clawing at his breasts. "Petey, didn't anybody remove these nipple phones?"

"Nope! Sorry! Forgot!"

"What the hell is a nipple phone?" the Captain asked.

Roee, painfully, peeled off, then handed the two fake nipples over to the Captain as he scratched at his own, apologizing for the rudeness but feeling much better.

"Miniature microphone-transmitter applications in the form of human male nipples," Petey proudly declared.

The Captain stared at the two nipples in his hand. Then sudden disgust caused him to drop them. "Petey, you're one sick puppy, do you know that?"

"Yeah. Break those, and it costs you ten grand per nipple."

"Sick puppy he may be, Captain, but a brilliant sick puppy."

"Ah—Fixxer!"

"The improvements you made to the satellite are amazing, but the fact that you could track us so precisely in the middle of storm clouds...."

"Easy, once I got a lock on the individual heat signatures of the planes, but did you really think he would go to this trouble to kill you? I mean, he could have just killed you on the ground."

"No, again, not perverse and grand enough for his type. When Mike returned with the report that he had found ammo in the San Simeon hanger, it became evident that Max was using it somewhere. If there was still a war going on in Central America, and he was still involved, that might have been the answer, but with no war, what's a warped bastard to do? War games with live ammo. We've known of such things before. Bea being found in Alaska—especially on the frozen Bering Sea—gave me another clue. Such war games must be played in very remote places. It was not much of a leap to figure that somewhere in eastern Russia was a likely place. Why else would he have an airfield in Nome? He wasn't in the business of giving tourist flights. He needed a private refueling station on the way there.

"So, knowing armed air battles were his pleasure, we gave him every opportunity to devise the idea as a fun way to get rid of us. Simple human psychology took over from there.

"But on to other things. Hamo, have you and Lydia had time to review the tapes?"

"Yes, everything worked fine. Lydia has plenty of material. It will make quite a brilliant exposé."

"And at any time, is either Roee or me recognizable on the tapes?"

"Only twice. Once when Max covered you with the camera himself. That part we have, of course, erased. The other time was when George kicked you. He kicked your face into a full-frontal view."

"Not such an easy section to erase," I said.

"That's not a problem. We can easily replace your face digitally with the face of the cop standing in for you."

"Yes, those police officers will come in for quite a bit of glory. I hope you'll play them up, Lydia."

"Are you kidding? Where's the glory for me if I do that? No, I think I'll just portray them as competent undercover cops. That's in the journalism, of course. In the movie version, I've got to have some hot sex scenes with the cop taking your role, so I'll have to expand it slightly."

"I also assume you'll be kicking some groin in the movie?"

"Sure. I can justify it dramatically."

"I'm sure you can. Now, what's the end of the story? Was Max's body recovered?"

"No," the Captain stated. "Found lots of debris from the plane in the ocean, but no body. But I think we can assume that Maxwellton James is dead."

"Can we?"

"Fixxer, don't get melodramatic with me. He's dead. Now what about this Enclave stuff? Do you buy any of it? Do you think it's real?"

"I don't know. Could be. The sentiments that Max claimed for it are certainly real among certain people. Some of them are undoubtedly powerful people. Whether those sentiments have been organized into the Enclave is something, I suppose, for further investigation."

"The question is," Roee said. "Who's going to conduct that investigation?"

"No, the question is, who will conduct it competently? Lydia's story will demand some action. It will also feed the Millennium need for conspiracies. It will play well among the masses that Max and Sara seemed to have disliked. If it's all real, are there then people in high places who can ensure that it remains just entertainment? Not a question we can answer today."

Mike, whose simple love for Bea Cherbourg was the author of the recent events we had been discussing, had sat during all this, quiet and still.

"Mike," I said, "how do you feel?"

"Strange, Fixx. Displaced, somewhat. You know what I mean? Here but not really here. I'm glad Max and Sara are dead, I'm really glad about that, but that's not very satisfying. I still don't see why Bea had to die. It's still, I don't know, still a bit surreal."

"Innocence harmed, always is," I said. "Or at least always should seem so to us."

Mike gave me a weak smile acknowledging my wisdom.

"Mike, I will send you back East to talk to Bea's parents. I want you to explain things to them. Share some grief with them, Mike. Share some, 'Good grief.' Once done, come back and get back to the newsstand and open your receptive ears. I still need your valuable information."

"You got it, Fixx. Anything, anytime, anywhere, you got it.

There is one other thing that bothers me."

"Speak."

"Did you have to destroy the Hollywood sign?"

"Unavoidable, I'm afraid. But it was looking shabby. This will allow them to bring it back to its former glory. By the way, was there any damage or loss of life in the crash?"

"One house," the Captain said. "Empty at the time. The LAFD got there quickly and extinguished the fire before it spread."

"Who did it belong to?"

"Oddly enough, to one Maxwellton James."

"You're kidding."

The Captain smiled—a rare uplift for him. "Yes, I am, but we've been studying irony in my creative writing class."

XX

Everyone then left except Lydia. We had a couple of cold vodka tonics and a large plate of feta cheese and olives.

"You know," I said, "for a moment, I thought Max had gotten to you. That the whole idea of the Enclave was seductive enough to recruit you."

"How could you think that?"

"Things said in the past."

"Yeah, I know. But, once it was all articulated by that nut, I could see, well, I could see that it was nuts."

"Care to elaborate?"

"No. Nuts is nuts, that's all."

"Oh."

Lydia took a critical look at my face. "You look worse than the first time you got beat up."

"Sorry to abuse your sense of aesthetics."

"Come back to Kassiópi, to my villa. To heal. I called Helen. She misses you."

"I miss her. Especially her lamb."

"Good, we'll eat lamb; you'll sit in the sun and heal; I can work on my expose; we can fuck. Maybe we'll like it so much we'll want to do it for a long time. Then maybe you'll tell me your name."

"My name is Nico."

"Oh, sure."

"For you, my sweet Greek, my name will always be Nico."

"Then you will come?"

"No. No, thank you. Not this time. I feel like staying close to home."

"Home? You call this slice of a high-rise box a home?"

"I do. It is."

"You went through hell for this Bea Cherbourg. Would you go through hell for me?"

"Depends."

"Depends on what?"

"Depends on the outside forces."

"You are—Fixxer—you are unfathomable."

"Thank you. I work hard at it."

"I'm going to kiss you now. I am not wearing Petey's lipstick. Let's see if we can conduct some electricity."

She did.

We did.

HOLLYWOOD
IS AN ALL-VOLUNTEER ARMY

27
THE RETURN OF GILGAMESH PAUL

After Lydia left and we excused and paid rather generously, our nurses, who then packed up their paperbacks and left, I turned to Roee and said, "Roee, wounded and recovering though you are, what's for dinner?"

"Didn't you just consume a large quantity of feta cheese and olives?"

"As Odysseus said to his host Alcinous, 'The belly's a shameless dog.'"

"Braised horse meat, then?"

"Roee?"

"Well, I suppose I could easily prepare some eggs and bacon."

"Turkey bacon, right?"

"Of course. My god is—"

"Determined to keep me from the pig flesh of my fantasies."

"How about the simplicity of fresh pasta with olive oil and garlic, garlic toast, and a fresh green salad."

I thought about that briefly, then said, "Sounds good."

xx

Of course, it was, and I even drank a wine recommended by

355

Roee. He said it would be more restorative than the vodka tonic I had requested.

During dinner, we discussed the adventure that had just concluded. It was Roee's opinion that we had done some good.

"Good, as you know," I said, "is so relative you would think Heisenberg's Uncertainty Principal applies."

"Certainly, bringing revenge to those culpable in the death of Bea Cherbourg was good."

"Roee, you are so Old Testament."

"I've never denied it."

"Yes, I suppose it was good. It was, in any case, my desire. I thought, though, you were referring to the destruction of two soldiers of the Enclave."

"No, I wasn't. Although, assuming the Enclave does exist, that can't be bad."

"Can't it? Maxwellton James was not wrong in this: The twenty-first century will be a bitch. You and I know that as much as any two people on the Earth."

"What century hasn't been a bitch, Fixxer? Isn't it a matter of how we handle the bitch?"

"Yes, I suppose so. Then it's a matter of figuring out what's good instead of, possibly, what's smart."

"Must the two be in opposition?"

"Well—as I'm not being paid to answer such questions, I'll be happy to leave it hanging in the air."

"Speaking of which, while you were—saying goodbye to Lydia, I was going over the accounts."

"A true Jew."

"Fixxer!"

"Sorry. It's the wine."

"You want pork; you are perfectly capable of going out to a coffee shop and getting it."

"I said I'm sorry. You don't need to be disgusting."

"I was reviewing the accounts and adding up what this little adventure will cost us."

"A pretty penny?" I inquired rather weakly.

"The backside of dollars leaving your accounts is never

anything but ugly, Fixxer. But, if you remember, I have set a deal with Jim Duncan to get him installed as the new president of Olympic Pictures. But we have to figure out a way to accomplish it."

"Roee, I can do that in a phone call. Get me Larry Lapham on the line."

xx

"What the hell do you want?" came Lapham's far from pleased voice. "Do you know Don Gulden's family is trying to sue me for damages? His fucking brother's a fucking lawyer."

"He should be recovering any day now with no side effects."

"Yeah, but—"

"Plus, he will be going to prison for a while."

"Oh, shit! You had something to do with this Sara Hutton thing, right?"

"Larry, how often have I told you I don't answer questions? Now, do you know Jim Duncan?"

"Yeah, I know him. I've worked with him. He's okay."

"Good. Your deal at Universal is about up. Your exclusivity ends in three months."

"Yeah, that's right."

"Then I think Olympic Pictures is the best home for you."

"Olympic! Are you nuts?"

"I think you can get quite a good deal there."

"I can get a good deal anywhere."

"Better than good, then. They would want you badly. You should tell them you would only feel comfortable at Olympic if someone like Jim Duncan ran the place, replacing the tragically late Sara Hutton."

"What? You want me to take this deal just so Jim Duncan can get back into the executive ranks?"

"I guarantee that if you do this, you'll both see success."

"God damn it, Fixxer! If I knew that using your services—"

"You did know."

"Not to this extent."

"Larry, for the first time in your career, the word auteur is starting to accompany your name, and you're still big at the box office. All thanks to me."

"All?"

"All enough for our purposes, Larry. Don't tell me you disagree." I made it sound like a threat, which wasn't hard.

"Yeah. Okay. I agree."

"So shut up, pay attention to your ego, and do as I say."

"Jim Duncan, uh?"

"Jim Duncan."

"He's a fine executive. I can work with him."

"I thought you two were a good match."

"You're so fucking perceptive."

"Yes, I am, aren't I? Goodbye Larry Lapham."

"Goodbye, Mr. The Fixxer."

I hung up the phone.

"1.5 million. In the Bank."

Roee seemed pleased.

The phone rang. Not The Phone, but rather the connection with the desk in the lobby of the building. This was odd, for it rarely rang unless we were expecting someone. The building staff was under strict orders not to call us in any other case.

Roee answered it. Spoke a few words. Then hung up.

"It's Anne Eisley."

"Anne? Well, yes, the film was wrapping."

"Landed at LAX from Australia just an hour ago. She's bringing up, uh, someone she found there?"

"What? Uninvited? She knows better than—"

"It's Gilgamesh Paul."

xx

The elevator doors opened, and Anne Eisley stood there, radiant, lovely, and not at all harried. You would not have guessed that she had just flown in from Sydney. Behind her stood Joe, the young man from the garage. He had a dolly, and on the dolly was a large cardboard box slapped silly with airport labels.

Anne rushed up to me and kissed me. It was long and generous. Upon pulling back from it, she noticed my face.

"You look horrible. Been having fun?"

"Anne, you know I don't like uninvited visits."

"Shut up. I come bearing gifts."

"And you're not even Greek."

"No, but we could talk about it. Roee, how are you? Oh, I see. Not much better."

"We're worn, but not the worse for it, I hope," he said.

"Stop the chitchat. Is this my gift?"

"You'll never believe it. I found them in a used bookstore in a small town in the outback. It seems a man who used to live there in the 20s ordered them by mail subscription. His grandson had just sold them to the store. A complete set."

I stared at the box. Disbelieving. Excited. Scared.

"Well, go ahead, open it up," Anne prodded. Joe took out a knife and began to slit the seal.

"Careful!" I said.

Joe was careful. Then he opened the box. I bent down and folded back the flaps. There they were. Twenty volumes of 'The Adventures of Gilgamesh Paul' by S.Z. Sharpton. The long-forgotten series of novels had been my quest to find. I pulled the first one out. It was *The Case of the Unnatural Predator*. I pulled out another. It was *The Case of the Shy Gun*. And one more: *The Case of the Malignant Rumor*.

"All but one have their original dust jackets," Anne said gleefully, excited, I think, to see my reaction.

I stood up. "Thank you," I said in a near whisper, all the volume I could manage. It's amazing the silly things we expend our emotions on.

"Yes, thank you, Anne," Roee said. "The torturous search for Gilgamesh Paul is now over. Care for something to eat? We have some pasta left."

"No, thank you, I'm tired. I think I'll go to bed." She then walked straight to my bedroom.

"She means your bed," Roee said.

"Obviously. Give Joe a tip, will you, Roee?"

Then I joined Anne in my bedroom. After all, the belly is not the only organ that is a shameless dog.

ABOUT THE AUTHOR

Before publishing ten critically acclaimed novels, award-winning and Amazon Bestselling author Steven Paul Leiva spent over twenty years as a writer and producer in the entertainment industry. He worked with such talent as Academy Award-winning producer Richard Zanuck; director Ivan Reitman; literary legend and screenwriter Ray Bradbury, and *Star Wars* producer Gary Kurtz. He even lent his voice to the Academy Award shortlisted (placing in the top ten) animated short, *The Indescribable Nth. https://vimeo.com/14857442*

Leiva produced the animation for *Space Jam*, putting together an ad hoc animation studio for Warner Bros in three days over the phone.

During this time, he wrote novels and a play, *Made on the Moon*, which premiered at the 1996 Edinburgh Festival Fringe, receiving a four-star review from *The Scotsman*.

After *Space Jam*, Leiva decided to concentrate on writing novels. Since 2003, he has published ten novels, a novella, and a book of essays.

His work has been praised by literary great Ray Bradbury, Oscar-winning film producer Richard Zanuck, NY Times bestselling author and Pulitzer Prize finalist Diane Ackerman, and *Star Trek: Enterprise* actor John Billingsley, the greatest bookworm in Hollywood.

Leiva received the Scribe Award from the International Association of Media Tie-in Writers.

You can find more about Leiva and read his blogs at https://tinyurl.com/ydgpkps8

BOOKS BY STEVEN PAUL LEIVA

Blood is Pretty: The First Fixxer Adventure

Meet the Fixxer—with wit and aplomb, he works the fruitful fields of Hollywood, fixing the sins and correcting the stupidities of the denizens therein. In *Blood is Pretty,* he comes to the rescue of "the most beautiful woman I have ever seen" to extricate her from the grip of the soul-sucking sexual desires of a producer born in slime and takes on the task of buying off with money and muscle a film geek who won't cooperate with a director of minuscule talent who wants to claim "V"—the geek's "Holy Grail" of a film treatment—as his own.

Hollywood is an All-Volunteer Army: The Second Fixxer Adventure

What those in the know in Hollywood really know is that if they need a dark deed done, if they need a sticky personal or professional problem "fixed," they can call upon the mysterious and dangerous Fixxer. Whether you are a successful comedy film director whose "art" has never truly been appreciated because the country's most important film critic has held a grudge against you since college, or you are a neophyte and naïve screenwriter who resents the professional blackmail she has just suffered, you call upon the Fixxer.

Traveling in Space

A unique first-contact novel from the aliens' point-of-view.

The last thing the factfinders—who call themselves Life—expected to find while traveling in space in "The Curious" on a mission from their planet, The Living World, was otherlife. But one day, they stumble upon the third planet out from a backwater sun and find it teeming with a vast diversity of life, including one sentient and cognizant, if primitive, species that they dub: Otherlife.

Being not only from "The Curious" but inherently curious themselves, they begin to study the Otherlife and their alien culture, discovering such strange things as marriage, intoxicating drinks, weapons of minor and mass destruction, the gleeful inhaling of toxic substances, two-parent families, layered language, genocide, non-nude bathing, and—the strangest thing of all—religion.
This first contact between Life and Otherlife, disconcerting for both, has moments of humor and moments of horror—and neither escapes the encounter unchanged.

The 12 Dogs of Christmas - A Novelization

Winner of the Scribe Award from the International Association of Media Tie-in Authors

Based on the beloved independent family film.

12-year-old Emma O'Connor is sent to live with her "aunt" in the small town of Doverville, where Emma soon finds herself in the middle of a "dogfight" with the mayor and town dogcatcher. To strike down their "no-dogs" law, Emma must bring together a group of schoolmates, grown-ups, and adorable dogs of all shapes and sizes in a spectacular holiday pageant. The *12 Dogs of Christmas* is a fun, heartwarming story featuring a diverse canine cast and is perfect for all those who love dogs, kids, and Christmas.

By the Sea: A Comic Novel

A modern comic adult fairy tale with an ensemble cast of Cinderellas. Instead of a kingdom by the sea, our story takes place in and around a residential hotel by the sea. The architecturally eclectic Briers Hotel is situated on Leech Beach, a not particularly inviting beach, being often fog-bound and always scruffy. But it's the perfect setting for our Cinderellas, male, and female, who put up with the scruffiness of life while striving to make it through their various personal seaside fogs. Theater; art; antiques; old movies; sex; more sex; death; fast and slow cars, chicken shit and cow poop; military bearing and erotic emissions—not to mention the wicked witch, the sea serpent by the sea shore, the village ogre, the village idiot, and several Prince Charmings—all figure into this merry tale with a multitude of happy endings.

IMP: A Political Fantasia

Thomas P. Powell's political ascension was both unusual and yet very American. From traffic cop to Vice President of the United States, his climb up the ladder of public service was often due to the push of random acts and not-so-happy accidents—although Thomas held the opinion that it was due solely to his singular innate moral authority. What matters is what's within; that's the Powell political philosophy. But, then, on the cusp of his grasping the last rung of the American political ladder, something truly within suddenly appears. A horrible homunculus, a wild imp, climbs out of Thomas's right ear to bedevil his nights, confuse his days, and take him on a crazy, wild, nauseating, and nuclear journey. It's like The West Wing was done as a Twilight Zone episode.

And you thought our last political nightmare was surreal.

Journey to Where: A Contemporary Scientific Romance

When a radical experiment into the nature of time is sabotaged, the scientific team finds themselves in an alternate universe where humans never became the dominant life force. Instead, dinosaurs evolved into intelligent bipeds, developing language and societal structures.

The scientists must learn to communicate with this alien species, who view them as unusual pets, and figure out how to recreate the original experiment in a non-industrialized world, so they can return home—assuming there's a home, or even a universe, to return to.

But the scientist who sabotaged them is trapped in this new world with them. And he's looking to rise to power, even if his quest means the death of his traveling companions. A contemporary scientific romance in the tradition of H. G. Wells and Jules Verne

Creature Feature: A Horrid Comedy

There is something strange happening in Placidville!

It is 1962. Kathy Anderson, a serious actress who took her training at the Actors Studio in New York, is stuck playing Vivacia, the Vampire Woman on Vivacia's House of Horrors, at a local Chicago TV station. Finally fed up showing old monster movies to creature feature fans, she quits and heads to New York and the fame and footlights of Broadway.

On her way, she stops to visit her parents and old friends in Placidville, the All-American, middle-class, blissfully ordinary Midwest small town she grew up in. But she finds things strange in Placidville. Kathy's parents, her best friend from high school, the local druggist, and even the Oberhausen twins are all acting curiously creepy, odiously odd, and wholly weird—especially the town's super geeky nerd, Gerald, who warns of dark days ahead.

Has Kathy entered a zone in the twilight? Did she reach the limits that are outer? Has she fallen through a mirror that is black? Or is it just—just—politics as usual?

Bully 4 Love: A Rather Odd Love Story

Adolphus Seruya is a happy, middle-aged, unambitious bachelor and History professor at a prominent community college. Then suddenly, SHE walks into his classroom. Lavinia Carson is beautiful in a unique yet compelling way. And radiant almost beyond description. Thus begins a rather odd story of love rejected, love ignored, love found— and cuttlefish pizza.

Extraordinary Voyages

What if a man wanted to go to the moon from the time he was an infant? Not a toddler, not a child, not a young man, but a babe in his mother's arms? What if Baron Munchausen traveled from 1790 to 1641 to take Cyrano de Bergerac to Mars? What if the man who wanted to go to the moon from the time he was an infant wrote some rude poems? What if the author of this book wrote his own Wikipedia page? Which he was sure Wikipedia would never publish. What if you bought this book and found out?

Includes the critically acclaimed novella *Made on the Moon*.

The Reluctant Heterosexual
A Tragicomedy in Four Movements A Prelude And An Interlude

With *The Reluctant Heterosexual,* Steven Paul Leiva concludes his thematic trilogy: **The Love, Sex, and Pursuit of Happiness Novels**. All three novels look at these essential aspects of the human condition, with each story focusing on one of the three. *By the Sea: A Comic Novel* looks at our unease when unhappy. *Bully 4 Love: A Rather Odd Love Story* takes a skewed view of this most revered emotion. And now, *The Reluctant Heterosexual,* as the title predicts, concerns sex, which is not always the same as love, nor is it always a happy situation. Subtitled *A Tragicomedy in Four Movements A Prelude And An Interlude,* each section of the novel, as in a musical composition, has its individual tempo, mood, and form as it tells the story—and stories—of Robert Leslie Cromwell and Sandy Smith—two *Homo sapiens sapiens* surviving and striving in the late 20th-Century.

Robert and Sandy are intelligent, creative, not unattractive, wealthy, married to each other, and in love. And yet their procreating bodies might as well be standing naked on a savanna in Africa in the late Pliocene Era. It's the sometimes comic conflict between ancient bodies and modern culture. Can there possibly be a happy ending?

The Definition of Luck
Or
The Post-Modern Prometheus

Khadambi Kinyanjui, a 6-foot-five Kenyan who grew up in London, is from a wealthy family. Joe Smith, quite a bit shorter, is a red-headed orphan who grew up with his Aunt Liz in a hole in the California desert. Both are brilliant scientists. One is a neurobiologist, the other an astronomer, who first meet in 2049 under the Tommy Trojan statue at the University of Southern California. They become the best of friends but a very odd couple. And yet, their brotherhood is more robust than most actual brothers.

Then tragedy strikes the pair. Death is near for one of them. What can fend it off? Can the mind, the *self*, be uploaded to some digital realm? Can one become more than a human and far less than an animal? Or will the fix be something unexpected and mysterious? Can this human survive? Can humanity? Can friendship?

Searching for Ray Bradbury: Writings about the Writer and the Man

Includes the title piece written for the *Los Angeles Times* and "The Man Who Was Himself," Leiva's memorial appreciation of Bradbury commissioned by the Science Fiction & Fantasy Writers of America for the Winter 2012/13 edition of their quarterly magazine, *The Bulletin*. Other pieces were initially written for *Neworld Review*, KCET.org, and Leiva's blog.
With a special foreword by Hugo and Nebula Award-winning author David Brin.

HOLLYWOOD
IS AN ALL-VOLUNTEER ARMY

www.ingramcontent.com/pod-product-compliance
Lightning Source LLC
Chambersburg PA
CBHW020511260626
47156CB00006B/1958